THE NORTH BEYOND

PART 4 : ARTORYNAS

P.M. Scrayfield

Pen Press

First published in Great Britain

All paper used in the printing of this book has been made from wood grown in managed, sustainable forests.

ISBN13: 978-1-78003-492-8

Printed and bound in the UK
Pen Press is an imprint of
Indepenpress Publishing Limited
25 Eastern Place
Brighton
BN2 1GJ

A catalogue record of this book is available from
the British Library

Cover design by Jacqueline Abromeit

CONTENTS

... the story began with:

THE NORTH BEYOND
Part 1: Numirantoro

THE NORTH BEYOND
Part 2 : Maesrhon

THE NORTH BEYOND
Part 3 : Haldur

VII DARKNESS

CHAPTER 48

Red-flowering thorn

The mountain mist swirled and drifted; and out of it, grey and insubstantial at first like the shifting cloud itself, the shadowy figures of men and women emerged. They walked in single file, quietly and without speaking, following a path that twisted through rocks and crags as it gradually dropped down to lower ground. Eventually the peat and sedge gave way to rough pasture where sheep looked up briefly from biting at the wiry grass, and then the path wound through hillside terraces built up to be tilled for crops before arriving at the floor of the dale. Here half a dozen young men detached themselves from the group and went over to a low, stone-built stronghouse; six others came out after a moment or two and set off in the opposite direction, up into the mist. It was late afternoon and down here the westering sun shone through breaks in the cloud; but the little valley, no more than a shallow bowl surrounded by steep peaks, was shaded early by the mountain heights that guarded it. Summer was passing and already the evenings were chilly enough. By ones and twos the group dispersed as people turned away to their homes, one young man heading across the bridge and up the slope towards the eastern side of the valley. Here there were dwellings cut into the face of the hill, only about a third of their length extending outwards into a type of large porch, timber-framed with windows let into the wall and thatched above with heather. Sitting on a chair outside the door of one of these homes, surrounded by children to whom she had been

1

telling a story, was a white-haired old woman. The young man drew near and stood beside her; he was tall, and she had to tip her head back to see his face.

'Here you are back then.'

'Yes, the others have gone up now: they'll add their own stones to the cairn before they take over the watch.' He looked down at her. He had never, in his whole life, seen Fosseiro sit idle, and his eyes moved from the wool she was spinning now to the shawl around her shoulders. 'I don't think you should sit out here this late, there's a cold wind getting up.'

'I'm all right. I like to enjoy the sun before it goes behind the hill. I'm better out here in the fresh air than cooped up inside. Plenty of time for that when the winter comes.'

He looked away. The sun's level rays fell on his face, which was thin and rather preoccupied. He knew what Fosseiro meant about fresh air: the hill houses were snug enough, but the damp could not be entirely kept out of them. Maybe that was how Torald had come by his cough. It was difficult to believe that Torald, so lean and tough, so resourceful, so unchanged by the passing years, was dead. He glanced around. It was largely thanks to Torald that they had managed to make a success of living in this refuge in the hills after escaping from Salfgard. His skills and knowledge had been invaluable, but now he was gone, dead in his bed from a chill on the chest. There was too little land here to spare any for a burial plot, so they took their dead up into the hills and laid them under cairns, everyone adding a stone; and Torald had been carried far up and left to guard the pass for them, the narrow trail that was the only way into their hidden valley. The young man sat on the ground and frowned at his feet. He wondered how old Torald had been: no-one seemed to know. He was not so young himself any more, soon he would be half way though his fourth ten years. For the first time in his life, he was conscious of the weight of his own mortality. He had sworn to take no wife and beget no child while they hid in the hills and Salfgard lay waste, and he would keep that vow; but now it came to him that maybe he would never have a child: neither son nor daughter, to lay the stones above him when his own time came. The shadow on his heart deepened as he thought of the old woman who sat beside him. At least he was childless by his own choice, which was something Fosseiro could not say. What would he do if she took sick like Torald? He clenched his fists. Fosseiro shouldn't have to live like this at her age, and it would be winter again before they knew it... When he turned towards her, he found her watching him with a knowing look.

'Run along now you youngsters, time you were all at home lending a hand before evening comes,' she said, and the children scampered off. The wrinkles deepened around Fosseiro's eyes as she smiled. 'What's the matter?'

'Nothing, really. Well, just the usual things you find yourself thinking after a burial.'

'You don't need to worry about me. I'm not going to die up here in the hills.'

He made a sudden movement with his hand. 'I wasn't... How... You shouldn't talk about things like that.'

'Listen, Cunoreth. I've known you since you came to us as a little boy at death's door, I nursed you back to life myself. I know what bothers you, without you telling me. I won't let go of life until we're back in Salfgard. Once we're home, it'll be different: it won't matter then. You'll lay me beside Ardeth, won't you?'

Cunoreth turned his face away to hide the tears that gathered in his eyes, but Fosseiro could hear them in his voice. 'Of course, if that's what you want.'

'Shall I tell you what I'd like most of all?'

Not trusting himself to look up, he nodded.

'If only we knew where it grows, I'd ask you to plant an *astorhos* tree over the two of us to draw its life from Ardeth and me. Ardeth loved this world, you know. He used to say it was so beautiful, he couldn't bear the thought of leaving it.' Now he turned, surprised to see the

3

thousand laughter lines crinkling again in Fosseiro's face as she smiled once more. 'I think he'd be glad to know that *astorhos* flowers opened above him and its seeds flew on the wind to spring up again. But there, maybe it's a tree that only blossoms in old stories, and I'm sure the hawthorn is just as lovely. Find a red-flowering thorn, Cunoreth, and plant it over us. Will you promise me that?'

'Yes, I promise. But if I ever found an *astorhos* tree, you should have that instead.'

A risk worth taking

Later that evening, after supper was over and children already asleep, Cunoreth sat talking quietly with Mag'rantor, Ethanur and a few others.

'I wish I could feel as sure as Fosseiro that we will go back and rebuild Salfgard, one day,' he said.

'Fosseiro's as strong as the hills themselves, in her own quiet way,' said Mag'rantor. 'If she's made up her mind she'll see Salfgard again, that's good enough to keep up my hopes too. Remember the night Ardeth died, Ethanur? I think it was something like that he was trying to say: he knew she'd bear up and hold us all together.' He fell silent for a few moments, busy with his thoughts; then he spoke again.

'I wonder whether any of those who tried ever did get through to the Nine Dales. But even if they did, it makes no difference for us. We've no choice but to stay here. We can't all follow them, and even if some of the younger fellows wanted to take the risk, we can't spare the manpower.'

'No, but we can't stay here for ever, either.' Ethanur glanced over to the corner where his baby daughter slept in her cradle; after his wild ride north with the warning of what had happened in Framstock, he had fled into the hills with the people of Salfgard and now was married to Escurelo whom he had known when they were children together during his foster-years. 'If our numbers increase, this valley won't support us.'

'If we can trust what Sigitsinen told us, maybe we won't have to stay,' said Cunoreth.

'You mean it might be safe to take another valley, if it's true Heranar's decided not to send soldiers after us again?' said Ethanur doubtfully. 'That's a big if: I'd trust Sigitsinen, for all I've only met him the once, before I'd trust Heranar with the memories I have of him.'

'That goes for me, too. I'd never trust Heranar. I've never forgotten the way he lied to Ardeth about what happened when Ghentar marked Maesrhon's face with his sword.' This was Mag'rantor's son Urancrasig, scowling as he spoke. He was a young man now, but in his memory he was a child once more, hiding under the river bank as the brothers' fight disturbed his fishing.

'Well, they're both gone now,' sighed Escurelo, shaking her head, 'but maybe you're too hard on Heranar. I never liked him, but looking back I can see he was easily led. Imagine him married and a father three times over! Maybe he's different now, he might have had a change of heart.'

It's the baby, thought Cunoreth; she thinks no-one who has a child can have bad in them. Suddenly he snorted with laughter.

'I wouldn't wish Heranar's marriage-parents on anyone, not even on him. I've seen a bit of old Gillavar in years gone by, and as for that wife of his...' Then gradually the laughter left his face and he turned to Escurelo. 'But I'll tell you something, I don't believe Maesrhon's dead. Sigitsinen didn't think so, and remember they trained together in the same military unit. Sigitsinen got right up here without us knowing anything about it before he suddenly showed himself, and he said Maesrhon passed out with higher honours than he did: it would take a lot to kill a man like that – well, Ghentar couldn't do it, for one. But anyway, I didn't just mean it might be safer for us up here if Heranar's called the pack off. I meant, going by everything Sigitsinen had to say, maybe it won't be long before things start to move, down there in Rossaestrethan and Rosmorric.'

He pronounced the hated names with a sneer, his mouth twisting in distaste.

'Well, I don't know.' Ethanur looked across again at his wife and child. He alone of them had witnessed the sack of Framstock and he had no wish to see more blood shed, however just the cause might be. 'I don't see any hope of success, no matter how many Gwentarans are in secret league. Even if they all rose up together, the Caradwardans would be too much for them, they'd be ruthless. If you'd seen the things I've seen, you'd realise.'

'Yes, but what about the Caradwardans? According to what Sigitsinen was telling us, some of them are in it too. Look what he said about the troops close to Valahald down in Salfgard – not to mention that every man from the auxiliaries who changed sides would be worth three rank and filers.' Mag'rantor leaned forward. 'Then there's Heranar. If it's right that he's lost the stomach for what he's being asked to do, he'd maybe not put up much resistance if there was a rising here in the north.'

'He's more likely either to be disposed of by that brother of his, or recalled in disgrace, and both would be a poor lookout for us, especially if we'd broken cover. I say stay as we are and don't trust any of them. Time enough to come down from the hills when we know for sure that it's safe. Let them fight it out among themselves, what do we care?'

This came from an older man who had so far sat silent on the edge of the group, listening to what the others had to say.

'But our own people, how can we not care about them?' put in Escurelo, wondering for the thousandth time what fate might have befallen Cottiro and Framhald and other friends of her childhood.

'This is it, this is what I mean,' said Cunoreth, looking earnestly round the group. He caught his uncle's eye for an instant and suddenly it occurred to Mag'rantor how much Cunoreth had changed since

Ardeth's death and all that had followed. The jaunty manner and devil-may-care personality had been replaced by something very much harder – for all that he still wore his hair in those silly braids, thought Mag'rantor, smiling inwardly.

'Sigitsinen told us this, that and the other thing,' Cunoreth went on. 'He said this was happening here, and that had happened there, and this man or the other would act so, or not, at such and such a time. I believe, and it seems we all feel the same way, that he is trustworthy. But how can he come up here to us again? His pretext is taken away, now that Heranar is persuaded there is no need to search the hills again. We need to find a way to stay in touch with him, or another who is similarly placed. One of us must go down from our refuge and set up a line of contact.'

'I'll go! Let me go, I'll do it!' Urancrasig was on his feet, lit up with eagerness.

'No, no. Come on, sit down. We know you'd be willing to risk it, but listen to me first.' Cunoreth pulled the lad back to his seat and Mag'rantor breathed again. 'You've got your mother and father to think of, and the rest of your family. And you've spent all your life either here or in Salfgard. We need somebody without ties, who's been up and down to Framstock a few times before. Somebody expendable, who's prepared to die before he speaks, if he's taken. I'll go.'

'You? With that hair, and the way you ride, you'd be recognised before you'd gone a day's journey,' said the sceptic in the shadows.

Cunoreth laughed. 'I don't think so. Give it a week, and see if you know me then. And who said I'd be on a horse?'

In disguise

Next morning the long braids that had swung behind him through many a wild ride were gone, lying about his feet in shorn locks as Fosseiro, with many silent misgivings at the reason for the request, snipped away until Cunoreth was left with a close-cropped head, his hair slightly longer at the neck where it grew low on his nape, and falling onto his brow in a short fringe. Before many more days were past, his jaw and lips were outlined by a new beard, darker than his hair. Mag'rantor thought it was not just how he looked that was completely different; he seemed older, changed in some way that was separate from his appearance. He's doing this for Ardeth and Fosseiro, he thought as they worked together one morning in the barn; and then he recalled that it was Cunoreth who had brought the news of Geraswic's disappearance. Thank the Starborn Ardeth never found out what happened to him, thought Mag'rantor, remembering the grim tale they had heard from Sigitsinen. He peeked at Cunoreth out of the side of his eye. Yes, maybe it was for Geraswic too. His mind ran on to other things Sigitsinen had told them, and eventually he cleared his throat and spoke.

'It seems just too much of a coincidence to me, that travellers should come south now from Rihannad Ennar, the first time since long before living memory. Surely this has to mean that some of our folk who dared the wilderness did get through to them.'

'Maybe. But if they did, they'd have had plenty to say about what's been happening down here; and if that's the case, then it follows that these men from the Nine Dales aren't telling the truth about the reason for their own journey.'

'Ye-es. Yes, I think I see what you mean.' Mag'rantor wrinkled his brow. 'Of course, we're also assuming that Sigitsinen gave us an accurate account of what he read in Heranar's report, and that what Heranar said in it was what he was actually told – that's before we get on to whether what he was told by his visitors was the truth or not.'

Cunoreth laughed at his uncle's face, screwed up in concentration as he wrestled mentally with all this. 'Well, you can see why I think we should try to get to the bottom of it all for ourselves and why it could be important to have some means of communicating quickly with Sigitsinen or others of his faction. In fact I'd say that's more or less what the men from the Nine Dales are up to: they're on a reconnaissance of their own.'

Mag'rantor thought this over for a while. 'Perhaps we should bide our time, then. I mean, once they've seen how things are, and gone back north with the tale… If we waited, it might be that a force would come from Rihannad Ennar next spring.'

Cunoreth straightened up from his task, rubbing his hands over his head and face where the new beard, and the unaccustomed short hair, were itchy as they settled down. He laughed again briefly. 'Maybe. And maybe not. Far more likely that those who came south won't be allowed to leave freely, now. There's six men who'll never see their homes again, I'd say. Look, Mag'rantor. I'll be off in a few days' time, but I won't say anything about exactly when. I'll just get my stuff together quietly and slip away. It's best people don't make a big fuss about it all.'

From the barn doorway, Mag'rantor watched him walk away towards the bridge. Yes, there was a big change in his nephew. Even his laugh was different: it was shorter, more cynical, nothing like the spontaneous, gleeful mirth of old. With a sigh, he turned back to his work.

At the bridge Cunoreth stood aside to give way to a young woman who had been drawing water from the stream. Astirano, although some years his junior, was easily of an age to be wed and yet, like himself, she had remained unmarried. They exchanged greetings as they passed, but after she had taken a few steps Astirano turned to look back. Cunoreth walked on and after a moment she picked up her bucket and continued on her way. The water was heavy to carry, that must be why her heart was beating a little faster than usual. Yet over the next few days, she remembered their encounter more than once and it came to her that there was something about this new Cunoreth that reminded her in some strange, small way, of Maesrhon. It was nothing about his appearance, although he too was tall and spare: rather something in his manner, some air of purpose, some hint of danger, some sense of dedication. She found herself watching for him as she went about her tasks, until a day came when he seemed nowhere to be seen; and when she enquired after him, as casually as she could, she was told he was already away.

The fugitive

Far, far away, the light of a new day began to creep among the trees of the forest that hemmed in the mine works of the Lissa'pathor. A fugitive parted the undergrowth where he had taken refuge and peered out. His hands were filthy, the grime of his labour ingrained upon them; and his eyes, red from lack of sleep, were wide with fear. But the apprehension turned to wonder as he saw the growing light, and the cool green world it revealed. In every direction trees stood rank on rank, mysterious and silent, their feet veiled in a drifting ground mist, their heads rising to an unguessed height where the summer canopy of leaves whispered far above. So the rumours that were handed on among the slaves were true, at least so far: it seemed the sun did rise upon the forest, and he had lived through the night to see the dawn. Maybe some others, driven by desperation to slip away into the trees as he had done, had managed to struggle through the tangled growth and escape completely. Well, good luck to them; his errand was different. He wiped sweaty palms on the rough cloth of his soiled jerkin and swallowed as fear rose in him once more at the thought of what he planned to do. Years had passed, although he was unsure of just how many, since Is-Avar had disappeared. Tales had filtered back of events in Caradriggan, of Is-Avar's botched revenge upon Vorynaas and the terrible price he had exacted in return, first upon the killer of his son and then upon Gwent y'm Aryframan itself. After that the work-gangs had filled up with Gwentaran captives and Gwentaran accents had been heard in the sleeping cages, but none from among his new companions in misery had taken the place that Is-Avar had held in his heart. His despair had been black indeed when he first realised that his only friend had gone for ever; but somehow he had dragged himself from day to day until an idea began to form in his mind.

Often he heard the overseers complaining how useless the Gwentarans were, how they sickened more readily than other slaves, how easily they got themselves injured, how they seemed to have no interest in whether they lived or died. All this was scarcely surprising, and comprehensible enough, but after a while the slaves began to hear about a new problem. When the head-counts were taken, the numbers would be found not to tally; and when a check was made, sure enough it would be those whose arms bore the corn sign who had gone missing. There were interrogations and beatings, and security was tightened, but it made no difference: everyone knew that some among the Gwentarans must have been prepared to risk the forest rather than end their days in chains at the mine. Then the old tale did the rounds again when men whispered in the cages at night, the story of how Maesrhon had melted away into the forest after defying Haartell; and eventually some of the slaves began to maintain that there was nothing there to fear: that it was only on the Lissa'pathor that the darkness lay, that the tales of horrors unknown lurking among the trees were lies spread by the Caradwardans. Staring about him now, the fugitive could not, himself, feel so sure of this. How could anyone know what lived in such a place? He had spent all his life either in the city or at the mine: to him his present surroundings were totally alien, an environment whose secrets and signs he had no hope of reading or understanding. But there was no need to waste any effort worrying about all that: it took no special skills to be able to climb a tree. As soon as he saw one that seemed suitable, he would do what he had come into the forest to do; and then not day or night, not hope or fear, not friend or foe, would matter any longer. He would be finished with them all, and quit of his slavery.

At that moment the breeze sighed across the treetops and carried upon it, distant but unmistakeable, was the rattle and thump of stones and earth being tipped onto a spoil heap at the mine. It needed no fieldcraft to know that he had fled only a short distance from the Lissa'pathor. Maybe he would try to force a path just a little further into the forest, to get as far away as he could while the day was still young. Then he would die in the light, and die a free man. Fingering the rope he had stolen and which was now coiled across his shoulder, he began to push his way fearfully through the undergrowth. After a while he noticed a persistent clamour of birds some way off to his right. This was different from the constant background of whistles and calls all around him in the leaves: it was a raucous cawing and shrieking which every now and then increased to what sounded like aggressive squabbling. He stopped, peering through the trees. Had he imagined it, or was the forest less dense in that direction? Maybe there was an open space where he could see the sky. He turned towards the sounds, his heart beginning to race as he anticipated maybe finding the kind of place he sought, but suddenly a shift of air brought a disgusting, unmistakeable stench to his nostrils. At the mine, when slaves died, their remains were disposed of down a disused shaft. On more than one occasion, he had been in a gang told off to tip two or three bodies down into the darkness and if the day was hot, and an earlier burial party had not been too particular with their lime spreading, he had caught the smell of what lay below. But here… He crept slowly forward, hearing a new noise now, a strange humming, droning sound. The ground was becoming rocky underfoot, the trees smaller where their roots had managed to find a grip among fissures and holes. Yes, there was a clearing ahead. And then he saw. His hands flew to his mouth as his stomach heaved and he turned away, gagging in horror.

For several long moments he stood, fighting the waves of nausea, and behind him the thing he had seen dangled from a branch, swaying a little as the crows and ravens and other carrion-seekers tore at it. Unwillingly, but as if he could not help himself, the fugitive turned again and looked. He had seen many dead men, but never anything like this. The soft parts of the body had been attacked first: the belly was opened up and shreds of flesh and offal lay on the ground below, where a dense black cloud of flies swarmed and buzzed. He looked up to where the rope was fastened, past the ruined face with its pecked-out eyes. He saw the mine-mark where the hair still clung to the shrivelled scalp; and then he noticed something more. The body's left arm had fallen and its bones were picked almost clean, but the right arm still swung by its sinews and the blackened hand was missing its two middle fingers. Now he knew who this was: he had been there when those fingers were lost in an accident with the winch. This grotesque, rotting puppet had been a man who toiled and sweated beside him, who lay near him in the fetid air of the sleeping-cage and who had disappeared without a word what, two weeks back. So this was where he had gone, and what he had done, when he slipped away from the rest of them. He too had gone into the forest to die alone. The fugitive stood rooted to the spot until a furious fight between two crows brought him to his senses. They were flapping wildly, both pulling at the same piece of nameless meat. He turned and plunged blindly back into the trees.

Night found him huddled into the cavity formed by the upturned roots of a fallen tree. It was no more than a burrow, but he could find nowhere better to rest. He was trembling with exhaustion, unable to estimate how far he might have travelled: surely not far, given the difficulty of forcing his way through the tangled growth of the forest, but he could no longer hear any sounds from the mine. He remembered that after fleeing from the scene of that lonely suicide, he had struggled over a ridge of high ground and down again, so now he must be in an entirely different valley. It had never occurred to him before that there were hills and dales in the forest, and valleys other than the Lissa'pathor. To him, as to all Caradwardans, the forest was simply Maesaldron: fearful, unknown and untrodden. What was he going to do? He lay down, his knees drawn up to his chest. If only he could sleep, and never wake again. Suddenly he started up. What if some beast of prey attacked him during the night? He began shivering uncontrollably and held his jaw with his hands to prevent his teeth chattering. Desperately he battled for coherent thought. Did it matter what happened? After all, he had come into the forest to die. He fingered the rope again, realising that he would never be able to nerve himself to use it, now; though surely being savaged and eaten while still alive would be worse, and death from starvation or exposure would take longer. The rope would at least be quick. Not if I get the length wrong, he thought; and how can I be sure of calculating the correct drop? But it was what he had seen that day that did most to weaken his resolve. He was revolted by it, as if his memory had been polluted by the sight. He wanted a cleaner death than that.

By the time dawn came once more he had no thought to spare for anything but his craving for water. He had never been so thirsty, not even after a long shift at the mine. There was dew on the leaves and he licked at it, but it barely wetted his lips. He was ravenous too, although hunger was something he had been forced to endure for so long that he knew he could keep going without food for a while yet. Lurching to his feet, he set off again, too preoccupied with his need for water to notice that he had begun to think like a man with life, rather than death, on his mind. At last, after hours of struggling through the thickets, he heard the sound of water and came upon a small stream. He drank and drank again, and then stripped off his ragged garments and washed himself, realising as the cool water stung and smarted in his hurts just how many cuts and scratches he had suffered as he pushed through the thorns and branches. With his thirst assuaged, he put his filthy clothes back on and sat resting beside the stream. He peered into it, wondering if there might be fish there, but saw none. In any case, he would have had no idea of how to go about catching one. And although, having lived now through two nights, he felt slightly less afraid that he would be mauled by some animal, nevertheless he realised that the forest must be full of creatures he could eat if only he knew how to snare or trap them. But he did not possess skills of that sort and had seen nothing but birds and one or two squirrels. He knew some mushrooms were poisonous, so dared not risk eating any; and had spat out various leaves he had nibbled, afraid when he felt their strange taste on his tongue that these too might cause a lingering death.

As he sat there, the little spark of hope that had lit within him dimmed and darkened. He was not going to survive, so while he was still able to make a rational choice, he must decide between a quick death or a slow one. His eye fell on the stream. It was too shallow here; he knew he would not have the strength of will to keep his face under water. But surely it must get deeper as it went downhill, and then perhaps he could use the rope to tie himself to a stone large enough to weigh him down. Wearily he got to his feet and began to follow its course. As the day wore on he noticed that he was moving into an area where the ground was rocky and the forest not so dense; it reminded him of the place where he had come upon the hanged man, but this time the new terrain was much more extensive. The trees thinned, and ash began to predominate, clinging to cracks in the rock. Beside him the stream babbled along, flowing noisily but scarcely more deeply than when he had first found it. And then to his amazement, with a swirl and a gurgle where it had worn a smooth curve in the rock, it simply disappeared underground at his feet. He stood staring, baffled and frustrated, and then slumped to the ground himself, incapable of walking any further.

Next morning came bright and sunny, with a fresh feel to the air. He was almost comforted, glad to know that his last day would be a fair one. This was the end: he knew he could not go on. Somehow he had to find the means to die today. He drank deeply from the stream before it plunged underground and then stood up, clutching at a branch for support as his head swam. Gradually the dizziness eased and he looked about him carefully. The few trees that grew out of this rocky pavement were only small and for the first time he could see something of what lay beyond and above them. Far away and slightly to his right, mountains lifted their heads into the blue morning sky. Slowly his gaze moved from the heights, across the middle distance where the slender ash trees moved gracefully in the breeze, until it rested upon a distant, dark green mass lower down, away to the left. It looked as though the forest was thick and dense again over there, and clearly the ground sloped away all the time from the mountains. That might mean bigger watercourses, maybe even a river, if he could just get across this strange landscape where the barren rocks swallowed streams in a single gulp. The going was difficult, as he found out soon enough. The limestone pavement was scored across with sharp-edged fissures and the pale rock dazzled his eyes in the noon glare, making him afraid of missing his footing. Whatever happened, it would not do to injure himself and be condemned to suffer a protracted end out here. At last he made it across into the shade of bigger trees and almost at once he noticed the sound of water again.

By the time he found the source of the noise, the sun was already westering. He staggered out into a large open space within the forest. Over a high crag, in an endless silver filigree, tumbled a stream upon whose spray a rainbow danced where the sun's rays fell. It seemed almost as if the water sprang out of the sky to throw itself sparkling into the embrace of the earth, for when he crept forward to look, he saw that it dropped in an unbroken span straight down into an almost completely circular hole in the ground. Bright green ferns sprang from crannies in the wet rock for a few yards below the edge, but beyond that was darkness where the light failed to reach. A soft, refreshing mist settled on his face as it drifted from the falls; around the edge of the glade the leaves swayed gently in the light breeze, fresh and green in the golden sunlight. Upon the face of the crag over which the water fell, flowers nodded above small rock-plants whose names were unknown to him. The fugitive stood up and looked slowly about him. This place of beauty and peace, made fairer still by the rainbow that shimmered over the falling water, this was the place he sought. He walked back towards the edge of the wood, and turned. A final surge of strength, a desperate exhilaration filled his whole being and lent him speed as he ran wildly towards the water. Only a few more paces now, a leap, a plunge, the earth would take him and it would all be over; but from nowhere something caught him by the ankles and sent him sprawling. He scrabbled in a fruitless attempt to regain his footing, and suddenly there was someone behind him, someone who raised him up, who was much stronger than himself and who had him by the arms in a restraining grip which there was no hope of breaking. A voice spoke in his ear.

'Easy, easy! There's no need for that. Steady now, easy.'

An Outland speciality

Valahald leaned his back against the parapet of the city wall and folded his arms. Although he was apparently staring down into the streets below, his gaze was focused inwards. Was Valestron never going to take himself off back to Heranwark? Was his power so secure that he could leave his command and hang around Caradriggan like this whenever he chose? He himself was not so lucky: if the chance he was hoping for, to whisper privately into Vorynaas' ear, did not come soon, he would have no choice but to travel back to his post in Framstock. This thought reminded him of something else. Why had he heard nothing from Heranar? The official confirmation that his letter had been delivered to his brother had come back promptly enough, but after that, nothing. Valahald turned the other way, to lean on the stonework with his elbows, frowning. If the boot had been on the other foot, if he had received a letter like that from Heranar, he'd have reacted quickly enough, that was certain. Perhaps he had been foolish to expect support from his brother. He could just imagine him, chewing at his nails as he read the letter, unable to make his mind up what to do. Ever since they were children, Heranar had needed someone to give him a lead to follow. Valahald's thoughts drifted on to Valafoss, excluded now from Vorynaas' inner circle, an object of ridicule to those with whom he had once been intimate. His frown deepened as he remembered how Valestron had taunted him, and then lifted as he recalled his own response. Pushing himself away from the wall, he strode off quickly. The time for decisive action had come.

The following evening he was sitting at supper with his father. The girl was nowhere to be seen; Valahald had insisted on her absence, if he was to enter his old home again, and Valafoss, though annoyed by this, had complied with the request in the interests of a reconciliation with his elder son. And so, after an exchange of polite but stilted notes, they were spending a few hours together. Conversation had not flowed particularly freely, and Valafoss had covered his awkwardness in gluttony even more conspicuous than usual. Valahald however seemed quite at ease and plied his father with food and drink whenever there was a difficult silence. Eventually the final course was served and the servants were given permission to leave.

'Don't you want any of these?' asked Valafoss, cramming two little sugary concoctions into his mouth at the same time and chewing vigorously.

'I'm not particularly fond of sweet foods,' said Valahald, lifting an eyebrow as his father reached for another item from the selection that had been set on the table. 'But I brought you this, which should complement the taste perfectly. Let me open it for you.'

He produced a bottle and poured a small measure of the dark golden liquid it contained.

'Oh! Well, thank you.' Valafoss sniffed at the drink. 'What is it? Won't you join me and have one yourself?'

Valahald smiled. 'Not for me, I find spirits don't agree with me too well. It's an Outland speciality. Do you like it?'

'Mm, yes.' Valafoss helped himself to another tot.

'Good.' Valahald got to his feet. 'Excuse me, I'll be back in a moment.'

He left the room as if going to relieve himself but trod softly down the corridor towards the servants' quarters. Hearing voices, he opened a door and beckoned a man to him. 'Where's the girl?'

The man looked round at his colleagues and back at Valahald. 'She'll likely be asleep by now, sir.'

Valahald took a step forward. 'Show me the room and be quick, before I make you sorry for it.'

The man scrambled to obey and Valahald followed him out, down the hall and up a flight of stairs until they arrived at an archway on the first floor. Waiting until he heard the footsteps descend again, Valahald walked silently up to a door, opened it quietly without knocking first and slipped inside. He glanced around: the room was almost in darkness, its corners lost in shadow, but a small night-light burned on a chest near the bed. Swiftly he moved across the room, wrinkling his nose at its musky perfume. The lamp-oil must be scented, he thought as he picked it up. The sleeping girl stirred slightly and then opened her eyes to see Valahald standing over her. With a cry of alarm she started up against the pillows, pulling the bedding to her. For a moment he waited, smiling slightly, enjoying her fear; then he put the lamp back in its place.

'You know who I am?'

'Yes.' The word was barely audible.

He stood there, a young man of medium height, average build, so unremarkable that his face would be lost in any crowd; and yet somehow threatening, curiously sinister in his lack of colour.

'Listen to me carefully. I'll be back in a few hours' time, early in the morning. You will stay here until then: you will not leave this room, you will not call the servants. Do you understand me?'

'Yes.'

Valahald walked back to the door, and turned. She was staring in fright, her eyes wide in a white face, her hands clutching at the counterpane. He smiled again. 'Good.'

When he returned to his father, Valafoss looked up from pouring himself another shot of the Outland spirit. 'You've been a long time.'

'Yes, sorry about that. Just thought I'd have a stroll round the old place, renew some memories. The house is looking well. I could do with a base of my own in the city.'

Valafoss peered at him suspiciously. Was he imagining it, or did he detect a hint of a very familiar musky perfume clinging to his son? And what did Valahald mean, a base of his own? Was he really looking for a reconciliation? But before he could even get started on sorting out his thoughts, Valahald leaned forward.

'And I've been having a little chat with that girl of yours.' His father's hand froze, the glass half-way to his lips. Valahald smiled. 'She'll be away out of here tomorrow.'

'You... you...' Valafoss gulped his drink and reached for the bottle again. 'You insolent young bastard, you...'

'What an unfortunate choice of words. Surely you're not insulting my mother's memory? But don't you worry about the girl, you won't be here to see her leave. Because there's something else I should tell you.' He reached to stop his father raising his new drink and their hands touched: Valahald's fingers were cold and dry on Valafoss' hot, pudgy flesh and both of them recoiled from the contact.

'That drink you're throwing down so enthusiastically. How many have you had? Three at least, I've seen that myself. Well, I did tell you it was an Outland speciality, and you know their reputation as herbalists. I'm afraid this particular concoction is poisonous. Slow-acting, admittedly, but deadly. And there's no antidote.'

Valafoss put his glass down. It rattled on the table as his hand shook. Colour flooded up into his face and then drained away, leaving him ashen. Sweat began to bead on his forehead and roll down his cheeks. His mouth opened, but for a moment no words came. Then a horrified whisper made itself heard.

'You spawn of Na Naastald. My own son.'

'Ah, but you're forgetting. You gave me to Vorynaas, remember? Now, about this drink. Actually, most people can tolerate a single measure; and the wandering *sigitsaran* are introduced to it in their cradles, they build up their resistance to it gradually.' Valahald laughed, as if recalling some pleasant memory. 'I've seen more than one young fellow in the patrols live just long enough to regret he ever bragged he could take as much of it as an Outland comrade. But for someone who's had three or more, like you have...' He paused.

'How long… how long does it take?' croaked Valafoss, trembling uncontrollably.

Valahald raised a finger. 'I was about to say, there's just an outside chance you might still get away with it, but you'll need to get moving.'

Valafoss sprang to his feet with an alacrity he had not shown for years, his eyes fixed on his son in desperate entreaty. 'Quick, quick!' he panted. 'Tell me what to do!'

Detaching his father's grasp from his sleeves and brushing carelessly at the creases in the material, Valahald sat back in his chair.

'Well, I'm told the only hope is to sweat it out before it gets a hold. I've heard that far away down in the southern Outlands, the *sigitsaran* perform a kind of dance of death.' Valahald laughed again. 'Almost literally, because I gather that it's not unknown for the participants to die from the dancing before the poison sees them off. It's your only hope, but I doubt whether you're able to move vigorously enough.'

'I can, I can!'

Sweat was already pouring off Valafoss, soaking into his collar and down the shoulders of his clothes; but in a frenzy of terror, with no thought now for his dignity, he began to jump up and down, pump his arms, run on the spot. Almost immediately his pallor was replaced by an alarming flush and the breath began to catch in his throat. Predictably, he was unable to sustain his exertions for more than a few moments and laboured to a halt, gasping for air, the rolls of fat on him vibrating visibly to the mad pounding of his heart. He looked at Valahald with a mute appeal, but his son shook his head.

'No, that's not nearly enough. You've got to really put yourself through it, or the poison will get into your system. If I were you I'd try some push-ups.'

'But I'm too heavy for that! I'll have to try something else!'

Valahald shrugged. 'It's up to you. But I really wouldn't waste time talking.'

There were tears on Valafoss' cheeks now as well as sweat. With a sob of despair, he floundered to his knees and began a doomed attempt to raise himself up and down using his arms. Panic lent him strength and he managed to heave his bulk off the floor three times, but by the fourth attempt his arms were shaking helplessly and he sank back down, fighting for breath.

'Come on, come on! You need to keep going.' Valahald broke off from apparently examining his nails to nod encouragement.

Valafoss rolled over, his sides heaving, and began again. He lifted himself once, twice, and then fell with a thud. Somehow he scrabbled to an elbow, his free hand tearing at the neck of his garments, his face contorted in sudden agony, his mouth gaping in a vain quest for air. His cheeks became mottled with blue, his eyes started in his head and a dreadful choking noise filled the room. Then once more he fell, this time onto his back, and lay still. All sound had ceased. Valahald stepped across to inspect him. As he stood looking down, his father's body convulsed in a final spasm and did not move again.

Valahald straightened up and stretched, pleased with the success of his plan. It had worked much more quickly than even he had anticipated. Then he sat down again and helped himself from the tray of sweetmeats, rehearsing the words of regret he would use in the morning to announce his father's death before he sent the girl packing. After that, there would be the funeral to arrange: expensive but tasteful. Suddenly, Valahald laughed for a third time. For some reason his mind had jumped back to his boyhood lessons in Tellgard. He imagined a new topic for the students to debate. *What caused the death of Lord Valafoss? Was it illness, greed allied with over-exertion, or murder? Give reasons for your choice of answer.* But maybe the actual cause was much simpler.

He selected a clean glass and poured himself a large measure from the bottle he had brought for his father. Inhaling its bouquet, he rolled the spirit round his mouth, savouring the taste before swallowing with appreciation. Yes, you could make a strong case for the theory that it was Valafoss' gullibility that had killed him. Valahald smiled, sipping again at his drink.

Chapter 49

Doubts and fears

'You've not got much to say for yourself this evening.'

Half a dozen or so off-duty soldiers were drinking together in the *Golden Leopard*; the man who had spoken was Tirathalt, now posted back to Caradriggan and based in the barbican garrison.

'He's been crossed in love, maybe. We should fix him up with someone,' laughed one of the group, glancing over to where some of the *Leopard*'s girls were peeping round the curtain.

'More likely he's been on the receiving end of Thaltor's temper,' said another. 'Come on Temenghent, spit it out. What's the matter?'

'Nothing's the matter. I was just thinking about something, that's all.'

'Thinking! The *Leopard*'s for drinking in, not thinking in. Talking of which, it's your round.'

Temenghent got to his feet with a laugh and replenished the drinks, but though the conversation drifted from topic to topic he still had little to say himself. Eventually by ones and twos men left the group to attend to duties and errands until only Temenghent and Tirathalt and an Outland friend of theirs known as Sigittor were left.

'You haven't really had a row with Thaltor, have you?' asked Tirathalt.

'No. Well, not with him personally. But I've been officially cautioned – and had my pay docked, too.' Temenghent had been staring down into his drink; now he looked up, checked that no-one seemed to be paying attention to their table, and lowered his voice slightly. 'I went in to Tellgard and asked to see the copy that's been made of Haldur's tale; and it didn't go down too well with them, up at Seth y'n Carad.'

'I bet it didn't,' said Tirathalt with feeling, his eyebrows raised in surprise. Then dropping his own voice below the background level of general conversation, he leaned forward. 'What did you make of it then? Do you think it's true?'

'I don't know what to think,' said Temenghent. He sat silent for a moment and then looked up sharply as something in the way his friend had spoken belatedly caught at his attention. 'Wait a moment – do you mean you've read it, too? How come you got away with it?'

Tirathalt laughed briefly, but without much mirth. 'It's different for me. I wasn't the only one from the barbican garrison who found a reason to slip down to Tellgard. If they'd disciplined us all, it would have made too much of an issue of it, they wouldn't want that. And anyway, my career prospects are over for good now, so far as they ever existed. I could see it was finished for me as soon as Valahald sent me back up to Framstock that time and sure enough, I'd hardly had the chance to unpack my gear before the orders came, shunting me back down here. One thing you don't want to do is get on the wrong side of Valahald. But you... you were taking a risk. What made you do it?'

'Oh, I don't know.' Temenghent shifted restlessly in his chair. 'I was there, you know, the day Haldur spoke out in Tell'Ethronad. I got the job of keeping him and the others away from everyone at the end, so they couldn't be questioned, and I could see Haldur knew it, but he just smiled. They didn't seem bothered at all. Then next morning I encountered another of them, Cathasar I think his name is. I gathered he's a professional archer, back home.' He lowered his voice even further.

'I get the impression there's more to these fellows than our top brass give them credit for. They're so... I don't know quite how to put it... so at ease with themselves, unruffled, yet they surely must have realised how things are... you know what I mean... Anyway this Cathasar actually suggested I went down to Tellgard with them, can you imagine...' He paused and took a pull at his drink.

'But afterwards I kept thinking about what he'd said, the way he spoke to me almost like one soldier to another but friendly enough; and by then everywhere you went you heard people talking about the tale they'd brought... and I thought maybe Cathasar was right when he said to me knowledge was power or some such thing, maybe it would do no harm to find out.'

Sigittor joined in for the first time, having listened in silence up till then. There were very few Outlanders among the regular troops and he had been one of the group of friends for so long that they never thought of him these days as any different from themselves. Now, though, his origins were brought forcibly to their attention, because he spoke in his own, incomprehensible language and then laughed at the look on their faces. 'It means, "Not knowing is no shame, but not asking is no sense." It's a proverb we have, away down in the south. So now you have asked, or at least found out, why do you doubt what you've read?'

'It's not that, exactly.' Temenghent rubbed at his face. 'Half the time I wish I'd not done it, or if not, that I could just forget about what I've learnt, but I can't. It goes round in my mind all the time. I see you've read it, too, though it took you long enough to tell us,' he added rather tetchily.

Sigittor smiled, but before he could respond, Temenghent went on. 'Of course, I suppose it could all just be a story they have up there in the north. They say it all happened in the dim and distant past – how could anyone know now for certain whether it's true or not?'

The hopeful expression vanished from Tiralthalt's face almost before it had time to register at all as he shrugged his shoulders. 'If Arval believes it...' he began, but Sigittor cut across him.

'Well, there's something that's struck me, something I'm surprised I've heard nobody else mention, because it could be the proof you seem to need. Don't you think it's odd that you can understand

Gwentaran speech, and that of these strangers from the Nine Dales? All right, they might use an expression or two in their own dialect, and they might have a stronger or weaker regional accent, but that's as far as it goes: you don't have a problem. Yet you can't understand the Outland tongue at all. Down in the southlands, we've a completely different language that comes to us as part of our birthright. That's because we were there already, from time beyond mind; whereas your own history tells you that long ago your forebears spread into this land from the east. Gwent y'm Aryframan was settled from Rihannad Ennar, by the account of its own people; and now we hear that men arrived *there* after fleeing from a homeland far to the east. I'd say this means you share a common ancestry and were all in flight from the same place and the same thing, and I think we've just found out what this was: *stirfellaerdon donn'ur*, as they seem to call it in the Nine Dales.'

The other two stared at each other. There was no need to ask whether their friend believed the tale: Sigittor's words had made it abundantly clear that he did. Then Temenghent laughed.

'Well, would you listen to him! Didn't know we'd been knocking about with the brain of Caradriggan all these years, did we, Tirathalt?'

'Yes, you've missed your way in life, you have,' said Tirathalt. 'Why are you wasting your time in the army? You should be debating philosophy with Arval.'

Sigittor looked at them out of the side of his black, hooded eyes for a moment. 'The ascetic life doesn't appeal to me: my mind works best on a full belly.' He sat forward, putting his elbows on the table so that he could drop his voice still further and still be heard. 'But would I be right in detecting a distinct, well, drop in enthusiasm for matters military among all three of us?'

'Steady on!' Tirathalt looked round nervously. 'You don't know who might be listening. In fact maybe this isn't the best place to be having this kind of conversation.'

'It's safe enough in here. This background racket will cover anything we might say if we speak quietly. Who brought Arval into it anyway? Not me. Now, here's your good deed for the day. That boy Escanic, you'll know him from your time over the border. He's on his year's compulsory service and temporarily quartered here in the city. You drop him a heavy hint that he wants to keep away from the young fellow among the Nine Dales party and keep quiet on the subject of Gwent y'm Aryframan. He can't hold his drink and he's being a bit free with his opinions on the problems up there.'

Tirathalt put his cup down slowly, his eyes on Sigittor's expressionless face. 'How, by all that lurks in the Waste, do you know…'

'We Outlanders keep our ears close to the ground. We've got our own methods of finding out what's going on. And I know somebody who knows his parents. They're quite elderly, he's their youngest; and the old boy doesn't want him adding to the strain on the family business, so he's putting pressure on him to enlist as a regular. They've been arguing about where all this is going to lead.' Sigittor's black eyes flicked upward for an instant as if indicating the louring sky and then turned back to his friends. 'As you've already observed, Tirathalt, it doesn't do to get on the wrong side of Valahald, so I'd remind Escanic of that.'

Temenghent now leaned closed to Sigittor. 'And *you* want to be a bit careful about where and when you use the name *Gwent y'm Aryframan* these days. *They* don't like it.' He jerked his head in the general direction of Seth y'n Carad and finished almost in a whisper. 'You don't want to find yourself in Assynt y'm Atrannaas.'

'I can guarantee you I'd finish myself off rather than let it ever come to that,' said Sigittor. Noticing the awkward silence that followed, he suddenly laughed. 'For one thing, the company in there would leave something to be desired. It'd be bound to include either Valahald or Valestron: we can all see a showdown coming between those two sooner or later.'

'Don't joke about it,' said Tirathalt with a shudder. 'This rumour that's going round, that Valafoss didn't really die of natural causes, that Valahald did him in … I'd have no problem believing that. And I doubt Heranar sleeps easy at nights with wondering what's going to happen to him and his family just as soon as Valahald gets round to it. Never came down to the city for his dad's funeral, did he?'

'Well, he couldn't,' said Temenghent, 'with Valahald being down here. He's got to stay put in the north and deputise for him.'

'But why's Valahald spending so long in Caradriggan?' said Tirathalt. 'What's he up to? It can't be anything to do with the men from Rihannad Ennar, or he'd have travelled with them when they went off south. I must say I was surprised when that was allowed – but didn't you say they'd not all gone?'

Temenghent nodded. 'Yes, that's right. Three of them stayed behind in Seth y'n Carad.'

'Stayed behind!' Sigittor snorted. 'You two, surely you're not still so trusting! They're being used as hostages, to make sure Haldur and the others don't try any funny business, or take it into their heads to make a break for home. Personally, I don't think any of them will ever see the Nine Dales again.'

Visiting Heretellar

This was one of the many fears that gnawed at Haldur. The season was far advanced now, but in spite of the dark skies that sagged overhead from one horizon to another not much rain had fallen: the roads were still open and passable. Could it be that there was no need to wait until the year turned? Maybe there was a chance that they could begin their homeward journey before conditions eventually worsened, as they surely would in the end. Although it was obvious that they would never get out of Caradriggan or across its northern border without this being officially sanctioned, he wondered whether they might be permitted to travel as far as Framstock before winter closed in… Mentally, Haldur reviewed what he had seen of the garrison and armaments under Valahald's command. If they did have to force their way out, was there any chance of success? He remembered what old Morancras had told them of the secret resistance, awaiting only the right moment to make a move. What if those men, and the slaves bearing the corn-mark, took their flight for the signal and rose in revolt before their own preparations were complete? How many might die then, whether they themselves escaped or not? Perhaps it would be better if they could somehow obtain agreement to the idea that they should quarter themselves on Heranar for the winter. They had seen that the governor of Rossaestrethan had no stomach for the responsibilities he carried. If they were fast enough and determined enough, they might rush the pass while he dithered over what to do about it. In his mind's eye Haldur saw Heranar, chewing at his nails as he worried about his family and his shaky authority, and again suppressed the little pang of sympathy he felt. Heranar had been complicit in evil, however much he might regret it now: he would have to take the consequences.

As these thoughts ran their well-worn path through his mind, Haldur finished dressing and glanced out of the window. Aestrontor was strolling across the courtyard with Heretellar's man Meremvor and Haldur smiled a little, imagining their companiable silence. They had seemed to hit it off well during these days spent on Heretellar's estate, though neither was a great conversationalist. Haldur took out his comb and set about his hair, but as usual failed to prevent it falling heavily back on to his forehead. He pulled a face at himself and was about to leave the room when he heard running footsteps and laughter from outside. Cathasar had come round the corner, bow in hand; and with him were a youth, also with a bow and a quiver at his back, and a small boy who dogged their steps hopefully carrying a toy bow of his own. I must get some practice in today myself, thought Haldur, enjoying the memory of how he had hoodwinked Valestron and his military cronies. Before travelling south to Staran y'n Forgarad, the whole party from Rihannad Ennar had been taken off to Heranwark where Valestron was in command. Here, as well as making very sure that they saw plenty of evidence of military might, capacity and resources, Valestron had challenged them to engage in various contests of arms with picked men from the garrison up in Rigg'ymvala. Haldur smiled again. Let them think he was unable to hit the gold, if they wished. They had no way of knowing he had set himself other targets, and hit every one; after all, it was the accuracy that mattered, and his aim was as true as ever. Sitting on the edge of the bed he pulled on his boots, wondering what had prompted him to conceal his skill. His own men had been surprised, and the only explanation he could give was the same instinct that had led him to persuade Ir'rossung to seem more hard of hearing than he really was: an intuition that somehow, these small subterfuges might yield them the advantage if a crisis occurred.

Haldur ran down the stairs and found Heretellar poring over a ledger on the corner of a table that was set for breakfast. He shut it as his guest entered the room and stood up with a smile, nodding to a servant to begin bringing the food in.

'Oh, I'm sorry, you shouldn't have waited for me,' said Haldur. 'I'm very late this morning, I see the others are already out and about.'

'Don't worry, if it means you slept well and late, I'm glad,' said Heretellar. He turned to the servants as they moved back from arranging dishes on the table. 'Thank you very much indeed. We won't delay you further, we can serve ourselves.'

They smiled back and Haldur saw again what he had noticed already, how all his people loved Heretellar. Though barely ten years Haldur's senior, he seemed older: it was partly the prematurely silvering hair, of course, but there was more to it than that. His forehead was lined as if he had much to worry him and his whole demeanour had a careworn air under the rather old-fashioned courtesy. Haldur, who had seen how the estate was run-down and had heard about the disappointing financial return from the night-blooming flowers, beautiful though they were, thought he understood Heretellar's worries. As they ate, he glanced across at where the ledger lay on a side-table.

'Time to tally up the accounts, is it?'

'Yes, I'm afraid so,' said Heretellar. He sighed, sitting back in his chair. 'They don't make good reading. We'll keep going, somehow, but it's the effect on my father that concerns me. He insists on staying in Caradriggan, though I've begged him to come down here with me; but he insists on seeing the books too. It will only be one more thing to worry him.'

Haldur came to a sudden decision. 'Listen, Heretellar. I'd like to give you a share of what I've brought from Staran y'n Forgarad.'

His eyes went to the window as he spoke, where he could see the lamp shining on the corner of the stronghouse where his wagons were stored.

'Not at all, I can't let you do that. You bought it for Arval and he needs help far more than I do. What you've got there will keep Tellgard going for a good two years, and by then…' Heretellar broke off, as if debating inwardly whether to continue.

He looked so despondent that Haldur wished he could confide in him fully. Instead he settled for simply saying, 'It's all right. Arval has told me a little of Maesrhon and his quest for Arymaldur's arrow. And I promise you that I will keep secret what I have heard.'

Heretellar looked up at his guest. 'Well then, you'll know that by then either he will have returned, or else we will have no hope at all left to cling to. Arval looks for his return, and my father stands with him, telling me to trust Arval and put my own hope in that trust. But it gets harder as the years go by.'

'I met a strange old man in Tellgard, who was most insistent that I should trust *you*,' said Haldur with a smile, trying to turn the conversation. Heretellar's attention was engaged; he seemed surprised.

'Yes,' said Haldur, 'a half-crazed old fellow, he seemed to me, barely clinging to life. So thin, you could see the bones through his skin, staring blue eyes in a hollow face. He came tottering out from some doorway, I couldn't make anything of most of what he was raving about. Some tale about his daughter, or his wife – it was hard to be sure which he meant, maybe he scarcely knew it himself any more. When he found out I'd be travelling south he got me by the wrist and wouldn't let go. "Don't trust anyone except Heretellar," he kept saying. "Don't make the mistakes I made, don't trust any of them, but you can trust Heretellar," and then just when I was wondering what on earth to do, another man came clucking in search of him and helped him back indoors.'

'That must have been Arythalt. I'm amazed to hear he's retained any memory of me, although maybe, after reconciling his differences with my father these last few years, my name has lodged in his mind. Merenald is devoted to him, and he's lucky to have refuge with Arval but, by the Starborn, I would not be in his shoes. I'm even more amazed to hear he's still alive, and he wouldn't be, after contracting the sickness that comes from the mine, if it wasn't for Arval's skill in medicine. Maybe it would be better if he had died, with all the sorrows that lie on his heart. His daughter was Numirantoro, the mother of Maesrhon – and, well, you'll obviously have heard that it's whispered *his* father was Arymaldur, not Vorynaas. My father saw Numirantoro, just after the baby was born… this was in Tellgard, you see, Vorynaas had just left her there… and he hated the child… My father told me once that he thinks maybe within Tellgard there is some, some gate, some path into the world of the As-Geg'rastigan. Maybe both she and Arymaldur were able to pass through it. But if Arval knows, he has never said anything.' Heretellar shrugged. 'It's difficult to explain what I mean, when I don't understand it myself.'

'You mean that Tellgard is a *numiras*.'

'What's that?'

'It's what we say in Rihannad Ennar, when we sense a place that has known the presence of the Starborn. All of us from the Nine Dales felt it in Tellgard: the feet of the As-Geg'rastigan have walked there.'

Heretellar's face lit up, his dark eyes brightening as the lines around them softened. 'My father will draw comfort from that.'

'We left a message for you with your father, when we first arrived in Caradriggan; did you get it?'

'Yes, I did, thank you. I was surprised by it, and very pleased. Tirathalt and I were boys together, but we drifted apart when he enlisted. I'd heard he had risen quickly through the ranks, so if an officer in Valahald's troops at Framstock is starting to ask questions, even if it's only in his own mind, that must surely be a good thing. At any rate, that's what I interpret his message to mean.'

Haldur hesitated. Should he say anything? 'Look, it sounds as though you've not heard the latest. Tirathalt's been demoted, he's serving in the barbican garrison now. One of my own lads was told by a friend he made as we travelled south. I just hope it's got nothing to do with what we found out in Framstock.' He lowered his voice. 'We had it from an old man, Morancras his name was: he spoke the rite for us. There's some kind of secret network of resistance up there, many of the slaves are in it and we've got reason to think maybe some of the soldiers too. According to Morancras, they're just waiting for the right moment... a word, a lead, something to spark them...'

'Morancras! I remember him from my foster-years. I don't like to think of him risking his neck in the way you describe.' Heretellar got to his feet and walked over to the window, speaking with his back to Haldur. 'But whatever is afoot, the secret must still be safe. If Valahald knew, he would act without mercy. He's quite ruthless, you know. There's the best part of twenty years between him and Valestron, so you'd think time was on his side, but his ambition won't let him rest. These rumours that he was somehow responsible for his father's death, I wouldn't be surprised at all if they turned out to be true. Anyway... in Caradward too, I feel a sense of, what? Disillusionment, regret, a hopelessness creeping now even among some of those who once were loud in support of Vorynaas. You might not think it of me, seeing me here in the Ellanwic trying to hold a decaying estate together, but

I urged action myself, once. It seems like something from another lifetime now, though it's not so many years ago. No argument that I or my friends put forward could sway Arval, who said that we risked greater evil in an attempt to bring about good, an attempt that we could not guarantee would succeed. Look at Meremvor there.' He turned back to sit down again as the man walked past the window outside.

'Quiet, isn't he? Rather dour, difficult to get to know. He's not always been like that. It was years before I got the story out of him, but I'll tell you what happened. He overheard Maesrhon speaking privately to me, and hid to listen. Maesrhon had got wind of the fact that our troops had infiltrated Gwent y'm Aryframan, taken prisoners, killed people – this was before the invasion. Meremvor's Gwentaran himself, originally: he said nothing, so when he asked me for leave to visit his family, I had no reason not to allow it. Instead he went straight to Val'Arad, the council in Framstock, and told them what he'd heard; and in reprisal, they voted to refuse to sell us corn at any price. You can imagine the panic and disorder this caused down here, fomented by Vorynaas. It was largely the reason that in the end he got the support he wanted for all-out war. But Meremvor didn't realise he'd not heard everything: he'd missed the first part of what Maesrhon told me, that our irregulars had spied out the land, left behind them a spider's web of secret rat-runs and refuges so that when the time came, they had surprise on their side and swept into the heart of Gwent y'm Aryframan before anyone knew they were there, let alone had any chance of organising to resist.

'Now Meremvor blames himself for what happened; he thinks if he'd not gone to Val'Arad, they'd not have refused us grain, Vorynaas wouldn't have got the vote for war… but who's to say he's right? Arval always maintains that even though events played into his hands, Vorynaas intended to take Gwent y'm Aryframan anyway; and who knows whether, if there'd been more warning, there'd have been even more death and destruction? It's only afterwards, when one looks back, that a pattern to events shows itself. At the time, it's impossible to predict all the consequences of any action.'

For a moment Haldur sat in silence, remembering his old impatience at what used to seem Carapethan's lengthy deliberations over weighty issues. He understood better, now. 'You're right,' he said, 'my father...' and then he broke off as there was a knock at the door, which opened to reveal Meremvor.

Heretellar went out to him and there was a short murmur of voices from outside; then he stepped back for a moment.

'Excuse me Haldur, there's a message I need to attend to. I won't be very long.'

He disappeared with Meremvor, leaving the door open behind him. Haldur wandered across to the window, thinking over their conversation. After a while he heard squeals of laughter from behind the outbuildings: the child he had seen earlier must be there with Cathasar and the other youth. Just then Heretellar came back and Haldur turned to him.

'Who are the two youngsters I saw with Cathasar?'

'That's my cousin. He's Ancrascaro's younger brother – you'll have seen her in Tellgard. The child is her son. Any excuse and they're out of the city and down here to stay.' Heretellar smiled rather ruefully. 'Ancrascaro and her husband Rhostellat are formidably intellectual but I don't think either of the children they have is going to turn out the same way.'

As he sat down his smile faded and Haldur suddenly realised how careworn he had looked when he returned from dealing with whatever message had arrived.

'What's the matter?' he asked. 'Has something happened?'

Heretellar chewed his lip. 'I don't want to say much in case it puts you in a position where you might feel you have to keep silent to shield me if you're questioned. But word's just come in that you've been tailed by Atranaar's auxiliaries, so Vorynaas will know already what your business was in Staran y'n Forgarad.'

'Oh, there's no need to worry about that,' said Haldur, relieved to hear nothing worse than this. 'We've been followed, watched, 'escorted' and generally herded about under surveillance from the moment we came out of the northern wilderness. It's only what I expected would happen.'

'I wouldn't take it too lightly. Vorynaas doesn't know yet your purchases are for Arval. His mood will be black when he finds out. But he'll have heard by now how you paid for them, and be filled with rage to think he was unaware of the amber you brought with you. He is a covetous and greedy man.'

Haldur shrugged. 'He told me in front of everyone in Tell'Ethronad that there was no commodity he was interested in buying or trading. You were there, you heard him yourself.'

'True, but he didn't know then what you carried, or what you intended to do with it. You'd think, with what comes to him from the gold mine … but amber has always been especially prized in Caradward. Every last piece was seized when the Gwentaran captives were taken. That old man Arythalt you met, his wife was from Framstock. It was a wonder throughout the land that she wore an amber drop in both ears, the second being his wedding gift to her. Men were still talking of that when I was a child, such a stir was caused by the fact that he had the wealth to purchase so precious an heirloom.'

'Listen Heretellar, there's one thing that bothers me. Am I putting Arval at risk by trying to help him?'

'I don't think even Vorynaas dares lay hands on Arval, although I don't quite know why. I was afraid, after what Arval said about Assynt y'm Atrannaas, that he would use his words as an excuse to throw him in there, but thank the As-Geg'rastigan, at least that hasn't happened.' Heretellar gave an involuntary shudder, and Haldur felt a chill strike his heart.

'What is this chasm of darkness? When we journeyed down from the north, we saw prisoners under escort heading towards a deeper blackness under the mountains and heard that name. Is it an actual place, then?'

Heretellar's hand came up in the sign. 'Oh yes. I've never seen it myself, and I hope I never do. Not long after our invasion of Gwent y'm Aryframan, in the lands around the Somllichan Ghent folk ran from their beds in terror one night when the earth itself awoke: there was noise and destruction as the mountains moved and settled again. When it was all over, there was something new to see. This was before our darkness began to creep and spread over the northern border, but there in the last slopes of the Red Mountains there was a blackness deeper than the darkest night, so impenetrable that no man knows what lies within or beyond it, though it quickly gained the name of Assynt y'm Atrannaas. They say that now it looms black even against the darkness beyond.'

'It does indeed. It yawns from earth to sky like a vast door in the blackest night,' said Haldur, remembering what he had seen. 'But what...'

'Wait, let me finish. Vorynaas thought he could turn this place of horror to his use. Those who oppose him, if they are too old, too young or too infirm for the mine, or if he wishes to make a particular example of a prisoner, they are taken there and consigned to the void.'

Haldur stared, aghast. 'What, you mean they throw them into an abyss?'

'No, the truth is far worse than that. They compel them at sword-point to go in. Some of the prisoners have run mad, turned and sought instant death on the spears behind them, but many more have been forced to enter the darkness.' Heretellar looked as if he was sickened by his own words. 'I told you, none knows what lies within or waits there for those condemned. Despite all the threats Vorynaas has made, even his own troops fear to go too close, and will not stay nearby. But there's no need to keep a guard. Not one of those who have disappeared into Assynt y'm Atrannas has ever come out again.'

For some moments Haldur sat, lost for words. 'I have faced hazards real and imagined since I left my home,' he said at last, 'and have felt both the bite of fear at actual danger, and the panic that comes with the onset of a peril unknown. But I have never seen or heard of anything worse than the wrongs men are capable of doing to each other. The day when I see Rihannad Ennar again cannot come soon enough for me.'

Heretellar got to his feet and began collecting up the remains of their meal, stacking the dishes and cups rather abstractedly.

'I know. Sometimes it seems to me that the heart is so rotted out of us that Caradward will simply collapse inwards and be forced to begin again, and I swear there are days when I wish this would happen, and soon. I count you lucky that you've your homeward journey to look forward to, risky though it may be – oh!'

A plate slipped out of his fingers and broke with a crash on the floor, and as the two of them scrambled about to find the pieces, a middle-aged woman bustled through from the kitchen, knocking on the door and opening it all in one movement.

'Now master Heretellar, what are you at! Leave off now, the pair of you, you'll cut your fingers on those sharp edges and then we'll have blood on the linen to deal with as well as broken plates.'

A younger woman and a boy appeared in her wake with a tray and a broom, and while she stood with hands on hips the table was cleared and the floor swept. She dismissed the underlings with a nod and turned back to Heretellar.

'That's sorted, then. Now why don't you two take yourselves off outside for a while and make sure those boys aren't putting each other's eyes out with their bows and arrows.'

Smiling sheepishly, Heretellar held up his hands in mock-surrender. 'All right, I know when I'm beaten. I'm very sorry about the plate.'

The woman clicked her tongue, laughing a little. Suddenly she stepped forward and pressed him to her in an embrace. 'Ah, my duck, you shouldn't feel you've got to take all on yourself.'

'I know, *is-iro*.' Resting his head briefly on top of hers, Heretellar returned the embrace warmly. 'Thank you for everything.'

She stepped back, looking up at him. Then with a shake of her head she adjusted her apron briskly and was gone.

'What can you do?' said Heretellar, seeing Haldur grinning broadly. 'She's known me since I was born: there's no point in trying to stand on ceremony with a woman who's had to clean you up after you've messed yourself. We'd better do as we've been told, and see what's happening outside.'

It was only much later that Haldur suddenly remembered something Heretellar had said earlier. He waited until they were alone again before speaking.

'What did you mean about Arval and Vorynaas? You were afraid because of something Arval had said about Assynt y'm Atrannaas.'

'Oh yes, that's right. Well, you've seen the two of them in Tell'Ethronad. Arval was vehement in his condemnation of what was happening, and Vorynaas in turn mocked and belittled him before the council. Then Arval stood up and foretold that Assynt y'm Atrannaas would devour more than the lives of prisoners, and would never be appeased until it received a willing sacrifice – presumably meaning, until someone walked into the darkness of their own free will. I was terrified, and my father also, that Vorynaas would turn on Arval and suggest that he did so himself; but he contented himself with sneering. But then, there are times, and that was certainly one of them, when Arval speaks with such power and authority, you would say you heard the voice of the As-Geg'rastigan.'

'And nobody has come forward yet.'

'Yet? You don't seriously think that anyone could bring themselves to do such a thing, do you?'

Haldur made no reply: he could see that Heretellar did not expect an answer.

Loss of face

In Seth y'n Carad, Vorynaas relaxed one evening in his private apartment. His feet, in soft indoor shoes, were propped on a padded footstool. He had enjoyed an informal supper with Thaltor, just the two of them; it had been almost like old times, in the years long ago when they were both young. Now Thaltor had gone to do a duty-round of the sentries before retiring for the night and Vorynaas, the lamp turned low, was sipping at a last drink and wondering whether to send for one of his women or not. No need to rely on one of the girls from the *Golden Leopard*, these days. On his payroll he maintained half a dozen or so rather higher-class women whose sole purpose was to service his various needs. When he tired of them they were replaced, paid off handsomely with a warning as to future discretion; but latterly any gossip would have been fairly tame as Vorynaas' appetites became less urgent. His mind wandered on to the news that had reached him earlier in the day, that Haldur was now bound for the city with wagon-loads of goods purchased in the south. It was surely too soon to stock up for the return journey to the Nine Dales and Vorynaas wondered, unlikely though it seemed, whether any of what was on its way was intended as a gift to himself. Though angered by the fact that clearly the northerners had greater purchasing power than he had realised, he smiled to think that maybe Haldur's old-fashioned ideas of courtesy might require him to make a generous reciprocal gesture for hospitality received, equivocal though his guest-status had been. Vorynaas smiled again, speculating now on the various luxuries he could soon be enjoying; and as he indulged these thoughts, his mind began to turn again to other pleasures. He put down his cup and swung his feet to the floor. Maybe this was just the night to send for that woman – what was her name again? – who, though still young and desirable, was experienced enough to be skilled in the more gentle, leisurely arts of her trade. He opened the door to where his manservant waited but before he could speak there was the sound of arms being presented in the corridor, followed by a murmur of voices. Then someone scratched at the outer door. Vorynaas nodded to the servant.

The newcomer was an Outlander whose dress and the small pewter-leaf badge proclaimed him a member of an auxiliary troop. He had the true *sigitsaran* features and accent, so that it was impossible to tell from his salute and formal greeting whether he was nervous or in any way overawed at being admitted to Vorynaas in person. After apologising for disturbing him late in the evening, he indicated that his message was confidential. Vorynaas gestured him through, with a meaningful stare at the servant as he passed, and as he closed the door behind the messenger, he heard the slight metallic noise as one of the armed guards came into the outer room from his post in the corridor.

'Well?'

'My lord, I have been sent by Valestron. I have intelligence that was not included in the information you received earlier today concerning the goods which the men from Rihannad Ennar purchased in Staran y'n Forgarad.'

Vorynaas raised his dark eyebrows. 'Really? And how do you know what I heard today?'

'Sir, I merely repeat what I have been ordered to tell you.'

'Hm. Get on with it, then.'

'Sir. You will be aware that six full wagon-loads are heading north to the city. But the men from the Nine Dales did not pay for all this directly with the merchants concerned. Haldur went first to a leading craftsman and dealer in jewels and precious metals. From him he obtained gold coinage in exchange for amber.'

Vorynaas had been lounging back in his seat, stroking his beard as he listened. Now he got slowly to his feet, his eyes narrowed.

'Let me get this straight. Haldur was carrying amber to the value of sufficient gold to pay for *six wagon loads of goods*? Was it worked, or raw?'

'My information is that it was a single worked piece.'

'By my right hand! A single piece, of such value! Did you see it?'

'No, sir. But word came to Valestron from a man who did that it was smooth and without blemish, deep in colour with a fiery core, burnished and perfectly round in shape, and the size of a child's fist.'

The description had obviously been learnt by heart and committed to memory, but its power to stun Vorynaas' senses was no less for that. He stood speechless, his heart beating so hard he could hear it in his own ears.

'Where is this amber now, do you know? And who was Valestron's informant?'

'Sir, all I know for certain is that the news came to him from among the auxiliaries. I can tell you nothing about what may have happened to the amber.'

Vorynaas stood brooding darkly. Impossible to know from the man's blank demeanour whether he was telling the truth or not, but it scarcely mattered. Vorynaas knew full well that the amber would never be found now if anyone went looking; it would have disappeared without trace into the spider's web of contacts the Outlanders maintained among themselves and their associates – might even have vanished into the pathless south with the wandering tribes. He forced a half-smile.

'You've done well, thank you. If you need food, go down to the kitchen and get a meal. I want you to stay at Seth y'n Carad tonight; I may need you to take a message for me in the morning. My staff will make a place for you to sleep in the garrison dormitory.'

The man saluted and took himself off, leaving Vorynaas pacing restlessly up and down the room, thinking over what he had just been told. Haldur would never have risked bringing an heirloom away with him on his perilous journey from the Nine Dales, nor would he barter such a thing in commerce. But if he was in a position to trade amber of the quality Vorynaas had just heard described, the implications were crystal clear. There must be more, very much more, amber in Rihannad Ennar. Thoughts, half-formed ideas chased each other across Vorynaas' mind; energy flooded through his body. Suddenly he felt twenty years younger and his pacing became a prowl. He craved action, not rest. He poured himself another cup of wine, drinking it straight down without noticing its taste. Then he remembered something and his face began to darken with fury. That young man Asaldron, the time he'd brought the travellers into Tell'Ethronad... *We have not come to trade.* Vorynaas could hear the voice in his mind, his fury giving it a sardonic edge the reality had never possessed. And he had allowed himself to be provoked into saying there was nothing the Caradwardans wished to buy or trade! Now everyone would know that these northerners were prepared to trade where it suited them, that their country was rich beyond belief in a commodity that all coveted, that they had made a fool of him in front of the whole council. He put the empty cup down, trying to steady himself. Suppose, just suppose Haldur was to say he had kept silent about the amber so that he could use it to repay Vorynaas' hospitality? Vorynaas had scant faith in this theory, but it could not be discounted. If it turned out to be true, after he confronted Haldur, he would lose face again. No, he must wait a while yet.

Abruptly, Vorynaas began striding up and down again. When he thought of the amber, a greedy desire surged within him; when he thought of Haldur and the men from the Nine Dales, he was consumed with rage. Fed by his sudden restless energy, the flames licked at him. Sleep seemed impossible: he wanted something, somebody, to vent his anger, his strength, his power upon. He thought of the woman he had been about to send for and laughed aloud. He had a better idea now. There was a new girl sleeping in his women's quarters, barely into adulthood, slim and shy. And she was afraid of him: he had seen the fear in her eyes. He felt his body thrill and tense in anticipation. His face flushed now with excitement, he told himself he would show that girl she was right to be afraid. He opened the door and beckoned his servant.

CHAPTER 50

Ruthless rivalry

'He gave me this.'

Vorynaas unlocked a drawer in the desk before him and taking out a gold arm ring he handed it across. Valahald turned it over in his fingers, feeling the weight of metal in it. His own taste in such things was different from that of Vorynaas, who tended to favour an elaborate, highly-decorative style. Valahald preferred a plainer effect, having discovered the impact that a certain stark simplicity could achieve. He would have been happy to wear this ring himself: it was only lightly ornamented but rich in colour and its heaviness alone was impressive, although it was clearly not to Vorynaas' liking. He passed it back.

'It's a quality piece. Must have been expensive.'

'No doubt. But expensive or not, it's effectively just a trinket to fob me off. Meanwhile that old fool Arval is sitting on a windfall beyond his wildest dreams.' He shot a venomous glance across the desk. 'If Heranar or you had had the wit to search their baggage… I don't take kindly to being made a fool of, Valahald.'

'Of course, absolutely. If it had ever occurred to me that Heranar would be so lax I would naturally have stepped in myself… but the fault is mine, too: I see now that I allowed brotherly feeling to influence my judgement.' The response came fluently: what an accomplished liar you are, thought Vorynaas.

'Naturally, I regret this,' Valahald continued. 'I feel that Heranar has dishonoured me, as well as failing yourself.'

Vorynaas noticed the slight hardening of tone in Valahald's voice. Skilled physicians had examined Valafoss' body and found no sign of wound or poison, but Vorynaas was certain that Valahald had killed his father. Briefly he wondered yet again how he had done it, and whether Heranar was now on his target list. Resolving never to consume any food or drink Valahald might offer without seeing it tasted first, Vorynaas tossed the ring back into the drawer and locked it again.

'So what did you want to see me about?'

'I have something for you.' Valahald lifted a small package and placed it on the desk. 'This gift has had to wait for my father's death before I could give it, but now, strangely enough, circumstances have conspired to make the time of its giving curiously appropriate.' He smiled, and Vorynaas was struck by the odd coincidence that Valahald should speak now of his father. Could be possible that he had sensed his earlier thought?

'We have mentioned family relationships,' Valahald went on, 'but what are ties of blood? A man may be engendered in a moment's drunken lust as readily as with deliberate dynastic intent. In a civilised society such as ours, surely the important bonds are those formed in loyalty by the mind. The only paternal relationship I acknowledge is with yourself: you are my father-before-the-law. I promise that the recent hurt to your pride will be assuaged, and this is a token of that promise.'

Vorynaas opened the package and the wrapping fell away to reveal the cup that Heretellar had once given to Ardeth, which Valahald had taken from the rape of Salfgard, which Valafoss had picked out for himself from the plunder. Valahald had replaced the plain horn cup with a new, silver-gilt drinking vessel but Vorynaas recognised the holder. His fingers touched the worked silver, his dark eyes feasted on the matched amber insets, glowing warmly in the lamplight.

'This is very generous of you,' he said. 'Should I thank both my sons-before-the-law, or does the gift come from you alone?'

'As I mentioned just now, Heranar has disappointed me. These days I do not consult him before I decide on a course of action. He and I have business of our own to sort out when he arrives in Caradriggan: I'm assuming that you will require him to come down for the meeting?'

'Yes.' Vorynaas stood up and moved over to the wine table that stood in an alcove. 'Well then, we two will seal the gift.'

They chatted for a while, Vorynaas wondering how long it would take before the true reason for Valahald's request for a meeting became clear. He seemed slightly taken aback to hear that Thaltor had already left on his journey up to the occupied territory.

'There's no point in hanging about,' said Vorynaas. 'I want Heranar in Caradriggan as soon as possible. Young Temenghent can stand in for Thaltor here: he's perfectly able for it, and the recent little fright he's been given should have steadied him up. Plus you'll be on hand here in the city to keep an eye on how he does. If he's got any sense at all he won't want you finding fault. And while it's true that normally I wouldn't count Thaltor as governor material, it's only for a very short time and all he's got to do is keep things ticking over until you get back. No difficulties up there, according to you, after all.'

Valahald heard the sardonic edge with which Vorynaas delivered this last remark, but hid his thoughts, noticing that no reference had been made to Heranar returning to his province. Did this mean that his brother was going to be replaced, or possibly even that he himself was going to be promoted to take charge of both Rosmorric and Rossaestrethan? Now that *would* be worth leaving Caradriggan again for!

'Correct. Well, correct up to a point.'

Vorynaas lifted an eyebrow. 'What's all this about? Is there a problem you've not mentioned?'

'No, not one I've not spoken of before. But I'm not happy about the fact that the auxiliaries are not under my control. How can I be held responsible for matters over which I have no authority?'

'Oh, for… You're not still griping on about that, are you?'

'The situation hasn't changed, so my reservations about it haven't changed either. Some of the men take their independence almost to the point of insolence, knowing they can't be touched.'

'Rubbish, man. If you come across anything like that, just report it.'

'But this is exactly my point: I feel it undermines my position. And, sir, I have to say I've always been uneasy about the auxiliaries being split off from central control.'

'Yes, you've said that before as well. Anything else you want to say again, while you're about it?'

'As a matter of fact, there is. I think there are too many *sigitsaran* among the irregulars.'

'Well, governor. It sounds to me as though what you're really saying, though clearly you don't have the nerve to come straight out with it, is that you question my judgement.'

Valahald's heart beat a little faster in spite of the calming draught he had swallowed earlier. He moved his left arm against the side of the desk so as to feel the reassuring pressure of the tiny bottle he carried in his sleeve pocket.

'Sir, I would never dream of doing such a thing. But it does worry me to think that before word reached you of what the men from Rihannad Ennar were up to in the south, an Outlander knew it, and it was reported to his troop commander, and then to Lord Valestron, before ever it came through to you. They all of them had the news before you did.'

There was a silence during which Vorynaas stroked his beard, studying the face of the man sitting opposite. So Valahald had simply been waiting for the chance to have another snipe at his rival. Though he had made a telling point, Vorynaas conceded to himself; while smiling inwardly at how Thaltor had said bluntly, before setting off for Framstock, that he would trust neither Valestron nor Valahald as far as he could throw them. When Vorynaas eventually spoke, it seemed he had changed the subject.

'And what do you think of that news?'

Valahald was surprised by this, but his quick mind saw an opportunity to press what he thought was his advantage.

'I think it proves that I was right about the men from the Nine Dales. From the start, my instinct told me not to trust them – of course, I'm not claiming I had any inkling of the wealth they kept secret.'

'Of course not.'

Valahald heard the heavy sarcasm and gritted his teeth. 'But Tellgard was the place for them after all, wasn't it? And in view of what's happened, I presume that's where they're going to stay?'

'Well, after what Haldur had to say to me, I wouldn't have him under my roof again if he begged me. Want another?' Vorynaas gestured towards the wine table, but Valahald declined. Pausing briefly to register surprise at this, Vorynaas topped up his drink and sat down again. 'So they must make their own arrangements. But yes, I anticipate they'll keep to Tellgard now while they're still in the city.'

'What did he say?' This was news to Valahald and he was agog to hear the details.

Vorynaas laughed harshly. 'The general drift ran along the lines of how they'd seen all they wanted to and they'd be off as soon as possible, so they'd be obliged if I'd do whatever was necessary to get them over the border. And also that, since I'd ruled out any question of trade so firmly and publicly, they had felt at liberty to make whatever merchandising arrangements they liked; and that being the case, it pleased them to help Arval out before they headed back north. But *of course* they recognised how generous my earlier hospitality had been – hence the bangle.'

While he had been speaking, Valahald had almost been able to hear Haldur's voice, as some hint of his speech crept unconsciously into Vorynaas' description of what had been said; but the final sentence was delivered with a sneer and a jerk of the thumb towards the desk drawer.

'I'll tell you this,' Vorynaas went on, 'and I mean what I say. If I see any man who is not already holed up in Tellgard with Arval putting so much as a spot of new paint on the woodwork, or replacing one cracked flagstone of the steps, that man will never work again.'

Valahald was scarcely listening to this: his attention had been caught by something else. 'Do they mean they want to start back straight away? Travel now, with winter coming on? They said before that they'd have to wait, so as to time it right for crossing the wilderness again. Why the change of plan?'

The dark, dangerous eyes surveyed Valahald as Vorynaas slammed his cup down angrily on the desk. 'It seems Heretellar's been telling them all about Assynt y'm Atranaas during their trip to the south: two birds of a feather there, him and Haldur! I remember Thaltor saying to me, years ago when you were all still boys, that Heretellar could hardly stand up under the weight of his own worthiness, or something along those lines. Anyway apparently the thought of it, Assynt that is, is too much for their delicate stomachs. Haldur gave me to understand that they can't stay here, after what they've heard. I suggested to him that if he felt that strongly about it, why not put one of Arval's more irritating pronouncements to the test by braving the dark himself. He didn't like that, I was pleased to see. But he informed me, as cool as you like, that his first duty was to his father and his people, which ruled out a gesture of that sort.' Vorynaas had been calming down as he spoke and now he laughed.

'I'll give him one thing, he had cheek enough to actually sound as if he regretted it. So the upshot of it all is that, the roads being still open and passable, they want to spend the winter with young Heranar up in Rossaestrethan. And no doubt you'll see why I need Heranar to come down here as soon as he can, first.'

Unwilling to admit he did not see where Vorynaas' thought was leading, Valahald inclined his head and nodded slowly in what he hoped was a suitably sage manner. Since he felt he should make some comment, he said, 'But that means Thaltor will have to miss the meeting.'

Vorynaas waved this off with a laugh. 'Thaltor wouldn't care if he never had to attend another meeting. He's like my own right hand, I know he'll do whatever I decide. And he knows I know he will. We go back a long way.'

'You mean you've decided anyway, whether we meet or not?'

'I certainly have: glad to see you worked that one out, at least.'

A jealous twinge had stabbed through Valahald, even though he knew there was no need to concern himself with Thaltor, when he heard the hint of indulgence in Vorynaas' laughter; but he forced himself now to smile as warmly as he could contrive. 'You and Thaltor are real brothers in arms. *He* would never let you down.'

'No, I don't think he would. But do you know something, Valahald.' Now it was Vorynaas' turn to smile. 'If he ever did, there's Assynt y'm Atranaas all ready and waiting; and I wouldn't hesitate to make use of it. For anyone, if I had to, from the lowest to the highest.'

Brotherly love

About a week after this, Valahald and Heranar were sitting together in the garden of what had until recently been their father's house. Heranar had arrived in the city the night before, and had spent the morning alone while Valahald had business in the barbican. He sat now silent, staring into the pool, miserable at his extended parting from his family, not knowing what to say to Valahald, uncomfortably aware that his brother's eye was on him. Eventually Valahald, growing impatient, stood up and took a turn or two around the pond.

'Come on Heranar! I wouldn't give you so much as a quarter-*moras* for your thoughts, but let's have them anyway. We need to be prepared for this meeting! We need to decide what we're going to say. And we should come to some arrangement about the house. Why didn't you answer my letter, when I wrote to you about our father making such a fool of himself? Fortunately it doesn't matter now, the way things have worked out, but I'd have thought you could have shown a bit more interest.'

Heranar looked up. The lantern above the fountain still played on the sparkling cascade as it fell, but he had seen no movement in the water beneath.

'What's happened to the fish?'

'What? The *fish*? They're still in there somewhere as far as I know. Look Heranar, we've got more important things than the damned fish to talk about.'

'I don't think they're still there. I've not seen one, and I've been watching for them.'

'Well, so what? Now listen. What exactly did Thaltor say about Vorynaas when he arrived in Framstock?'

'I told you: he just said he'd come to cover for me while I was in Caradriggan for this meeting. He never said anything about Vorynaas that I can remember, except that he wanted me to travel south. I hope whatever Vorynaas wants me for won't take long. I want to get back to Ilmarynvoro and the children.' He chewed his nails for a moment. 'You'll be coming back to take over again in Framstock when this business is over, won't you? You've been down here long enough, surely.'

Valahald stood in front of his brother. 'I might remind you that I've had a lot to deal with down here that I didn't expect, what with all this domestic mess to sort out. And I was right about the men from the Nine Dales: all my intuition told me there was something they were hiding, and now we know what it was. You should have had them searched. You've done yourself no favours there with Vorynaas, Heranar. He's furious to think you let them slip through your fingers still carrying all that amber.'

Heranar turned his head with a half-shrug. 'I can't do anything about that now. It's easy enough to be wise after the event. They arrived in friendship, after all. Haldur in particular was really nice to the girls. Ilmarynvoro said she liked him and if I'm honest, I did too.'

'This is worse than I thought.' Valahald sat down and leaned forward. 'What's the matter with you? You've had your status handed to you on a plate, you're a son-before-the-law of Vorynaas, but look at you. You can't command the respect of your subordinates, you can't even make a decision and stick to it: what about all that vacillating over whether to sweep the hill country? You've got no ambition, and you've tied yourself up in a marriage that's beneath you.'

A mixture of anger, fright and embarrassment battled within Heranar, causing the tell-tale flush to rise to his cheeks. He forced himself to look Valahald in the eye.

'Don't talk about my wife like that. What would you know nothing about things like these? You think of no-one but yourself. Wait till you're a married man too, you'll see the world differently then. And you can leave my ambitions out of it as well. I know what I want, all right?'

Valahald smirked. 'No, really? Let's hear, then.'

Heranar's hand closed on the edge of the seat to steady himself; he had not meant to speak out like that. His brother was the last person he would have chosen to confide in; but the problem had been eating at him for so long, and who else could he tell? He dropped his gaze to the pool again and lowered his voice.

'What I'd like most of all is to come back here to Caradriggan and bring Ilmarynvoro and the children with me.'

This was definitely not what Valahald wanted to hear. His voice had an edge to it now. 'Oh, so now we're getting to it. You think you're entitled to the house, just because you've produced a brood of children? Well, think again! I'm prepared to discuss selling it and dividing the proceeds, or I might consider buying you out. But under no circumstances am I going to look for another place while you sit pretty in here.'

To his surprise, his brother laughed at this.

'I knew you wouldn't understand,' said Heranar. Suddenly he felt easier, more confident. 'You can have this place if you want it, I don't care. I've never liked it, I realise now. And our mother hated it, she was always unhappy here. Remember where we lived when we were really young? Remember the garden, and that summerhouse against the back wall, where we used to play before the old man started to use it himself? That's what I'd like: somewhere lived-in and welcoming, with a garden for the girls to run about in, where Ilmarynvoro could sit in the sun.' The enthusiasm died from his voice and face as he finished. 'Only, there's no sun now; and anyway, I'm not sure Ilmarynvoro would want to leave her own people to come and live down here.'

'I can see why you got on well with Haldur,' sneered Valahald. 'But by my right hand, Heranar! No wonder you're out of your depth running a province if you can't even make up your mind what to do about your own family. If you want something, just tell this wife of yours what you're going to do, and then do it.'

'But that's just the point, she *is* my wife, so I can't simply ignore her wishes, or upset her by making her think she's keeping me in the north for her sake, against my own inclination. And, while I'll admit I don't get on too well with her mother and father, the fact remains that they're my marriage-parents, so I've got to consider them as well.'

'Listen to me, Heranar. You need to realise that if you're going to get on in the world, you have to put yourself first. Never mind your marriage-parents! If you'd had any sense at all you'd never have tied yourself up with a family of backwoods smallholders and goat-herders from some forsaken hole in the hills. Remember you're a son-before-the-law of Vorynaas.'

Heranar shook his head. 'I know I wouldn't be where I am today without it, but all that business was forced on me. I've never felt comfortable about it, the way you do. In my heart I'm still the son of Valafoss, which is what I really am.'

He glanced over towards the house. The whispers had reached him and he thought his brother more than capable of disposing of their father: now his flesh crept as he tried not to imagine what might have happened here, in the very house under whose roof he was sleeping. He looked down at the pool once more, and this time he saw something in the water: something pale, slowly rising up from the depths. Belly-up, whitish, with staring eyes and gaping mouth, a dead fish came to rest just below the surface, moving slightly as the fountain ruffled the water.

'Oh, it's dead!'

Valahald whipped round and exclaimed in disgust when he saw what his brother was looking at. He yelled for a servant and a man who had been standing just within the large courtyard doors hurried over.

'Get rid of that before it starts to smell.'

The man fetched a basket from the toolshed and scooped the fish from the water.

'My brother here seems curiously concerned about the fish,' said Valahald, with a touch of languid amusement. 'Take that away and then get a stick or something with a long handle. Stir the water up, see if you can dislodge the others from wherever they're lurking.'

'Sir, I'm afraid this was the last one left.'

'Oh? What's been the problem, then?'

Valahald lounged on the seat, enjoying his role as master of the house, but Heranar saw that the servant was afraid and unsure of what to say. The man shifted from one foot to another and cleared his throat.

'Sir, Lord Valafoss always used to feed them himself when he took the air before his own mid-day meal.'

Valahald sat up slowly. 'And how was I supposed to know that?'

There was a painful pause. The servant stood, his eyes cast down, the basket dripping water on to the ground beside him. His silence spoke volumes and all three of them knew it. So Valahald had failed to feed the fish, which had eaten each other one by one until the only survivor died of starvation right under his nose. But although this was a genuine, if careless, oversight, the household staff had been afraid to intervene because they had assumed his cruelty was deliberate. What could the man standing before them possibly say? Heranar's heart hammered. He was certain now that the rumours were true, that Valahald had killed their father. Panic rose in him at the thought of his wife and children, so far away. He must get back to them!

Valahald spoke. 'I told you to take it away. You will present yourself in my study in an hour's time, and you will wash the stink of fish off yourself first.'

The man backed off at speed. Valahald watched him go with narrowed eyes and then turned to his brother.

'Fools! If I had the time to deal with it, I'd get rid of them all and start again with staff of my own choosing. Well, the rest will have to wait, but I'll have him on his way at least before evening.'

Heranar heard his own voice as if from a great distance. 'What did you do to the girl?'

'I didn't do anything to her. I simply showed her the door and packed her off as soon as her sugar-daddy was dead.' Valahald laughed unpleasantly. 'I got the impression she couldn't get away fast enough. She seemed positively petrified with fright every time I spoke to her – I can't think why.'

Afterwards, Heranar never quite knew how he came to blurt out what he said next. 'I've heard the rumours, Valahald. About you and our father.'

Valahald smiled. 'You'd not seen him for quite a while, had you? Overweight, unfit, you've no idea the state he was in. He and I dined together here, in his own house, the food and drink prepared in his own kitchen. He stuffed himself until the sweat ran off him and died in front of me with his mouth still full. Don't you know he was examined afterwards by the most eminent medics Vorynaas could get hold of? You shouldn't listen to whispers, Heranar.'

'But don't you even care that this is what people are saying?'

'Why should I? I'm ambitious, I don't waste my energy worrying about what people think. And anyway,' he smiled again, and again Heranar's flesh crept, 'I find it's not such a bad thing, actually, to be able to strike a certain note of fear in people.'

Heranar twisted his fingers together and in spite of all his efforts to prevent it, his voice shook slightly. 'I know you're not going to admit it, or tell me how you did it, but I know it's true. I know you killed our father.'

'Oh, pull yourself together Heranar,' said Valahald contemptuously. He flung himself down onto the other seat. 'You know what Vorynaas told me, only last week? That if he had to, he would send even Thaltor to Assynt y'm Atranaas. Thaltor, Heranar, even Thaltor. You think about the implications of that. That's how strong you've got to be, if you want to get to the top and stay there, the way Vorynaas has done. True power lies with him alone – and I'm his son, before the law. Of course, that applies to you too,' the smile reappeared on Valahald's colourless face, 'but only technically speaking, as it were.'

'You know who you remind me of? You sound like Valestron.'

'Now get this straight, once and for all.' Valahald spoke quietly, but with such menace that the stressful flush ebbed from Heranar's cheeks, leaving them mottled and blotchy.

'Whether he realises it or not, I have the advantage over Valestron in several ways. I am younger than he is, I am more calculating than he is, I am more intelligent than he is. And I can be more ruthless than he is, if I feel it's necessary: I've learnt that from Vorynaas. It's his example I follow, not Valestron's. I know something about Vorynaas that only a son would know, a secret he told me himself. He once made a vow, swearing to do a certain thing or be devoured by the blindworms of Na Naastald: he wasn't afraid to make such a bargain with fate, or to fulfil his oath; and neither should I be, if I had to.'

At this Heranar's arm came up almost of itself as he began to make the threefold sign: the gesture, once second-nature to him, that he had not made in years. He caught himself doing it and dropped his hand back down to the bench, but his brother had noticed.

'Well, well,' sneered Valahald. 'Do you know who *you* remind *me* of? You're like Haldur and his merry men from the north, and *he* puts me in mind of Ardeth and the other peasants who wasted our boyhood years. You must have picked it up from your marriage-family. I wonder why you *really* changed your mind about having the hill country searched. Maybe you knew something about fugitives hiding there? Maybe you didn't want them found?'

The flush crept up Heranar's neck again. 'I don't have to justify my decisions to you. My report went to Vorynaas, all right? And anyway, a reconnaissance was carried out, by a senior auxiliary officer.'

Valahald laughed sourly. 'These Outland bastards who seem to be taking over the auxiliaries can tell me till they're blue in the face that the rabble from Salfgard aren't lurking up there somewhere, but I know better.' He stood up. 'I'm going in now to deal with the fish-feeding idiot. Listen, Heranar. You need to shape up and sharpen your ideas, and to do it quickly: I won't be pleased if you let me down in front of Vorynaas at this meeting tomorrow.'

Temenghent panics

Temenghent had been granted a morning off-duty, since he would be in sole charge of the garrison in Seth y'n Carad during the afternoon hours when the other commanders and senior figures were closeted in secret session. He had scarcely got into uniform again after arriving back in his quarters when Valahald materialised silently in the doorway.

'I'd like an explanation of why you've been in Tellgard again.' Valahald's voice was quiet and his demeanour neutral, but Temenghent felt himself beginning to sweat.

'No, sir! At least, not in the sense you mean, I …'

'I want to know why. And I want to know now. Make it quick, I don't have much time.'

Temenghent swallowed, surreptitiously wiping his palms against the cloth of his uniform. 'Sir, I was off duty this morning and I saw what I thought at first was just some old bundle of rubbish lying in a corner of the street. But then I heard moaning and I went to look closer and it was the old man Arythalt. He was just lying there, as if he'd collapsed; I can't think how he managed to get that far from Tellgard… Anyway I thought the best thing to do was get him back there as quickly as possible, so that's what I did.'

'Why do it yourself?'

'I was afraid he might die on me right there if I didn't move him straight away. My own grandfather…' Temenghent bit off what he'd been going to say when he saw the look on Valahald's face: an appeal to family feeling was not a good idea in view of the rumours one heard. He ploughed desperately on.

'And sir, he was across the road from your own house – I thought, what if he'd been heading there, confused you know, thinking it was still his? And maybe going to make a scene that might have been embarrassing for you? So yes, I could have told somebody else to deal with him but I could do it quicker and quieter, so I did. He's so frail, he weighs no more than a child.'

For a long moment Valahald contemplated Temenghent, a curious expression on his face. Then he pulled up a chair and sat down.

'Commendable consideration on your part. But I'm curious to know how someone who by your account is practically at death's door could do anything to "make a scene", as you put it. Tell me more.'

Fragments of thought scurried through Temenghent's mind like frightened mice. Was it just coincidence that Valahald had found out about his visit to Tellgard, or did he have him under observation? Why was Valahald sitting about here, when he'd just been going on about being short of time? What about this meeting he was supposed to be attending?

'Well, it… it was the way he was sort of talking to himself – almost raving, he was,' stammered Temenghent, fear spurring his powers of invention. 'I thought, what if he attracts attention, and then who knows what he might have come out with, rambling away like that?'

'Was he saying anything coherent?'

'Not really sir, there was no sense to it, it was just…'

'But you must have been able to make something of it, otherwise why be concerned? You're contradicting yourself, that's not good in a military man. Come captain, set your thoughts in order.'

Temenghent looked into the colourless eyes of the man sitting opposite. A bead of sweat trickled down through his hair and soaked clammily into his undershirt. He could see some private amusement in Valahald's face and knew that his superior was toying with him, but what was behind it all? *One thing you don't want to do is get on the wrong side of Valahald.* Tirathalt's words came back to him as the conversation they'd had in the Golden Leopard flashed across his mind. What did Valahald want to hear? Panic lent him inspiration.

'Well, most of what I heard was probably stuff from years back. Names, you know? He kept repeating names... Family memories, I expect.'

'Names. I see. What about the men from Rihannad Ennar: did any of their names come into it?'

'Oh yes.' Temenghent nodded, improvising rather wildly along the lines Valahald was so helpfully indicating. 'Yes, he mentioned them, and Arval, and he was muttering something about his daughter's foster-years in Gwent y'm Aryframan – as it was then, I mean. And there was a lot of stuff I couldn't make much of, except that I suppose he was thinking about his time at the mine, because he kept going on about the forest.'

'The forest?' Valahald paused as if considering this, his head slightly tilted. 'Maesaldron. Are you sure it wasn't Maesrhon you heard him mention?'

'I don't think so, sir, it was the darkness that he...'

Valahald cut across this. 'But family memories would surely include his grandsons, no? I put it to you, captain, that it seems very likely you misheard the old man's ramblings.'

It was obviously best to agree.

'I could have got it wrong, yes,' said Temenghent. 'He did mention Ghentar, certainly.'

Valahald stood up and glanced out of the window. 'No doubt you're anxious to get started on your rounds.'

Temenghent stood, too. 'Sir, there was something else I wanted to say about Arythalt.'

'Yes?'

'It's just that, well, you know what old folk are like: they remember things from years back much clearer than what happened yesterday. And people say his mind's completely gone. I mean, he's probably very confused.'

Valahald smiled. 'Possibly. I see they're beginning to arrive for the meeting now. I must be getting along.'

Vorynaas gets his way

By mid-afternoon, Valahald was witnessing something he never remembered seeing before, and had certainly not expected: Vorynaas arguing his case against opposition from some of his closest supporters. No time had been wasted in coming to the point. The Nine Dales were to be invaded, Vorynaas announced. Annexed, if it seemed worthwhile; destroyed, if not; but in either case, all existing amber was to be seized and brought back to the city and its source found and secured for Caradward. Then he called on his associates to outline to the meeting how best they considered this operation was to be successfully carried out. Vorynaas sat back and waited as the other men around the table looked at each other. Heranar chewed at his nails, his face flushed; his brother, pale and composed, said nothing but was as watchful as Vorynaas. There was no knowing what might be passing through Atranaar's mind, but Valestron was frowning and his subordinate commanders, summoned from their posts in Heranwark, Staran y'n Forgarad and the border headquarters beside the Red Mountains shook their heads and muttered together. One of them looked up and caught a raised eyebrow from Vorynaas:

he broke off his exchange with his colleagues and all three glanced at Valestron as if hoping he would give them a lead.

'Well, gentlemen,' said Vorynaas eventually, 'why this reticence? Let's have your ideas on the table. Valestron?'

'In principle, I think the venture you describe has many points in its favour. But, and I say this with regret, in practice I do not believe we can succeed in it.'

The officer from Staran y'n Forgarad leaned forward, emboldened by these words. 'My lord, it pains me also to say this, but I have to agree with Valestron. Rihannad Ennar is so far away; our resources would be too stretched.'

'Yes, it's a basic rule of military strategy, after all.' This was Rhonard, the man from Heranwark. 'The longer your lines of supply, the greater the risk.'

Vorynaas glared at Rhonard, silencing him instantly. 'I don't need a lesson in strategy. There are risks, and there are calculated risks. What have *you* got to say?'

'Well, I… I…' floundered Torilmarap from the border garrison. 'It's a question of heart against head, my lord Vorynaas, and I feel we should follow our heads, in this particular instance.'

'So it seems, then, that none of my most senior military men has any suggestion as to how we are to accomplish what you all claim to want to achieve. Most disappointing.' Vorynaas sat back in his chair, one hand stroking at his beard, his eyes moving from one man to the next. He waited, allowing them to wonder whether he was going to give up his plans, and then suddenly raised his voice: Heranar and Rhonard jumped visibly.

'How pathetic! Listen to me. I will not tolerate an independent power lurking unsubdued beyond our northern borders. If six men can get here, then it follows that the Nine Dales cannot be so far away that we can discount any threat from them, and by the same token they must be near enough to be within our reach, if we are properly prepared.'

'Could I say something?' Heranar's words were hesitant, almost apologetic.

'Please do,' said Vorynaas, his tones dripping sarcasm. 'It would be a pity to have come as far as you have, and for me to have had to send Thaltor to mind Rossaestrethan for you, only to sit here with your mouth shut.'

Heranar blushed painfully, looking down at the table to avoid seeing his brother's expression of contempt.

'Yes. Well, what I wanted to say was this. I questioned Haldur and his companions about their journey as soon as I had them within my power…' – here he faltered slightly, hearing a hint of suppressed mirth from somewhere to his right – '…and from the description they gave me of the wilderness they had travelled through, I would agree with their belief that the route would be impossible for a large body of men. Na Caarst: it's not just dry and barren, they said the ground's not safe underfoot; there's places where it's caved in – Haldur reckoned whole armies could be swallowed up and lost.'

'Well of course he did! He fed you all the horror stories you could take, to stop you getting any ideas about trying to follow him. You're so gullible, Heranar, and I know who you inherit that from.' Valahald paused to savour the slight frisson that went round the group at these words, and then turned to Vorynaas.

'I'm sure that when he's thought things through, my brother will be just as keen to support your latest venture as I am, Lord Vorynaas. It's unfortunate that we must be without Thaltor on this occasion, but I assume he is with you in this?'

'Yes, he cast his vote before he set off for Framstock.'

'We could all of us have counted on that, surely.' The light, knowing voice belonged to Valestron. 'Making a career out of being a right-hand-man generally precludes the possession of an independent mind.'

Though he concealed it, Vorynaas heard this with more than a little surprise. So the enmity between Valestron and Valahald had now reached such a pitch that Valestron was prepared to risk a public insult to both Thaltor and Vorynaas in order to score a point over his rival. Well, if it came to barbed shafts, Vorynaas could throw them with the best.

'Whereas the mind of a left-hand-man is much more interesting to those who can read it – as I am able to do, Valestron.'

The black, hooded eyes in Atranaar's expressionless face slid from Valahald's smirk to Valestron's studied indifference. Impossible, as yet, to pick a winner between these two; but it had not been necessary, in the end, to choose between Ghentar and Maesrhon. In the years since then, Atranaar had risen to the top of his own military specialisation, and Vorynaas was still secure in power. His attention switched back to the man at the head of the table. Maybe there was a way to appease all of them.

'I have a suggestion to make, sir. Let picked men from among my troops carry out a reconnaissance. I am confident that the best of the auxiliaries would be capable of overcoming whatever difficulties they might encounter in Na Caarst.'

Rhonard jumped in, eager to restore his loss of face. 'Now there's an idea. The irregulars are the men for this job. We need to gather all the first-hand information we can, before committing ourselves to an operation as big as this. We can set up a forward base for them in Rossaestrethan. They'd be ready to move in the spring, if everything's put in place over the winter. You could sort that out, couldn't you Heranar? No problem.'

'Well, I… Yes, but…' Heranar's heart sank as he foresaw the impossible situation he now seemed likely to be placed in. Did he dare request a recall to Caradriggan now, while he was still in the city and could speak alone with Vorynaas? But what if this was granted and he had to send for Ilmarynvoro and the children without having had the opportunity to explain things first? He sat there, preoccupied with his private worries, and around him the debate went on. When he began to attend again, matters appeared to be almost settled.

'Why not simply use the auxiliaries to lift the amber? Once they're in place, they'll know where it comes from and goes to. Let these northerners keep on doing the work of getting it, and then relieve them of their efforts. Minimum risk, maximum result.'

This was Valestron, clearly pleased that the specialist troops in his control were recognised as capable of such a dangerous and complicated mission, and warming to part at least of Vorynaas' original strategy.

'Yes, we've done it before, after all,' said Torilmarap, enthusiastic now. He and Rhonard exchanged knowing grins: both had served in the auxiliaries earlier in their careers and had seen action in Gwent y'm Aryframan.

Heranar looked at Vorynaas, wondering in some surprise whether he would allow himself to be talked out of his stated complete objective. Vorynaas did indeed find himself tempted. He brooded for a while, as the others waited for him to speak. In spite of what he had said, he did not truly view Rihannad Ennar as a credible threat to Caradward. The desire of his heart had been to conquer and lay waste, with plunder as an agreeable bonus: he was smarting still at being slighted by the men from the Nine Dales. But he had already decided not to lead any expeditionary force himself, being both reluctant to absent himself from the centre of power in Caradriggan and (although he did not admit this, even to himself) too old now for active participation in such a risky venture. No, he would remain here, and maintain control. However, failure was not to be countenanced; and it seemed that those he would be relying upon to carry out his plan were not persuaded of its successful outcome. The fingers of his right hand moved involuntarily as he imagined caressing globes of worked amber such as the piece which had been described to him but his mouth, hidden behind his left hand, set scornfully at the thought that his most senior lieutenants were such cowards that they would only support him as far as raiding, but drew back from the greater prize of conquest. Or was it that they were too complacent, too comfortable? Then a new thought struck him.

The debate had gone this way and that for two hours and more by now, but Valahald had not had much to say. There had been the predictable sniping between him and Valestron at first, the one scoring points off the other. But since then, Vorynaas now realised, Valahald had kept pretty quiet. Was he really going to let his rival carry the day by getting Vorynaas to agree to the less ambitious plan of plundering rather than destroying? He'd been devious from boyhood, as Vorynaas had reason to know. There he sat, self-contained, silent, secret. And far too confident. As Vorynaas considered his elder son-before-the-law, it came to him suddenly that Valahald was concealing something momentous and instinctively he acted to seize the initiative.

'Well gentlemen,' he said, fixing Valahald with the dark, dangerous eyes that had cowed so many men over the years, 'before I make a final decision, perhaps the governor of Rosmorric will do us the courtesy of sharing his thoughts. I see that he came here this afternoon with the intention of telling us more than he has said so far.'

Slightly disconcerted by this, but hiding it successfully from all but Vorynaas, Valahald inclined his head.

'You are as perceptive as ever,' he said. 'In the Nine Dales I think there is a prize which you will find even more to your liking than amber. I urge you to go north to take it.' He paused for maximum effect, looking round at the others present. Once again Heranar felt his flesh creep as his brother smiled. 'Yes, indeed. I have reason to think that Rihannad Ennar may be harbouring the traitor Maesrhon.'

CHAPTER 51

Last days

Arval sat at the tower window in Tellgard, as he had sat so many times while the years had come and gone. He had been reading, but although the book was still open his eyes were turned away from it, down towards the scene below. Cathasar was taking an archery session while Tellapur and Asaldron were helping some of his own people repaint the woodwork of the colonnade outside the workrooms to the left. Across the courtyard the windows were lit up in a study room where he saw Haldur talking to Ancrascaro. There was no sign of the other men from the Nine Dales, but Aestrontor had proved an able instructor in swordsmanship and Ir'rossung too was more than willing to help out where and when he could. The book slid from Arval's hand unnoticed as his mind ran over the unexpected treasure-trove of materials which had rolled into Tellgard as a result of Haldur's generosity: not just foodstuffs and stores, but woods and metals for the craftworkers, medical supplies, inks and fine leather to repair and restore worn bindings in the library. And, locked safely away, gold coins of great value to help with future need. Arval smiled to himself as he savoured the pleasure he and Rhostellat had found in listing and laying up all these good things. Almost, almost he could pretend that the old days had returned; that Tellgard had shaken off its pall of despondency as a snake sloughs its skin, waking up to a new spring of warmth and growth.

He saw Merenald heading back from the kitchens, carrying a covered tray with food for Arythalt. Against all the odds the old man still clung to life, but his condition was causing Arval renewed concern. He had been behaving with increasing strangeness: it was as if the revitalised atmosphere within Tellgard had unsettled him in some way. He seemed anxious and agitated, and had several times evaded the watchful care of Merenald. More than once they had found him, confused and rambling, in some far corner of the precincts; and one day he had disappeared altogether. Merenald, beside himself with worry, was still desperately searching every nook and cranny in Tellgard when Temenghent, of all unlikely people, climbed the steps of the colonnade, carrying Arythalt over his shoulders. From what he told them, it seemed he had found the old man in a state of collapse, across the street from his old house. Arval had been unable to shake off a feeling of unease about this, but now as he watched Merenald disappear through the door of the guest wing his thoughts turned back to the men from the Nine Dales. He had little doubt that it was their presence that had at least partly contributed to Arythalt's condition: sometimes he would address Haldur as Ardeth, as if scenes from his own youth were uppermost in his mind; at other times he would stare fixedly at Tellapur and then mutter to himself. Arval had heard the names of Ghentar and Maesrhon during these confused ramblings, and guessed that Tellapur's youth had brought the faces of his long-lost grandsons back to Arythalt's bewildered memory.

Now that time was short before the northerners would be leaving, Arythalt seemed even more disturbed. No doubt he was aware of the increased bustle of activity as preparations for departure were made, but who knew what he made of it all. Past and present were so scrambled in his head that for all Arval could tell, maybe in his less lucid moments he thought he too was to leave Tellgard and was afraid of what might happen. Arval made a mental note to speak to Merenald about Arythalt's medication: it would do him no good at all to be continually over-excited. Ah, but all too quickly the guests would be gone and the air of vitality their presence had conferred would dwindle away. Although Arval had half-hoped Vorynaas would refuse them permission to leave so soon, this was not to be. One morning when he and Haldur were deep in conversation, there had come a knock on the door and Forgard looked into the room.

'Here you are. Have you two eaten? No, I thought not. Come on down, there's no need to go without now, thanks to this young man's generosity.' Forgard smiled, nodding at Haldur. 'And I've some news for you. I ran into Heranar earlier. How he holds his job down I've no idea, he seems a bundle of nerves; but although he was patently keen not to be seen talking to me, I did gather that he'll be going back north within the week, and that you'll be travelling with him.'

With a sigh, Arval turned to his book again but the words swam meaninglessly before his eyes. His mind ranged over all the new knowledge he had recently acquired as a result of meeting Haldur: how dearly he wished he could have talked it all through with Artorynas! Haldur had told him how abashed Artorynas had been, when he found out the truth that they had pushed from memory behind those deceptive little words 'the bad time'. Yes, Artorynas would have felt the shame deeply, as indeed did he. He longed for the day when the two of them could debate and discuss this and other matters to their hearts' content. And who knew what wonders Artorynas himself might tell of, when once he returned! But this thought brought another, much less welcome, in its wake. Arval abandoned his attempt to read and set aside his book. Haldur, who after all had a much clearer picture than he did of the northlands into which Artorynas had gone alone, and who had spent time with him much more recently, was none so sure that his friend was ever coming back. He tried not to show it, in order not to worry Arval, but the old man was far too astute a reader of men's thoughts not to have seen the doubt he was attempting to suppress. Suddenly solitude weighed too heavily on Arval's heart. The windows opposite were dark now; Haldur and Ancrascaro must have finished talking and gone their separate ways. Arval got to his feet, intending to seek company, but as he stepped into the corridor there was Haldur himself coming towards the study.

Haldur wanted to know if he might see the books Numirantoro had made. He had heard about these from Artorynas and Arval too had mentioned them, urging him to examine them while he had the opportunity. For a long time he sat, turning the pages slowly in silence, feasting his eyes on the richness of the work before him. At last he paused and looked up: Arval saw that the book was open at the picture of the huge grey standing stones.

'I've never seen anything to compare with this,' said Haldur. 'Artorynas has a way with words, but even what he told me fell short of the reality.' He glanced at Arval. 'Is he very like his mother?'

'Yes, he is. Although as he grew older, in appearance he began to favour Arymaldur more.'

'You know, the very first time I saw him, I thought he was one of the Starborn. Especially as he was in a *numiras*.'

Arval's dark eyes seemed fixed on something far away. 'Rihannad Ennar is fortunate, to be so hallowed with these *numirasan* of which you tell me.'

Haldur dropped his head and Arval heard the ache in his voice when he spoke. 'Yes, I can't tell you how much I wish our journey was over, and I was back there.'

The final few days passed in a whirl of activity and preparation: Haldur, thinking ahead, felt that anything needful for their eventual journey beyond Gwent y'm Aryframan should be purchased or made ready now, rather than left until they found themselves in Framstock under Valahald's eye. Who knew what restraints and restrictions might be put upon them once they were far removed from the general gaze of Caradriggan? They were particularly careful and choosy in the horse-market when selecting animals for the long road home, remembering that Heranar had kept them confined to quarters when they travelled south, and not knowing whether he would do the same during the winter months they planned to stay with him.

'Whatever is the matter with him?' Tellapur wondered aloud one morning, when he, along with Haldur and Aestrontor, encountered

Heranar in the street. Buoyed up by the thought that they would soon be on their way north again, they greeted him in friendly fashion and Haldur wanted him to join them in a drink at the *Sword*; but Heranar, obviously uneasy throughout their conversation, seemed positively stricken at this idea and took himself off at speed, mumbling excuses.

'Who knows? Who cares?' Aestrontor pulled a wry face. 'I'll tell you what though, it'll be heavy going, stuck under his roof again.'

'True enough,' said Tellapur, 'but rather him than his brother. Maybe it's just the thought of travelling as far as Framstock with Valahald watching him. I'd certainly sympathise, if that's the case.'

'Yes, me too.'

Haldur laughed, but there were frown lines on his forehead. What *was* the problem? He watched Heranar disappear around the nearest corner like a rabbit bolting for cover. They knew that he had been summoned from his posting to attend a meeting: Cathasar had heard this from Temenghent on the day he had rescued Arythalt – and suspected that Temenghent had said more than he meant to, in mentioning that Vorynaas had gathered his chief subordinates to him. Haldur found himself wondering, not for the first time, what had been going on up in Seth y'n Carad.

Marching orders

Heranar on the other hand would have much preferred not to know, especially given the amount of time it seemed he was going to be spending with the men from Rihannad Ennar. None of his protestations that one of the first things he had asked them was whether they knew anything of Maesrhon had been the slightest use: Valahald had once again accused him of excessive credulity and Vorynaas, now that he had been given a scent of his quarry, was clearly not to be deterred from a chase to the death. Heranar, having seen the signs of obsession in the past, had no difficulty recognising them now. The plans were quickly laid.

'No, no,' said Vorynaas, in response to Valestron's urging that Haldur and his companions, or even Arythalt, should be arraigned and interrogated. 'That would only create an unnecessary stir: in fact it would just serve to spread the rumour, which is the last thing I intend to happen. No, as it is, if anything leaks out, people will simply put it down to the old fool's ramblings and leave it at that. And it's fortunate that these northerners are so keen to put city life behind them and scurry back home: as soon as they're away from Caradriggan, we can begin preparations. Then once they move on from Framstock, we'll start shifting all the men and gear up there, to make it our main forward depot for the advance force of auxiliaries quartered on Heranar. It gives us almost an extra half-year. Come the spring, we'll be ready for them to begin setting up a chain of stores dumps and communication posts. And then, with everything in place, we'll make our move the spring after that. And when the moment comes, gentlemen, you can tell your troops that the reward still stands, but if Maesrhon is taken alive, the bounty will be doubled. I want to see him, one final time. By my right hand! I have sworn to bring him to account, and I will.'

Valahald went about the city with a new spring in his step, elated at what he saw as a victory over Valestron. So what if it was the auxiliaries who would be crucial to the success of the plan? If Valestron had had his way, they would only have been used for what amounted to petty raiding. Valahald was a man who craved power much more than wealth. Invasion, conquest: these would advance him in pursuit of it, and enhance his status with Vorynaas. What a stroke of luck that business with Temenghent had been! Valahald smiled to himself. He'd put the frighteners on the young man, right enough, so that he responded readily to a little coaching; by the time he was brought before Vorynaas and the others, the story of what he'd heard and what it was likely to imply had firmed up nicely. And yet, thought Valahald, sitting back at the desk where he was working, I should give some credit to myself. A man may make his own luck if he keeps his wits about him. I've never believed that Maesrhon died in the forest, and there was something about these northerners that made me suspicious, right from the start. The Hounds of the Starborn, indeed! With a snort, Valahald tossed his pen onto the paperwork he was checking and clasped his hands behind his head. Across the room the military clerks were careful to continue their work without looking up. In his heart, Valahald conceded that actually finding Maesrhon was unlikely. But sometimes a long shot did hit the target, and if that happened in this instance, his stock with Vorynaas would rise so high that Valestron would be finished once and for all. And as a good second-best, it would not be difficult to trick some captive from the Nine Dales into believing he could buy his life with a plausible tale of Maesrhon's arrival and subsequent death there. Which reminds me, thought Valahald, bending to his work again. Quickly completing his list of requisitions for the imminent journey back north, he snapped his fingers for a military posting docket to be brought to him. I must get that fellow Temenghent transferred to my staff, he said to himself as he filled it in; I need to keep him under my eye for a little while yet.

Word that Temenghent was to leave Caradriggan was not long in filtering through the various military establishments in the city. The talk went round in the messes and taverns where soldiers gathered. While the more ambitious men eyed the post that would need to be filled at Seth y'n Carad, and wondered whether anyone was in line for it, most of the speculation centred around the reason for Temenghent's transfer. What had brought him to Valahald's attention, and was the move for better or worse? Though no-one was bold enough to come straight out and say it, clearly the majority opinion was that catching Valahald's eye for whatever reason was not a good idea, even if it did lead to promotion. Temenghent's friends kept out of the discussion as far as they could, but they read the worry in each other's faces. Why was he avoiding them? He had not been seen since the news broke. One morning Sigittor found himself in Seth y'n Carad, having been ordered to escort a consignment of gear into the stores from the main depot in the barbican. The day was chilly and while his men unloaded the wagon, Sigittor stepped over to a brazier to warm his hands and take a quick cup of mulled ale. He turned to stand with his back to the heat and came face to face with Temenghent as he emerged from a nearby doorway.

'You've been lying low! What's the story on this move to Framstock then?'

Sigittor spoke cheerfully enough but he was struck immediately by his friend's agitated manner, and looking more closely he noticed how pale and worried he seemed. Surely he was thinner, too?

Temenghent looked quickly around the compound. 'I've got to talk to you, but not now in case Valahald notices...'

'Valahald's in the barbican, I saw him there as I left with this lot. Come and get yourself a cup of ale. Nobody will think anything of it if we exchange a quick word and if they did they can't hear what we say out here. What did you want me for, anyway?'

'You know that time you and I and Tirathalt talked about – well, there's no need to go into what we talked about. But you said,' Temenghent glanced about him again and lowered his voice, 'you said you'd never let yourself be taken to Assynt y'm Atrannaas. You're an Outlander, everyone knows they've got ways and means. Can you get me what I'd need?'

'What? Surely they're not...'

Temenghent shook his head impatiently. 'I can't go into all that now. I need something small, something easy to keep hidden about me. I've got to be sure it will bring a quick death. I can pay whatever it costs. Can you get it for me?'

'Yes.'

'Good. Listen, two nights before we go north, I'm off duty that evening. I'll meet you in the *Leopard* and when I give you the nod, slip out of the back door. There's a little shack behind the privies, nothing in it except old rubbish and rat poison. I'll make sure it's open, we can talk there.'

He walked off without another word, leaving his drink barely touched. Sigittor's face gave nothing away, but he clasped his hands around his own ale-cup and stepped up close to the brazier as if he felt the morning turn colder than before.

'Trust me.'

At noon that day Valahald ran into Heranar and swept him into the *Sword and Stars*. As they crossed the courtyard towards the main door, an Outlander emerged from the entrance to the bath-house. Valahald eyed him with a certain automatic distaste, not liking that he could afford such an expensive establishment especially as he seemed young – so far as it was possible to tell with these *sigitsaran*. Then he remembered the old crone who had supplied him with certain drugs and who was also an Outlander. Maybe *sigitsaran* had a taste for women who looked old enough to be their grandmothers. Or maybe, he thought, his good humour returning, maybe she *is* his grannie and they like to keep it in the family: I wouldn't put anything past them. But Valahald's expansive mood began to evaporate as his brother sat there glumly, picking at his food.

'What's the problem today, then?' he asked. 'Look, this is your big chance, but you've got to be ready to take it! You must be confident we can pull off this campaign, surely? We're Caradwardans, we can do it.'

'Oh yes, it's not that.'

As one who had been there when Gwent y'm Aryframan was overrun, Heranar had no doubt of success again in Rihannad Ennar.

'Well then, what? We'll be on our way north in a few days now – I thought you couldn't wait to get back to that wife of yours? There's no pleasing some people.'

Heranar ignored the jibe. 'It's all very well for you, sitting pretty in Framstock empire-building. What am I supposed to tell Haldur when all the men and equipment starts arriving in Rossaestrethan? When auxiliaries start pouring in and setting up camp? It's just not realistic to expect me to get right through the winter with him and the others on my hands without them guessing what's afoot. What explanation can I possibly give? And then of course it'll be my fault, according to you, if our troops get to the Nine Dales only to find them ready for us.'

As he reached for his cup, Valahald took a sideways peek at his brother. How could anyone be that naïve? Or was Heranar just plain dense? He sipped at his drink, weighing things up. Heranar's anxiety did seem genuine, therefore his innocence must also be genuine. Unbelievable! Well, it was useful, as the rest of them had all agreed, so he might as well do what he could to reinforce it. He spoke quietly.

'Listen, see how you like this.' Heranar looked up, his brow furrowed with doubts.

'You do a good job on this one,' said Valahald, 'by which I mean, make sure everything runs smoothly up on your patch for our boys, and keep the northerners sweet: and if you want, I'll put in a word with Vorynaas for you about bringing you back to Caradriggan when it's all over.'

'Really?' A blush of pleasure began to spread over Heranar's face, but then the sandy eyelashes drooped again and he chewed at his nails once more. 'But how can I... I mean, what can I tell them that'll be convincing? What if they guess, they'll...'

'Heranar.' Valahald sighed. 'You do worry, don't you? Why do you work yourself into such a state? You must get it from our mother, she was a worrier too.'

'But if they don't believe me, what am I going to...'

'You'll have help, don't worry about it.'

'Help? How do you mean?'

Valahald gripped his brother's arm. 'I told you, there's no need for you to worry about it.' He gave the arm a little squeeze and then got to his feet. 'Trust me.'

This reassurance was partial at best as far as Heranar was concerned. He was sleeping badly again, waking from the old nightmare of blood in the streets of Framstock only to see his brother's colourless smile in his mind's eye. Now he suspected he would also hear those two words *trust me* drifting in a whisper on the night air.

In the *Golden Leopard*

A couple of evenings later, the *Golden Leopard* was packed to the doors. It was hot and rowdy, and there had already been two fights over a girl. Temenghent caught Sigittor's eye.

'I can't stick this, I'm going outside for a breath of air.'

The room was so noisy that the words were partly mimed, but the message was plain enough. He shouldered through the throng and disappeared.

Sigittor drained his mug and pushed it across to another man in the group. 'It's your shout. I'll have the same again, I'm just going to make room for it while you set them up.'

The privies were at the left side of a narrow yard behind the inn, but beyond them was a small store, nothing more than a windowless shed. The door was unlatched. He slipped inside. It was pitch black, but he could hear Temenghent's breathing.

'Have you got it? I've brought the money.'

'Yes. Here.' With a faint chink of coins, a tiny object, no bigger than a thimble, changed hands. 'It will break easily if you bite it, and you'll be dead before you hit the ground. Now tell me why you think you're in danger of Assynt y'm Atrannaas.'

'Valahald panicked me into telling lies,' whispered Temenghent. 'No, I'll not say what they were, but I was too afraid not to do what he wanted. He made me do his bidding, but he knows it was under duress. That'll be why he's had me transferred to his staff: he's only taking me north so he can watch me. He'll find a way to get rid of me. But though I'm ashamed to have been such a coward, I've made my mind up to put things right before I die. They've decided, up there in Seth y'n Carad, to take Rihannad Ennar. The plans are all laid:

they're going to do to the Nine Dales what they did to Gwent y'm Aryframan. Well, there's nothing anybody can do to stop that. But there's something else, something that Heranar doesn't know; they've not told him because they don't think they can rely on him not to give the secret away.'

A breath of laugher escaped Sigittor. 'I saw the brothers together the other day, going into the *Sword* as I was coming out with what you wanted. What a pair! The viper and the rat.' His Outland accent seemed accentuated by the whispers and the darkness.

Temenghent reached out and grabbed his sleeve. 'Listen, we've got to be quick. Maybe Haldur and the others will suspect what's going on anyway, but it won't make any difference, because they're going to be murdered before they get even half a chance of making a break for the Nine Dales with a warning. Keeping it dark from Heranar is so he'll act normally and they won't guess, but as soon as they get up there in Rossaestrethan, well away from anybody who'll even think of objecting...' Temenghent broke off to make an unpleasantly descriptive slicing noise.

'Why are you telling me this?'

'You've said yourself the Outlanders have their own ways of getting and passing on news. There'll be thousands of auxiliaries moving north soon, with *sigitsaran* in numbers among them. Get the word on to the network. You must know someone you can trust.'

A sudden commotion broke out in the yard. Temenghent put his eye to the door and saw that another brawl was under way: men were fighting and shouting, and the bouncer had his hands full ejecting one of the belligerents. He turned back to his silent companion.

'Right, this is your chance. Slip back in now while this rumpus is afoot and no-one will notice you've been a long time. If they do, say you found me throwing up and then left me to get on with it. I'll wait till this dies down and come back in then.'

Sigittor paused, his hand on the latch. 'I do know someone I can trust. But how do you know you can trust me?'

'I just do. Go on, quick.'

But as Temenghent stood alone in the dark shed, waiting for the right moment to make his own move, he realised that although it was true to say he trusted Sigittor, he no longer really cared. He had done the only thing he could think of to avert the planned evil deed. It was no good hoping he would ever get near enough to Haldur to warn him directly, and even if the men from the Nine Dales somehow found out for themselves, or had reason to suspect what was going to happen, what could they do? They would need help, which was what Sigittor's Outland contacts might be able to provide. His friend had let enough hints drop for Temenghent to be certain that some kind of subversive organisation existed. And Sigittor himself should be safe from reprisals: his brain worked quickly, and he could hide his thoughts. But if suspicion fell upon himself, if he was found out and they came for him... well, he had tried his best now to atone for his lies: a burden was lifted from him. His fingers closed round the tiny phial of poison. At least they would never get him as far as Assynt y'm Atrannaas.

A sleepless night

So time passed until only one night in Caradriggan was left for those who were to leave the city. In Tellgard, Haldur and his companions stood in the ancient hall with Arval's folk to hear him renew the pledge; then after a final check of all their gear, they ate supper together and went to their rest. Yet Haldur was unable to sleep and eventually, in the deep of night, he rose quietly and went out into the emptiness of the exercise court. Even though he knew he would see nothing, instinct made him tilt his head back as if to search the black sky overhead for stars. How he missed them! A slight sound behind him made him turn swiftly, his senses at full stretch, to see Arval, emerging from the tower door.

'So you are wakeful, too,' said Arval, and Haldur could hear both the smile and the sadness in his voice. 'A vigil is easier to bear if one is not alone. Let the two of us talk together while we still have time.'

They went silently up the stair and into the dark study, where Arval turned from lighting the lamp to see Haldur's face full of a new idea. 'Arval, why don't you come home with us? You could establish a new Tellgard in Cotaerdon! You would be more than welcome.'

'I can't do that, and leave my people here. I have to stay, I have to show them we can hold together. And anyway, Artorynas will return; I must be here as I promised, when he does.'

For a moment or two Haldur hesitated, then he spoke. 'I think I ought to tell you something. I asked Artorynas to come back to Rihannad Ennar, before he returned to you here in the south. It was because it was so hard to see him go, alone; I wanted so much to go with him, but I couldn't: my duty is to my father, and the Nine Dales. And so I thought, if he came to Cotaerdon first, at least we'd see each other again, even if it was only once… but now it seems to me that maybe I shouldn't have done that; perhaps it will delay him when time is running short.'

'But he promised to do what you wanted, didn't he?' Warmth stole into Arval's heart as he looked at the concern on the young face that gazed so earnestly into his own. He was glad to see that Artorynas had found a true friend during his quest. 'I'm sure it's a pledge he will want to fulfil, and for reasons more important than simply obligation.'

'Well, he did tell me that the Nine Dales felt like home to him. That's partly why I wondered whether you would like to…' Haldur broke off as Arval shook his head, but was taken aback by what he said next.

'Tell me why you think Artorynas will not return.'

'I… I… It's not that I think he won't. But I know my father believes he has gone to his death.'

'How do you know that?'

'Because Artorynas told me himself – although he bore no malice, he agreed with Astell our lorekeeper, who said the Nine Dales were the true love of my father's life, and everything he did sprang from that. So after Artorynas had gone, I sought Astell out and spoke with him. He wouldn't say much, I could see he felt he should honour the confidence Artorynas had placed in him; but I gathered that the Hound of the Vow had given Artorynas certain assurances, which he trusted. And I would trust Cunor y'n Temennis myself, not to mention that if anyone could find Asward donn'Ur and come back from north of the Somllichan nan'Esylt, it would be Artorynas. But, well, I suppose it's that I'm so afraid he might not; I daren't let myself hope too much.'

'Keep fast to your hope, Haldur.' Arval smiled. 'You know how to play on an old man's weakness! How I would love to meet your lorekeeper, and talk to the Hound of the Vow!'

'Oh, that's not why I...' Haldur looked so dismayed that Arval laughed aloud.

'I know, I know. Now, since I must forego the pleasure of debate with the learned men of the Nine Dales, you must stand in for them, one last time. Tell me again of Rihann y'n Temenellan and the Cunorad y'm As-Geg'rastigan, but go slowly so that I may record your words.'

The hours passed unnoticed as Haldur spoke, and Arval wrote, occasionally pausing to put a question. Beyond the lamplight the room was shadowy and still, filled only with the scratch of Arval's pen and the two quiet voices; but faintly Arval felt it once more: that other-worldly thrill of life dancing upon the air, present to the senses yet tantalisingly just beyond reach. At last Haldur fell silent and Arval put down his pen. He tilted the page to the lamplight, waiting for the ink to dry, and then closed the book, lightly touching its binding as it lay on the table. The hour of parting drew near, and both men felt its pain lie heavily upon them. Then Arval broke the deep quiet of the room with a question.

'What advice are you going to give your father when you return home?'

Haldur answered slowly without looking up; his eyes rested upon the closed book, and the old hand that gently caressed it, without really seeing them.

'My father was already unwilling to take up the sword Sleccenal, as we say in Rihannad Ennar. He will be even more reluctant when I tell him that I've seen enough now to know that we could never hope to prevail against the armed might of Caradward if we were to march south. He will grieve for our kinsfolk in Gwent y'm Aryframan and even feel sorrow as I do for those in Caradward whose hands are clean, but when he hears about Assynt y'm Atrannaas his mind will be set. He is the father of his people: he will do nothing that risks bringing this darkness into their hearts, or this blackness into the skies over the Nine Dales. And I will support him in that resolve. At least, that's how I feel at the moment.'

'You think your mind may change, then?' asked Arval.

Haldur looked across at Arval and was struck by the old man's air of alert concentration. His thin features were thrown into sharp relief by the lamplight, but the dark, deep eyes were bright and shrewd, filled with wisdom. The night was passing, yet such dawn as there would be was still far off: it was the low hour when sick men die, when all the world lies fallow and lifeless, but Arval showed no signs of fatigue. How often, wondered Haldur suddenly, had his companion sat alone in this room, wakeful in his search for knowledge?

'There is something that bothers me,' said Haldur. 'Valahald was suspicious of us from the start and we have crossed Vorynaas in public. We know they have been consulting with their associates these many days now. What are they talking about, up there in Seth y'n Carad? They are men I would not trust one quarter of an arrow-shot from me, and I doubt their intentions, in letting us leave apparently freely; but even worse, what if we have made a mistake in coming to Caradward at all? We took the risk, to see for ourselves what was really happening here, but maybe our arrival has only served to prove the existence of Rihannad Ennar. I am afraid that now Vorynaas will think it possible that we are within his reach and will come to take us, bringing the darkness with him to the Nine Dales.'

'And what would you do then?'

'Well, we are prepared for the defence of our land. If it came to it, we could defend it to the last child able to draw a bow although I doubt, now, whether this would be enough. But anyway, this would mean that an army was already at our gates and there is one thing of which I am absolutely sure: whether we are the wronged party or not, I do not want the fight to be upon the soil of Rihannad Ennar, which up until now has remained free of such taint. If we were ever to have warning that Vorynaas and his men were advancing against us, I would do all I could to persuade my father that we should go out to meet them before ever they came within striking distance of the Nine Dales.' Haldur paused, turning away from Arval's gaze. 'And I can tell you what I should keep from him, that I think we would pay with our lives and still be unable to stop them.'

'There is something which you have not mentioned, but I wonder whether it is in your mind,' said Arval. 'If Artorynas finds the arrow he seeks, matters may fall out in ways none of us has foreseen.'

Haldur looked up. 'Yes, I suppose so.'

Maybe Arval expects a more positive response, but what can I say, he thought. He realised that although he had tried to cling to the hope that Artorynas would return, he had never truly believed that he would bring the arrow with him, or really considered what it might mean if he did. He guessed now that Arval knew this, especially when the old man spoke again.

'I will share with you the hope that was left with me,' said Arval. 'Arymaldur told me that there is always hope, if men know where to find it. I have reason to think that this is the quest upon which Artorynas has gone. I trust the promise that Arymaldur made, and I trust Artorynas to fulfil it. I am certain that he will find the arrow, that he will come back, that hope will return with him; though the form it may take is hidden from me. Now, the night is almost over but you have taken no rest. You have a long journey to begin today, and you bear a leader's burden. Though you have confided in me, you have spared your companions from sharing your fears, I think? So come with me now and take what help I can give you.'

Arval led the way along the passage within the wall and into the secret sanctuary. Never before, in any other *numiras*, had Haldur been aware of such an unseen might held in hidden check: it took his breath away. From a high shelf beside the lamp Arval lifted down a flagon and offered Haldur a tiny measure of the spirit it contained. Haldur took it with a shaking hand, trembling with awe at the power he sensed within this small, silent chamber. They drank, and Arval smiled a little. As Haldur looked at him, he realised to his amazement that he could see youth in Arval's face. Or no, not youth, for his features were as venerable as ever; but now he discerned what he had not been aware of before: an ageless quality, a strength and vigour that was serene, timeless and untouchable. Suddenly it hit him that after today he would never see Arval again and he bowed his head to hide the pain he felt. My brother, my mother, my friend and now my new-found teacher and guide, thought Haldur in a rare moment of self-pity. Is it always going to be like this? Meetings, partings, sorrow and loss; and somehow I must find the strength to bear them all publicly when the day comes to take my father's place. He felt a touch at his elbow as Arval indicated that they should leave the sanctuary. This time, they went down through the resonant emptiness of the hall before emerging into the open air once more.

After the darkness of the hall, it seemed almost light outside to Haldur as he paused for a moment beside the door. Within two hours at most now they would be on their way. He looked up and saw that the first murky glimmers of Caradriggan's day were beginning to show, giving grey substance to the thick blanket of louring cloud. All was quiet and hushed, but then a new sound floated across the stillness. Heedless, careless, unseen in the gloom that still wrapped the city, a robin greeted the approaching day. Bright, jewel-like, the cascade of wistful notes fell upon Haldur's ear; and as he turned towards the sound, a slight shift of air brought the smell of new-sawn timber to him from the workshops. He stood, his senses quickening to the sweetness of both wood and bird. The life within this earth, the life of men upon it: surely they should be at peace with one another, not at odds, he thought. Then the first noises were heard from the street outside and the fleeting moment passed.

'I shall be working in the medical wing this morning, so I will say farewell now,' said Arval. He took Haldur's shoulders. 'You will be strong enough for what awaits you, Haldur. May the As-Geg'rastigan go with you.'

An ill-omened departure

The moment of departure arrived and the men from Rihannad Ennar assembled outside Tellgard; but glad as he was to be away at last, Haldur's heart was heavy at the thought of never seeing Arval again. Soon Valahald and Heranar rode up with a small escort to find him and his companions waiting to join them. Heranar had barely breathed a sigh of relief at Arval's absence when suddenly, as the party began to move off after the bare minimum by way of greeting, there was a clatter of hooves behind him and a shout of alarm. He turned to see one of the troopers struggling to control his horse, which was rolling its eyes, plunging and fighting the bit with ears laid back. The cause of its panic was a wraith-like figure which had materialised out of nowhere and was now reaching up with unsteady hands, apparently trying to catch hold of the nearest bridle. Arythalt! If this was what the mine-sickness did to a man, thought Heranar, was Arval doing him any favours by keeping him alive? He stared at the wasted hands, the waxy pallor of the sunken face.

Haldur, reacting quickest, jumped down from his horse. What bad luck that the poor, confused old fellow had eluded his carers to witness their departure. But bad immediately turned much worse as Arythalt, seeming to find what he was searching for, grasped at Tellapur in entreaty.

'Maesrhon, don't leave me again!'

With the tail of his eye Haldur saw Tellapur looking wildly at him for guidance and did the only thing he could think of to get him out of Valahald's sight.

'Fetch Arval,' he said curtly and the boy gratefully dismounted and sped off, taking the colonnade steps two at a time.

Haldur moved forward to support Arythalt, who sagged against him, his skeletal frame almost weightless, the ribs sharply defined even through his garments. Running footsteps heralded the arrival of Merenald, breathless with anxiety: not before time, thought Haldur, and then immediately felt ashamed of himself when Merenald began to stammer out his thanks. But Valahald had left his place at the front of the group of travellers and now sat looking down at them from his horse. Just as it seemed he was about to speak, the eyes opened in Arythalt's emaciated face. He saw Valahald, and began to struggle in Merenald's arms.

'Armed men! Salfronardo!' The reedy old voice trembled and cracked, breaking off in a spasm of coughing. Gently Merenald wiped his mouth but Arythalt pushed the hand away. His eyes wandered vacantly and then suddenly focused on Tellapur's riderless horse. 'Where's Maesrhon gone? I want him to stay, don't let them take him back to the north!'

'Hush, hush now,' murmured Merenald, 'don't upset yourself, sir. It's not Maesrhon, you're all mixed up again. Come on now, let's get you settled.'

'Wait.' Valahald nudged his horse forward a couple of paces to block Merenald's path. 'This sounds most interesting. Let's hear some more.'

'Oh, leave him alone Valahald,' said Heranar, 'you can see his mind's gone. Let's get on and get moving.'

'Don't tell me what to do.'

Valahald sat up with a jerk as Haldur spoke, and his horse startled slightly. Merenald jumped out of the way, caught his foot against the lowest step of the colonnade and Arythalt, slipping out of his arms, fell with a cry of pain. Haldur stooped to help, but Merenald had already seen the unnatural angle of his master's body as he lay moaning and knew his thigh was broken. Furiously, he turned on Valahald.

'This is your doing. He'll not last till tomorrow, now. I just hope Arval's skill can calm his mind so he dies in peace. How many more old men are you going to speed to their graves? We can all see he doesn't know yesterday from today, but you – you just couldn't leave well alone, could you? "Let's hear some more", indeed!'

Valahald's face set. 'I want to hear no more from you at any rate,' he said, beckoning a couple of his troopers. 'Arrest this man and bring him along, we'll turn him over to the guards as we pass through the barbican.' He turned back to Merenald. 'You can save anything else you've got to say, and tell it to the darkness in Assynt y'm Atrannaas.'

'Valahald! It was only a few words of cheek when the man's upset – you can't do that to him!' This was Heranar, embarrassed but sufficiently shamed to speak out. Merenald was speechless, pale with horror.

'You think not? Let me show you.'

Valahald had grabbed hold of Merenald, intending to drag him over to the two men he had indicated, when a new voice rang out.

'Let him go!'

Tellapur had reappeared, but Arval was before him. He stood at the top of the steps, his black eyes fixed on Valahald, his face taut with anger. Valahald, still grasping the cloth of Merenald's jacket, glanced around at his men; but they had backed off when confronted by Arval, leaving Valahald isolated at the foot of the steps and surrounded by the six from Rihannad Ennar.

'Well, you could have had the drain on your stores lessened by two mouths today, but if you insist on keeping this one, I won't stand in your way.' Valahald let go of Merenald, making a great play of dusting off his hands.

Arval advanced down the steps until he was face to face with Valahald, whose horse fidgeted nervously, and his words fell into a breathless silence. 'The darkness in you is deeper by far than any within Assynt y'm Atrannaas.'

Valahald, feeling all eyes upon him, opted to brazen things out. 'Oh, save it. We've got a long way to go today, so we'll leave you to your soothsaying.'

He was tugging on the reins to turn away when from the ground at his feet there came a cry of fear. Some hint of what was afoot had penetrated Arythalt's mind as he lay groaning in pain.

'No, no! Not Assynt y'm Atrannaas! Not that, I've done nothing…' He broke off, racked with coughing, and then appealed wildly again. 'Don't take me there! Arval, don't let them, let me die here…' His eyes began to wander, his voice wavered and dropped. 'Help me, Merenald… Maesrhon!'

The words died away in a whisper. It was like seeing a dead man speak, thought Heranar, the hair lifting on his head as he stared at the cadaverous face, the bony hands stretched out in desperate, terrified entreaty.

'Merenald, get someone to help and take him indoors,' said Arval; but Valahald turned back again.

'Wait a moment.' He leaned down towards Arythalt, malicious amusement in his voice. 'Maesrhon might be found one day, who knows? So don't die just yet, or you'll miss what will happen if he *is* ever brought back here.'

Arval straightened from bending over Arythalt, his eyes burning with wrath. 'Listen to me. This is the second time that Tellgard has been fouled, the ground sullied upon which the feet of the As-Geg'rastigan once walked. For the sake of the innocent child you once were, Valahald, I warn you now: do not be the cause of a third such defilement.'

'Are you threatening me?'

'Have you no ears, as well as no shame?' Haldur remembered what Heretellar had said, that when need arose Arval could speak with the voice of the Starborn. That power and authority were present now for all to hear.

'I am warning you. And I have a warning also for those who follow you.' Arval's gaze swept over them, but not a man there could meet his eyes. 'If you would have hope of the dawn, do not place your trust in a man whose heart is blacker than the night.'

Valahald smiled, but it cost him an effort and he knew that Arval had seen it. As he gave the order to move off, hatred bit silently at his inmost self, worming its way to an ever closer and more secret bed in the darkness of his heart. Without another word, Arval turned away.

CHAPTER 52

Guarding the wagon park

The room was beginning to empty as evening wore on towards night: soon it would be time to go outside to take up station by the watch-fire. Cunoreth knuckled his eyes and yawned. He was sitting in the common room of the main *gradstedd* in Rihannark, where for a couple of weeks now he had been employed as the night guard for the wagon park. His body had not yet properly adjusted to sleep during the day and wakefulness at night, but in a way he was glad, because at least it took his mind off how hungry he was. The door banged as several more patrons of the inn sought their beds, and he stood up, careful as ever not to stretch in case this drew attention to his height and lanky frame. So far as he could tell, no-one had given him a second glance since he came down from the secret refuge in the hills, but there was no point in taking unnecessary risks. He walked out into the darkness and over to the glow of the fire. After exchanging a word or two with the man whose shift was now over, he did the rounds of the paddock fences, checking that all was well with the unattended wagons and with the tethered animals who either lay or grazed placidly, and then returned to sit with his back to the brazier. Cunoreth's stomach growled, sounding loud to him in the quiet of the night, and he dug about in his pouch for the scrap of leather he had taken to chewing in an attempt to fool his mind into forgetting food. What I need, he thought, is some of that Outland stuff you hear about that's supposed to keep your brain active while depressing your appetite; but then, who's to say that's not just a story people put about. You heard such strange claims made about the *sigitsaran*, especially those in the auxiliaries.

Cunoreth sighed and moved around to the other side of the fire. He had taken on this job so as to have a reason for staying in Rihannark. The town was situated in a valley to the east of the main route north through Gwent y'm Aryframan, but its road was good nevertheless and was often used by auxiliary troops when moving about between postings. The owner of the *gradstedd* actually had a special store, filled with provisions only to be used when the irregulars quartered themselves upon him. They expected the best, when not living off their wits on exercise or active service, and could turn nasty if they didn't get it. At least, that was what Cunoreth had been told. The store was kept locked and he had never seen inside it, but he had tormented himself often enough with imagining what it held. The fare on offer for other folk, especially those of lowly status like himself, was meagre and poor in quality. He chewed more vigorously, trying not to think about food. He'd been spoiled by the luck of his early years, eating like a lord in Salfgard with Fosseiro in charge of the kitchen. Even up in the hills, it could have been worse. There was game, and fish in the streams; every family tended its own small vegetable plot and worked in the three fields held in common. They were treading a fine line between survival and disaster, he knew, and their meals were spare enough; but what wouldn't he give now for a bowl of broth with mutton and beans in it, thickened with barley! Suddenly his mouth watered at the memory of honey. Their bees roved over mile upon mile of heather, you could taste it in the sweetness on your tongue. Cunoreth spat into the fire, hearing the hot embers hiss.

Tonight's supper, now – or breakfast, as it was for him. Roasted turnip flavoured with half an onion or so, and they'd had the nerve to claim it had bacon in it. Maybe a couple of lumps of fat, and maybe not. And one miserable little undersized egg. If I could get into that locked storeroom, thought Cunoreth, I swear I'd eat the half of what's in it. He stood up and began walking slowly around the paddock. He had been a fidgety child who found it difficult to sit still for any length of time and even now, thinking came easier to him when he was on the move. Pacing softly to and fro in the quiet night, he reviewed what he had discovered so far. It seemed to him to amount to very little. He had drifted from one odd job to the next, lending a hand in gathering the paltry harvest here, mucking out a stable there, minding a market stall, washing pots in a tavern kitchen. Gradually moving south, he eventually arrived in Framstock to find Thaltor of all people occupying the governor's residence; and through attentive listening had found out that both Heranar and Valahald were away on business in Caradriggan. Every so often a new rumour would surface: he had heard it said that Heranar was under something of a cloud and had been sent for to explain himself to his superiors, that the men from the Nine Dales had got on the wrong side of Vorynaas. Even a story that Valahald had somehow killed his own father had done the rounds. Well, there was nothing so surprising about that to a man who had known Valahald as a youth, as Cunoreth had. It was easy enough to see that everyone was afraid of him. It was all very well for Sigitsinen to claim that disaffection and rebellion were smouldering and only wanted the spark to set them alight, but if the exiles were to take the risk of joining in, they would need to be sure any rising could succeed and as yet Cunoreth was not convinced of this.

A sharp little breeze gusted across the wagon park, its cold fingers brushing Cunoreth's thin shoulders. He flapped his arms and pushed his hands up into his sleeves for warmth. Autumn was passing: surely if Heranar and Valahald were going to return to their commands, they must travel soon. As for the men from the Nine Dales, Cunoreth spared them little of his thought. Maybe they would come back this way eventually – and maybe not, if he was right in his hunch that they would not see the Nine Dales again. But mild and dry though the weather had been, it must turn soon; and if he had not managed to make contact with Sigitsinen by then, a difficult decision would be before him. Should he take the risk of staying down here through the winter, or set out for the safety of the hills? He would have to make a move before snow fell, blocking his way and leaving his tracks for all to see. Cunoreth sat down beside the brazier again with his back to the heat, scratching at his chin. He would be getting rid of the beard as soon as he no longer needed the disguise, but now he pulled and picked at it in frustration. Perhaps it had been a mistake to stay in Rihannark, where despite his hopes there seemed to be almost no troop movement going on. Perhaps the auxiliaries were already dug into winter quarters. Perhaps he should try to find them, rather than waiting for them to come to him: he'd learnt a lot from Torald and could move cross-country stealthily enough if he had to. Yes, but not as expertly as the irregulars. Supposing he was intercepted, and not by Sigitsinen's company? Cunoreth grimaced to himself in the dark, pulling his hat down over his ears.

A chance to seize

Three mornings later, he was hanging about the inn yard after his shift was over, thinking that if he lingered and kept his ears open he might pick up something worth knowing. The sound of horses approaching reached him and then from the stables there was a bustle of activity. He heard voices, trampling, hurrying footsteps, doors banging inside the inn. Just as he turned to go indoors himself to see what he could find out, he was stopped in his tracks by a shout from behind him.

'Hey!' One of the stable hands was calling to him. 'If you're not away to your bed yet, can you come in here and give us a hand with this lot?'

The man ducked back inside and Cunoreth joined him, to discover that there was news at last.

'What's going on then?' he asked as he worked with the man to unsaddle and rub down a horse.

'Big troop movements, according to what I've just heard,' said his companion, indicating with a jerk of his head a group of men who were disappearing in the direction of the entrance to the *gradstedd*. 'The governors are coming back from the south: there'll be staff coming with them to fresh postings and others leaving to go the other way, likely. Plenty of traffic on the roads, while they're still passable. It'll mean more work for us, but there'll be more chances of a tip here and there. Money in my pocket to brighten up the Midwinter Feast – there's something to look forward to.'

Cunoreth glanced over the horse's back in surprise. 'You still keep the feast, here in Rihannark?'

'No, no, I just used the name out of habit. We've nobody here to lead the rites, and not likely to have either, after what happened to the old fellow in Framstock.'

'Why, what did happen?' asked Cunoreth, when it seemed the man was not about to elaborate.

'Oh, didn't you hear about it? Mauled to death and half-eaten by a pack of wild dogs, so the tale goes.'

He picked up a bucket and went off to the pump, leaving Cunoreth, who well remembered old Morancras but was not going to risk revealing this, standing in sickened silence. Coming back from the yard, his companion turned from tipping the water into the trough and laughed.

'You've gone a bit green in the face! Not going to throw up your breakfast on me, I hope.'

Cunoreth looked up. 'No, I don't get so much to eat in my job here that I can afford to waste it by puking.'

'Yes, I know what you mean. Look, if you're not ready to sleep yet, what about giving me a hand with cleaning this tack? I've an idea that might appeal to you. My name's Ellic, by the way. What's yours?'

'Avarath.' Giving the false name he had settled on for use during his mission, Cunoreth gathered up an armful of bridles and reins and followed his new friend into the tack-room. Ellic heaved the saddle he was carrying on the stand and the two of them set about the leatherwork.

'Well, what I was going to say was this,' Ellic went on. 'The advance party who came in this morning say there's a company of irregulars coming up the valley road and likely to pass through here in a day or two; and that being the case, I'd be very surprised if there aren't a few *sigitsaran* among them. I know some people don't like them too much, but I'd not be one of them. For one thing, if you've got the money, they can supply certain commodities you can't get hold of any other way. And for another, they all seem to know each other, so if you want something, even if it's not available there and then you've only to put the word out. Last time we had Outlanders in here, I let it be known that I'm after some of that stuff people say they use when they're on the march or on exercise to keep them on their feet without sleep or food. But I don't want it to stay on my feet, exactly.' He laughed, giving a knowing wink. 'You follow me?'

'I'm not sure,' said Cunoreth, rather baffled.

'Oh, come on! They say it gives you staying power in more ways than one. You're not married, I take it? Well, I am. It's not that I wouldn't recommend it, but you do get bored after a while. Now, you know the *Fox in the Spinney*, the other inn over the bridge? There's a girl in there I've had my eye on for a long time.' Ellic drew his breath in appreciatively and winked again. 'Just as soon as I can work myself an afternoon off from here, I'm going over to the *Fox* to try out the combination of this girl and the Outland concoction I'm hoping to buy. I've heard you can keep going for hours – and if it's as good as they say, I'll have my way with the wife as well, when I get home, and she'll be none the wiser. Now do you take my meaning?'

'Oh yes, I'm with you now all right.' Cunoreth laughed as lewdly as he could manage, but he was wondering if the chance he had been hoping for was about to present itself under a most unexpected guise. He breathed on a piece of metalwork and attacked it with the rag and polish. 'And you're hoping one of these new arrivals will be bringing you a supply of this stuff?'

'That's it. I've the money saved up, just in case. And what I wondered was – well, how can I put it. You seem to keep to yourself, pretty much: I suppose when you're on the night shift that goes with the job. But I can't see that you've much to spend your pay on, so I wondered whether, if the opportunity's there, you'd be interested in buying some too and then we can do a deal, just the two of us, to split it between us.'

'Well, I don't know.' As Ellic was speaking, Cunoreth's memory suddenly filled with a picture totally unexpected: he saw Astirano's face, as he passed her when she drew water at the stream; Astirano whose hopeless love for Maesrhon had cast a shadow on her life. Without warning an urgent surge of desire shot through him, leaving behind it a kind of new trackway in his mind, almost as if it had been burned on to the surface of his thoughts. The image came and went in an instant, and he returned to the present to see Ellic looking disappointed. Cunoreth pulled himself together.

'But I'll think about it, that's for sure,' he added, 'and maybe I could join you, if you're drinking with one of these Outlanders you're hoping will be here? If it was early enough, I could come along one evening before I start my shift.'

Ellic cheered up again. 'Yes, no problem. We'll keep in touch, then.'

There was no room for thoughts of hunger during Cunoreth's next few night-watches. Ellic's remark that word got around among the *sigitsaran* in the auxiliaries had made him wonder whether he could use this network to make contact with Sigitsinen, and he racked his brains for some hint he could let fall, if the anticipated meeting should take place. But he was distracted by new thoughts of Astirano, memories of her that he had never realised were carried hidden in his heart. Round the picket-lines he walked, his stride as restless as his thoughts. Clear in his mind now he saw what he wanted: to have Astirano love him, to marry her and mend both their lives, to live together in peace and plenty in Salfgard restored. So what needed to happen, to make all this possible? For Salfgard to live again, life must return also to Gwent y'm Aryframan. That could only be, if the pall of gloom and despair was lifted from both the land and the hearts of its people. Cunoreth walked over to the fire and sat down again, facing away from its light as usual. To dispel the darkness, surely the Caradwardans must be destroyed. Strange to think he was Caradwardan himself, by birth. A log settled in the brazier behind him; instinctively Cunoreth turned at the noise, to see a little flight of tiny golden sparks fly up from the embers, glowing briefly before they died, and a new idea came from nowhere into his mind. The gloom lay on many Caradwardan hearts too, anyone could see that. How could more destruction bring anything except more despair? It was help they needed, all of them, but who would bring it to them? Suddenly Cunoreth jumped to his feet again, and began to pace about once more. Hadn't Torald told him to hone his wits with use, to make sure he kept them always sharp? He felt his old, devil-may-care self beginning to return. Why worry, why plot and plan: look what had happened already. The unexpected conversation with Ellic had shown him a possible opportunity. He would make sure his wits were about him, and trust his instinct; and then, if the chance came, he would take it.

A message passed

More than two weeks passed before Cunoreth knew for certain that his chance had indeed come, and been taken. As promised, Ellic included him when a group of auxiliaries turned up to drink at the inn; and sure enough, there were *sigitsaran* among them. Soon Ellic was waving Cunoreth over to a corner where he sat deep in negotiation with a dark, youngish man who wore a plain pewter leaf badge at his shoulder.

'Here, Avarath,' said Ellic with a grin. 'I've got the stuff, look. Now how about it? Why don't you buy some, too?'

Cunoreth whistled in disbelief when he heard the price. 'I don't have that sort of money to throw around. And anyway, I'm not sure I'd want to buy until I've heard your verdict on whether it works or not.'

'Yes, you try it out for us, Ellic,' said another fellow who worked in the stables, 'and let's see what kind of state you're in the next morning.'

One or two others joined in the ribald laughter at this, and a man at the edge of the group leaned forward. 'When I was stationed in the barbican, down in Caradriggan, they reckoned that was what old Valafoss was taking, otherwise how else would he have been able to see to that girl he had?'

'I know, but I heard it said too that it was another Outland concoction that Valahald fed him, to get rid of his dad when his goings-on started to spoil his prospects.' This came from one of his comrades.

'Steady on!' Ellic looked around him in some alarm, but the man laughed.

'Don't you worry, we say what we want in the auxiliaries, when we're together. And I don't mind telling you now, in front of Sigisstir here, I'd think twice before I swallowed down any of his Outland stuff.'

'Think twice, eh? That would be a first, for you.' Ellic's supplier stowed away the payment and tucked his pouch out of sight. He surveyed the group with black, hooded eyes. 'There's no need for any of you to get worked up, I'm keeping the rest for myself. From what we hear, I might need it before this operation's over and I get back home again.'

Cunoreth noticed how none of them laughed at this: clearly they took Sigisstir's meaning to be that his need might occur during active service rather than in more pleasurable circumstances. He began to pay closer attention.

'Ah, what would you know about it?' said the man who had been on the receiving end of Sigitsir's sarcasm. 'But *I* know well enough what's the matter with you. You thought you'd be promoted to second when we got up to camp, but then you found out Sigitsinen's still got the green badge and you've been in a bad mood ever since.'

'See what I mean, you others? There he goes again, thinking once but not twice. Sigitsinen's been decorated by Atranaar himself, yet he's still up here as second to Naasigits. What does that tell you? It suggests to me that those in charge don't want to split up a crack team for some reason, and that's what makes me think something big could be afoot.'

His heart beating fast, Cunoreth joined the conversation. An idea had suddenly come to him: it was a slim chance, but one worth taking. 'This Sigitsinen you mention. He's an Outlander, I take it? And you're moving up to join his company? Is he stationed near here, then?'

'If he was, we wouldn't tell you. Nothing personal, you understand.' The man who had been put down twice in front of his friends tried to restore his loss of face. 'Why do you want to know, anyway?'

Cunoreth shrugged, trying to appear off-hand. 'Oh, it was just that I think I might have met him, one time. The man I remember by that name had the green enamel leaf on his badge, he was dark but his eyes were unusual for an Outlander, a kind of pale greenish grey.'

'That's him all right.' Sigisstir contemplated Cunoreth. 'Where did you meet him?'

'Away up north, months back. I was working up there, then. A man like me has to move around if he wants to put food in his mouth, and I take what work I can get, wherever I can get it. I'd got to know a fellow who seemed to be friendly with this Sigitsinen and that's how I saw him a few times. But he's dead now, this Torald that is, and it was after that I moved down south and fetched up here.' He swallowed the last of his drink, and stood up. 'Come to think of it, I'd better be getting myself across to the wagon park to start my shift, if I'm going to be in funds next time you want to do a deal – sorry, Ellic.' Cunoreth turned to Sigisstir.

'Maybe, if you're going to be seeing Sigitsinen, you'd tell him old Torald's gone.'

Cunoreth makes his mind up

The company of auxiliaries moved on next morning. About five days later, Cunoreth was woken in the middle of the afternoon by a hubbub outside, and looked out to see that an unusually large number of wagons and other traffic had arrived. When he rose in the early evening to get ready for another night-shift, he saw that the park and paddock were full: a mixture of civilian and military vehicles was taking up a good two-thirds of the space, with pack mules and draft animals tethered in several picket lines. As he ate, it began to rain and before he had finished it was teeming down outside. The inn became crowded as more and more men hurried in to seek better warmth and shelter than their tents and wagons could provide and Cunoreth gathered that a merchant's caravan and several lone travellers had linked up to travel under the protection of a big military supply train. Evidently stores and equipment was on its way north in some quantity: he frowned as he wondered what lay behind all these manoeuvres. Cunoreth had more pressing concerns of his own, however, as he pulled his cloak and hood close about him. He hated wet nights. There was a miserable little wooden shelter for the watchman to use, but lighting its undersized brazier meant leaving the upper half-door open. Rain blew in and hissed on the fire, making it smoke and spit, and the only seat was a damp, uncomfortable plank; but when he complained, he was told that plenty of others would be glad enough to take his place if he thought himself too good for the work he was employed to do.

After a couple of hours, Cunoreth decided that keeping warm was his main priority, even if it meant getting soaked. He walked gloomily up and down, relying on the exercise to set his blood moving, occasionally retreating to the hut when the downpour intensified. Why bother with a watchman, on such a night as this? There was so much movement and activity, as men hurried through the rain from *gradstedd* to wagon, or from tent to privy and back, that the animals stamped and snorted restlessly and surely no hunting predator would come near. And as for human felons, if anyone was so desperate as to venture out on a night like this in the hope of stealing what was not his, well good luck to him, thought Cunoreth. In any case, how could he be expected to tell one dark, muffled figure from the next? They passed to and fro, huddled into their cloaks, with an occasional greeting or a shared curse about the weather, and all were as alike as beans in a bowl. He tweaked sharply at his hood, sending a shower of water to join the falling rain, and getting his hands wet in the process. Back to the shelter for a few minutes then, to chafe his cold fingers over the brazier. He squelched across the muddy park, head down, and from the darkness of a small, nondescript wagon nearby a watching figure slipped out and followed. Cunoreth bit off a yelp of fright as a hand tightened on his arm.

'Quiet!' hissed a voice in his ear. 'Stand right at the back and keep your eyes open. I'll stay out of sight below the door. Now, what's all this about? What are you doing down here, sending me messages about Torald?'

Peering into the dark angle of floor and wall behind the brazier, Cunoreth could hardly believe his ears. 'Sigitsinen?'

'Of course. Hurry up.'

'It was the only thing I could think of, so that you'd know the word came from someone out of Salfgard; although it's true about Torald, he is dead. I've been here a few weeks now, in the hope of making contact. Before that I've worked here and there since I came down from the hills. We feel we've got to know what's happening, that's why I wanted to get hold of you. Can't we set up some kind of link for passing on information? Something's going on, isn't it? I've heard all kinds of rumours, and now there's all this movement of men and supplies.'

'Oh yes, there's plenty going on, and more planned. Listen, how do you feel about joining those of us who're going to try and stop it?'

'Well… Can't you tell me a bit more, first?'

'I need to get the men from Rihannad Ennar away. If you can still handle a horse like the way I saw you ride up in the hills, then I think I can see a way to rescue them, if you're willing to help.'

Cunoreth chewed his lip. Daring the possibility of death for the sake of Mag'rantor, Fosseiro and the others was one thing, but now he thought of Astirano and knew he had no wish to risk his life, especially for strangers who meant nothing to him. 'Why do we have to worry about them?'

'Because dead men are no use to us, and they're going to be murdered unless we can get them out in time. We need them to make it back to the Nine Dales, so they can tell what they've seen down here and even more important, take a warning of what's in store. You want to know what's going on? I'll tell you: the invasion of Rihannad Ennar, that's what. If that goes ahead, we can forget about help from the north – and we're going to need help from somewhere, if we're to put paid to Vorynaas and the rest of his companions in darkness. The lord of the Nine Dales will listen to his own people, surely. That's why we have to get them home, to bring us hope of aid. And if we can get them back to Rihannad Ennar before the winter stops us, we won't just save their lives, we'll buy ourselves some time, too.'

Cunoreth looked out over the half-door into the drilling rain. The night had a raw, wintry feel to it: the weather could be already breaking. Did he want to spend the rest of his life hiding in the hills, even with Astirano? No, he wanted to bring her back to the sunshine of Salfgard. Suddenly he felt elation course through him and he laughed, quietly but with almost his old reckless abandon.

'What's the joke?'

'Nothing, really.' Cunoreth laughed again. 'It's silly, I know, but I was just wishing I'd not had my hair cut short.'

'Meaning?'

'You get me a horse, I'll ride it.'

Heranar in haste

To the enormous relief of Haldur and his five fellow-travellers, their journey back north unfolded without incident once its inauspicious start was behind them. They drew near Framstock eventually, Tellapur and the others in high spirits at the prospect of shaking off Valahald at last and beginning the next stage of their return home; but Haldur, who had more on his mind than they did, was pensive as he thought over the events of their embassy and pondered the advice he would give his father when the time came. He glanced across at Heranar, who was chewing his nails as he rode, looking like a man who carried the woes of the world on his shoulders. Spending the winter cooped up with him was something too dire to even contemplate, and Haldur forced himself to think of something else. Maybe there would be time, while they were in Framstock, to seek out old Morancras once more. It would be almost two months too early, but perhaps they would be able to persuade him to speak the Midwinter rite for them, seeing as how there would be no chance of hearing it under Heranar's roof.

'I feel as though years have gone by since we last sat here,' said Cathasar, looking around the hall where the companions ate their evening meal on the day they arrived back in Framstock.

'Yes, I know what you mean.' Asaldron suddenly laughed. 'Remember the morning when you and Aestrontor had that little set-to with Valahald in here, Haldur? At least we've not had to put up with him tonight. No doubt he's holed up in the governor's residence with the worthy Thaltor. I expect that's where Heranar is, too.'

'I wonder how soon we'll be off again to go north with him,' said Haldur. 'Let's hope the spring comes early next year, so we can get away from him too as quickly as possible. Though you know, in a strange way I feel a bit sorry for Heranar.'

'Well I don't! And I don't think I ever could.' Tellapur seemed almost indignant with his leader.

Haldur smiled at the young man. 'I did say I felt *a bit* sorry. I'm not wasting all that much sympathy, believe me. But I think he's got caught up in something that's too big for him, and can't see a way out. It's not a pleasant situation to be in.'

'Maybe not, but it's his problem, not ours.' Aestrontor stood up and stretched. 'I'm for bed.'

Next morning he and Haldur were walking up the street together on their way to seek out old Morancras when they were surprised to see Heranar himself hurrying after them, calling Haldur's name. He grabbed Haldur's arm, almost too out of breath to speak.

'I need to get home straight away. If only I'd had the message last night, I'd have set off today…' He broke off, trying to get his breath back. 'We'll be leaving first thing tomorrow, so make sure you're ready.'

Haldur and Aestrontor looked at each other. 'What's the sudden rush for?' asked Haldur.

'My daughter is ill. We'll be travelling as fast as we can manage.'

'But you've three daughters. Which of the little girls is it?' said Aestrontor.

'I don't know! They can't even tell me that …' Again Heranar broke off, but this time Haldur heard the catch in his voice and with a jerk of his head indicated that Aestrontor should carry on alone to call on Morancras. He drew Heranar away with him, suggesting that they walk down to the *Salmon Fly*, but Heranar shook his head and turned back out of Water Street, hurrying towards the bridge.

Haldur caught him up in a few strides. 'Steady there, calm down. Tell me what's happened. How did you hear?'

They were on the bridge now and Heranar suddenly stopped, turning to face Haldur in one of the embrasures. The flush was fading from his cheeks, leaving him pale underneath the stressful blotchiness.

'Thaltor. Well, Gillavar. It was Gillavar who sent the message, apparently. My own marriage-father, and he couldn't even use his grand-daughter's name! They're of no account to him, he wants grandsons… and then Thaltor, who cares for nothing and nobody but himself, Thaltor doesn't think it worthwhile to send word to me in Caradriggan, doesn't even remember about it when he sees me last night! It was only this morning, suddenly he said "Oh by the way, one of your youngsters hasn't been too well" and I had to drag what information I could out of him. Not that there was much: Gillavar evidently couldn't be bothered to send the kind of details I wanted to know, just mentioned it in passing; he'd show more concern if it was one of those damned dogs he takes everywhere with him… Not even her name!' Heranar twisted his fingers together, staring away at the water below.

Astonished at this open display of emotion, Haldur felt another small surge of sympathy for Heranar. 'I'm very sorry,' he said, 'but maybe you're worrying unnecessarily. After all, it sounds as though this is old news. The little girl is probably well again by now.'

Heranar turned right round and gripped the edge of the stonework. He was silent for a moment or two and then spoke with his back to Haldur. 'But anything could have happened since then. For all I know, she might even be worse.'

'Listen, Heranar.' Impulsively, Haldur got him by the shoulders and turned him round. 'We'll be happy to go north just as fast as we can, you can be certain of that. And I'm sure you'll find your daughter will be well again. Don't you think a message would have come from your wife, if anything was really wrong? Thaltor hadn't heard from Ilmarynvoro, had he?'

Heranar looked at him doubtfully. 'No, that's true, I never thought of that. But we'll still be leaving at dawn tomorrow.'

'We'll be ready. We're in just as much of a hurry as you are.'

The others were delighted when Haldur returned with the news that they were to prepare themselves for travelling on immediately. They began sorting out bags and baggage, intending to get everything ready before evening so that they would all be free if Morancras was willing to speak the rite for them, but the banter died on their lips when they saw Aestrontor's face as he appeared in the doorway.

'I've been in the *Fly*,' he said, 'and that's where I found out what happened. The house in Wide Westgate's been pulled down, there's a new barracks there now. They told me Morancras was found shut in with three stray dogs. They'd been … well … they'd been chewing at him. Nobody knows whether they'd actually killed him or not.'

'When was this? Did you find that out as well?' asked Haldur eventually.

'They found him the day we left for Caradriggan.'

Tellapur jumped up from where he had been kneeling on the floor, re-packing a saddlebag. 'Valahald had something to do with this, I just know it!'

'Quite correct, in a way.' Valahald himself had materialised silently behind Aestrontor. They could hear the sly amusement in his voice. 'It was actually two of my men who found him: not a pleasant experience for them, I'm sure you'll agree, but at least they succeeded in killing the dogs.' A slight smile appeared on Valahald's face. 'I hope you'll enjoy your stay with Heranar. I gather you'll be making an early start tomorrow, so no doubt you'll want to be early to bed tonight; and as I've a pile of paperwork waiting for me, I'll bid you farewell now.'

Next morning they were away so early that scarcely a passer-by was abroad in the streets to see them go. Up the northern road they went, at such a pace that Haldur, who had begun by being preoccupied as to why Valahald should have sent men to call on poor old Morancras on the very day their backs were turned, began to worry about the effect on the horses and mules they had bought in Caradriggan. He was unsure what the choice of livestock would be like, if they had to change mounts again before they finally set out for home, and in any case had not budgeted for a double purchase. They would just have to hope that the rest over the winter would be sufficient. Meanwhile Heranar pressed on as if demons from Na Caarst were on his tail and on the last day of their journey he commandeered a fresh horse for himself from a posting-station and galloped off ahead alone, leaving the rest of them to make their own speed. By the time they arrived themselves and were heading for the quarters they had used on their downward journey, there was no sign of him: presumably he was once more restored to the bosom of his family. Haldur stopped a passing member of the household staff.

'Is all well with the children?'

The fellow looked at him. 'The governor's little lasses? Of course, they're fine. The eldest was a bit peaky there, a while back, but nothing to worry about. I've youngsters myself, but he's like a broody hen with those girls of his. Should've been a woman.' He laughed and tramped off.

Defences lowered

For the next few days gales and rain swept down the shallow valley where Heranar's headquarters were situated. The men from Rihannad Ennar stared out of the windows, bored to distraction as the slow hours crawled by. Haldur looked at his companions. A whole winter of this! Three months, at the very least. They would never be able to stick it, there'd be trouble of some kind. He came to a decision.

'I'm going to see if they'll let me in to talk to Heranar. We've got to get him on our side.'

In the event, when he reached the porch of the governor's residence he could hear Heranar's laughter over the shrieks of children at play, leaving the servant at the door without any chance to claim his master was occupied with business. Suddenly one of the little girls burst into the corridor, the other two in hot pursuit, giggling; but catching sight of Haldur, they instantly fell silent, staring. Wondering what had happened, Heranar stuck his head round the door and saw Haldur, standing there under the survey of three pairs of huge brown eyes. The children flew back to their father's side, leaning against him as Heranar caressed their long dark-red hair. Once again it struck Haldur forcibly, how different Heranar seemed now from the man who blushed and chewed his nails when his brother or his troops had him under their eye. He smiled at the four of them.

'I can see this might not be the best time, but I need to talk to you, Heranar.'

Heranar seemed to hesitate for a moment, then he stepped aside. 'Come in.'

In the corner there was a low table with a board game of some kind on it and small, child-size chairs around it. 'Play over there quietly for a while,' said Heranar, and the two eldest girls did as he asked but the smallest climbed on to his lap.

'I'm glad to see they're all in good health,' said Haldur. 'You never did tell me their names, you know. Who's this, for instance?'

'This is Rhosantoro,' said Heranar, rocking the toddler on his knee, 'and that's Tiranesco and Elethilmaro.'

Haldur smiled. 'Beautiful names, for three beautiful little girls. There'll be plenty of competition for their favours, when the time comes.'

Beaming with pleasure, Heranar relaxed visibly. 'It's a good thing they take after my wife, rather than me.'

Unable to think of a convincing response to this, Haldur settled instead for a question. 'And have you always lived here, since your marriage?'

'Yes. You see, I was a single man when I was posted here – when I was made governor of Rossaestrethan.' The flush began to creep into Heranar's face again at this. He paused and swallowed. 'I was travelling round my new province when I first saw Ilmarynvoro, the daughter of my host for the night. You've met my marriage-father, Gillavar.'

Haldur remembered Heranar's outburst against his marriage-father on the bridge in Framstock: clearly no love was lost there. 'I should have said before, I'm sorry you recently lost your own father. Your sorrow is a grief to me,' he added formally, making the sign.

'Thank you.' Heranar had not heard those words used in years; now he found them strangely comforting. Suddenly he began to speak almost freely.

'You know, when I was a very small child, my parents lived in one of the oldest parts of Caradriggan. When I look back now, I realise the house was probably smaller than I remember. It fronted onto the street, but behind it there was a long walled garden with a gate at the bottom into a narrow alleyway, and at the far end there was a little summerhouse built against the wall. I expect the garden was overlooked by the upper windows of the nearby houses, but children don't notice things like that: to me it seemed a secret world. You could hear noises from the street, and people passing along the alley, but they didn't know we were there, my brother and I. We used to play in the summerhouse; it was semi-derelict. But then my father had it repaired, and used it as a kind of office; and then,' Heranar smiled rather sadly, 'then as he, well, I suppose I'd have to say as he rose in the world, we moved to a bigger house.'

Haldur was taken aback by this sudden unexpected candour. He hesitated, wondering if this was a moment to play on Heranar's weakness. 'Please don't be offended by my saying this, but you don't seem a happy man, to me. Why not resign your commission and go back to Caradriggan, if that's what you really want?'

Heranar shook his head, his eyes downcast. 'It's not as easy as that.' Did Haldur know of the whispers that Valahald had been responsible for their father's death? Surely he must: it had been widely enough rumoured. 'What is it people say? "No man can turn back time." No, indeed you can't. All you can do is go on. And there's my wife to consider; her people are here.' He looked up. 'Please don't mention this conversation to her.'

'No, of course not.' Sensing that Heranar was about to clam up on him, Haldur decided to press on quickly with what he had come to say.

'Well, maybe I'm fortunate: I don't want to turn back time, I just want to go back home. I can't tell you how much I want to see the Nine Dales again, come the spring, and that goes for all of us. But in the meantime, could we not have your permission to ride out occasionally? Why do you need to keep us caged up in here? It was bad enough before, but the thought of spending the whole winter like this is unbearable.' Heranar made no answer and Haldur tried again. 'Look, we'd keep to ourselves, we won't try to mix with the locals.'

The silence lengthened above the chatter from the little sisters over at their play table. Haldur ran his hands through his hair and then spread them wide in appeal. 'What's the problem? What is it that worries you? Surely we all know where we stand, after what's been seen and said over the past few months.'

As the telltale blush began to creep over his face at this, Heranar stood up, sliding his youngest daughter from his knee, and turned away in an attempt to hide it. 'I'll think about it,' he muttered.

'Is there no hunting around here? You could send an escort out with us, if you feel you must keep us under guard,' suggested Haldur, trying to pin down the concession he wanted.

'I've said I'll think about it, all right? I'll speak to you again when I've made a decision.'

There was an edge to Heranar's voice: clearly the audience was over. But left alone once more with his children, Heranar was no longer of a mind to join their play and they began to bicker among themselves, causing him eventually to send them packing with a servant. As they went, Elethilmaro turned in the doorway, pouting.

'I don't like that man who came in here. He made you sad and now you're cross with us.'

Heranar scarcely heard her. He sat in the empty room, chewing at his fingers, and the thoughts ran to and fro in his head like cornered rats, gnawing at the frayed remains of his peace of mind.

CHAPTER 53

Forewarned

'But why? When? Why has he told us? What's he going to do now? Never mind him, what are *we* going to do?'

The voices were kept down, but incredulity and anxiety could be heard in them as the questions flew to and fro. They looked from one to another, eyes wide in alarm, searching for reasons, for answers; but none came, and gradually the shocked muttering died away as every face turned to Haldur. He shook his head.

'To be truthful, I've been afraid for a while now that something like this was being planned. But for him to tell us!'

'Go over it again,' said Asaldron. 'Slowly. Everything he said.'

'Well…' Haldur's fingers combed at his hair in agitation, and as usual it fell heavily straight down again. 'I got word that Heranar wanted to see me. I assumed he'd decided whether or not he was going to let us take a bit of outside exercise, so I was surprised at first when he brought me out of his office and started walking up and down in the courtyard. Obviously, I realise now he didn't want to risk being overheard. Anyway I couldn't fail to notice how terrible he looked. It's only a few days since I spoke to him last, but I'd swear he's thinner and hasn't slept much either. Suddenly he stopped dead in his tracks, cut straight across the conversation we were having and blurted out "I've made up my mind to tell you something. Rihannad Ennar is going to be attacked." I think he was almost tempted to bolt straight back indoors, but I wasn't going to have that: I left him in no doubt that if he was prepared to tell me that much, he'd better tell me what else he knew. He said it was decided before we left Caradriggan. They're going to spend most of next year in preparation, setting up secret lines of communication and supply, digging in, so as to minimise the risk of crossing the wilderness; then the all-out assault will come in the spring after next.'

'And you've been feeling sorry for him!' said Tellapur bitterly.

Haldur looked at the young man. 'Yes, and I think you might, if you'd spoken to him as I have. He's not so much older than I am, but he's burdened with regrets, haunted by past misdeeds and feels trapped without hope of escape. At least he's been brave enough to do one thing he thinks is right. But anyway, we've got to look out for ourselves, now.'

'But why's Heranar telling us? I can't see what's in it for him, to betray his own people.' This came from Cathasar.

'All I could get out of him was some mumbling about how he himself doesn't agree with what they're doing, but can't stop it or get out of being a part of it, but feels we deserve a warning.' Haldur shook his head again. 'Heranar's in over his ears, he doesn't know where to turn. I don't think he'll come through this alive.'

Frowning in thought, Asaldron spoke slowly. 'So we'll have a year to prepare, once we get home, before we have to face them.'

'I'm not going to sit here wasting time after what I've been told.' There was a new, harder note in Haldur's voice. 'We've got to use the warning we've been given, we owe it to the Nine Dales. If we make a break for it now, we just might be able to get back before the weather stops us. We've got to try.'

'What? Get out of here, where we're guarded night and day, up to the pass and through it without being stopped? We haven't a hope, Haldur.' Cathasar began pacing up and down. He turned and flung out his arms. 'Not to mention the small matter of crossing the wilderness. I take it you've not forgotten how carefully we prepared before we came south? And now you're suggesting we tackle it without any gear or supplies? Because that's how it would have to be – how could we possibly get stuff together? Everyone would know what we're up to, we'd have Heranar's men on our tail before we were out of sight of his walls. And you're talking about the weather stopping us!' He laughed rather wildly and sat down again. 'I hardly think we need to waste our energy worrying about the weather.'

'No, that's right.' Haldur kept his voice down, but he spoke coldly. 'Nor on useless rage. You're angry with the Caradwardans, with Heranar, with the plight we're in, with me, with yourself. Save it, Cathasar: it will stop you thinking clearly. Now listen to me. If we're to do this, we'll have to do it soon. Of course it's a huge gamble, so we've got to reduce the risks as far as we can. We'll allow ourselves one week. Every day we'll get together to share any information we've been able to pick up, any ideas that occur to any of us. Any and all of them, no matter how unworkable they might seem. We'll make the best plan we can, and then the first chance we get once the week's up, we'll be gone.'

'Haldur, I want to say something.' Ir'rossung felt the words sticking in his throat, but he had been included in the party for the wisdom of his age and he knew it was his duty to speak. 'If we're captured, they'll kill us; and then there'll be no warning at all for our people. I don't think we should all go. I'd only slow you down, for one, so why not leave me and some of the rest of us here and just you and, say, Aestrontor try to get away?'

Aestrontor had sat silent as usual up to this point, weighing up the odds, but now he spoke. 'Two is not enough to dare the wilderness. If there should be an accident, it would leave one alone with no help at all. Three should go, at the least. Maybe Cathasar should come with us.'

Tellapur looked around at the others. As the youngest, he would surely be one earmarked to stay, and he felt sick with despair at the prospect. But then Haldur laughed grimly.

'Ir'rossung's right that if we're taken, they'll kill us. But what do you think would happen to those still here, if some of us got away?

It would be a death sentence for those left behind. No, we came into this together, we're going to get out of it together, or not at all. And we will: all of us will see the Nine Dales once more. Rihannad Ennar will call us home.'

But days slipped by, and though Haldur racked his brains, he knew he was no nearer to making a plan for escape that had any hope of success. He had not seen Heranar again: no doubt he was avoiding further contact, maybe by now even regretting what he had done; but in any case as governor he must be fully occupied with business in view of the sudden upsurge of activity within his headquarters. By keeping his ears open Haldur gathered that the newcomers were preparing the ground for a base which was to be established somewhere away to the north-east.

'Goodwill visit, huh!' grunted a fellow aggrieved enough to exchange a word or two with him. 'We've all heard that kind of thing before. All it ever means is more work for us: they'll want this, and they'll want that, and they'll want it all at the double with no account taken of any local difficulties. Yes, somewhere over towards the mountains, that's what I heard. Well, as long as I don't have to go there. You hear tales that would make your hair stand on end, no wonder they say that's where the toughest irregulars get posted.'

Meanwhile the visiting officer was sitting with Heranar at his desk, enjoying the governor's hospitality and relishing even more his superior's obvious discomfort as he ran over the schedule of activity planned for the next six months or so, laying plenty of emphasis on the assistance that Heranar would be expected to either provide or organise. Finally he gathered up his documents and it seemed he was preparing to leave.

'Is there anything you'd like me to go over again?'

'No, no, that's all quite clear, thank you.'

'What about these fellows from the Nine Dales? Not causing any problems, I hope?'

Heranar felt his face beginning to flush and twisted his hands together under the desk. He stared at the paperwork in front of him to avoid meeting the other man's eyes. Here was another who scarcely bothered to conceal his lack of respect: though junior in rank, he was the older of the two and was no doubt of the opinion that Heranar had been promoted far beyond his abilities. By the way he was speaking and behaving, anyone would think he was the one conducting the interview, not the governor. It was probably a trick he'd picked up from Valahald, thought Heranar miserably.

'I've no difficulties with them,' he muttered through clenched teeth.

'I'm glad to hear that, sir. However, I've instructions from Lord Valahald to help out, if you want me to. I could have some of my lads take them out for a bit of a breather, for example.'

This came as enough of a surprise to make Heranar look up. Suddenly he remembered something Valahald had said to him one day, back in Caradriggan: something about how he would have help in dealing with the northerners. Maybe this was what his brother had meant. He began to feel happier.

'Yes, I'd appreciate it if you'd arrange that. As a matter of fact, they have asked me whether they might exercise outside the walls. I agreed to consider the request but it would have meant getting an escort together to send with them. If you'll take the job on, that sorts things out. Perhaps a day's hunting?'

The office shook his head. 'I don't think so, sir. Not hunting.' He smiled. 'Can't have them armed, when they're mixing with my men, now can I? But we'll take them off your hands, shall we say three days from now?'

Haldur heard this news with mixed feelings. All his instincts told him that this was their chance, if they were to get away. He thought back over their journey south, and recalled the distant mountains they had seen while crossing the wilderness, the mountains which Cathasar, with his keen eyesight, had thought were clothed with forest. In Tellgard he had looked at old maps of Gwent y'm Aryframan which Arval held and he estimated that here, where Heranar had his headquarters, was not so far from where Salfgard had stood, albeit further north and west. If they could get across the river and into the hills on this side of the range, maybe they would be able to find a way back by picking a path through the mountains and thus avoid using the pass at all. But somehow they would have to shake off pursuit, and the only glimmer of hope there seemed to be the hint that for some reason the common soldiers were afraid of the terrain into which they would be going. Against this of course was the fact that he had also been told it was land used by the irregulars. Haldur grimaced in frustration: maybe trying to escape now was just too desperate, too likely to fail. He sensed that the mood of his companions was beginning to turn against the idea, especially now that they had been told no weapons of any kind would be permitted when they rode out. None of them but himself had been able to think of any stratagem and even his own thoughts were scarcely worthy to be called a plan.

Treachery

He was sitting in silence, wondering whether after all they should wait until the spring, when the door to their quarters opened and Ir'rossung came in, bringing with him some news that changed everything. He rushed over to Haldur.

'It's a trick! I heard them talking! As soon as they've got us away from here they're going to kill us all!'

'Steady now, steady.' Haldur's stomach was churning and his words were as much to calm himself as the others. 'Let's hear it, Ir'rossung.'

'I thought I'd take my horse over to the smithy, get the shoe that needed seeing to sorted out today rather than leave it. No sooner was the job under way when one of Heranar's men appeared, and along with him a fellow I recognised as one I've seen going about with the officer in charge of this visiting detachment. They made it very clear they weren't best pleased to have to wait, so rather than have to listen to them I shut the door and left them outside. Well of course in no time I found it uncomfortably hot, but rather than open the door again, or go outside and be on the receiving end of more snide remarks, I moved away to the window. And standing there, I found I could hear what the two of them were saying, where they sat on the bench outside.' Ir'rossung paused. He had been gradually becoming less agitated as he spoke, but now he took a deep breath.

'They were still griping about being in a queue behind me, and then Heranar's fellow said, "Mind you, if this lot's a sample of what we'll have to deal with when we move against the Nine Dales, we shouldn't have any kind of a problem. I can't wait! If the pickings turn out to be half as good as the rumours suggest, I'll be well set up." There was a kind of startled noise from the other man and he said, "Keep it down, can't you? We don't want them getting a hint of what's afoot." Heranar's man had a good laugh at this. "That old fool?" he said. "There's no need for you to worry about him, he's as deaf as a post. Bad luck to him, getting in ahead of us. Don't see why we should have to wait, but the smith's so bloody-minded, once he's started a job nothing will shift him till it's finished."

'After that neither of them said anything for a while, but I reckon the other fellow was narked at being laughed at and was thinking how he could get his own back, because eventually he said, "It's not just your time he's wasting you know, it's his own. There's not much need to have your horse re-shod when you won't need it any more before the week's out, is there?" "What are you on about?" said the first man. "I thought you lads were taking them out on exercise?" "We are," he said, "but we'll not be going far. Just a few miles, all nice and friendly so's they don't suspect, and then… that's right, I see you get the picture. There's more than one meaning in taking a man out, eh? Then we'll dump them somewhere for the kites to feed on. You can trust our top brass not to take the chance of them ever arriving home with any kind of warning."

'I could hardly stand still. There was a much longer silence this time, and I was afraid they'd not say anything else before the smith had finished with my horse and I'd have to leave. Then the fellow from the garrison here spoke up again: he'd obviously been doing some hard thinking. "Why are your lot doing the job? I know for a fact that Heranar's turned down more than one request for the prisoners to ride out, even under escort. We've kept them close in here; we could have eliminated them any time, if that was the idea."

'This time it was the other fellow who laughed. Then I heard him spit. "Heranar!" he said. "Listen, let me give you some advice. If you're ambitious like you say, you want to put in for a transfer to Valahald's staff. He's the coming man, not his little brother. Heranar knows nothing about this. He wasn't told, because the other commanders don't rate him. They were afraid he might give the game away by dithering, let alone not have the nerve to get the job done, as you put it, himself. This way, dear governor Heranar's innocence is the perfect cover." Then they drifted off into speculation about whether or not the rumours were true, that Valahald killed his father; and they were still talking about that when the smith finished and I had to come away.'

'We've got no chance now. All we can do is play for time. Maybe we could say we've changed our minds about going outside the walls,' said Asaldron.

'What, sit out the winter just waiting for our throats to be cut one night?' Haldur shook his head. 'No, the decision's been made for us now, thanks to what Ir'rossung's found out. We've no choice any more, so no need for doubt. And we do have one chance, so we must use it. We've got the advantage of knowing our enemies' plan, without them realising it. They think they're going to fall upon us without warning, but they'll be wrong. And as for the means to do it, I think I can see a way for us to have weapons of a kind, even if we actually appear unarmed.'

Thank the Starborn, thought Haldur, that I had the idea of playing up to Ir'rossung's deafness. The subterfuge has been well rewarded.

For remembrance

That evening, Haldur and Heranar spoke together again. It was a strange meeting, which took place at Haldur's request when he heard that Heranar would be away next day for a stint up in the fort at the pass. Vividly in Haldur's mind ran the memory of their first meeting, up there at the edge of the wilderness. Something had changed between them, since then, some subtle shift born of Haldur's pity and Heranar's change of heart: but now it was likely enough that they would never meet again. Was it simply that Haldur knew he could be looking death in the face, whereas Heranar was ignorant of it, that gave the younger man what he felt to be an advantage? Or was it that the courage he brought to this situation gave him a strength that Heranar, knowing himself the weaker character, instinctively clung to? For the second time in as many days, it seemed to Heranar that he was sitting on the wrong side of the governor's desk; but now, rather than resentment, the thought brought with it only an enormous sense of fatigue. Heranar felt worn out: tired, beaten, defeated. A wild desire to confide in Haldur tormented him, but he had no idea where to even begin. His mind shied away from what he had already said: every time he thought of it, he was gripped by panic at what he had done. Now to his deep dismay, Haldur brought up this very subject.

'I don't think I said this before, I was too taken aback at the time. But I would like you to know that none of us will ever betray you by revealing that you told me what's going to happen.'

A fresh surge of panic coursed through Heranar at the use of the word 'betray'. He sat in miserable silence for a while, fighting the temptation to say he wished now he had never spoken. But the truth was much more tangled and complicated than that. He heard the words in his mind: *I wish I could turn back time.* How lucky was Haldur, who said he was not troubled by thoughts of this kind! Two more wishes added themselves to the long, impossible list: that he need not be involved in the coming invasion, and that Haldur could have been his friend.

'What's the matter?' Heranar looked up to find Haldur watching him.

'Nothing. Well, I... I just...' Heranar shook his head and gave up. 'Nothing.'

'You're worrying about what you've done, aren't you? Calling yourself a traitor? Don't think like that, Heranar. How can it be wrong to take a stand against evil? You know there's no justification for attacking Rihannad Ennar. You were right to tell me, you've done a brave thing. But if you're afraid now, you should ask Arval to help you.'

'Arval! It's too late for that. You were there, you heard what he said when we left Caradriggan.'

'It was Valahald he warned, not you. You stood up to your brother in front of all of us, do you think Arval won't know? Listen, Heranar. You were still up here at the time, but you must have heard what happened when we were brought before Tell'Ethronad. Arval wrote out *Stirfellaerdon donn'Ur* as I spoke it for him and he'll have had more copies made by now. Send to him for one, read it, arm yourself with knowledge. You owe it to your children.'

At this mention of his children, Heranar buried his face in his hands and a kind of muffled groan broke from him. Haldur looked at the bitten finger-nails and again pity stirred in him. He was glad to know that Heranar was innocent of the plot to kill them. Suddenly he knew what he was going to do; after all, it was thanks to Heranar that at least they had warning of the danger to Rihannad Ennar. He reached into his pouch, took out the fist-sized lump of raw amber and put it on the desk between them.

'Here's something to remember me by.'

Heranar took his hands away from his eyes and gaped in amazement. 'No! I can't take this, I can't. It would feel like payment for what I've done.'

'It's not a gift to you.' Haldur smiled. 'Let's say I'm leaving it with you in trust for your little girls. Even divided up, it will make three heirlooms of great value. Keep it safe for them while they grow up. No-one need know.'

He stood up and took his leave, walking back to his companions almost light of heart. There was nothing more they could do, now. The plans were laid, they would have to trust to fate. Behind him Heranar sat on alone, the room growing cold around him as time passed and still he sat, putting off the hour of rest.

Death or freedom

And so the day of death or freedom for Haldur and his companions arrived. They were ready early, having none of them slept too well; and by mid-morning, after being looked over to see none of them carried weapons, were riding under escort at a steady pace, heading away from close confinement at last. Haldur moved over to speak to the officer in charge.

'Thanks for arranging for us to get out for a few hours – we've not taken kindly to being cooped up all the time. Your new camp's over in that direction, I gather? Would you agree if we don't ride within sight of it? We're more used to the outdoor life, back in the Nine Dales, and I don't doubt we'll see more than enough of barracks and soldiers and four walls around us before the winter's out and we can set off for home.'

'No problem. We'll take you over the river towards the hills, that should suit you, eh?'

With the tail of his eye Haldur saw some of the troopers exchanging smirks. He forced himself not to grip the reins, to keep a relaxed seat, to look easily about him as if all was friendly, but the racing beat of his heart filled his throat. It had been agreed that the others were to leave it to him to pick the moment when they would try to break away; but not knowing when their escort would choose to set upon them, it was vital that they were ready for an instant response if the attack came before they made their own move. They had ridden out of one valley, that where Heranar's headquarters were situated, and were now descending the slopes of another. Here and there smoke rose from isolated homesteads and people scratching at little fields looked up sullenly as they passed. Haldur moved his shoulders, trying to ease the tension from them. Maybe they were safe here; perhaps the idea was to wait until there would be no witnesses or any chance of intervention. He remembered the knowing looks that had been exchanged. As they splashed across a ford where the river ran in several shallow channels between gravelly banks and ridges, he tried to steady himself. It would surely be soon: now was the time for the first pre-arranged signal. Half-way up the further slope, he drew his horse across towards a stand of tangled thorn bushes all wound about with brambles.

'Won't be a moment. Nature calls.'

Immediately, Cathasar followed him. 'Me, too.'

The others ignored them and simply walked their horses on, and after a moment's hesitation the escort followed suit. Behind the bushes, with frantic speed Cathasar unwound the sling from round his head and crammed the concealing hat back on; from the ground at his feet he grabbed half a dozen stones and pushed them into his sleeve pockets. The smooth pebbles he had seen at the river-crossing would have been better, but there was no time to waste in wanting what he could not have. Haldur cursed under his breath as in his haste he fumbled: the noise of metal on metal seemed deafening. The day before, he had filched two old horseshoes from the heap of scrap metal outside the forge and attached them to a long leather rope made from tearing up a shirt. This improvised bolas had been concealed under his clothes and now needed to be pulled out from where it lay across his shoulders and down his sleeves. He shoved the horseshoes onto his left wrist, pulled the sleeve down over them and climbed back on his horse, tucking the leather thong under the skirt of his tunic. With his right hand he felt behind his neck and saw Cathasar do the same. Yes, they could reach the half-size sparring staves roughly sewn into the lining of their jackets. It had taken them hours to cut through the staves, working in the night using only knives, but it would be worth it if Asaldron's idea worked. A desperate, hopeless wish for his bow flashed through Haldur's mind.

'Ready?' Cathasar nodded wordlessly. 'Come on then.'

They trotted up to rejoin the others and soon they were riding over the crest of the valley and looking over the land beyond. It seemed not so dark and murky here and Haldur, straining his eyes in hope to pick out their best course, found he could see further than he had expected. The country was wild and bare. He could see no sign of habitation, just a rather barren expanse broken up by numerous rocky outcrops. Instinct told him the attack was imminent. He cleared his throat and began to speak the words they had agreed on, his voice sounding strange in his own ears.

'It won't be long now until the Midwinter Feast in *Rihannad Ennar*!'

He cried out the name of their homeland, and instantly they sprang into action. Aestrontor, who had ridden with the Cunorad in his time, lashed his horse to the gallop and in the surprise of the moment opened up a gap between himself and the rest. His companions also dug their heels in, spreading out in different directions so that for a precious moment their escort milled about in confusion, yelling as much at each other as at their intended victims. Haldur had counted on this.

'Now!' he shouted, throwing the bolas. It whirled through the air and wrapped itself around the forelegs of a trooper's horse, the iron weights whipping the leather thong tight. The horse stumbled and fell, throwing its rider who hit the ground heavily and lay still. At the same time Tellapur, Asaldron and Ir'rossung hurled their cut-down staves, using them as they would aim throwing sticks at a flock of birds. Two more soldiers fell and a third was hit on the shoulder: his wild scream of pain panicked his horse, which bolted with the man clinging desperately to it with one hand, half out of the saddle. But the leader was unhurt, and still mounted, and now he began to rally his men. They were all armed, but Haldur was not so concerned about weapons for hand-to-hand fighting. It was the archers who worried him. Out of the corner of his eye he saw Aestrontor circling back towards them: this too was part of the plan, that he and Haldur would form a rearguard behind which the others could retreat and Cathasar, who was most skilled with the sling, would have cover to fire.

'Go on, go on!' he shouted at his cousin, and Asaldron wheeled away with Ir'rossung and Tellapur. He and Aestrontor pulled out their staves and galloped to and fro, using all their skill on horseback to swerve and turn so as not to present too easy a target.

'Take out the bowmen if you can,' panted Haldur as Cathasar rode past him in a cloud of dust.

Aestrontor threw his stave. It missed his man, but clouted a horse to the side of its head, bringing it down and its rider with it. Stones flew from Cathasar's sling. Some found their mark but others missed, and he was running out of shots. Suddenly through the noise of hooves and shouting Haldur heard the troop leader ordering his remaining archers to aim at the horses. Desperately he yelled at Cathasar to give Aestrontor his unused stave.

'Get back, get more stones!' he gasped, and then dragged his horse round again, calling to Aestrontor to follow his lead. They charged directly at the remaining troopers, brandishing their staves like madmen. For an instant or two the soldiers wavered in the face of this crazed assault, but their discipline held. They spread out, baffling Haldur's attempt to unsettle them. Their commander sensed that the impetus of the attack upon them was waning and he still had a numerical advantage. His bowmen took aim, and two horses fell: Cathasar's, and Tellapur's. Haldur saw Asaldron skid to a halt and go back to Tellapur, who had staggered to his feet and now somehow clawed his way up to share Asaldron's horse; but Cathasar was left isolated, scrabbling on the ground for more sling stones. In a moment that seemed outside time, Haldur's and Cathasar's eyes met through the swirling dust, and each saw death in the other's face. Then Cathasar leapt up, swung his arm and let fly. His cast was true and another archer fell. But the troop leader laughed aloud: there were two archers still unharmed and both of them now took aim. This was the end, then. Everything had happened so quickly, probably only a few moments had passed but it was over now.

'Get him up, quick. Ride, keep moving.' Haldur spat the words out at Aestrontor, but though he heard the sounds as Cathasar was heaved across his saddle-bow and the laboured breathing of the horse under its double burden, his mind was now detached and curiously calm. So he was to die here in a strange land, never to see his father and his beloved homeland again? Well, if it had to be: but he would sell his life dearly to give his companions the best chance he could. He set his horse to the gallop and hurtled forward, riding straight at one of the archers, reckless, heedless, as if on a wild dawn chase with the Cunorad. Maybe something of this showed in his face, because it seemed he saw doubt creep into the man's eyes as he aimed. Then suddenly, it was as if an invisible force struck the archer: his head jerked back, his arms flew wide. The bow dropped from his grasp, the arrow skittered harmlessly away, the horse backed and plunged; and the man toppled forwards, his feet trapped in the stirrups, one hand almost brushing the dirt, an arrow lodged between his shoulders. Before any of them had had time to do more than gape at this, another arrow came whistling after the first, and another soldier was down, blood pouring through his fingers from the ruin of his face. A third arrow passed overhead harmlessly and one of the troopers pointed.

'Over there! Behind those rocks, that's where they're hiding!'

The officer in charge made a snap decision. His prisoners were escaping, but they would not get far. They'd lost two horses and were effectively weaponless; they had no supplies and they were in hostile territory. They could be rounded up later. Meanwhile, his men were under attack. He wrenched his horse round, bellowing at them to charge whoever was lurking in ambush. He had barely given the order when their assailant burst from cover. Haldur had a fleeting impression of a slight figure on a grey horse who tore off into the distance, clinging low on the animal's neck, twisting, turning, leaping obstacles, already gaining on his pursuers. Not even among the Hounds of the Starborn had he ever seen anyone who could ride like that, but this was no time to stand and stare. He hastened after his companions.

'Come on, we must make what speed we can. We've got to get into the hills if we're to have any chance at all. We don't know whether they'll come after us.'

The secret road

Haldur thought it best not to share his worry that they might be intercepted by irregulars, but before long he had other concerns. Their progress was too slow for his liking: they shared the extra riders out, changing frequently, so as to spare the horses as much as they could, but it was obvious that their mounts were almost spent. It would be no use forcing them and ruining their fitness for the days ahead, but he wanted better cover before they stopped to rest for the night. As for hunger, the sooner they got used to empty bellies the better. Every man carried a bag of meal concealed in his clothes but that was all they had until they reached more promising country where they might hope for success in setting snares. Haldur put Aestrontor at the head of the party, to pick out a path and set the pace, and took up a position at the rear both to act as guard and to encourage Ir'rossung, who was visibly flagging. There was little talk, just the creak of leather harness and the occasional sharp sound of a hoof striking a stone, but then the silence was broken by a strange voice.

'So far, so good; but you are out of your way.'

They started in fright, and turned to see a man standing behind them. A dark man, an Outlander by his looks, but how had he appeared out of nowhere? Then they saw the badge at his shoulder. An officer of the auxiliaries! The man noticed their dismayed reaction and smiled slightly, slowly raising empty hands.

'This is not an arrest. I am alone, and I am here to help you, Haldur son of Carapethan.'

They looked at each other and Haldur rode back a pace or two, staring down at the man. He had unusual, pale eyes that contrasted strangely with his otherwise dark looks.

'I've seen you before, haven't I?' said Haldur. 'You were a guest in Heranar's house, before ever we went south to Caradriggan. You wear the green badge, and yet you say you will help us? How? And how do we know we can trust you?'

The man had still not lowered his hands. 'Yes, we've met before. On that occasion you told the company that the torc you bear has two eyes, one to look into your own heart and one to look into the hearts of other men. If you are worthy of this heirloom, you should know whether I'm trustworthy or not. As to how I will help you: I will save you from Valahald's men and set you on the path for Rihannad Ennar. My comrade has drawn the pursuit away, but we cannot delay for long explanations. I can take you to a refuge where you'll be safe, and we can talk there if you wish. You must come with me now, though, or it will be too late.'

Haldur hesitated for another moment or two only. 'Lead the way, friend of the Nine Dales,' he said.

Turning away in a new direction, the man led them swiftly across country. He had refused the offer of a horse, moving at an easy, tireless lope that was more than equal to any speed their weary animals could manage. The terrain became more difficult, breaking up into stone pavements and rocky outcrops. After a few miles they found themselves staring down into a pothole. A yard or two back from its edge an ash tree grew from a crevice in the rocks. Their guide produced a rope and made it fast to the tree; then he turned to them.

'This is where you lose your horses, I'm afraid, but better that than lose your lives.'

'Down there? Oh no, I'm not going down there.' There was sweat on Cathasar's face and the horse he rode, sensing his fear, began to toss its head and back away.

Haldur dismounted and took a few steps nearer the edge. There was the same raw, rank smell rising from the depths that he and Aestrontor had noticed when they crept close to investigate the sink hole in Na Caarst. His own palms were clammy but he did his best not to show that he too was afraid. 'We have to climb down the rope into that? Why? Tell us what awaits us down there.'

'What better way to elude your pursuers than to vanish into the earth? This shaft connects with an underground system of caves and passages which will bring you out again to the refuge I mentioned.'

'How will they not simply pick up our trail and follow us down the rope?' asked Aestrontor.

'I'll be taking the rope with me, when you're all safely down, and I'll drive the horses off in different directions. There won't be any clear traces left to lead them here, once I've finished my work.'

Cathasar appealed to his leader. 'Haldur, don't make us do this. There must be some other way! We'll be stuck down there without the means to get out again, if he's going to take the rope, and how will we find the way through if he's not coming down with us as a guide?'

For a moment Haldur stood without speaking. At the edge of his sight, the pothole gaped dark and he avoided looking into it, glancing instead at the badge of rank their guide wore. Surely their rescue could not be an elaborate trick, not when the mysterious rider had killed two men before he broke from ambush? He forced himself to look at where the ground fell away. 'There's someone else down there, is that it?'

For answer the Outlander stepped up to the brink and called down, and from below a shout echoed in reply. He looked at Haldur. 'Correct. It's not so far to the bottom, maybe thirty, forty feet. The guide has waited for you in the dark, but he'll light a torch for you to climb by.'

Suppressing a shudder as he wondered how long the man underground had waited without light, Haldur addressed his comrades. 'At least three men have risked their lives to help us. How can we not trust them? And we swore to stick by each other, whatever happened.' He looked directly at Cathasar. 'I told you before, and I promise you now: we will all see the Nine Dales again.'

Now he turned to the Outlander who waited beside the rope. 'It seems we're to go on from here with a new guide. We owe you our lives: may we know your name before we part?'

The man smiled. 'We will meet again, all being well. Time enough then for names and such.'

Disaster strikes

So one by one they clung to the rope and made the descent, and when they all stood safely on the wet rock at the bottom the man who had waited for them called up the shaft. The rope jerked about as it was untied from the tree and then it was hauled out of sight.

'Here.' Their new guide was rummaging in a pack, and took out what looked like a bundle of leather. 'Tie these on. There's one or two places where the passage is low and we have to crawl.'

They saw then that he was wearing knee-protectors, thick leather pads that were plastered with mud; his jerkin too was smeared with clay across the shoulders and there were smudges on his face. He took the torch from where it had been wedged.

'Ready? Follow me, and keep close.'

They set off, feeling the chill strike through their clothes, putting out their hands to steady themselves, touching the walls of the passage, rough and wet. There were pools here and there underfoot, icy and often unavoidable. Before long their feet were numb with cold. The torch flared and dimmed and flared again and in its uncertain light they saw one or two gaps in the rock to their left, no more than fissures with a hint of impenetrable blackness beyond them, but so far at least there was no doubt that this was the only path to follow. They could hear the sigh of their breath on the cold air, the drip of water falling invisibly, and somewhere beyond all this, a constant, muted murmur, but no man spoke: they were all afraid. After a while their guide broke the silence.

'This is the first low place.' He held up the torch and they saw a rock wall before them with a dark opening at its base, no more than the height of a child not yet into its second ten years. 'It bends to the right, but there are no turns, you can't mistake the way. The thing is though, it's too low for the torch. I'll go through first, light up again and wait for you.'

Haldur swallowed. 'How far is it?'

'Not as far as it will seem. My advice is to breathe slowly, and count. You should be through in about sixty breaths, if you can steady yourselves.'

Asaldron squatted down and peered into the tunnel. 'That noise we can hear is louder through there. What is it?'

'It's just water. There are three rivers that run through the cave system. When there's rain in the hills they come through in spate; in fact in the winter this low place is usually submerged. It's lucky you got away before the season turned.'

Forcing down his fear, Haldur organised his men. He put Asaldron, who seemed steadiest, at the front, followed by Tellapur and Ir'rossung. It seemed best to go in the middle of the file himself, where he could keep contact with both front and back; and behind him he placed Cathasar with Aestrontor to bring up the rear. All too soon it was his turn to drop to his knees and begin crawling, worm-like, into total blackness. He was a couple of yards in, both expecting and dreading to hear Cathasar creep in behind him, blocking his escape, when disaster began to unfold. There was a confused noise of scuffling and shouting which, confined and magnified by the rocky walls, sounded almost like fighting. Suddenly Aestrontor called down the tunnel.

'Haldur! Cathasar won't go in, he says he's turning back!'

Haldur scrambled out as fast as he could, stumbled and clutched at Aestrontor to steady himself. 'You go through, explain to the others,' he panted, 'and I'll go after him.'

He set off back the way they had come, feeling his way in the utter darkness, hearing the sounds of Cathasar blundering along somewhere in front of him. Several times he hurt himself against the protruding rock and once, by the noise, Cathasar fell headlong. At last a dim light began to show itself and finally he burst out of the tunnel to find himself once more at the foot of the shaft. Cathasar was standing there, his chest heaving, eyes dilated and dark in an ashen face: Haldur would scarcely have recognised him.

'I can't go in there. Don't try to make me do it! I can't, Haldur, I'm sorry. I can't do it, I just can't.'

Cathasar wiped his forehead with his sleeve, leaving his face smeared with dirt; there was blood on his cheek already where he must have hurt himself when he fell. Haldur remembered that Cathasar had seemed more disturbed than any of them at the Lissad nan'Ethan's hypnotic, thunderous plunge into the dark abyss, and sought for some way to calm him.

'Take it easy, we'll wait till you feel better. We don't have to go through until you're ready. Try to breathe slowly, like he told us.'

'Breathe slowly! What about the rest of what he said? What if the water comes through? It might be raining in the hills now, how would we know? Say we're in that tunnel, and the river rises and it fills with water!'

Cathasar suddenly doubled over and turned away, heaving as the fear rose in his throat and made him retch. He spat out a mouthful of bile and straightened up again. 'I'm sorry, but I mean it, Haldur. Go through if you want, but I can't. I'll have to go back.'

'How can you go back?' Haldur stood there, baffled and thwarted. Should he reason with Cathasar, show sympathy for his fear, try to talk him round, or simply tell him to obey orders? 'Going back alone isn't an option. You wouldn't make it. You'll either be picked up and killed, or you'll die slowly in the wilderness somewhere. We're all afraid in here, don't worry about it. The others have all gone through, we'll get out all right. Come on now, Cathasar.'

'No! Don't touch me! You can't make me do it.'

Cathasar backed away, his voice ragged with panic. Before Haldur could stop him, he began a desperate attempt to climb up the side of the pothole towards the dim sky above. Bits of rock, loose stones and clods of earth came rattling down.

'Cathasar, no! You can't get up there without the rope!'

Haldur ran across to the foot of the rock face but before he himself could begin to climb a shower of soil caught him in the face. Wincing, he mopped at his streaming eyes, and by the time he was able to look up again, Cathasar was almost two thirds of the way to the surface. Glancing down, he tried to move faster when he saw Haldur reaching for a hold on the rock, but his right hand lost its purchase as his fingers slipped on a patch of algae, bringing all his weight temporarily onto his left foot. Up here, nearer to the lip of the shaft, earth had been washed into the pothole over the years as the ground eroded. Cathasar's foot was resting not on hard stone, but on an accumulation of soil bound together only by the roots of rough grasses and now this suddenly gave way. With no time even to cry out he fell, straight down onto the solid rock at the bottom. The horrible sound of the impact told Haldur all he needed to know. He stared in disbelief at the blood pooling behind Cathasar's head, the unnatural angle of his broken body as it lay spreadeagled and still. His eyes were wide open, but in spite of what Haldur had promised, they would never look upon Rihannad Ennar again.

CHAPTER 54

The refuge

A bright beam of sunlight drilled its way through the gap between the shutters and fell on Haldur's sleeping face. His eyelids moved a little, and he turned over in the warm bed; but his dreams were broken, and as his mind began to rise towards waking, gradually the sounds of the new day came into focus. There was a quiet, continuous fluttering of leaves, a crooning and clucking of fowls, and then someone walked past, feet crunching and a pail handle squeaking slightly. Suddenly a rooster crowed, his assertive challenge cutting through the gentler, soporific background noises. Haldur woke to the comfort of woollen blankets, rough but clean; the smell of woodsmoke; and the indescribable blessing of sunlight. Lifting the window panel in the shutter, he pegged it in place and looked out. The air that came in was cold, bringing with it a hint of the forest smell that was so familiar to him. Leaves, brilliant with autumn colour, were moving in the light breeze and falling in an endless cascade of russet and gold, loosened by the overnight frost that still lingered blue on the ground. There were trees all around the small clearing with its settlement of snug roundhouses, animal pens, log piles and fodder stacks. Hens picked about here and there, folk went quietly about the first business of the day; and a low, red sun rose slowly into the sky, its warming rays shining level through a slight morning mist.

Haldur's face broke into a wide grin of pure, delighted joy. He could have stood and gazed all day, and never tired of filling his eyes with the glorious sunlight and the clean blue sky above. Then, as on the two previous days when he had awoken in this hidden refuge, memory too awoke. His head drooped to rest on the wood of the shutter. He squeezed his eyes shut; but though he could close out the beauty of the new day, he was unable to blank from his mind the sight of Cathasar lying dead at his feet, or to banish the weight of failure he felt at losing one of the men under his command. Voices drifted across to him and he looked up to see Tellapur and Asaldron already heading across to the large central building where most of the cooking was done. Haldur reached for his clothes. Nothing could bring Cathasar back, and he still had a responsibility to his other companions. There was no time to spare for indulgence in grief or regret: they were still far from home, with a dangerous journey before them for which plans and preparation must be made. But in spite of himself, he was quiet over their morning food and afterwards went to stand alone at the place where they had buried Cathasar. It had been a struggle to bring his body with them through the cave system, and Haldur ached and smarted in more than one place from the effort of the task. The new grave was the third in the little plot set aside at the edge of the clearing; only a few yards away, the small trees of the woodland edge began and behind them the forest stood, secret and solemn.

A slight noise made Haldur turn, to see Morancras approaching.

'Your sorrow is a grief to me,' said the old man, making the sign.

Haldur nodded, forcing a half-smile of acknowledgement, and Morancras stepped forward to stand with him at the graveside.

'The death of a follower is one of the loads a leader must carry,' he said, 'and like other hard things in life, they say it gets easier to bear with time and experience; but I think for you it will always be a burden. Honour him with your sadness, but don't blame yourself for his death.'

Still Haldur stood without speaking. He looked up from the grave, at the gently-falling leaves as they turned in the golden autumn sunlight, at the high snowy peaks standing like sentinels above.

His heart ached for Cathasar, from whom death had snatched the chance of looking upon such loveliness, whom they must leave now to lie here without ever seeing his home again; and for himself, for the vain promise he had made that his comrade would come safe to Rihannad Ennar. The torc sat heavily upon his neck: Morancras was right, lordship brought burdens that others could not share. At this, his thoughts turned to his father: to Carapethan waiting every day for news, for word of how they fared, hoping against hope for their safe return. He began to walk slowly back towards the dwellings, drawing Morancras along with him.

'You're very kind. I'm glad you were able to lead the rite for him,' he said. Then in spite of all, he laughed a little. 'I can still scarcely believe we found you here!'

It had indeed been not the least of the surprises of an exhausting day: the strain of riding with would-be murderers, the desperate fight to escape; the shock of rescue by an apparent enemy; the horror of Cathasar's death, the black crawl through the caves; the overwhelming relief of safety deep in the mountains – and then, of all people, to come face to face with old Morancras: to find him hale and healthy, with new flesh on his bones and a new strength in his voice, when they had thought him dead, had recoiled in horror from the tale of his mauling by maddened dogs. Haldur laughed again, remembering.

'I thought, when we first saw you, I really thought for a moment that something in the darkness underground must have affected my sight, or maybe even my mind!'

Morancras smiled at this. 'Yes, I can tell you there's many a time I pinch myself, not believing it's true I'm safe here. And I'm not the only one, as you'll have found out by now. Some of us owe our lives to Sigitsinen, like I do; others have made their way to us with the help of our network of secret contacts. We've even a few who've escaped from the gold mine.'

'When Sigitsinen left us at the caves, he hinted that we might see him again,' said Haldur, 'and I should like to thank him for his help.

We too owe him our lives. But I'm anxious not to delay: we must be off again as soon as possible.'

'Oh, you'll see him all right, if he said you would.'

Harsh lessons

The short day was drawing to a close, with stars winking in the deep blue above and frost already crisping the leaves underfoot, when word came that Sigitsinen had indeed appeared among them. Haldur had seen not the slightest sign of his arrival and wondered how he had travelled to their refuge. He began to realise just how expert the auxiliaries must be at moving across country. He found the Outlander sitting alone, but there was a jug of mulled ale on the hearth and cups beside it.

'I hear you lost a man in the caves,' said Sigitsinen. 'I am sorry.'

'Those of us who came through to safety here owe our lives to you,' said Haldur, 'and to whoever the man was who drew off pursuit. But yes, Cathasar is dead. You'll remember, he was reluctant to even begin the journey through the caves, and it was the first low passage that caused the trouble. He panicked at the prospect of crawling through in darkness, tried to climb the wall of the shaft, lost his footing and fell.'

'If he had obeyed your orders, he would be alive today.'

Haldur looked up. The unusual pale eyes were fixed on him. 'He trusted me, and I promised him he would see his home again.'

'If he trusted you he should have done as you told him. This was the first man you've lost? I thought so. It's one of the most difficult lessons of leadership, to take a loss and move on from it. You're not home yet, and if you succeed in reaching the Nine Dales with all your remaining companions, you will have been very fortunate. I see you think me harsh. I play a dangerous game with very few rules: sometimes it is necessary to be harsh, even ruthless. Maybe you've wondered how old Morancras was spirited away from under Valahald's nose. The man Valahald thought was Morancras was a member of my troop. I killed him myself, shut up the body with three hungry dogs and then brought Morancras out of Framstock. A perfect false trail: the body mutilated beyond recognition, the real death faked to look like a training accident, and Morancras saved from the arrest and interrogation that Valahald had intended for him, after you'd spent time with him on your journey south.'

Sigitsinen paused here as if waiting for a reply, but none came. He leaned forward, speaking more gently. 'You seem shocked and no doubt if our places were reversed, so should I be. Forgive me for saying I think you've been fortunate, if you've not yet been faced with the kind of difficult choices some of us have had to make. What do you think Valahald would have done to Morancras, if he had taken him? What if Morancras had been tortured into speaking? Both you and I would likely have been dead by now along with many others who risk their lives daily to keep hope alive. But if Morancras had simply vanished, all Valahald's suspicions would have been aroused: at least one dead man was essential if the plan was to succeed. You must know the old saying: never leave a bad apple in the barrel. The man I killed was one such. He was causing trouble among his comrades; sooner or later he would have been disposed of anyway through the admittedly rather rough justice of the irregulars. If a man had to die, was it not better that it should be him, rather than Morancras?'

The fire fluttered into little flames as a draught passed across the hearth. Haldur sat staring into the embers, trying to sort out his thoughts. He felt hopelessly young and inexperienced compared with the man who had been speaking: Sigitsinen was right, he had been lucky not to have to pick his way through the kind of moral maze he had just heard described. What would he do if life brought him such choices in the future? The strange, bright eyes were still watching him. Suddenly Sigitsinen smiled, his teeth showing white in his sallow face.

'Here, let's not let this drink get cold,' he said, reaching for the jug and pouring. 'It must seem a long time, since we met in Heranar's hall;

months of weighing every word before you speak, of suspicion and doubt. You can let your guard down here, where we are all friends. We need to make plans, but you can take a couple more days to recover and settle yourselves before you go on again.'

Haldur took the proferred cup and wrapped his hands around its warmth. 'Why are you helping us?' he asked.

'That's easily answered. We need you to get back to Rihannad Ennar alive, because we want *you* to help *us*. We can't topple Vorynaas and his people alone. We need aid from some outside, unexpected source. Otherwise, while it's true that sooner or later there may well be a rising, it will be born of desperation and ruthlessly suppressed: there are too few of us to succeed alone. And if we're to have help, we must have it quickly, for two reasons. First, with every day that goes by, the risk increases that our secret league will be discovered. It might have happened already, if we'd not managed to rescue Morancras. If any word leaks out, we will be hunted down without mercy and who then will support the men from Rihannad Ennar when they arrive? Yes, as you see, I am certain men from the Nine Dales will indeed come to help us. You won't know this, but more than once, fugitives have risked crossing the wilderness in the hope of reaching your land and appealing for aid. No help came, so it would seem that none of those who tried ever lived to see Rihannad Ennar. And then who should appear out of the north only yourselves! Now hear the second reason why time is running out. You don't know yet what Vorynaas is planning. In the spring of the year after next, his army will be upon you. Do you want his murderers at your door? This is why we will help you to reach your home before the snows come, because it gives us time to outwit him. If he is allowed to press ahead with his invasion of the Nine Dales, it will be too late: there will be no help you can bring us then. Haldur, you've seen what things are like in the south. If Vorynaas is not stopped, Rihannad Ennar too will go the way of Caradward and Gwent y'm Aryframan. You must persuade your father to send us aid!'

Sigitsinen had assumed that Haldur would react immediately to his words and was astonished when he sat without speaking. He watched him closely, seeing that his silence was one of preoccupation rather than shock.

'You're taking this more calmly than I expected,' he said.

'That's because it wasn't news to me,' said Haldur. 'I denied this when I was asked outright, but we have indeed taken in refugees who begged for our help. Twice, in fact. My father gave them sanctuary but is unwilling to take up arms unless his hand is forced. Instead, he sent me south to find out what I could. I'm returning with darker tidings than either of us imagined. But in the meantime, I think I might have rather a surprise for *you*. We already knew that our homeland was to be attacked. I was told this, by Heranar.'

'Heranar!' In his amazement, an exclamation in his own Outland tongue escaped Sigitsinen. 'Heranar! What sort of a game does he think *he's* playing?'

'One he has little hope of winning, I'd say. I take it I can safely assume he's not numbered among your associates?'

'Absolutely not. I'll need to pass this piece of news on; I can see we might need to think again about Heranar.' Sigitsinen brooded for a moment and then turned his pale eyes on Haldur. 'Presumably this was why you made your own break for freedom, even before our attempt at a rescue began?'

'Well yes, partly. But there was a more pressing reason, in that we knew if we didn't get away, we were going to be murdered out of hand. No, we weren't told about that, in fact Heranar didn't know about it. We found out – Ir'rossung found out. He's been pretending to be much deafer than he actually is, and there's been more than one occasion when he's heard careless talk. Lucky for us, especially this time, but we still might not have made it without your help. Who was the man who lay in ambush and then rode off like one of the Cunorad? Is he in the auxilaries too?'

'No, he's from away up beyond the Gillan nan'Eleth,' said Sigitsinen, thinking to himself that maybe Haldur and his men were rather shrewder and more daring than he had given them credit for. 'He's one of the leaders of a small community, the folk from Salfgard who managed to get away in time when Gwent y'm Aryframan was overrun. But they're all part of it, along with those here in the forest; and there's others too as you heard from Morancras earlier in the year. Slaves, of course, but some among the military as well. Some quite highly placed, including my own senior officer Naasigits. You'll gather from his name that he's an Outlander like myself: a fair few of us are involved, and that's particularly useful for passing information around the network. The man you saw, his name's Cunoreth. He acts as the link between me and his people up in the hills, but he was needed in your case for his skill on horseback, so that we could be sure he'd lead the pursuit away and then make his own escape. Which reminds me – who are these Cunorad you mentioned?'

Sigitsinen listened in silence as Haldur explained, and at the end he raised his hand in the three-fold sign. '"Let the Hidden People show themselves,"' he echoed. 'Yes, I too could wish that. Tell me, have you found any *numirasan* here, when you walked in the forest nearby?'

'No, not yet at any rate,' said Haldur. Encouraged by Sigitsinen's response, he decided to continue. 'But in the heart of Caradriggan itself you have in Tellgard a *numiras* more hallowed by the presence of the Starborn than any other I have ever known.'

Again Sigitsinen made the sign. 'Well, maybe that's not so strange. I'm sure you've not spent time in the south without hearing the name of Arymaldur whispered.' He looked down at his drink as he swirled it round in the cup. 'And that of Maesrhon too, though I think I could make a guess that you've no need to rely on whispers, given that you were eventually quartered in Tellgard itself. If anyone knows the true story, it has to be Arval.' Suddenly Sigitsinen glanced up and caught the expression on Haldur's face. He laughed.

'Don't worry! I'm not going to fish for anything that's better kept secret. But I trained alongside Maesrhon for the auxiliaries and I know what I saw in him. It's my belief he truly was *as-ur*. Vorynaas always hated him: in fact there's a price on his head, and I've heard that one of the reasons Vorynaas is set to assail Rihannad Ennar is because he is persuaded that Maesrhon may be found there.' Sigitsinen laughed again.

'But Maesrhon didn't go north. We *sigitsaran* know more than Vorynaas. Some of my own people, Outlanders who live in the far south beyond Caradward, wandering east to west and back with the seasons, gave shelter to a man who with their help passed through the marshes of the Haarnoutan and travelled on west alone. This man said to them, "Maesrhon will not be seen again in Caradriggan, but Artorynas will return". It's my belief that this wanderer, who disappeared into the west alone, was Maesrhon himself; because before Maesrhon vanished from among us, he taunted Vorynaas in his own hall with the words "Remember Artorynas". If only Maesrhon could send us this Artorynas, whoever he is… If he's anything to do with the As-Geg'rastigan, Caradward might fall without a blow being struck. But it's no use wishing. We've got to rely on our own efforts if we want to make it happen.'

Haldur sat without speaking, feeling his heart beating fast. He was glad that Sigitsinen, though he had clearly noticed the consternation in his face, had not fully read his thoughts. When he heard the Outlander speaking the name of Artorynas, Haldur had been tempted to tell Sigitsinen all, but he forced himself to resist. I swore an oath to my father never to speak of Artorynas, he thought, and I promised Artorynas to break that silence once only, to Arval alone. I must be true to them. To cover the awkward silence, he asked a question.

'Why does Vorynaas think Maesrhon is in Rihannad Ennar? Do you know that?'

'Oh, that's Valahald. Spawn of Na Naastald, that one, if ever anyone was. But he's a clever man who knows the power of a well-directed whisper. Let me tell you there'd be no holding Vorynaas, once he got it into his head that the vengeance he craves might be within his grasp.' Again Sigitsinen laughed.

'And that's in spite of the fact that Valahald, and Heranar too come to that, had previously followed Maesrhon's trail as far as the forest. That's what most people think, that he went into Maesaldron and died there. But he'd been in there before, when we were still doing our training together: he would know how and where to lay a false scent. The Caradwardans are born with the fear of Maesaldron in their blood.'

'Yes, we noticed that. Why is it, do you know? Are we in the forest, here?'

Sigitsinen shrugged. 'Who knows, I don't. But no, this isn't Maesaldron. You're still within what was Gwent y'm Aryframan here, although deep into the Somllichan Torward. Tomorrow I'll show you on the map and you can make a copy for when you come south again. Then I'll have to return to base, but we've got guides organised to set you well on your homeward way.'

'You seem very sure that we will be coming back.'

Leaning forward, Sigitsinen tapped his finger against the inward-facing finial on the torc at Haldur's neck. 'You know what this sees in your heart.' He stood up. 'Come on, let's go and eat with the others.'

Mistress of the *Corn Dolly*

Having been without weapons, tools or food – barring the bag of meal which each of them carried secretly – when they were rescued, the men from the Nine Dales were all very conscious that their benefactors were drawing deeply on their own reserves to equip them for the journey ahead and keen to do what they could to help replenish what they were taking. There were boar and deer in the forest, and they used the bows they were given to aid in the hunt. About thirty people lived permanently in the secret clearing, with some like Sigitsinen who came and went from time to time on errands of their own. Most of those who lived there were Gwentarans, but there were others: a dark and silent Outlander who made what shift he could to produce, improvise and repair tools and other metalwork; and a scattering of Caradwardans who in their youth had married Gwentarans and now found that in middle-age their loyalties no longer lay with the land of their birth. One of these couples had worked in a *gradstedd* over in the Rossanlow in happier days: she now oversaw much of the cooking, and her husband took charge of the livestock. Most activities were communally organised, which made for a more efficient use of resources when there were so few people in the group. There were Caradwardans too among those who had been slaves in the gold mine and who were instantly recognisable from the way their hair would no longer grow along the brand of the mine-mark. The refuge was hidden deep in the mountains, guarded by towering peaks and thick woods, and there were only two ways into the valley where it lay: either underground, through the caves, or over a high and difficult pass.

As they went about the settlement and trod the forest glades, foraging and hunting, Haldur looked about him with a more informed eye, matching what Sigitsinen's map showed, and what he had told them, with what he saw for himself. Today he was on foot with bag and basket, gathering what he could find of late berries and fruits and the mushrooms of the forest floor; but yesterday he had been among a successful hunting-party. How good it had felt to test his hand and eye once again! Haldur spotted some cloudberries and guiltily ate a few, enjoying their intense sweetness, reliving in his mind the draw, the aim, the release, the sound of the arrow speeding unerringly to its target. He glanced up at the ice-clad summits glistening against the sky. There was just one place where he saw cloud, or mist, drifting across the unbroken blue. He had been told that there were hot springs which prevented snow from blocking the path: it was steam he could see, up there beyond the trees, where soon they themselves would climb, toiling up the steep ascent on the first steps of their final push for home. But how soon? It could be scarcely much more than a month now to the Mid-Winter Feast and he chafed to be away, afraid they would leave it too late to beat the weather. Sigitsinen though had made it very clear that the arrangements must be left to him and Haldur knew they had no option but to trust him. He began to work his way back, foraging as he went, and at the edge of the clearing encountered Tellapur, who was gathering firewood.

'Sigitsinen's here again,' said the young man, 'and Hafromoro's really going at it with the cooking; she's obviously planning something a bit special.' He grinned at Haldur, suddenly back to his old, boyish self. 'I think maybe we'll be off tomorrow!'

Tellapur turned out to be correct. They sat down to plates of rich venison stew, thick with mushrooms and chunky roots. There were new-made oatcakes to go with it, and afterwards frumenty flavoured with berries from the forest. Haldur took Hafromoro's arm as she carried a steaming bowl past him.

'You'll never get rid of us if you spoil us with meals like this,' he said. 'I'll bet your inn was never empty while you did the cooking.'

She beamed with pleasure. 'Well, yes, it's fair enough to say that. The *Corn Dolly* was known far and wide on all the drove roads. Here you are.' A generous extra portion was ladled onto Haldur's plate before he had time to protest.

'Steady on! Don't stint yourselves by overfeeding us.'

Hafromoro was a wide, motherly woman as befitted her name; but Haldur had seen that though still ample of bosom with forearms brawny from a lifetime of kneading and grinding, her face was deeply lined and wrinkled and the flesh sagged on her. She had somehow shrunk inside her skin as if she had lost a lot of weight in a short time: life was hard, here in the forest refuge.

'You eat it up,' Hafromoro said. She made to move on, still smiling, and then turned back to Haldur. Letting the ladle rest in the pot she carried, she put out her free hand and briefly touched his cheek. 'We can't have you setting off hungry. Get home safely, all of you. We'll be watching out for you, come the spring.'

Later that evening, Sigitsinen called the companions together. For each of them there was a pack with basic rations for the trail: simple, subsistence foods to add to the meal they had brought with them. In addition every man received a bow, a quiver of arrows, a sling, and a set of snares; and Sigitsinen suggested they should cut themselves staves from the forest before they set out. When they tried to express their thanks, he cut them short.

'These are all things we can get more of, or make for ourselves, but we have little to spare in the way of tools or weapons. However, you have none at all, so we must share as we can. I can let you have three knives and two hunting-spears between the five of you. Now, tomorrow one of us will guide you on the first part of your journey. Within a couple of days you should reach the river valley leading to the hidden pass out of the mountains and another man will meet you there with riding mules.'

Over the pass

And so they set off once more, climbing up and up through the trees until the forest thinned and the going became steeper and more difficult. At first Haldur's thoughts had been taken up with sorrow for Cathasar, left to lie in his lonely grave, and with regret that he had discovered no *numiras* during his wanderings in the forest; but soon all his concentration was necessary to make sure of his footing on the narrow, rocky path. More than once, used to mountain journeys though he was, Haldur had swallowed hard and looked away when all he could see below his feet was a blue gulf of empty air. At noon they stopped for a breather and a bite of food. Aestrontor, who had wandered off for a few moments, came back and beckoned to Haldur. Only a few yards from the path, they rounded an outcrop of stone to find a small, level space on the mountainside. Up here they were not far short of the tree-line, but they were facing south with a rock face behind them. The noon sun warmed the little sheltered nook, barely six paces across. There was grass at their feet, and a young holly sapling had sprung up, its leaves green and glossy against the grey of the mountain. In a hollow of the rock a tiny pool of water reflected the blue sky above, and around it crystals of quartz and garnet glinted silver and blood-red in the stone. Far, far below they glimpsed the settlement, as tiny as a child's toy; and around them stood the mountains, their snows wrapped in the silence of the high places. Haldur and Aestrontor looked at each other: there could be no doubt. Haldur went to fetch their guide.

'You know what we mean, those of us from the Nine Dales, by a *numiras*? Well, I've been asked if there were any here. I found none nearby in the forest, but this is such a place, here on the mountainside. Will you tell Morancras, and Sigitsinen next time you see him?'

The young man stood silent for a moment, his thoughts impossible to guess. He looked about him. 'I'll tell them, but Morancras would never be able to climb up here.'

'I suppose not, but he'll be glad to know about it. Now we need to make an offering before we go on.'

'If you must. I'll wait for you on the path.'

The other two exchanged glances as the young fellow turned away. Apart from telling them his name was Haldas as they set out, he had had very little to say; but the mine-mark was branded into his hair, which perhaps explained the rather bitter, closed-in set of his face. Aestrontor and Haldur hunted about and found a small oval pebble, smooth and creamy white. They spoke the words and let it fall to the bottom of the little pool where it lay gleaming in the clear water. Then they went on, up through the sulphurous steam of the springs; up to the pass and over, down into the trees again; up to another less lofty pass and down once more. They slept in rough shelters constructed from fallen boughs and covered over with brushwood and leaves, but the cold broke their rest and dawn found them chilled with numb fingers and toes. During the third morning Haldas waited for Haldur to come alongside him as they walked downhill through the woods.

'By early afternoon today we'll come to the river, and our contact should be waiting there with the animals.'

When they emerged from the trees beside a wide, strongly-flowing river, there was no sign of the man who was to meet them. However Haldas seemed unperturbed. He sat down on a fallen log, taking food from his pack, so the others followed suit. As they finished, they heard a shout and a man came into view from around a downstream bend with six mules on leading-reins.

'All well?'

'Well enough, but there's only five of us now. We lost a man in the caves, killed in a fall.'

'Ah, that's tough.' The fellow tipped his hat back and scratched his head. He was small and leathery-looking, with several missing teeth. 'Well, a ride's no good to you, on the paths you'll be treading back to the valley,' he said with a nod to Haldas as he worked to unclip the leading-reins, 'so I'll take this one back with me. We can always use an extra mule.' He climbed into the saddle. 'No point in hanging about, I'll be off straight away. Always more difficult to hit a moving target, eh?'

With a cheerful laugh and a brief lift of the hand he turned the animal and rode out of sight as suddenly as he had appeared.

'Breezy sort of character,' said Haldur. 'What's his name?'

Haldas shrugged. 'I don't know, I've never seen him before. Sigitsinen made all the arrangements.'

Asaldron turned from adjusting the girths on his mount. 'Where've the mules come from?'

For the first time, a faint smile showed on Haldas's face and a hint of warmth crept into his voice. 'That's Cunoreth. If we need riding animals, he steals them. He can do anything with horses and such. Well, this is where I turn back, so I'll bid you goodbye now.'

'Take care, then. Our thanks to you, and to Sigitsinen, and remember us to Morancras and Hafromoro and all the others.'

Rough comforts

The valley ran not much east of north and before long the sun was hidden behind the mountains. Darkness closed in about them and with it bitter cold, in spite of their fire. The chill kept Ir'rossung wakeful, worrying about what might happen if the weather worsened, as surely it must, or if he weakened further. He had kept his thoughts to himself, but he was shivering at nights when he should have been sleeping, permanently tired as well as never warm enough. Every day brought winter nearer, and he was already dreading the bite of cold that came as evening closed in, earlier with each day that passed. Haldur too lay sleepless, listening to the sound of the river, still wide and deep even this far upstream. In his mind he reviewed the map he had been shown, and of which he now carried a copy. From that it had seemed to him that they would not have far to go before they reached the head of this pass hidden deep in the forest, but now he began to doubt the distance. Sigitsinen had said they were making for a pass much lower than the one guarded by the fort, but the river must rise on this side of it. Surely the water ought to be narrower, shallower, more turbulent if they were really near its source? It must be broad and mighty indeed where it flowed into the plains of Caradward. Haldur wondered at the strange name the Caradwardans knew it by, Lissad na' Stirfell, and wondered too that though they had the skill to bridge it, they were so fearful of the forest from which it emerged. But a piece of luck for us, he thought, trying to let the voice of the flowing current soothe him to sleep.

By mid-morning of the following day, Haldur's unease was spreading. The going was relatively easy, with plenty of fairly open, level ground near the river and the mules picked out a path at a steady pace, allowing for conversation as they rode along.

'I just don't understand this,' said Asaldron. 'If the road's as long as it seems it's going to be, why didn't Sigitsinen tell us? Maybe we should try to move a bit faster while we can.'

Aestrontor was staring around, trying to get a feel for the lie of the land, but although the valley where they rode was fairly broad and its gradient only gradually rising before them, it was hemmed in by tall mountains cloaked in forest that shut in any view of the country beyond its bounds.

'Well there's one thing, if it's all as easy as this, it's fortunate the Caradwardans have never found it; although I'll admit I'd feel happier if I had a better idea of what's ahead of us. Do any of the rest of you get the feeling that the land we're moving into now is changing a bit? Look over beyond, there: look at those rock formations, and the rock itself is different. And that slope rising up ahead of us, which side of the river is it? I can't decide whether it's part of the range on our side, or a spur coming down from the mountains across the valley.'

The sun was almost at the noon, shining directly onto the huge shoulder of rock where Aestrontor pointed. Shadows were at their shortest, making it difficult to get any kind of helpful perspective. *If only we had not lost Cathasar, his keen sight would have helped us here,* thought Haldur sadly, when suddenly there was an eager shout from Tellapur.

'Hey, you know what? I think that shoulder of rock *is* a spur of the mountain on the other side of the valley, and if it is, then the river must flow round it. When we get round the bend it makes, we might be able to see better where we're making for! From here, it's blocking our view, so we can't get a glimpse of what lies ahead.'

'Come on! We'll keep going until we get a sight of what's in store for us before we stop for a break.' Haldur dug his heels into his mount, urging it forward, and the others picked up to a trot behind him; but when he saw what faced them he halted, all thought of rest and food forgotten, and his companions stood staring alongside him. Not far ahead, beyond the last curve in the river's course, the valley came to an end in a wall of stone: and out of this the water surged, pouring out already deep and strong from a dark cavern in the rock.

'By the Starborn!' exclaimed Asaldron. 'We surely don't have to follow the river into that?'

'No, that can't be it. Not with animals, and without lights or guides. But what are we to do?'

'There must be a way over. We know we can't have gone wrong so far, with the river to follow. And it's too wide and strong to cross, even here, so the path must be on this side.'

Haldur shaded his eyes, scanning the huge barrier that reared before them, blocking the valley and barring their way. He saw that the face of it was creased with faults and fissures, some large and deep enough to support shrubs and small trees; in one place there had been a landslip where huge grey blocks of stone had tumbled one on another.

'Look, over there.' Aestrontor was pointing away to the left. 'See that big rock? Look up beyond it, past the dead tree, then there's three, no four, smaller rocks in a row with a bush or bramble or something at their right-hand side. I think we could pick a path up that way; there might be some kind of a trail winding across the slope that would bring us to the top eventually.'

'A trail for goats, maybe. It's all very well for you and Haldur to talk about getting up there, but not all of us rode with the Cunorad.' This was Ir'rossung, but it was obvious from their faces that he spoke for Asaldron and Tellapur too.

Haldur dismounted. 'We don't have to ride. We'll go on foot and lead the animals. You go first, Aestrontor, and I'll bring up the rear. We'll get the climb over with before we eat: our food will taste all the better for it.'

So up they went, cautiously and fearfully, gradually gaining height until the roar of the river as it poured from underground became muted and softened and its waters, sparkling in the sun, were far below them. Aestrontor led the little cavalcade from right to left and back again, picking out the easiest, most level ground he could find. At one point a wider space leaned back into the slope and he waited for Haldur to come up.

'See that?' On the softer surface where soil had accumulated there were hoofprints. 'Somebody's been up here before us, going in both directions as well.'

Slightly cheered by this sign, they inched their way upwards until, with a final scramble, the climb levelled out. To their surprise, they stood not at the head of a pass looking down on lower lands, but in a kind of dry valley: at least, barren slopes rose up on either hand, but there was no watercourse and they guessed that they were now above the river where it flowed underground. In spite of their plans to stop for a while, they decided instead to press on while daylight lasted in the hope of a more hospitable camping-place for the night with water for the animals. They reasoned that, since their route had been described to them as a pass, sooner or later they must start to descend again; and as afternoon drew on, the land did indeed begin to slope down and where there had been only boulder-strewn hillside, now they saw trees gradually thickening into a renewal of the forest.

'We'd better go down into the trees before we stop, hadn't we?' said Tellapur. 'There'll be more shelter, and wood for a fire.'

'Yes, I suppose so, but I don't want to go too far.' The light was fading fast, but Haldur was keen to get the best idea he could of the land ahead, which meant looking at it from a high vantage-point before the view was blocked by trees. It would have to wait for morning now, and he was unwilling to use up time making a longer back-track than was absolutely necessary. 'We'll stop as soon as we find a stream.'

'I can hear water now,' said Asaldron, looking up to his left.

He led the way round a gaunt outcrop of stone, but then reined in so suddenly that the mule following nudged into his own mount and there was a moment's scuffle as the others brought their animals under control again. There was indeed water, pouring down in a small cascade to run chattering across their path and away into the forest; but it was what they saw on the far side of the stream that stopped them in their tracks. The trees screened a small space sheltered by the rocks of the mountainside. Where some of these had fallen, they had been built up into a low but sturdy shelter whose rear wall was the stone face of the hill itself and whose roof was rough heather thatch, roped down and pegged. There were no windows, but the door stood open to reveal a glow that hinted of firelight; and sitting outside on a boulder, leaning casually against the wall with arms folded, was a man who was obviously enjoying their amazed silence.

'Good timing, gentlemen. I've a pot of hot beans on the fire ready. It won't be up to Hafromoro's standard, but there's a brace of ptarmigan I bagged this afternoon to make it a bit more interesting.' Suddenly he burst into gleeful laughter. 'I wish you could see yourselves. I'm so glad I persuaded Sigitsinen not to say anything, it would have really spoiled the surprise.'

When Haldur saw the man's long, lanky frame unfurling as he got to his feet, he laughed in turn, shock turning to relief. 'You must be Cunoreth! We're in your debt already, as well as Sigitsinen's. And you're right, he never said a word about you meeting us here.'

'Yes, that's me. But don't let's stand here yarning, come on over. Let's get the animals seen to and then we can close the door between ourselves and the night.'

The little hut was not much more than a bothy, cramped and basic; it was pungent with smoke and the smell of animals who shared the one roof with their riders. But it was warm, and the comfort of fire and food made up for the lack of other amenities. There were two sleeping places built up with logs against the walls, and Cunoreth fetched a few armfuls of bracken from a lean-to shed to soften the floor for those who had to make their beds on the ground. He had brought more provisions to replenish their packs and help them on their way, and with a flourish also produced a hatchet, two smallish knives, a dagger and a rather handsome hunting knife in a worked leather sheath, waving away their protestations.

'Pinched them off Caradwardans. More use to you than them,' he explained airily.

As the evening went by he kept up an engaging flow of talk liberally spiced with jokes and anecdotes which had them laughing in response. Tellapur was clearly captivated by Cunoreth's devil-may-care insouciance, although Haldur saw that their host for the night was not so young in years as he was boyish in manner and sometimes his voice would harden as he told them of his life with the fugitives from Salfgard, his work with the partisans that brought him through the forest and up to this little eyrie in the hills, his hopes for the future. Nor was it lost on Haldur that Cunoreth too seemed certain that the Nine Dales would respond to the call for aid when the spring came. But eventually the fire died down and they made ready to rest; Cunoreth banked the embers for the night and blew out the small horn lantern that hung from a beam and one by one they dropped off to sleep.

Much later, Haldur woke with a start as if some noise had disturbed him. He listened, his eyes wide in the dark, but all he heard was the soft sighing of the breeze through the trees of the forest, and a rustling as the mules moved quietly in the straw. His thoughts drifted back over the evening's conversation. Cunoreth had been unable to shed any light on his own growing conviction that the river they had followed was none other than the same they had seen plunge into the abyss far to the north, the same that he and Aestrontor had heard flowing underground in the wilderness.

'Maybe you're right,' was all he could say. 'You know more about Na Caarst than I do, after all. The old fellow who taught me my field-craft was the only other person I've ever met who'd been in there and come out alive. He knew about the canyon with the falls, because he made sure I explained about that to the runaways we tried to help on their journey north.' Then he corrected himself. 'Well actually, there was one other, now I come to think of it. Old Torald only ventured in after he heard that Maesrhon had been there. You've heard about Maesrhon, I don't doubt? Yes, I thought you would have. Apparently he used to ask Torald about the wilderness: Ardeth was beside himself when he knew that's where he'd been. A strange character, even as a lad, which is how I remember him. Poor old Ardeth, he was never quite the same after the boy left Salfgard.'

Where was Artorynas now, wondered Haldur. Ardeth, Sigitsinen, this Torald character, even reckless, jaunty Cunoreth: somehow he had touched them all. Was it possible he could be already back in Cotaerdon when they arrived there themselves? Unwilling to dwell too much on this idea, Haldur turned his mind back to the question of the river. Imagine if their very own Lissad nan'Ethan, running so placidly through Cotaerdon, flowed all the way south through gorge, cave and forest to pass eventually through Caradward as the Lissad na'Stirfell! It would mean that every time they had drawn water from it, they had somehow made contact with home. Smiling in the darkness at the comfort of this thought, Haldur turned over and settled for sleep again, but had barely closed his eyes when he heard what must have awoken him in the first place. From behind him, where Ir'rossung lay, came a bout of coughing. He realised immediately that Ir'rossung must be awake too, because the sound was suppressed as if he was muffling his face in his blanket. After a moment's silence, the coughing began again, quiet but persistent. It occurred to Haldur that Ir'rossung had been rather subdued during the previous evening. He raised himself onto his elbow and whispered.

'Are you all right? Can I get you some water?'

'I've got some. It's just a tickle from the smoke.'

'Right. I can't wait for the morning, so we can set out again. It won't be long now before we're back home.'

'No. Better get some rest if you're going to be fresh for an early start.'

'Yes. Good night, then.'

With an effort, Ir'rossung choked back his cough until he heard from Haldur's breathing that the young man was asleep again. He had not told the truth to his leader, and now he swallowed cautiously, trying to ease his sore throat. It was getting more painful all the time, but worse by far was the sensation that had been growing in his chest since mid-afternoon. His lungs felt like caverns of fire, every breath more difficult than the last. Ir'rossung had lain awake long enough by now for his sight to adjust completely to the dark. He could see a tiny red spark where an ember had burned through the turves that

Cunoreth had put over the fire and the minute flower of light winked before him like a golden star. There had not been a single day of their journey when Ir'rossung had not longed for the time when he would see his home again: the hope of returning to Cotaerdon once more had sustained him through many a gloomy hour. Now he found himself dreading the dawn and the onward struggle. His exhausted mind could conjure one thought only: a desperate wish that he could stay where he was and rest; that he need not leave this rude mountain hut, mean and rough though its comforts were.

Chapter 55

New responsibilities

'Soaked. Right through to the skin.' Vorardynur peeled off his undershirt and rubbed at his dripping hair with it, but gave up almost immediately and bundled up the sodden garment with his wet outer clothes. 'I'm going to get some dry things on.'

Carapethan turned from where he had been staring out at the drilling rain. 'Not like that you're not. Get those boots off first.'

Vorardynur laughed as he tugged at his mud-caked footwear. 'You surely didn't think I was going to risk a clip round the ear from Aldiro for trailing all this muck through the hall? I'm not that tired of life.'

Even in his bare feet, Vorardynur was a head taller than Carapethan. The lord of the Nine Dales looked up at his nephew, standing there stripped to the waist with an armful of wet clothes, his hair tangled and damp and his face still pink from exposure to the raw, stinging rain, and laughed in his turn.

'That'll be the day, when Aldiro clips you round the ear. Not to mention she'd need to stand on something to reach.'

He was pleased with Vorardynur, who had been a great support to him in the months since Haldur went away south. After a shaky start, when the young man's quick temper had sometimes been a problem, they had worked well together. It could not have been easy for him, reflected Carapethan. He must have known how much I missed Haldur and wanted him with me, but he's been tactful and grown well into his role without putting himself forward unduly. If

I'm to be honest with myself, I'd have to admit he's surprised me. And he's popular with the people, too. By now Carapethan had his own boots off, but when it seemed he was not going to follow his nephew, Vorardynur caught him by the arm.

'Come on, let's both change before you get delayed by some business or other. You shouldn't keep those wet things on longer than you need. I don't know why you insisted on going round the town on a morning like this. Surely it wouldn't matter so much if you missed a day?'

'Same reason you insisted on coming with me, I expect. Yes, all right. I don't want an ague any more than the next man, especially with the feast coming up.'

They moved off, chatting companionably, but Carapethan wished he had not mentioned the Midwinter Feast. It wouldn't be the same, this year, with Haldur not there. And now it looked as though even the weather would be unseasonal. Although snow had fallen unusually early in the Nine Dales, causing them to shovel it from the streets of Cotaerdon a full month before the usual time, it had been followed by a sudden thaw which had sent meltwater flooding through the town; and now for a week or more they had endured constant sleet and rain, driving in torrents on a bone-chilling wind. Vorardynur too was thinking about the feast. He wanted the chance to speak privately to Aldiro about the arrangements, which this year needed handling with some delicacy. It would not do to let the absence of Haldur and the others spoil the general mirth, but at the same time the concern of parents and friends must be respected. And I must be careful about my own demeanour, thought Vorardynur. He had been disappointed at not being included in Haldur's venture. He had wanted to go, felt himself a suitable, indeed essential, choice; and at the time, to be left behind had seemed like a snub, even with the consolation of deputising for Haldur at home. But as the months had gone by, he had discovered a change in himself. Working closely with Carapethan on a daily basis he had come to a deepened respect for his leader and now found that he enjoyed his new role. Of course it was unwise to look too far into the future, but these days he knew in his heart that when the time came for Haldur to take up the lordship of the Nine Dales in his turn, he hoped his cousin also would want him at his side.

A world unravelling

Trying hard not to quicken his pace, not to seem as if he was bolting for sanctuary like a fox to its earth, Heranar walked across the courtyard of the fort towards his office. Closing its door behind him, he leaned against it for a moment in relief, savouring the privacy. How he hated his stints up at the fort, where it was so much more difficult than at headquarters to avoid scornful glances from the men under his command. He especially dreaded times like the present: the regular shifts when he was stuck there for several days on end so that night duties could also be included. There were still two more days to go before he could put it all behind him for this time. He sat down at his desk and almost immediately caught himself fingering the amber Haldur had given him. Afraid to leave it behind him, even locked in the governor's safe, afraid to carry it with him in case it was accidentally discovered, he had decided eventually on the latter course as the less risky of the two. The precious gift was kept close in a secure belt, hidden under his clothes; but he had found it impossible to stop himself constantly touching it, checking to make sure it was safe. He put his hands firmly on the desk and clenched his fists. I wish I hadn't taken it. I shouldn't have taken it. But worked up and polished, how lovely it would look when worn by his beautiful daughters! The brief solace of this thought was banished by a panicky reflection on the number of years that were likely to pass before any of them was of marriageable age – years of worrying about whether his heirloom was still a secret. Then it occurred to Heranar that this particular problem might well solve itself. If the attack on Rihannad Ennar was a success, and he had no doubt it would be, he could say he came by the amber in the Nine Dales. After all, it would be the leaders of the invading force who took the best pieces. All he had to do was be extra careful for, what, barely another two years and no-one need ever know it was a gift from Haldur. Then shame washed over Heranar and he hung his head. I wish Haldur hadn't given it to me, he thought. I hope that smooth-talking fellow of Valahald's will arrange to take the northerners off my hands again soon. Maybe he would keep them in his own camp for a few days – then I wouldn't have to see them about the place at all. Heranar sat staring at his bitten fingernails, never for a moment imagining that behind him down the valley his world had begun to unravel.

When he heard of the botched assassination attempt, Wicursal, the officer who had so irritated Heranar, wasted no time. He listened aghast to the tale his demoralised captain had to tell when he returned and then, after issuing orders for a burial party to see to the dead troopers, immediately sat down to compose a report. Within a couple of hours it was on its way by the fastest military courier service, heading straight for Valahald. Never mind that up here he was operating within Heranar's province: the governor of Rossaestrethan could wait. Wicursal knew which brother his money was on, and was determined whatever happened to keep well in with Valahald. In spite of his need to get word to him as soon as possible, he took care to phrase his report so that plenty of emphasis was laid upon what he saw as his own unimpeachable conduct. Then, apprehensive nonetheless at what might happen once Valahald got the news, he set about his own investigations into the affair.

In Framstock, Valahald took the despatch behind closed doors before he broke the seal. He read it with incredulous fury, his eyes moving ever more rapidly over the text. Throwing it down on his desk, he jumped to his feet so violently that the chair tipped over and fell; but he ignored it and stood, breathing heavily, whitened knuckles raised to his gritted teeth, his mind racing. Then slowly he raised his head; the expression on his face would have given good reason for fear, had anyone been there to see it. Very gently he picked up the chair, replacing it on its legs with delicate precision, and then from a drawer he took a tiny flask at which he sipped briefly. He opened the door and called for his secretary.

'I want no interruptions for the next hour. During that time I wish to work alone: you will close the corridor so that I am not disturbed by noise, and at the end of the hour I shall be sending an important and confidential document to Lord Vorynaas. Arrange for a courier to present himself to me here then, and make sure instructions are issued that the fastest possible service is to be used at every stage between here and Caradriggan.'

Valahald sat down at his desk and began methodically, deliberately, to set his thoughts in order. Rage started up again within him when he thought of what had happened within Heranar's jurisdiction. What damned bad luck that the roads were open so late this year, forcing him to alert Vorynaas before he had had a chance to take action himself. But there was no time to waste on anger. Valahald forced himself to be calm, feeling the Outland potion he had used beginning to take effect. He had purposely given himself only a short time in which to think, in order to concentrate his mind. Maybe he could turn the situation to his advantage? Heranar had embarrassed him once too often now: this could be the moment to rid himself of his brother, as he had disposed of their father. Carefully and slowly, he read through Wicursal's report once more, noting what it said and what it implied, testing his suspicions against what he could infer from its contents. When he was ready to write to Vorynaas, his message was as brief as he could make it. Relaying the facts as Wicursal had set them out, he assured Vorynaas of his own unwavering loyalty. Further, he asserted his belief that he could find and punish whoever had been responsible for the breach of security; and to that end, he requested permission to use whatever means he felt necessary. Off went the despatch, and Valahald settled down to lay his plans, anticipating at least a week before any kind of word came back from Caradriggan. But barely four days later, an exhausted rider came hammering up the road from the south. Vorynaas had outdone his son-before-the-law in terse brevity.

'Do whatever you think fit,' he wrote, 'but get this mess sorted out. Otherwise I shall send Valestron to take over.'

He would have much enjoyed the small, unpleasant smile with which Valahald folded this document and locked it away.

When Heranar arrived back at headquarters he could scarcely believe that so much had happened during his short absence up at the fort. Shame at what he now learnt about the plan to kill Haldur and his companions jostled in his mind with anger that he had not originally been told; but his secret relief that they seemed to have escaped was far outweighed by panic at the thought that they had got away while in his custody. No matter how often he told himself that he could not be blamed for what he had known nothing about, that he had done his duty by keeping them close, that it was only with Valahald's permission that he had allowed them to ride out, still the fear rose in his throat. His hands shook as he leafed through the papers on his desk again. So Wicursal had already conducted a preliminary investigation, without bothering to send a message for him up to the fort; and Valahald was on his way, with authority from Vorynaas to take whatever measures he wished during his own enquiries. Heranar's eyes fell on the phrase 'breach of security' and terror leapt into his mind, freeing it from the paralysis of shock. This was the end for him, he knew it. His heart was beating so hard that its racing pulse made the chain of office tremble where it rested on his chest. At best he would be demoted, stripped of his governorship, disgraced; at worst, Valahald would find out what he had done and then anything could happen.

Heranar's mistake

'Why? What for? I don't want to. And the girls don't like it there, you know they don't.' Ilmarynvoro stared at her husband, puzzled and more than a little alarmed. Late that evening, once they were alone together, Heranar had told her that the next day she and their daughters must go to her family home and stay there until he sent for her again.

'Because of what I told you about. Valahald's on his way here, the whole place will be in an uproar. You've not seen him recently like I have: believe me, he's more unpleasant than ever. I don't want you to have to put up with his insults, and I don't want him upsetting the children. You must realise somebody will be made to pay for this business over Haldur, and I think it's more than likely that that someone will be me. I want you well out of the way of any trouble that's in store and if you go to your people, I can say you've gone to keep the feast with your parents. Valahald knows your father follows the old ways; he won't find it strange, he'll just sneer. And if you're going, you'll have to go straight away, before he arrives and while the roads are still passable.'

'How can it be your fault that Haldur and the others escaped?' Ilmarynvoro frowned, watching Heranar as he sat chewing at his fingers. 'You can't be blamed for that. There's something else, isn't there? Something you've not told me. I know there is.'

'Valahald will be looking for a scapegoat and using me would be exactly the kind of thing that will appeal to him. But yes, there is something else. It's this.' Heranar produced the amber and Ilmarynvoro's eyes widened in amazement, but he stopped her as she began to speak. 'Don't ask me any questions. Keep it hidden with you always, don't ever mention it or show it to anyone, even the girls. If people knew about it, they might easily jump straight to some wrong conclusions.'

Ilmarynvoro was frightened now. She took the amber, warm from the heat of Heranar's body, and felt it immediately beginning to cool in her cold hands. 'I should be here with you if you're in trouble. Did Haldur give it to you?'

'I told you not to ask me about it.' Heranar held Ilmarynvoro to him, closely so that she could not see his face. 'Just remember, always keep it secret.'

Trust betrayed

Wicursal maintained a respectful silence, waiting for Valahald to speak. What a change since the last time he had sat in this office! He remembered how Heranar had mumbled and fidgeted, seeming so ill at ease. But now Heranar was effectively under house arrest, because Valahald was acting as governor in his place; and he, Wicursal, was promoted to the new position of senior aide. Who knew what might come of this, if he acquitted himself well? A high-ranking command, surely, when the time came for the invasion – or maybe Valahald would want him to act as deputy while he was away in the north? Now that would be worth staying behind for. Steady, he told himself, steady. He wondered what Valahald was thinking about. By my right hand, he said to himself, I would not be in Heranar's shoes today.

Although apparently gazing impassively out of the window, Valahald was not really watching what he saw of the day's business as it went on within headquarters. His mind was turned inwards, reviewing the events of the past few days since he had arrived here in the north. A slight smile showed on his face as he recalled Heranar's state of panic. His brother had been positively gibbering with fright, but obstinate in his insistence that the escape must have been organised from outside, that the ambush proved that the men from the Nine Dales had been aided independently.

'Oh, I think you're wrong there.' Valahald had kept his voice and manner light, having discovered that this was often more intimidating than bluster. 'Surely you remember what Wicursal put in his report: that his captain states the ambush took them all by surprise. Haldur attacked his troops first, with improvised weapons: the decision to make a break for it had obviously already been taken. What interests me is why the men from Rihannad Ennar should risk attempting to escape in the first place.'

'Well don't look at me. How could it have had anything to do with me? If it hadn't been for Wicursal... He more or less implied that you'd authorised him to take them out under escort. You can ask him; he knows I'd kept them close until then. But when he said you'd told him to help, I thought… Remember how you promised me, back in Caradriggan, how I'd have help in dealing with them? I thought this must have been the kind of thing you meant.'

'I've no idea what you're talking about.'

'You must remember! It was in the *Sword and Stars*, we were eating there together. You said I'd have help, you said I could trust you.'

'I don't remember any such conversation.'

'But you must do!' There was sweat on Heranar's face and a catch in his voice as if he was on the verge of weeping. 'It was at the *Sword*, you said to trust you. If there's been a breach of security, as you put it, I'm not responsible. I've said nothing, how could I? I've told no-one anything.'

Valahald smiled to himself again, recalling this exchange as he gazed through the window. Yes, you can trust me, little brother, he thought. For example, you can trust me to notice how fervently you protested your innocence. Unless I'm losing my grip on things completely, no-one has actually accused you personally of any betrayal – not yet, anyway: all I've pointed out is that *somebody* must have tipped off the northerners. But if I had a silver *moras* for every time you swore you'd said nothing, the drinks would be on me all over again at the *Sword*. Then there's the convenient absence of the lovely Ilmarynvoro. What a coincidence that she should decide to visit her family at just this time. I wonder what she might tell me, if she thought you were in danger? Or what you might have to say, if you thought your lady wife was under threat? Valahald drummed his fingers on the desk for a moment or two and then turned to Wicursal.

'You did the right thing in calling in a unit of the irregulars to form a search party, but I want another sweep made of the country between here and the mountains.'

Valahald brooded for a moment, remembering the fruitless efforts made by the auxiliaries to smoke out the folk of Salfgard. It seemed to him that there had been two separate betrayals of confidentiality: one to Haldur, but another to whoever had organised the ambush, and maybe the fugitives had had something to do with that: he was still convinced that they were hiding somewhere up in the hills.

'There must be something to find, and if all they could manage to round up was three loose horses, then I think it's time to let someone else have a crack at it. And this time, I'm going to have my own men do it: men from Caradward, without any Outlanders among them. While that's taking place, I've got another job for you. It's an important task, and it's one that's got to go right, with no hitches. Are you ready to take it on?'

'Absolutely, sir.'

'Good. Gather a small escort, not too many, but enough to deal firmly with trouble if you encounter any. I want you to bring Ilmarynvoro and the three children back from old Gillavar's place. Tell them Heranar and I want them to spend the festival here with us. She might make a fuss about travel arrangements for the youngsters, I don't know – maybe there'll be a nursemaid or someone who needs to be brought along. You can agree to anything of that sort, within reason, but there's to be no delay; get them back here as quickly as you can. If anyone shows signs of serious opposition, don't mess about: your orders come from the acting governor and anyone who doesn't comply with them takes the consequences. Ideally, keep everything as friendly as possible and if anyone asks, you can say Heranar and I are working together while he helps me with my enquiries. Pick your men carefully: make sure they can either keep their mouths shut or dissemble convincingly.'

Wicursal hurried off to put his instructions into action and Valahald turned his mind to the matter of organising the detachment of troops who were to comb the country into which Haldur and his companions had vanished. Once they were gone, and Wicursal and his men had set off on their errand, it would be time for his next move. He smiled to himself as he pulled out the drawers in Heranar's desk, looking for the forms he wanted. Where did Heranar keep his paperwork? Ah, here it was. He took out a blank docket and began filling it in. It would never do to allow a reunion of those two love-birds. He must make sure Heranar was away before Ilmarynvoro was brought back, so maybe it was a good thing after all that travelling was easier than usual this year. Two days later he was in the bath-house when he heard the shouting of orders, the jingle of harness and the trampling of feet and hooves; and by the time he emerged, immaculate in freshly-laundered clothes, the dust of departure was already settling again in the courtyard. Heranar, heavily guarded and more afraid than he had ever been in his life, was on his way south to Framstock, to be held in prison there at Valahald's pleasure until the governor of Rosmorric's business was concluded in the north.

Midwinter in Cotaerdon

In Carapethan's great hall, the seating arrangements, set out formally for the festive meal, had long become disarranged. Earlier in the day there had been the rites and the traditional storytelling and entertainment, and then the feast itself. But now that evening was well advanced, people were gathering in smaller groups for talk and laughter and moving about the hall exchanging greetings with friends. Carapethan himself, together with Aldiro, had unobtrusively withdrawn from proceedings and retired to his private quarters; and many of the older folk had also already left to return to their own homes. Vorardynur was careful not to sit at the high table once Carapethan had left it, but strolled from one conversation to another, drink in hand. Every now and then he could hear the sound of the stormy night outside, even over the noise of the hall. He was about half way down its length when a sudden cold draught lifted his hair and he turned to see that one of the guards had come in. Whatever it was he had to say clearly caused consternation: men put down their cups and jumped to their feet, and

Vorardynur saw heads bumping together as a babble of excited talk broke out. He began to push his way towards the doors but before he got there, the guard went out again followed by half a dozen others: sleet flew in, spattering on the floor, and the wall hangings flapped wildly as the hall doors, left unsecured, banged back and forth in the gale. As Vorardynur reached the foot of the hall, ignoring protests from those he shouldered aside, four men were helped in from the porch. They were drenched, shivering, and unkempt, and seemed barely strong enough to look about them. Vorardynur had been staring at them for several moments before, with a shock almost like a physical blow, he realised who they were. He raced back up the hall, taking the steps to the dais in a flying leap, running down the passage beyond, shouting for Carapethan. The two of them collided in a doorway, clutching at each other.

'Haldur's back! He's here, in the hall!' gasped Vorardynur.

Without a word, Carapethan pushed past him and ran, Vorardynur behind him and Aldiro, temporarily forgotten, bringing up the rear. They burst into the hall, men scrambling out of Carapethan's path as he rushed up to his son. Haldur was sitting down now, his head hanging; someone had pushed a drink into his hand and his companions were being fussed over. Tellapur was in his parents' arms, both of them weeping openly in the relief of his unexpected return. As his father arrived before him, Haldur raised his head. The lord of the Nine Dales looked at his son, unable for the moment, in his shock and joy, to speak a single word. He was forcibly struck by Haldur's resemblance to his mother: Ellaaro's eyes looked back at him from the boy's face. Somehow Haldur did seem boyish, younger than he remembered; but then, as the leader in Carapethan began to take over from the parent, he saw that he was mistaken. He noticed a change in Haldur, something new that was more significant than his wayworn appearance and thin face. Those misty-grey, dreamer's eyes held a haunted look. Instinctively, Carapethan knew Haldur brought bad news which it would be better to hear privately first. He found his voice.

'My son! I've been foolish enough to look for your return every day since you went south, but I never hoped for it before spring at the earliest. Now here you are, already back by midwinter! This is one feast-night that will never be forgotten. Whatever tidings you bring can wait until tomorrow; for tonight, I will simply say: welcome home.'

There was an outburst of cheering and clapping. People hammered on the tables and stamped their feet and the children present, allowed to stay up late for the feast, began running about in excitement. Haldur barely seemed to notice. He waited until the enthusiasm died down and then spoke.

'There are no words to express how glad I am to be here; I could embrace the very earth of Rihannad Ennar. Now that I have returned to my homeland, I wish with all my heart never to leave it again. But when the year turns, I must leave the Nine Dales once more.'

Carapethan's heart lurched. 'Tomorrow, we'll talk tomorrow. But there's something I need to know tonight. Where are Ir'rossung and Cathasar?'

'They are dead, both of them. Cathasar was killed in an accident.' Haldur glanced round at the listening faces. 'I can tell those to whom he was dear that he was buried with honour by friends. Though they never knew him, they laid him among their own. His grave is far away in a strange land, but it is overlooked by a *numiras* on the mountainside. Ir'rossung took sick. He was too ill for the kind of journey we were making, but what could we do but press on? He wouldn't hear of causing us delay and maybe putting ourselves at risk of sickness also and he was probably right: there was no shelter we could have made that would have saved him; the cold and wet would have killed him whether we had tried to sit it out or carried on. Somehow he clung on to life until we looked on Rihann y'n Devo Lissadan once more, and then he died. It was almost as though he could let himself go once he had seen his homeland again. We carried him to the ferry village, and Sallic's people gave him the rites.'

Raising his hand in the threefold sign, Haldur looked at his father. 'I am sorry that I return to you without two of those I led out. Both of them more than played their part. Indeed I don't believe the rest of us would have come back safe had it not been for their help.'

Other hands moved now, and for the first time Carapethan embraced his son. 'This sorrow is a grief to us all, it is a loss we all share. I know without needing to ask that every man who went south with you fulfilled the trust that was placed in him.' He nodded at Vorardynur. 'Make sure they're looked after with food and whatever else they need, then come through and join us.'

Drawing his son with him, he began to head back up the hall. Haldur looked about him, checking the faces in vain for the one he had most hoped to see even though he knew there was no need. If Artorynas had returned, he would have been there to welcome him.

A timely warning

By the time Vorardynur came back to Carapethan's chamber, Haldur was installed by the fire with Aldiro fussing over him. She had made him put on a winter-weight sleeping shirt and over it a fur-edged house robe belonging to his father. As Vorardynur came through the door Haldur was fending off his stepmother, who was now hovering with blankets and wanting to know what she could bring him to eat. The two young men embraced, grinning at each other.

'Sorry I didn't even speak to you in the hall,' said Vorardynur, 'but all I could think of was fetching your father as quickly as I could.' He held his cousin away from him. 'By the Starborn! You've lost some weight, your shoulders feel like a clothes-stand. Surely you want more to eat than that? He's going to need feeding up, Aldiro.'

Haldur shook his head, sitting down again and pulling the fur collar open at his neck. 'It's hot in here. I'm not used to it, and the same goes for food. Take it from me, in a few days' time I'll be putting it away with the best of them, but this is all I want just now.' He broke another piece off the small crusty loaf he was eating. 'Believe me, there have been nights when I thought I would die happy if only I could taste fresh bread again.'

Behind him, Carapethan and Aldiro exchanged glances as Vorardynur sniffed incredulously at the steam rising from the hot milk, sweetened with honey, which seemed to be all Haldur was drinking. On the hearth there was a pan of mulled ale and he poured for himself from this before sitting down beside Carapethan.

'Well come on, we're all ears.'

The lord of the Nine Dales gazed at his son and those shadowy eyes looked back at him from a thin face that was subtly changed, although Haldur's wet hair still flopped heavily down in its old way. Carapethan leaned forward, suddenly conscious of how quiet the room was. The background roar of voices from the hall had faded to no more than a murmur and even the noise of the storm outside seemed muted now.

'I can see before you speak that there's more to this than the sorrow of two lost companions. Never mind what I said in the hall when men were listening. Tell me now what it is that cannot wait until tomorrow.'

'Yes, it's bad news, as you've already guessed.' Haldur paused for a moment, glancing into the glowing heart of the fire. 'There were more reasons than one for pushing ourselves so hard to get home. We'd all have been dead by now, if we'd stayed. Ir'rossung found out we were to be murdered, so we'd nothing to lose and everything to gain by escape; but in any case we had already decided we must try. The Caradwardans are planning to attack Rihannad Ennar. If we don't do anything to prevent them, by the spring after next, their army will be upon us. We forced ourselves to go on, to endure all the hardships of this winter journey, so we could bring you a warning. We've bought you time. When the spring comes, we must be ready to make our move before they make theirs. We must go south again to stop them.'

A small catch of the breath from Aldiro was the only sound that greeted this. Haldur looked up to see all three of his listeners staring at him in shock, Aldiro's hands to her mouth.

'No,' said Carapethan eventually. The word sounded indistinct; he cleared his throat and spoke again more strongly. 'No. They've made one attempt to kill those who came to them in peace; I'll not send anyone south knowing they'll face an army. If they come against us, we'll defend ourselves here. But do you really believe they can cross the wilderness in sufficient force? Can they do this?'

'Oh yes, without a doubt.'

'Well then, thanks to what you've found out and the speed with which you've brought us a warning, we'll be ready. Every man, woman and child who can draw a bow will defend our land. They may reach our borders, but they will not pass them.'

'Father, no. You must listen to me. If you had seen what we have seen, heard what we have heard… If you knew of Assynt y'm Atrannaas, where prisoners are forced into a darkness like nightfall at the end of the world, if you had met their commanders: Vorynaas, who is ruthless and without mercy, Valahald, who murdered his own father to further his ambition! They have long ago closed their minds and their hearts, they knew nothing of *Stirfellaerdon donn'Ur*. You sent me to discover whether what we had been told was true, and whether the Nine Dales themselves were in danger. I tell you, nothing you have heard could prepare you for the reality, for the darkness and despair that follow wherever the Caradwardans go. Believe me, we must not let them bring this anywhere near our borders! Only Rihannad Ennar stands against them now. We have to stop them. You must call for the Releaser, put on Sleccenal!'

Vorardynur looked from Haldur to Carapethan, eagerly waiting for his uncle's response. He had never heard Haldur speak like this before and wondered whether Carapethan, who had resisted all his own arguments for intervention, would now be swayed by this emotional appeal from his son. Carapethan sat silent, thinking of the day he had shown the sword Sleccenal to Artorynas. Had he not said then that his only reason for going forth with war would be if Rihannad Ennar itself was threatened? And now here was his son, who, he reflected with a horrified shudder, had almost paid with his life for the knowledge, telling him that this dreadful moment was at last upon them. Eventually he stirred in his chair and forced himself to speak.

'Leaving aside any other considerations, what makes you think you can defeat this evil on its own ground? From the way you speak of them, our enemies would seem to be invincible.'

For the first time, Haldur smiled. 'Because there are indeed other things to consider. Look at this, and then hear the rest of what there is to tell you.'

He unbuckled one of his saddlebags and drew out the precious, tattered map that Sigitsinen had given him. By the time he had finished speaking, the lamps were dim and the fire had died down to embers. Carapethan watched Haldur fold up the map. He was sure of one thing above all others, which was that Haldur would not leave his side again: he would not risk his only son a second time. But there was no need to mention this now.

'It's late, and there's much to do. The time of year prevents us sending for the whole council; but this is something that we can't wait to discuss, so in the morning Vorardynur and I will send the word around. Meanwhile you need to get as much rest as you can so that you're ready to address Haldan don Vorygwent by tomorrow afternoon.'

Plans begin

Before Carapethan had even come home on the following day, Sallic and his father Devorhon arrived in Cotaerdon. Having seen at first hand the desperate lengths to which Haldur and his companions had gone to reach home, their decision to brave the weather and struggle up the valley in order to hear the news had been an easy one. With them was one of the Gwentarans who had brought the first appeal for help to the Nine Dales and was now settled with Devorhon's people;

and by the time the mid-day meal was served, Arellan the champion archer from Rihann y'n Riggan had also blown in on the storm. When the hour came for Haldur to speak, so many had gathered to hear him that Carapethan delayed the start of the council while he gave orders that his guest-hall was to be made ready. One glance at the faces of those assembled had been enough to show him that word of momentous tidings had run wild like the wind that howled round the eaves, and there were many present whose return journeys could not be made before nightfall. They crowded round Haldur, shaking his hand, clapping Aestrontor on the back, welcoming Asaldron and Tellapur, smiling with pleasure to see them safe in spite of their anxiety at what they might be about to hear; and Carapethan, coming back to his place, felt his heart still raw with guilt that his love for Rihannad Ennar had so nearly cost the life of his son. Indicating that all should resume their seats, the lord of the Nine Dales bade Haldur speak.

Prompted occasionally by those who had accompanied him, Haldur embarked on an account of his embassy: their journey south, their time there, things seen and said, people met. The tale wound on, taking in the treachery that prompted their desperate bid to get away, the help that had enabled them to succeed, the deaths of Cathasar and Ir'rossung, the struggle against time and weather to bring a warning of the danger that faced Rihannad Ennar. Here Haldur paused, and as one man his listeners turned to Carapethan; but he nodded to his son to continue.

'On my last night in Tellgard, I talked with Arval,' said Haldur. 'He asked me what I would advise, once I returned home. I told him I had seen enough to realise that we could never defeat Caradward's army in open war and that, reluctantly, I would speak against the idea of intervention in the south. But I also said that if ever it happened that Vorynaas should come north to assail us, then rather than let battle despoil our land, I would argue that we should advance against him, choosing attack rather than defence.' He looked at his father. 'And I told Arval that if this came to pass, I would hide from you my belief that we would die in the attempt to stop him.'

Carapethan's bright blue eyes widened: Haldur had said nothing of this the night before and the shock of what he had just heard brought the colour up into his face. Now his son smiled slightly as he returned his father's gaze.

'However, that was then. Things have changed, since that day; and so have my thoughts. When I spoke with Arval, I did not know that an invasion was indeed being planned. But now, we know we are to be attacked; and we know when. Further, we know of the secret resistance, the partisans who have helped us, who wait only for our help in return as their signal to act. And, having been in Caradward, I know what the Caradwardans fear. Our knowledge is our strength: their fear is their weakness. We must use the one against the other. Look at this, and I will show you how.'

Haldur unfolded his map, and eager hands reached forward to smooth it out on the table.

'When we went south, we went through the wilderness, and here on the northern borders of Gwent y'm Aryframan is where we were intercepted from the fort that guards the pass. But there is a better way, a secret way that leads to the heart of Caradward. See, we will ride down the east bank of the river, and after it plunges into the earth, we will keep to our course east of south until we reach the forest at the mountains' feet.' They craned to see, as he traced the line on the map with his finger.

'The forest hides an easy pass through the mountains. Only the partisans know of it: they will be keeping watch, waiting for us. We will follow the river valley south. Who would ever have thought that the Lissad nan'Ethan flows so far? But its waters burst from the ground again and carve a wide and fairly open passage through the forest. This is what the Caradwardans call Maesaldron. They are born with the fear of it bred into their bones, and only greed and force will make them enter it – for instance, to work their gold mine, which you see marked *here*. Sigitsinen and his comrades however will guide us through the forest until we arrive at the head of the dark valley where the mine lies.

'With surprise and fear on our side, we will secure the mine and free the slaves, sweep down the valley out of the forest and take the bridge. Meanwhile, the signal will have been given and within Caradward itself and the occupied territories, the rising will begin. In the far south are the Outlanders, with no love for Caradward; many of them are in the plot to destabilise its forces from within. To the west and north, governors Valahald and Heranar will be cut off by our advance. To be honest, I can't see Heranar having the courage of his convictions and changing sides, but I'd say it's likely that he might panic and desert his position. Valahald is a different proposition altogether, a ruthless man who will fight if cornered. However we must hope that if Heranar lets him down, and the Gwentarans rise in sufficient numbers, he can be overwhelmed before too many lives are lost. We've seen for ourselves that many of his own men hate him. Which brings me to Vorynaas.

'Valahald emulates Vorynaas, who rules by fear and envy. His close associates are jealous of each other and scramble for his favour, but even they are afraid of him. They know that he will eliminate those who step out of line because he can buy others to take their place: it's his grip on the gold that gives him power in the first place, and he uses this hold to create fear, which in its turn reinforces his power. But you see the weakness of his position.' Haldur tapped the map.

'Take away his gold, and he will be as a man without the use of his right hand. When we emerge from Maesaldron, the mine and the bridge in our control, and advance on Caradriggan, his aura of invincible might will vanish like an illusion; the fear of him will melt away, his power will be gone. The one thought his supporters will have then will be to disassociate themselves from him as fast as they can.

'If we simply trust to our defences, if we allow the Caradwardans time to perfect their plans, we will be overwhelmed and enslaved like the Gwentarans were. But this way...' Haldur waved his hand over the map. 'We've seen what it's like in Gwent y'm Aryframan; we were taken to Heranwark and shown what goes on in Rigg'ymvala; we travelled as far south as Staran y'n Forgarad. Heretellar once said to me that he felt the heart was eaten out of Caradward, that it was like a fruit that had rotted on the bough. This way, we can jolt the tree so that it falls of itself.'

They looked at each other. Carapethan waited to see who would speak first; and Haldur avoided his eye, wishing he could tell the council what Arval had said about the quest to find the arrow. But it was no use: he could hardly choose this moment to reveal the only occasion on which he had disobeyed his father. Then Devorhon cleared his throat.

'I take the points that Haldur makes,' he said, 'but we'd better think about the practicalities of all this.'

As soon as he spoke, it seemed everyone wanted to have his say. Questions, comments, doubts flew to and fro. It took all Carapethan's authority to impose some order on the discussion, but he was prepared to let them talk themselves out and the hours went by almost unnoticed. Eventually there began to be long pauses for thought between the questions; and here Poenellald, ever down-to-earth, returned to the concerns that seemed most relevant to him.

'How many men should we have to send? Not to mention horses and supplies.'

'We need carry only provisions enough to see us as far as Caradward,' answered Haldur, 'because once there, if we prevail we will have the use of all that Vorynaas keeps stockpiled under guard. If we are defeated, well, dead men do not need to eat.' He heard the sudden movement his father made at this, but did not look round. 'As to horses, agility and endurance will be more important than speed or strength, so ...'

'So why not use the horses bred for use by the Cunorad?' broke in Maesmorur.

Haldur remembered how Maesmorur had spoken once before in favour of a small force of chosen companions. How long ago that debate seemed now, even though not much more than a year had passed since then. But now Astell caught his attention.

The lorekeeper was leaning forward, his rather predatory face pointing its sharp beak at Carapethan. 'Why not, indeed? And furthermore, why not send the Cunorad to ride them?'

'Yes! I've seen them and I was afraid, even though I knew who they were.' This was Cureleth, alight with enthusiasm for Astell's suggestion. 'So imagine – how would you feel if you'd never seen them before?'

As he turned in surprise, Haldur saw that Astell was now watching him, almost as if he guessed what he would say. He gripped his sleeves under the table, steadying himself.

'Sigitsinen believed Caradward might fall without a blow being struck, if only the Hidden People could show themselves. To him, this was just a dream... but if Artorynas were to find the arrow he seeks...' Haldur swallowed. 'If Artorynas comes back to us in time...' He left the sentence unfinished in the face of his father's obvious displeasure.

Carapethan's brows were drawn down, accentuating his penetrating gaze. He looked slowly round the table. Suddenly it struck Haldur how quiet it was. The wind had been howling as it swooped and beat around the hall, but now all was still: the storm must have blown itself out while they sat talking. He looked up to find that his father's bright blue eyes were now resting upon him.

'Those who go seeking Asward donn'Ur do not return,' said Carapethan.

VIII LIGHT

CHAPTER 56

On the Golden Strand

The new day stole delicately into a silent sky, gently as a petal drifts from the flower to the ground, and looked down upon the slumbering earth. Quiet and peaceful she had lain, cradled in the arms of night; but now sunrise warmed her ancient face, restoring anew its maiden freshness unsullied. Beneath the blue sky spread a wide blue sea, little waves fretting playfully against golden sands, a dazzling path of light laid upon its waters from shore to horizon. As the sun rose higher it shone down upon a gleaming strand where wading birds ran to and fro or wheeled above, twisting and turning with flashing wings, their plaintive cries piping above the distant sigh and sough of the sea. Where land met shore stood low, crumbling cliffs, their grassy outcrops bright with pink sea-thrift; and far away inland, snowy mountains lifted their heads into the sky where rosy clouds floated like fish with golden fins. The air carried a mingled scent of flowers and grass, salt and sand. Untouched and unspoiled, the earth lay open to the hushed, still morning; and nowhere was there any trace of the work of man, nothing to show that any had ever walked there.

But not far from the foot of the cliffs, what was it that moved among the tumble of grey boulders? The new day broadened and the sun climbed, its light running like the tide among the rocks and crags; and it shone upon a man. He lay face down, one arm stretched out, but the light roused him: for his fingers moved as though they explored the texture of the soft, warm sand; and the rhythm of his breathing changed. Into his senses crept an unfamiliar briny smell and suddenly he moved abruptly, pulling back his outflung arm and huddling all his limbs together as if in response to some threat. The morning breeze lifted his hair from his face: loose, dark locks with one white strand among them, flowing back from a lean, strong-boned face with hollow cheeks and a high forehead. For a moment he stayed so, propped on one elbow, staring downwards as if dazed or confused. Once more he touched the sand, letting its fine grains sift back through his fingers. Gradually he sorted dreams from reality, aware now of new sounds: sounds as strange to his ears as the salty tang was on his lips and the pungent smell of wrack and rockpool in his nose. He heard the murmur of an elemental voice, a voice that called to him and would not be gainsaid. He staggered to his feet. Golden eyes, their amber sun-sparks waking, looked upon the sea: stared, and stared again, as if their wonder could never be assuaged.

So Artorynas stood, alone in the new day: land behind him, sea before him, sky above. He stood, gazing on the sea, listening to its voice, and about him the wild creatures went unheeding about their business. Small blue butterflies danced on erratic wings in the warm air against the cliffs, bees buzzed in the sea-pinks, rabbits nibbled at the grass. Birds without number soared overhead or probed the sandbars. Artorynas recognised redshank and curlew, their long legs and bills seeming to waver in the warm haze that now shimmered over the beach; and the ravens that croaked about the cliffs, sending rabbits bounding for cover, were familiar to him; but a myriad smaller waders, and the white birds of the ocean that swept by on outstretched wings, he could not name. They cried to him of secret, lonely places, of wide grey waves surging far from land. Now he turned away from the sea, looking about him in every direction. Far, far away the everlasting snow of the mountain-tops gleamed pure and white in the morning sun. Their distance was impossible to guess, but he sensed besides some unusual quality to the light, a strange touch in the air.

The frown lines deepening between his eyes, Artorynas stared doubtfully at the cliffs behind him. They were low, earthy, broken up by gullies where little streams wandered down from the land behind to lose themselves in the sand. Silvery driftwood and wave-washed boulders lay at their feet, and sea-kale grew; on their ledges, where soil had accumulated, were the mats of pink thrift; and at the top, small trees and bushes overhung the streams, and the grass grew sweet and green right to the edge. Land's end met sea shore in balanced blend, with no clear line to mark where one ended and the other began. But surely, when he had pursued the As-Geg'rastigan in that wild, desperate chase... when he had run like a madman, calling to them, and they had swept away from him over a wide, golden sea... when he had leapt after them, a hopeless yearning in his heart... *those* cliffs had been mighty bastions whose feet stood in the moving waters, whose sheer faces denied the waves, whose proud heads towered high above and looked straight out to the far horizon? Artorynas felt despair growing within him at the questions for which he had no answers. What was this place where he now found himself? How had he come there? Had it all been a dream or some kind of delusion? And where now could he ever find Asward donn'Ur?

Abruptly he turned away, looking out to sea once more. Then, drawn by its call, he began to walk slowly towards its margin. Nothing he had ever read, or heard tell of in tales, had come close to even hinting at the majesty of its wide waves. He stood and gazed upon the sea, awed by its vast extent and might. That power was sleeping, on this benign, sunny morning, but he sensed its presence in the depths. Little wavelets frilled about his feet in a lace of foam, and he felt rather than heard the regular suck and shock of the ocean-surge against the stacks offshore. Now Artorynas noticed that the water seemed to be retreating from him, leaving wet sand and shells where the shallows had curled, and remembered boyhood lessons of rising and falling tides: low water must be still some time away. For a moment he caught his breath, thinking there were swimmers far out in the glittering water; but looking again he realised he saw more wonders from his schoolroom days brought to life before him. Those must be seals whose dark heads bobbed in the waves not far from rocks now revealed above the receding tide. As he watched, several hauled out to sun themselves on the drying reefs and sandbanks. He smiled at their ungainly progress, but the lowing and barking of their calls, carried mournfully to him over the water, brought him back to thoughts of his predicament.

With a sigh he began to retrace his steps. Was he to turn back inland, or continue his search along the shore? And if the latter, in which direction should he go? He sat down on a huge rock that lay half-embedded in the sand. Absently he passed his hands over its smooth, warm surface, gazing about him again; and it struck him that what he felt was not weariness, but peace. I am at the mid-point of land and sea, he thought, and the heavens arch above me with no blemish to mar either earth or sky. I have never imagined any place so fair, and now not only do I see it, but I am here within it, partaking of its loveliness. Again that strange breath, as of an air from another world, seemed to brush lightly over him but he put it from his mind. His resolve had not broken so far and therefore now too he must force himself to continue the quest, as he had willed himself to do before. He trudged back, thinking to scramble up the cliff in order to get a higher vantage point from which to survey his possible onward course. And then, as he stooped to gather up his gear, he saw. It was as if a sudden, immense silence fell: as if earth and sea were still, as if no bird cried, no breeze blew, as if his own heart had ceased to beat. There before him it lay, the thing he had toiled so hard, and walked so far, to find. He dropped to his knees, and put out trembling hands to take up the arrow Arymaldur had made.

Eventually Artorynas dragged his eyes away from the precious thing he held. Was it the same sun, that still shone down? For him, everything had changed: he could not have said whether it was only moments, or whole ages of time, that had passed. Slowly his numbed mind began to work again. It broke upon him that his search was over, for surely this *was* the Golden Strand! He was standing on Porthesc nan'Esylt, he had found Asward donn'Ur! Now he knew the crystal brightness of its light, now he realised what other-worldly life it was that had breathed upon him half-recognised. But then where were the Starborn, what of the As-Geg'rastigan? He leapt up and looked wildly round. Then, the arrow blazing in the sunlight where he still clutched it in his hand, he ran out from the cliff, calling and seeking in vain. At last he slowed and trailed back. Slumping to the ground, he stared out over the shore. There before his eyes was the evidence of his own presence: his footsteps were plain to see, a clear track leading down to the sea and back, and then great ragged impressions in the sand where he had run desperately to and fro; but nowhere was there a sign that any other foot had left a print. What was it Arval and Astell had said? *The As-Geg'rastigan may walk unseen.* But he *had* seen them! Somehow, for however brief a moment, their world and his had been sufficiently at one for them to save him when he fell, to bring him to this place. He looked again at the arrow. The Starborn must have been beside him: how else could the arrow have been beside him? The As-Gegrastigan had been with him, but they were there no longer. He had found them, and looked upon them; but they – staying for neither speech nor succour, they were gone. They had left him. He was alone.

Something changed in Artorynas' face as he realised he had not the strength to resist the pain that was growing within him. All his life he had fought what he saw as weakness; even as a child he had striven to keep his features stern and his feelings hidden. He had faced down the taunts of Vorynaas, and stored up Arval's praise to live on in secret, alone, and met both with the same apparent calm. There had been occasions when he had been almost overcome, when tears had stung his eyes, but never once had he yielded. But he could deny himself no longer. The ache grew till it seemed his chest would burst, rose to his throat, twisted the old scar on his lip. Tears welled from his eyes, rolled down his cheeks, splashed onto the backs of his hands as he crouched; they dropped onto the sand and were lost and still he wept, unable to stop himself. Caught in a storm of grief, battered by the pent-up emotion of years he wept, silently at first as the tears fell too fast for him to dash them away; but the hurt inside him was like a savage beast now freed from its cage. It ripped and tore at him with merciless teeth and claws until the pain was unbearable. He began to groan, breathing in helpless gasps; and though he clenched his teeth in shame at the sounds he heard himself making, he was powerless to prevent them. Alone amid the beauty of Asward donn'Ur he lay and sobbed hopelessly as if the hurt could never be washed away no matter how many tears might fall.

Memories, faces, fragments of thought flitted randomly across his mind. Again Ardeth welcomed him to Salfgard; again he stood with bleeding face as Ghentar and Heranar ran away into the dawn mist. Isteddar stared at him in the hayloft of the *Sword and Stars*; Vorynaas denounced him before Tell'Ethronad. He smelled the perfume of Heretellar's night-blooming flowers, tasted Torald's mountain trout, heard the storm-cock under the louring sky of Caradriggan. Alone, he rebuilt a hillside wall once more; once more, while others slept, he worked at figures and reports, alone. Alone. The very word seemed to increase his pain. He felt he would have paid any price for the comfort of a companion's presence. He yearned for the tender sanctuary of a mother's arms, which he had never known from Numirantoro; for the reassurance of a father's manly hug, denied him by Vorynaas and impossible from Arymaldur; for the warmth of a true friend's embrace, felt only in farewell from Haldur; for the close rapture of desire, which neither Astirano nor Torello could ever have from him nor he in turn from Esylto. Blinded by tears, he fumbled for his gear, tipping it in a careless heap. He clutched the empty pack to himself, instinctively needing something, anything, to put his own arms round in a desperate attempt to keep the loneliness at bay. But with a cry, he flung the pack aside. It was too small, too insubstantial. The pain that gnawed him from within somehow seemed to demand a tribute of pain inflicted from without. He heaved at a rock, worrying at it like a dog, pulling it from its sandy bed. Pressing his cheek to its unyielding surface, he wrapped his arms around it and gripped until it hurt him, bruising his ribs and arms. Wordlessly he keened, lying broken-hearted and alone, weeping as though the anguish would never cease. His eyes were closed now, but still the tears welled from them, flowing down without number through the dark lashes that lay wet against his face.

When he came to himself, the sun was sinking huge and red towards the horizon, lighting a bright pathway across the endless sea. There was no sound but the quiet lapping of waves and a golden evening lay over all. It was plain that the water did not reach this far up the strand, at least not during the gentle weather of summer, for here the sand was fine and dry. The cliffs returned the sun's heat in a long after-glow, warming the air. Artorynas sat up. Was this the evening of the same day, or had several passed? He neither knew, nor much cared. He felt as insubstantial as a ghost, empty and wrung out, but he was master of himself again. The tears of a lifetime had washed over him in one bitter flood: he would not weep again. He looked at the driftwood that lay, bone dry along the high-water mark. There was no need here to be afraid of what fire might bring. Twilight set in as he gathered wood, stacking it high, and in the deep blue dusk the flames leapt up. Artorynas fed them through the night, tending a beacon of defiance that flared against the dark. Morning found him sitting beside the dying embers with staring eyes, amber eyes that smarted as they had never done before from tears, smoke and wakefulness. He stood up and once more walked down to the water's edge. Stripping off his travel-soiled garments he waded into the sea, warm in the shallows where it flowed over the sand. For the first time he felt the buoyancy of salt water, letting its eddies bear him where they would: sometimes swimming against the tide, sometimes floating with it. Emerging at last, he pushed the water off his body and let the sun dry him, noticing the salt left behind as the rivulets that ran from his wet hair evaporated in the morning's warmth. He wondered vaguely when he had last eaten, and after going a little way up the nearest stream until he found water to drink that was without a brackish taint, he took food from among his store. Then, having methodically re-packed everything that he had tipped out, he sat down with Arymaldur's arrow across his knees and set himself to consider what best to do.

But his bruised mind was not ready yet to address itself to practical decisions of time and travel. The days to come, and the deeds that must be done, would have to wait a while. His thoughts turned instead to Arval and the teaching he had imparted, to things learnt from Astell, to Numirantoro and Arymaldur and the mysteries of the As-Gegrastigan. What was it the lorekeeper of the Nine Dales had said? That men yearned for the Starborn from instinct, as if knowing they could be as one, were it not for the flaws that marred them; that the As-Geg'rastigan were hidden from the Earthborn in a world that was perfect, as they were. But when he had asked how then could they pass from one to the other, Astell was able to offer no answer. He himself had no explanation for how he came to sit here, on Porthesc nan' Esylt. How could he have gone from the desolation of the wilderness to the beauty of Asward donn'Ur between one step and the next; how plunged in a breaking fall and yet found himself safe and unharmed on the Golden Strand? It could only be that for a brief moment, the worlds of the Earthborn and the Starborn had been one. As he remembered what he had heard and seen, his heart was wrung with pain once more and the sunlight seemed dim and weak. That glimpse of glory had lasted for so short a time! Maybe both Arymaldur and Numirantoro had been among the host of As-Geg'rastigan that he had seen as they swept into the sunset, but how could he ever know?

This bitter reflection turned Artorynas' thoughts to the mother he had never known. When he had been injured, Arval had taken him through Tellgard's hidden door: the door that only the Starborn, or those who shared in the life of the As-Geg'rastigan, might use. His mind's eye saw that shadowy court once more, its *astorhos* trees fragrant in the starlight. He had recognised it immediately as the place of Arymaldur's and Numirantoro's fateful meeting. Artorynas frowned. All the tales he knew that dwelt upon the fate of the As-Urad told that there was no outrunning *maesell y'm as-urad,* as Carapethan had been so keen to remind his people. Arval's own father had been *as-ur,* a man who in spite of having wife and child had been powerless to stop himself leaving them to search for the Starborn. Who knew whether he ever found them; and if he did, whether it brought him peace. But if Numirantoro, a daughter of earth, had been able to find and pass the secret door, surely this must mean, as Arval had surmised, that she was already in some way numbered among the Starborn? And now he recalled more of what Arval had tried to make him understand: that Arymaldur had shown Numirantoro, mind to mind, that the life of the As-Gegrastigan could indeed be hers; but that if she would have it, she must pay the ultimate price. Now that Artorynas had seen the As-Geg'rastigan with his own eyes, he understood more clearly what he had struggled to grasp when Arval had revealed his parentage to him. He heard Arval's words in his heart once more: *The love of the As-Geg'rastigan is an all-consuming loss of self: their union is a radiance of light.* Numirantoro's love for Arymaldur must indeed have been too great for her to bear if she had willingly gone to meet the fate she knew awaited those who embrace the Starborn in all their majesty and might.

And yet somehow she remained among us long enough to bring me to birth, thought Artorynas, even though the same day that saw me born took both Arymaldur and Numirantoro from us. Did she linger for my sake, or for Arymaldur? Or did he wait for her, before he returned whence he came? Or was it simply that Arval sustained her with the spirit of which only he knows the secret, whose strength is so potent that it has prolonged his own life across such a span of years? He told me once that he was waiting, without knowing why; but when he saw my mother, he knew she was the reason. So then, if she had to live long enough to give me life, it was all for me. It is not who I am, but what I am, that signifies. I was born so that when the day came, I could undertake this quest. Arymaldur told Arval: let that which I leave seek for that which I take; when the two are united, hope will return. And now at last I have the arrow! I have found what I sought for so long: my quest is achieved. I should be filled with joy, borne up by gladness; but instead my mind is dull and my heart downcast. Why is this so? It is because the task is not over yet, he reasoned. I have yet to fulfil my promise to Arval. Only when I stand beside him once more with the arrow in my hand will hope somehow return. The long road back must still be trodden, and I must set out soon. The days are passing by, time is running out. He sat gazing seawards, but his eyes scarcely saw the beauty around him. Finally he sighed. Let me at least look at what I hold, he thought; and began, almost reluctantly, to examine the arrow.

Many times, he had heard it described; but there were no words known to him that were worthy of its wonder. He turned it over in his hands, a thing both delicate and deadly. There was a life locked within it, a force barely contained that he sensed beneath his fingers. This was made by my father, he said to himself; but though he deliberately used the word he could not invest it with the meaning it should carry. Suddenly, as Artorynas gazed upon the arrow, it occurred to him that he held not only a work of his father's hands, but also bore a precious thing of his mother's making. From its secret pocket he took out the As y'm Ur. Tiny, exquisite, it lay trembling in the palm of his hand. On the night he left Caradriggan Arval had given it to him, telling how Numirantoro had made it and entrusted it to him to keep for her son, along with his true name. All his life until then Arval had kept it safe for him, and surrendered it only at their parting. It hung on a chain, but Artorynas had always carried it hidden next to his heart. All through the years and long miles of his journey north it had gone with him, a gem he had treasured as a lodestone. Since Arval gave it to him, he had shown it to no other: not even with Haldur had he shared its beauty and significance. Now, laying down the arrow, with infinite care he loosed the minute hinges to reveal the layers of meaning concealed within the As y'm Ur.

Outwardly, it was a sphere whose filigree of greens and tawny-russet was a blend of malachite and tiger's eye swirling one into another; but it opened to show an inner surface of dark blue lapis and misty opal inset with diamonds as tiny as pin pricks. Artorynas had never seen any work of craft so small and intricate and he marvelled at Numirantoro's skill. Yet there were more wonders still to see. The outer case contained an inner globe of red gold, absolutely round, pure and plain; but this too opened. Within the glowing gold, at the very heart of the gem, lay a core of sky-steel. Artorynas sat and feasted his eyes on his mother's vision of this world: the earth, robed in green and blue and brown, its lands washed by the restless sea, warmed by the golden sun, with the sky and its myriad stars over all. This world, beneath whose placid bosom beats an ardent heart of fire. This world, itself star-born in the deeps of time, still carrying within the signs of its true nature, which even now those who will may read. The As y'm Ur, so small, yet charged with such a freight of meaning. And I hold it in my hand, said Artorynas to himself. He raised his head, this time truly seeing the beauty of what lay around him as he sat on the Golden Strand, perceiving that what was caught in the As y'm Ur was the fairness of Asward donn'Ur, even though this was a place Numirantoro had never seen.

Or had she? He remembered the huge circle of stones he had passed by as they brooded on their lonely upland plain. Numirantoro had not looked on these with her waking eyes, yet she had brought them to the page in perfect detail. *As silent as standing stones*: he could see the book in his mind even now. He had wondered if Arymaldur himself had brought the arrow to him, whether he had looked upon his son; maybe Numirantoro also had stood beside him. Artorynas glanced at the ashes of his fire, the fire that had said: a man is here. Now he looked up at the morning sky. It was blue and empty above him. *Let the Hidden People show themselves.* It had been the Earthborn in him that prompted him to defy the darkness in the way men have ever done, but it was his Starborn nature that told him now he had deceived himself about the shadow on his heart. This was not cast by the thought of the long road back to Caradriggan. It came rather from the fact that he was now face to face with the choice he had known he must one day make. Ever since he was ten years old, broken-hearted at the prospect of leaving Arval to spend five years in Salfgard, that choice had been waiting for him: mysterious at first but gradually moving into focus until at last, with sudden clarity, it had been revealed to him on the night he set out from Tellgard. Not for him the fabled sorrow of the As-Urad, caught forever between two worlds, doomed to yearn for both. Whether because of the choice Numirantoro had made, before he was even conceived, or for some other reason yet to be revealed, he must choose, once and for ever, to which kindred he would belong.

This was a decision by no means as clear-cut as it might have appeared, had he read it in a story or heard of it in some old tale. The small scar on his lip showed white for a moment in his sun-browned face as Artorynas smiled a little, remembering Arval's reassurance to a despairing small boy that he would be happy in Salfgard. Arval's wisdom had spoken truly: the Salfgard years had been filled with love and the warmth of family, and had given him what he had never known in Caradriggan, a taste of the joy that can bless the Ur-Geg'rastigan. And in the Nine Dales he had found a sense of home, and with it also a friendship that would endure no matter what. His smile broadened, lighting his face with that same inner life that would sometimes show in Arymaldur's austere features, and then faded once more as darker thoughts filled his mind. He wanted to believe he could be content, working alongside Ardeth or the old fellow up in the Golden Valley, but was this not a delusion? Would he not lie restless at night, yearning for something more? He saw the pain in Astirano's eyes, the tears on Torello's cheeks; remembered the long anguish of Geraswic's life. And now he allowed himself to think of Esylto, whose outward loveliness was only matched by the radiance within. Where had he heard words like those before? It was what people said about Numirantoro, reaching for the only comparison they could make, the same one he had made when he had first seen Esylto: she is as fair as the Starborn. Esylto knew him for what he was, but her eyes were fixed on the As-Geg'rastigan themselves: she had looked past him, as he had looked beyond Astirano and Torello. Only sadness could follow any union he might make with a woman of the Earthborn, no matter how much she might want him, or he desire her, in the beginning.

To Artorynas it seemed that the truest bond the As-Urad might hope for was with a comrade, as he had found friendship with Haldur. But here too, time and change were doomed to lay their hand. He could almost hear Haldur's voice, insisting he would be steadfast and always want Artorynas beside him for advice and support. But despite their best intentions, reality would dull the brightness of this ideal. Haldur would be lord of his people one day; he would have a wife and children to claim first place in his heart. Or supposing they both wed, but Artorynas, like Arval's father, was unable to find peace? Haldur's wife would not be pleased at the constant presence of an unsettled friend to disturb her husband's content. And what of Haldan don Vorygwent? Who knew how Haldur's counsellors might resent his reliance upon one adviser more than others. Carapethan's fears of discord in Rihannad Ennar were well-founded, bitter though it was to admit this. No, it would be better if Haldur and he were to remain as they were now, true brothers in heart. If I may be numbered among the Starborn, thought Artorynas, then they are the kindred I choose. But I will go to them with Haldur in my heart, and that will bring him joy even in his sadness, because he yearns for them too: he would have taken the vow, and remained with the Cunorad for life, if his fate had not intervened to prevent it. And now I too have a destiny to fulfil, and promises to keep. I have made my choice, but before I am free to follow it, I must return first to Cotaerdon, to see Haldur one last time; and then I must bring the arrow south to Caradriggan, before the seven years are spent, and stand beside Arval again as I swore to do. How what has been foretold will come to pass once I am there, or what I must do to make it happen, I do not know, any more than I can see how I am to achieve my choice. Must I find the As-Geg'rastigan again? Have I any reason to hope that they would stay for me, when they would not wait for me on Porthesc nan'Esylt?

With this Artorynas stood up and looked out over the sea. His amber gaze, bright in the noon sunshine, slowly swept round the horizon and back. The strand stretched as far as he could see in both directions. He could not decide his path, for if he turned inland again, how could he find the way when he did not know how he had come there? In any case, he could not bring himself to turn his back on the sea. Its movement drew his eyes, its voice whispered in his ears, its call played upon his heart. He was fascinated by its every mood, unable as yet to tear himself away. The days passed, and he lingered in the balmy air of the Golden Strand. He floated in the warm waves, and lay indolent on the dry sand, and the soft sea breezes kissed him by day and lulled him to sleep at night. Yet from the north he sensed a different air, a hint of something too elusive to describe: otherworldly, from a north beyond. Not cold, yet clean as the whitest snowfield, pure as ice, fresh as if never breathed; clear and keen, it touched his face and lifted in his hair, and he felt the secret life that moved within it. Time and again he would look that way, or sit at evening gazing on the stars that woke in the deep blue of the northern sky. When he had seen the As-Geg'rastigan they had hastened northwards down the golden path of sunset, and though the sun had moved round since then, instinctively he looked to the north in hope to see them again.

But although no sight or sign came to him and each dawn found him still alone, almost without his realising it, the fact that he had now made his choice had removed a burden from his mind. He had spent most of his life in the deepening shadow of its looming approach, and the years of his search had not been made any easier by the knowledge of how hard a decision lay ahead: but that was all behind him now. Like a sword-blade, forged and tempered by fire and water, so he too had been tried and tested. Though battered and beaten by the storm of emotion that had broken over him, he had emerged from it somehow cleansed and stronger than before, as metal is refined from the ore in a crucible of extremes. Artorynas knew now that when the moment came, he would implement his choice without hesitation, whatever might be required of him to answer the call of the As-Geg'rastigan; and as for when the call might come, that he was content to take on trust. He had food in plenty: fish from the streams and the sea, crustaceans and shellfish from the rockpools; there were sea-kale roots to roast, and samphire to add savour to his meals; blackberries and nuts in the gullies that ran down to the beach. Sometimes he would sit for hours, seeing the Starborn again in his mind. Then he would take out Arymaldur's arrow from its place among his own, marvelling that its life-force did not consume them to ashes, and drink in the details of its perfect, simple purity of form and construction. On other days he would wander along the water's edge, picking up shells left behind by the ebb or enjoying the play of light that woke in the tiny, jewel-bright pebbles as the tides ceaselessly sieved them to and fro.

One evening he lay, propped on his elbow, playing idly with his little treasure-trove of shells. Gradually twilight deepened towards night, blending earth, sea and sky; but trails of phosphorescence marked the place where the small wavelets splashed and spread on the sand. Artorynas stared seawards, his eyes wide in the darkness, still turning the shells over in his fingers. He had been musing on their infinite variety, their shapes ranging from wide and flat to deeply convoluted, their textures from silky smooth to ridged or spiny. He realised that life within the deeps of the ocean must be as multifarious as that on land, and suddenly it pierced his heart that Arval had never seen what he now beheld. How eager he will be to hear all I have to tell when I return, he thought; but if only he could be here himself to share the beauty of Asward donn'Ur with me. That night it was long before he slept, and he woke with a start as dawn was breaking. Although no detail now remained, somehow he knew the dream that disturbed him had been of Caradriggan. Who could say what might be happening there? Had Haldur arrived yet, had he spoken with Arval? Artorynas looked at the light of sunrise dancing on the sea. Every day the sun moved a little further south as the year turned: the berries and other fruits he was gathering warned him that earth's seed-time was approaching. The temptation to stay any longer must be resisted. He had left it late, but he must set out; and since his errand was now to the south, he would walk that way along the shore while he could and trust that fate would put his feet on the right path. Yet though he shouldered his gear and moved off, for all his resolve he went slowly, turning many times to look back north; but all he saw was the line of his own footprints lengthening behind him on the sands of Porthesc nan'Esylt.

A day came when the wind rose, whipping the waves to white crests, picking up sand to blow stinging along the shore. As the gusts became stronger Artorynas, looking doubtfully at the sky, began to think of shelter. Turning inland at the next stream outfall, he scrambled up until he found a small area of level ground at some height above the water. It had been carved from the cliff as the stream changed its course over the years and now, backed by the rock-face, was carpeted with grass and flowers. These were now bending before the gale as Artorynas quickly dismantled his pack and re-formed it into his emergency shelter. He was glad of the small protection provided by the cliff behind him, for the wind buffeted his tent, plucking it from his hands and making its fastenings dance wildly in the air; but at last all was secure and he crawled in. From here he could look out over the wide expanse of water, now beginning to rise in ever-angrier waves and billows. He stared in awe, only now fully realising the immense power that lay hid in the boundless deeps. The wind howled, the ocean-going birds screamed as they rode upon it, and the sea gathered itself into surge upon surge of dark, roaring water. The breakers crashed upon the shore in a thunder of flying spume as the first of the season's high tides greedily reclaimed the summer strand. Nearer and nearer the water swept: it reached the cliffs, spreading out, fretting among the rocks. Soon these were submerged as the level rose, until now the sea in all its restless might was pitted directly against the steadfast land.

By now Artorynas was on his feet. He had expected rain to come with the wind, but although clouds raced overhead, it was salt water that spattered on his face from the violent turmoil below him. The little stream now flowed directly into the sea, its waters backing up in eddies and cross-currents where the two met. Shafts of sunlight came and went, brilliantly illuminating the waves in green and blue where they stabbed down, withdrawing to leave a menacing expanse of dark, steely grey broken only by lines of white foam. Artorynas looked anxiously at the hungry waters heaving and tossing. He could feel the shock in the ground beneath him as they rolled in and hurled themselves at the cliff and wondered whether he should move further inland. But eventually it seemed the tide had reached its highest point; though the waves still slapped and smashed below, they had stopped rising. It was almost evening before he was sure the ebb was running. The sun sank into deepening banks of sullen red cloud and then the rain began, falling at first in huge, single spots and then merging into a continuous downpour. For hour after hour, lying in his makeshift tent, Artorynas listened to the deluge. The water-level in the stream rose, making him thankful he had picked a spot well above its banks. He could hear its voice change as the torrent increased, raging past him seawards. When dawn came at last, he crawled out into a new world.

The sea had retreated once more, but though it sparkled in the low sun under a pale, washed-blue sky, it was somehow flattened out by the rain, its voice subdued, its temper moody and withdrawn. Beside Artorynas the swollen stream still rushed down in spate. He noticed the discolouration in the waves where its brown, peaty current mingled with the sea. There was a new high-water line, with different flotsam scattered along it; the rockpools were refreshed and brimming. The sand was dark and damp, ribbed and rippled where the water had moulded it; and the strand was scoured clean, with every trace of his footprints washed away. Well, thought Artorynas, there could not be a clearer sign than that. It seemed the lazy days and tranquil nights were over now. Packing up his camp, he backtracked until the stream was narrow enough to cross, and then returned to the coast. He reckoned the shoreline was at least a path he could not mistake, if he was careful not to be caught by the tide, and negotiated any rivers or streams inland rather than where they flowed across the beach. It would not do to be mired in quicksand, or cut off on a sandbar.

So south he went as the days gradually shortened. There were no more great storms, and the air was still mild and soft, but rain fell frequently to swell the inland waters on their journey down to the sea. Often Artorynas could tell from far off when a river would bar his way, because long before he reached it he would see its silt as a stain on the erstwhile unbroken blue of the waves. One day he was scrambling down to walk along the sands once more, now that the retreating tide had left them uncovered, when something caught his eye. In a small pool among the rocks a white flower floated, moving slightly as the breeze ruffled the surface. Artorynas picked it from the water in amazement. There could be no doubt about what it was: the creamy white petals, with golden stamens, formed a central rosette that was surrounded by a delicate outer ring of identical but smaller florets like living lace. Only one tree had flowers like this, and only once before had he seen them: in the secret court within Tellgard where he had awoken under Arval's care. That had been mid-winter and still the flowers opened above him, because they bloomed on the *astorhos* tree, which old lore said was the only tree that flowered in all seasons, even when its branches were bare of leaves.

Artorynas climbed back up the low cliffs to look around him. The bushes and trees were showing autumn tints now, here and there; some mornings if he crossed a stream or river early in the day he would see its currents flowing golden with leaves that had fallen overnight. It was said that the *astorhos* tree was found only where the Starborn walked, so it was likely enough that it grew here in Asward donn'Ur, but he had seen none and he saw none now. If there were any, maybe they were further inland, so how had this flower come here? He looked again at the bloom in his hand. It must have been borne on the sea, to have been left floating in the tidal pool where he had found it. Artorynas gazed out across the waves, scanning the far horizon. Was it possible there was an offshore island where the trees grew, where maybe the As-Geg'rastigan themselves might be found? He stood and stared, and gradually the eager light left his face. Even if such an isle existed, how could he come there? The sea birds wailed and cried as they soared above him and he wondered if they knew the answer, wishing he could ask them. With a sigh, he went down to the strand once more to continue his journey; but this time, he walked as near the sea's edge as he could and when the tide began to turn again, later in the day, it brought two more *astorhos* flowers drifting in upon it. Artorynas bent to gather them up and as he straightened, thinking to retreat inland ahead of the moving water, he thought he saw, far away to the south, the outline of higher land near the coast. Was it taller cliffs, or a seaward mountain standing alone, or only towering clouds forming where land and sea met? He peered into the misty distance, frowning, forgetful of where he stood until a wave crashed about his knees and sent him floundering hastily up the beach.

Gradually over the next few days, what he had seen slowly resolved itself into a huge, craggy headland that jutted far out into the sea. Artorynas wondered if there was any way around it, or whether he would be forced into a long climb. As he drew nearer, this seemed the more likely course, because he noticed how the offshore currents were pushed far out to sea. He could see the different colour in the water as it swept away in a wide arc before flowing back in towards the land. Maybe there was another river beyond the headland, one larger than he had so far crossed. If so, he might have to travel some distance upstream before he had any hope of crossing it, and the sooner the better before it became swollen with more autumn rains. But as these thoughts ran through his head while he prepared for rest one evening, some half-forgotten words he had once heard from old Cunor y'n Temennis came back into his mind, and with them a sudden idea. With morning he walked more swiftly, striding along purposefully, possessed by new hope. He saw that the promontory ahead of him rose to sheer, mighty cliffs at its far end. There was no way around: the waters would be deep and dangerous with a treacherous undertow. He would have to climb, then, and his eye picked out a likely place where the land seemed to dip. From half-way up the slope he looked down at the waves curling below. Probably as the years went by the rocks would erode until the sea broke through and made an island of the higher outcrop. Meanwhile, best keep his concentration focused on the next secure crevice for a handgrip, the surest ledge for a foothold. At length he reached the top and lay panting on the springy turf.

Before him lay a wide estuary through which a river wound in several curving channels to the sea. Directly below, where the current had changed its course at some point in the past, there was a small area of saltmarsh fringed with sea lavender and buckthorn; but further upstream the greensward grew right to the water's edge. The valley was sheltered and faced south-west and it held what he had been almost sure he would find. On a level terrace above the near bank, out of reach of winter floods, stood a grove of *astorhos* trees. They moved gracefully in the breeze and as Artorynas watched, a small cloud of white flowers blew from them to settle spinning on the clear-flowing river. So the old legend told to him by the Hound of the Vow had been true: that if a man walked beside the Lissad y'n Cunorad far enough, he would find the tree of the As-Geg'rastigan growing. This was Rihann y'n Temenellan! All he had to do was follow the river upstream and it would bring him back to the Nine Dales. It might have been an easier road, thought Artorynas, if I had simply let the river lead me: maybe I could have stood where I find myself today with a good deal less effort. But it was surely unwise to assume this much. All his instincts, and all the counsel he had received, had told him to turn his face to the north. He had done this, and his quest had been successful. Perhaps if he had taken a different way, he would never have seen the As-Geg'rastigan; perhaps it was necessary for a man to have their help if he would find the Golden Strand. Artorynas studied the valley before him, wondering how far he would have to travel before he saw the blue smoke rising from Seth y'n Temenellan's hearth. Well, it would be foolish to take any unnecessary risks now. Autumn was drawing on, but the climate, as Astell had surmised, was benign in this hallowed land. He would press on while he could, and then, if he had to, he would dig in once more to wait out the winter when it came. After all, he reasoned, Haldur surely cannot return before spring at the earliest, and I promised I would not leave without bidding him farewell.

Artorynas got to his feet and was on the point of clambering down when he paused and turned. He looked back over the way he had come, back over Porthesc nan' Esylt. On a sudden impulse he shrugged off his pack and drew out Arymaldur's arrow. He held it up, and as it flamed in the sun, he felt the As y'm Ur move slightly against his throat. In Asward donn'Ur he had worn it on its chain and now he undid this, taking the gem in his other hand. Let the Starborn return, let the Hidden People show themselves! My mother went to Arymaldur without hesitation, he thought, even though she knew the price would be her life, her child, her place among the Earthborn. She did not falter, once her choice was made, and neither will I now I have made mine. If only I knew what I must do! Artorynas stood gazing northwards and then from far away it was as if he heard Arval's voice once more, reminding him of the words Arymaldur and Numirantoro had used in foretelling their son's fate. He opened the As y'm Ur and the minute core of sky-steel at its heart, tiny though it was, flared with an overwhelming brightness. He looked at the sky-steel of the arrow's point. *Only sky-steel can pierce sky-steel*: the old adage came back to him from his boyhood lessons. Artorynas' face set, stern yet serene, and the frown lines smoothed out between his golden eyes. Now, at last, he understood. Closing the As y'm Ur once more, he hid it away: how fortunate that Haldur had never seen it. He replaced the arrow in the quiver where his own were stowed, hefted his gear and moved off without looking back again. It seemed that he and Haldur must journey together after all, when the time came to set out. Skill with the bow such as only his friend possessed would be needed once they arrived in Caradriggan.

CHAPTER 57

Cousins

As Haldur tramped down the butts to retrieve his arrows, the sun sailed out from behind a cloud and he felt its warmth on his cheek. By the time he had come back to the line, he was uncomfortably hot in his wadded jerkin and he unfastened it, sitting down on the bench, staring sightlessly at his feet. What was the point in going on with his practice, when all he would be doing was staying behind? There would be time enough, more than enough time to kill, when the others were away south: off to the south on their mission to save the Nine Dales, while all he did was sit at home. A burning surge of shame rose within him, adding its heat to the warmth of the sun, and he flung off his jerkin and tossed it on the bench beside him. It seemed that even the weather favoured their enterprise. Once the storms that raged, one on the heels of another in the days after his return, had blown themselves out, a light snowfall had been followed by weeks of clear skies and hard frost. The lower passes had stayed open, making winter travel possible by horse-sled. Carapethan had sent out the word: the champions of each dale were to send their ten best archers who were both free and willing to go; they themselves were to stay, unless they had no family commitments and could also find a deputy skilled enough to take their place. In addition, any who had ridden among the Cunorad and who were likewise eligible were asked to answer the call. Ninety-two bowmen had presented themselves, for Carapethan had decided that his best female archers would be better deployed fighting to the last for their homes, if it should come to that; but there were women among those who had once been numbered among the Hounds of the Starborn. Fifty-three of these had come in, and all were quartered now in Cotaerdon while the final preparations were made.

The ground at the butts was trampled and churned where practice had gone on all morning. The grass, already growing strongly, was bent and bruised but its sweet smell only tormented Haldur further. He scowled down at it. Only those currently in the Cunorad were yet to arrive from Rihann y'n Temenellan, only the last of the specially-bred light horses to be rounded up, only the remaining provisions and equipment to be gathered in – and then, in this early spring sunshine, they would be off. He should be glad: glad that he had brought the warning in time, that his father was acting upon it and had taken his counsel. He should be happy that there was a chance that the Nine Dales would be saved. He should even be pleased that Carapethan valued him too much to risk his life again. But knowing all this made no difference: no matter how many times he repeated all the arguments to himself, he could not shake off the black cloud of shame and disappointment, the terrible feeling of uselessness. He had begged and pleaded with Carapethan, he had made his resentment plain; angry words had been spoken, but his father had refused to budge from his decision. Vorardynur was to lead in Haldur's place, which meant that of the six who had set out the previous year, only two would make the journey again. Tellapur had not demurred, when his parents asked him not to go: Haldur knew only too well how the young man had hated what he had seen in the south; and Cathasar and Ir'rossung were dead. That left Asaldron and Aestrontor, both of whom were to ride. Haldur clenched his fists in frustration. He knew Asaldron would have preferred to stay in the Nine Dales, but Carapethan had said he must go to advise and guide Vorardynur – as if I couldn't do that, thought Haldur bitterly. I wouldn't have cared whether I or Vorardynur was to lead, if only I could have gone too. As for Aestrontor, he had claimed his place on three grounds: that he had ridden in youth in the Cunorad, that he had been one of the six, and that he was a member of Carapethan's household men, several of whom had been included. Haldur hacked at the ground with his heel. All those reasons apply to me too, he thought, but none of them was a strong enough argument to persuade my father.

And then there was Artorynas. *Those who seek Asward donn'Ur do not return.* Carapethan's words repeated themselves endlessly in Haldur's mind; he could hear them in the background of all his other thoughts. In spite of everything Arval and Artorynas himself had said, in spite of his own hopes and beliefs, he knew he was afraid that his father would turn out to be right. But worse than this was the possibility that Artorynas would come back to find Haldur idle in Cotaerdon while others risked their lives for their homeland; and worst of all was the fear that he would return successful, the arrow of his quest in hand, only to discover that no help could be offered to him either from the Nine Dales or from the man who had sworn himself the brother of his heart. Haldur gritted his teeth as the inward battle raged in his mind. He told himself they could not afford to delay; what would have been the point of that desperate struggle to get home if they were now to wait, when no-one, not even Artorynas himself, could know when or whether he would ever return? And in any case, had he not long ago faced the sorrow of knowing that Artorynas, if he lived, would journey back to Caradriggan whereas his own destiny lay in Rihannad Ennar? Yes, said his thought; but Arval hinted that if Artorynas found the arrow, matters might fall out in ways none of them could foresee... and after all, whether people here realise it or not, this is about more than the survival of the Nine Dales. Suddenly he was gripped by an overwhelming conviction that they would fail unless Artorynas rode with those who were to go; that so much was at stake, they would only succeed if he found the arrow. And with that, a memory flashed into Haldur's mind: a memory of that sad farewell between himself and Artorynas, of a cold, grey sky, a tumbledown old barn, and something his friend had said, something about how he might be able to help him, one day. He jumped to his feet, meaning to go straight to Carapethan for one last attempt at persuading him to wait in the hope of Artorynas' return, and then, realising he had left his jerkin forgotten on the bench, turned back to snatch it up and saw Vorardynur heading towards him.

'The Cunorad have just come in,' said Vorardynur without bothering with any greeting or other preamble. 'I thought you'd rather hear it from me.'

'Oh.' Haldur sat down heavily, his elbows on his knees and his fingers in his hair. 'Yes, thanks for coming to tell me. A week at most should see you set off, then.'

'I'd say so.' Vorardynur hesitated for a moment, and then sat down on the bench beside his cousin. 'Look, I just wanted to say... I mean, I'm sorry about how... that you're not... What I mean is, I'm sorry I'm going in your place. I mean that, I want you to know I mean it.'

Haldur sat up and put his arm across Vorardynur's shoulders; his hair, released from the grip of his fingers, turned in the sun and flopped down on his forehead. He managed a smile. 'I know, don't worry about it. You're the man for the job, none better. You wanted to come with me when the six of us went south, and my father wouldn't allow it, so it's only fair for you to go now.'

Vorardynur smiled back and then sat in silence for a while. The two young men had always got on well and both of them now had some insight into the weight of the decisions Carapethan was called upon to make on a daily basis. Clearing his throat, Vorardynur, sounding slightly awkward, spoke again without looking at Haldur.

'There were a couple of other things I wanted to say while I had the chance. I wanted to thank you for all the help and advice you've given me. I'm sure that wasn't easy, especially knowing I'm going in your place, but thanks for not making me feel any worse about it than I already do. And there's something else I thought you might like to know. When the six of you went off, well, yes, I was angry not to be included. I didn't want to stay here, I... well, to tell you the truth, I felt rather slighted. But the funny thing is, once I got used to it, I was quite glad. It was …' Vorardynur's voice tailed off as he made a vague gesture with his hands. He began again, trying to express what he meant.

'It's difficult to put into words. When I began to get over the disappointment, when I started to understand your father's duties and responsibilities better… He took me with him, when he rode round the dales last summer; my respect for him grew greater every day. And I, well, I began to realise something I would never have believed of myself, that I could take satisfaction from the problems as well as the pleasures of lordship. So now, if Carapethan had said I must stay once more and he was sending you south again, I wouldn't have minded at all. It's strange, isn't it? You want to go, and I'd really rather stay here. We'll have to accept your father's decision, but I wish we could exchange places.'

With a laugh, Haldur clapped his cousin on the back and then took his arm from his shoulders so that he could look at his face. 'Well, I don't. I wish we could both go!'

'Oh, come on. There was never a chance of that. This is hardly the time for Haldan don Vorygwent to start risking a possible new lord-line.'

'They wouldn't need to, not if Asaldron stayed here.'

'Mm. Well, that's true, I suppose.'

'Listen, Vorardynur. I don't know if you realise, but Asaldron's unhappy about going south again. He doesn't want to go. He'll not let you down, but if I were you, I'd keep him close so you can steady him if you have to.'

Vorardynur chewed at his lip, frowning. 'Right, thanks. I'll remember that. Oh by the way, I forgot. I was going to mention this straight away, but then we started talking about other things. The Hound of the Vow himself has come in with the Cunorad.'

'But he can't be going to ride with them!' exclaimed Haldur. 'Why has he left Seth y'n Temenellan?'

'I don't know. As soon as I saw them arriving, I came to find you, but perhaps we should go back to the hall now.'

'Yes, come on.'

The two young men stood up and Haldur strode swiftly off, feeling suddenly much lighter at heart. He had spent hours with Vorardynur over the past months, telling him everything he could think of that might help him in the desperate venture that was planned, but an awkwardness had hovered between them that only their conversation today had dispelled. And now, if he could not see Artorynas again, this unexpected chance to talk once more with old Cunor y'n Temennis was the next best thing. Somehow Haldur found Astell, erudite and learned though he was, rather unapproachable and forbidding. He yearned for the converse of a gentler, unwounded heart, for a kinder wisdom, for the quiet understanding he had always been offered by the Hound of the Vow.

The empty precinct

There it was at last. Artorynas paused for a moment, gazing up the valley. Ahead of him, now no more than another hour's walk distant, lay Seth y'n Temenellan. After all the weary miles of wandering, the days and nights under the open sky, the months with only a turf-built shelter to keep out the winter cold, soon he would be within that ancient precinct. He would show the arrow to the Cunorad, but the details of what he had seen in Asward donn'Ur would be for the ears of the Hound of the Vow only, at least at first. He quickened his pace, eager to embrace the old man once more, to share an exchange of lore, to rest, if only briefly, in the comfort of his serenity. But as he came nearer, doubts began to grow in his mind. There was no-one working in the fields, even though the spring sun shone down and it was the season for sowing and new growth. Perhaps, thought Artorynas as he approached the outer wall of the intake, perhaps the Cunorad had ridden out today and were now far away in some other valley or high on a distant mountainside. Maybe: but why was there no smoke drifting blue on the morning air? The frown lines appeared as Artorynas stared, the amber eyes moving slowly over the old red roofs and mellow walls, the stables, stores, guest-hall, the sanctuary itself. The paths were empty; the buildings seemed deserted. The valley was always quiet, but suddenly he felt its silence oppressive. He was walking through the fields now, looking about him as he went. He saw that all was well-tended: where the new crops were just beginning to show, they had been kept free of weeds; but where were the hens he remembered, who had been free to roam and forage, where were the sheep that used to graze the valley's upper slopes? With beating heart, Artorynas reached the buildings and looked into the stables. They were empty, and he saw at a glance that the horses of the Cunorad were not expected to return to them. There was no water in the troughs, no fodder in the racks, no bedding on the floor. All was swept clean and bare. He looked in the hen-house, the goat byre, the pig sties and saw that these too were all out of use. The various stores seemed intact, if somewhat depleted, but the fuel-stack was full. Although there seemed little point, Artorynas unlatched the door of the guest-hall and glanced around, seeing only what by now he expected: no sign of life. There was only one building left to check now. He could put the moment off no longer. Artorynas walked towards its steps, began to climb them; reached the wide porch, saw the doors before him. They stood open, fastened back wide to the walls. He halted, looking once more into the room he had seen first in a dream long before he ever beheld it in waking life.

The tables and benches were in their accustomed position, but the room was empty of all else. There were no bowls of golden unguent, no garments hanging on the walls, no boots below, no pitcher of water, no lamps on the shelves, nothing. Nothing except what rested upon the table facing him at the higher end of the room, where light shone flickering from a bowl placed at its centre. Artorynas stepped into the room, and as he crossed the threshold a strange sensation passed over him, as if he had gone from one world to another. The air within the room felt different: cold and still, but somehow charged with life. He walked forward and stopped before the bowl of fire, looking down into it. The flames rose and fell within, dancing brightly without sound or source, burning with no fuel upon which to feed and giving off light but no heat. Time unmeasured passed as Artorynas stood there. Eventually he raised his head, turned from the fire and slowly walked out again. He paused outside, looking up at the sky, and suddenly his face changed. It had seemed rapt in some vision, but now it was taut and alert. He ran down the steps of the porch. The sun was westering, but who knew whether this was afternoon of the same day? He remembered well the Hound of the Vow telling him how a man might stay on his feet indefinitely, so long as he was sustained by looking into the heart of the *itanardo*. Artorynas hastened back down the valley as quickly as he could, long strides eating up the way as he began to climb to the lower pass. Why had the Cunorad y'm As-Geg'rastigan gone? Where had they gone? He pressed on through dusk and darkness, following the track by the moonlight reflected from the snowy slopes above, and dawn found him at the gates of a small upland farm tucked into a fold of the hills.

A rooster was crowing in the yard and he heard children's voices; then he saw a man come round a corner of the building carrying two pails. Beside him capered a skinny little black sheepdog and three youngsters, two boys and a girl. Artorynas called out a greeting and the man put down his buckets, the children pressing closer to him as the newcomer approached. A coil of smoke rose up from the house chimney as someone within stoked the fire ready for the new day.

'Good day and good health to you and yours,' said Artorynas. 'Can you tell me why the Hounds of the Starborn have left Rihann y'n Temenellan?'

'They're away to Cotaerdon.' The man stared curiously at Artorynas. Who was this, who seemed to know nothing of recent events? 'Er... You'll be...?'

'My name is Artorynas. I was a guest in Carapethan's hall until last spring. I have been on a journey and now I'm returning to Cotaerdon myself, but why have the Cunorad gone there?'

'Lord Carapethan sent for them. If you've come over from Trothdale, you must have made a very early start. Won't you take a bite to eat? There'll be fresh milk, and my wife would be pleased to put up something for the day, if you're going further.'

Artorynas considered the man before him, a typical son of the Nine Dales: strong, sturdy, open-faced. His fair hair looked as though his wife cut it for him using a bowl to guide her: it stuck damply against his forehead where the sweat of the day's toil already lay. Life was hard, up here in the hills, and yet he had not hesitated to offer hospitality.

'You're very kind, but I can stay only for tidings. What is happening in Cotaerdon?'

The farmer shifted his feet, suddenly uncomfortable. Artorynas... He'd heard that name. This was the fellow who'd gone off on some mysterious errand, the one Carapethan had said would not return... the one they said was *as-ur*. He swallowed audibly and then noticed his children gazing up from him to Artorynas, open-mouthed.

'Here, you three, take the pails and start on the milking while I talk to the gentleman.' They ran off, looking back curiously, and the farmer waited until they had disappeared into a barn before he spoke again. 'Haldur came home and brought word the Nine Dales are in danger. Haldan don Vorygwent decided to send a force south: picked men only. Carapethan sent for the best archers, as well as some who've ridden with the Hounds in their time, and those who're in the Cunorad now.' He jerked his head in the direction of the farm buildings.

'I didn't want to say anything in front of them, but those like us, with small children – we can't leave them, and they're too young to send – we've to be ready to do our bit in defence of our homes. If Vorardynur doesn't come back, we'll know there's nothing for it but to sell our lives as dearly as we can. The wife's as handy with a bow as I am.'

His heart began to race as the implications of all this dawned on Artorynas. A hundred questions clamoured in his mind. 'Vorardynur? Is Haldur not going?'

'No, they say Lord Carapethan wouldn't risk his son again. I heard the young fellow was angry about it, but he couldn't persuade his father. Carapethan refused to let him ride with them.'

'You don't mean they've already gone?' Artorynas was breathless with apprehension, unable to keep the urgency out of his voice.

'Well now, I'm not exactly sure. They might be away, but often it's a while before news comes to us here of what's doing in Cotaerdon, especially this early in the year.'

'When did the Cunorad leave Seth y'n Temenellan?'

'Ah, I can tell you that. It was two days past a week ago. I've some of their hens and sheep here with me; they'd to make arrangements for the livestock, you see, and …'

'A week and more! Sir, forgive me if I seem abrupt, but I must get to Cotaerdon by the quickest possible means. Can you lend me a horse? I'm sorry that I can't offer you anything for its hire, but I give you my word I will have it returned to you immediately.'

The man hesitated and then seemed to change his mind about what he was going to say. He cleared his throat. 'Yes, I've a horse. Over here.' In the stable he untied a very ordinary gelding and handed Artorynas the rope. 'You can be getting to know him while I fetch the tack.'

They emerged into the yard once more and Artorynas began to walk the horse up and down. The farmer hurried off but something made him turn at the door of the tack-room. The sun was still low in the sky and its level beams fell directly upon Artorynas as he circled with the horse. Maybe it was nothing more than the dust stirred up by its hooves, motes that glistened and glinted in the early morning air; but to the farmer it seemed that this tall, lean stranger with amber eyes moved within a nimbus of golden light. His mind made up, he ducked under the low lintel of the house door and when he returned to bring the saddle and bridle, with him came his wife and children. After an awkward silence, the man of the house spoke up.

'There's been talk about you since you first came to the Nine Dales. That Cureleth, he started the rumour, and then everyone was saying it: Artorynas is one of the *as-urad*. I don't reckon to know a lot about these things, but… All my life I've looked for the Hidden People to show themselves, and now today… I think you're more than *as-ur*. You are one of the Starborn.' He made the threefold sign and then spread his hands as if making an offering. 'Lord, if you need a horse, it's yours to take. The honour is mine.'

Artorynas looked at the five faces turned to him. He asked their names, and smiled when he heard them: old-fashioned maybe, but time-honoured with use and repeated a thousand-fold up and down the land. Into his mind came a memory of the old couple who had shown him kindness away up in the Golden Valley, and with it a great love for the Nine Dales and its folk.

'I must go now,' he said, 'every moment counts. But I leave a promise with you: Rihannad Ennar will be safe. I give you my word that no harm will come here.'

Taking up Sleccenal

The time had almost come. Carapethan knew he could put off for only a few moments more the fateful act he had never imagined he would have to perform during his lordship of the Nine Dales. But it was for him, as leader of his people, to call for the ancient sword Sleccenal and arm himself with it in ceremonial and formal indication that a state of war now obtained. All through the weeks of debate and preparation since midwinter, the scene about to be enacted had played itself out in his mind and haunted his dreams. He told himself over and over again that he was not the aggressor: that if Vorynaas had assailed them without warning, he would not have hesitated to take up the sword and rally all to the defence of their homeland. It was only the warning that made the difference, he argued inwardly; all it meant was that they were striking before they could be struck: after all, they knew for certain that the blow was coming. When he thought of all Haldur had told them, of the darkness and despair in the south, of the horror of

Assynt y'm Atrannaas, of the treachery his embassy had so narrowly escaped, of the unwarranted attack planned upon him, his doubts would be swept away in a confident surge of anger and certainty. And then he would wonder whether they were mad to think the small force he was sending could possibly succeed, whether the strategy they had decided upon was the merest fantasy, a wild delusion, and all the doubts would come flooding back. The discord between himself and Haldur had also upset and disturbed him, and the Hound of the Vow had not helped, either. Carapethan had looked for words of comfort and reassurance from the old man, for his help in reconciling Haldur to his lot, but he had been disappointed. Instead, Cunor y'n Temennis had irritated him by supporting the idea of waiting for Artorynas to return, suggesting that if he brought the arrow with him, matters might wear a different face.

That was a cunning seed to plant in my mind, thought Carapethan. He knows me well: he knows I do not want to take up Sleccenal, and seeks to make me hope that this mysterious arrow will save me from that choice. There he sits now, with Astell and Haldur near him, of course: dreamers, dealers in riddles. Who knows what visions of unreality they have conjured before my son's eyes. Well, they will find out what I have told him: those who go seeking Asward donn'Ur do not return. And we cannot wait; speed and surprise are our main hope. I must give the word, now. He looked over those before him: Vorardynur, the Hound of the Vow with the twelve Cunorad behind him, Astell, his other senior counsellors from Haldan don Vorygwent, Asaldron and those who would be leading companies when the expedition set off, Haldur. My son, thought Carapethan. Whatever happens, I will keep my son beside me. If things turn out as we hope, he will see that my decision was right and all will be well between us once more; but if the worst should come to the worst in the end, then we will stand together and die together. For a long moment, he and his son gazed at each other, not heeding the others present. Then Carapethan gathered himself. How much time had passed, while he sat in silence? Maybe not more than a moment or two, longer though it seemed to him. He stood up, and all eyes followed him.

'Open the doors,' said Carapethan.

Men pushed them back, and the sunlight streamed in. All followed Carapethan as he emerged from his hall; they spread out beside him on the porch and looked down at those who had been waiting outside. At the foot of the steps were the archers and riders, the members of the lord's household and a great crowd of folk from Cotaerdon and nearby villages. A kind of sigh rose from them as Carapethan raised his hand.

'Bring me Sleccenal.'

As they waited, Haldur could feel his own heart beating. Then Vorardynur returned, bearing the ancient bronze sword. He laid it before Carapethan. The lord of the Nine Dales stared down at it like a man in a dream and then turned wordlessly to Vorardynur, who lifted the swordbelt over his uncle's head. Carapethan eased it on his right shoulder, adjusted the buckles, settled the belt at his hips, felt the empty scabbard against his left thigh. Now his eyes were fixed on the sword once more. Take it, he said to himself, take it. In that last moment of hesitation, some part of his mind registered the sound of hoof-beats, a headlong gallop as someone rode at frantic speed towards them through the empty streets of the town. It woke a memory in Carapethan of the night when he had sent men to fetch Haldur back from his farewell to Artorynas. The noise came nearer. Carapethan looked up, caught his wife's eye, noticed heads turning at the back of the crowd. He put out his hand, wrapped his fingers round the hilt of the sword, felt the amber pommel warming in his grasp. He lifted Sleccenal, and heard the intake of breath from those watching. He steadied himself to speak the words required by tradition.

'This is Sleccenal, the Releaser, the Freedom-Giver. I am Carapethan, by your consent Lord of Rihannad Ennar. Before you all, I ...'

He paused for what seemed an eternity. Another memory had flashed into his mind. The last time I held this sword was the day I showed it to Artorynas, he thought; and with that memory came the recollection also of words spoken then by both of them. He forced himself to go on.

'Before you all, I now…'

The attention of his audience was distracted by confusion and movement behind them. A spent horse stumbled to a halt in a cloud of dust, head hanging, flanks heaving; and the man who had thrown himself from it was desperately pushing his way through the people towards the hall. Who was this, this fellow with no respect for the solemnity of the occasion? With a fierce glare, Carapethan raised the sword. Do it, just do it, he told himself. Finish the words, set the sword in the scabbard and there will be no going back.

'I now… I now take…'

'Wait, wait!'

At the foot of the steps stood Artorynas. Thin and wayworn though he was, there was something in his face that checked Carapethan, an authority in his voice that all heard. 'Lord Carapethan, there is something you should see before you take up Sleccenal before your people. I bring this with me from Asward donn'Ur.'

He held up the arrow. It blazed in the sun, the sky-steel at its point as brilliant as a star of noon. A ripple of movement, like barley bending in the wind, passed across the throng as every hand moved in the sign. Carapethan glanced quickly round and was struck more than anything by the demeanour of the Cunorad y'm As-Gegrastigan and of those others who had ridden with them in their time. Suddenly it came forcibly home to him what a devastating impression they might make on an unprepared foe, especially… yes, he had to admit it to himself, especially if Artorynas was at their head. He looked again at the arrow and for the first time a small glow of hope warmed his heart. Slowly and deliberately he laid down Sleccenal and looked Artorynas in the eye.

'This is a day that I think will always be remembered among us while men still live in Rihannad Ennar,' he said; and then he too made the sign.

Decisions revoked

Within hours, the news was spreading up and down the valley and Cotaerdon itself was working like an ant-heap as rumour and speculation were given full rein. Clearly there would be a delay of at least a day or two now, as plans were revised; and trade was brisk in taverns and eating-houses where people gathered to gossip. Meanwhile Carapethan was closeted with his counsellors and it was not long before he found himself wrestling with a new problem. Artorynas had joined them to hear an account of Haldur's embassy to the south and to relate in turn how he had fared on his own quest. This narrative had been brief and unadorned with much detail, but Carapethan had noticed the reactions of Astell and the Hound of the Vow in particular to certain points. Eventually the discussion turned to those who were to march upon Caradward.

'Do you think we are courting disaster, to send so few?' asked Vorardynur. 'Have we any hope of success?'

'You have every hope, given who is to go and what you tell me of how matters stand in the south,' said Artorynas. Then he turned to Cunor y'n Temennis. 'Will you permit those who once rode in the Cunorad to be as one with them when the time comes? A day of destiny approaches: when it dawns, will you let them too array themselves in the gold?'

Carapethan switched his attention to the Hound of the Vow. The old man seemed rejuvenated: he looked like a man who had been granted his heart's desire. His faded brown eyes lingered on Artorynas' face as he answered.

'If you wish it my lord, then certainly they may do so. May we hope that you will ride with them?'

All around the room, men leaned forward. The question to which all of them most wanted an answer had now been asked. Artorynas exchanged a brief glance with Astell before he spoke.

'Haldur asked that I should come back here, when my errand was over,' he said. 'I have kept one promise today, but now I have another vow to fulfil. I must keep my oath to Arval. By some strange chance, I returned to you before it was too late, and my way also now lies south. Those who go to Caradward will be riding with me, rather than I with them.'

The air of relief in the room was almost palpable. They sat back, smiling at each other, filled with new hope. But it seemed Artorynas had not finished speaking.

'I have a request to make, Lord Carapethan,' he said. 'I have been told that your son is to remain here. I urge you to reconsider this decision.'

Haldur had been sitting with downcast eyes, but at this he looked with almost painful entreaty at his father, the colour flooding into his face. Carapethan's thick fair brows came down; the bright blue eyes were fierce.

'No! My decision is final and I will not change it: Haldur will stay here. Vorardynur will go in his place.'

Vorardynur shifted awkwardly in his chair. 'Uncle, I would happily remain in Cotaerdon if it meant that Haldur might go. He and I have spoken, and I know…'

'There will be no more discussion of this!' Carapethan brought his fist down to emphasise his point and an uneasy silence followed.

'In that case, I have something else to ask,' said Artorynas. 'I was given generous assistance by a farmer in the hills between here and Rihann y'n Temenellan. He is a poor man with a young family who helped me without hesitation and I have ruined his horse in my haste to get here in time. Will you replace it for him? May I go now to choose another animal to send to him with my thanks?'

'Of course, of course,' rumbled Carapethan. 'We'll talk later. I shall want to know his name and I'll add something of my own to show my gratitude too.'

Artorynas left the room but the tension within it barely diminished; indeed it increased when Astell's voice was heard. His face seemed even more predatory than usual as he turned his penetrating stare upon Carapethan.

'We all understand your wish that Haldur should stay here,' said Astell, 'but you are the father of your people as well as the father of your son, even as I am lorekeeper of Rihannad Ennar as well as simply one of its folk. I speak now in that capacity. As it is worse than violence that threatens us, so it is more than a conventional military array that we send in response. In our time of darkest danger, we have had recourse to subtlety rather than brute force; and I wonder whether we would have been bold enough, or wise enough, to make this choice, if Artorynas had not lived among us. If we had heard only the tales of those who fled to us from Gwent y'm Aryframan, would we have sent an embassy to the south? Yet it was as a result of this decision that we gained a warning and time to act upon it. Now, at the very moment when you were about to take up Sleccenal, Artorynas has come back to us. Can we dismiss this as mere chance?

'Carapethan, I see your unwillingness to wear the sword of war and I honour your reluctance: you have never forgotten the lessons of *Stirfellaerdon donn'Ur*. I see also that you thought Artorynas would not return, but I pass no judgement upon this error: there were others who made the same mistake. Yet he is here again, one who has walked upon Porthesc nan Esylt, one who has beheld wonders we can only dream of. He has found the arrow of his quest and we have seen it, this awesome thing made by the very hands of the Starborn. Your men will ride behind him who bears it! Do you not think he must have good reason to ask you to send Haldur also? Do you not think it worthwhile even to find out what that reason is? I perceive that Artorynas will seek you out again and when he does, I urge you, Carapethan, to put your love for the Nine Dales above all else in your heart.'

Customary though it was for men to speak their minds before the lord of Rihannad Ennar, none of those present would have dared to address Carapethan as Astell had just done. They waited uneasily for what might happen next. Haldur glanced at Cunor y'n Temennis and saw that the old man was watching his father with affection and understanding. Carapethan sat silent, determined to master his emotions before he answered Astell. He had barely contained his anger at some of what the lorekeeper had said, but could not deny that he had made some telling points. That final barb about the Nine Dales had been well aimed. Carapethan's heart bled within him from fear at what might befall his beloved land if he made a wrong choice now. At the same time he was assailed by painful memories of other confrontations with Astell, other pronouncements he had made: all enigmatic, all ambiguous, all filling him with dread for his son. Who can I turn to, thought Carapethan. I must stay strong. It will bring bad luck if I show weakness now on the very eve of departure, but if ever a man needed counsel and guidance, that man is myself. He looked up, straight into the kindly eyes of the Hound of the Vow, and his brow cleared. It was more than he could manage to smile at Astell, but he turned to him calmly.

'Thank you; you have spoken well, as befits the lorekeeper of Rihannad Ennar, and I will consider carefully what you have said. Meanwhile, I wish to speak with Cunor y'n Temennis, alone.' He glanced around the rest of the company. 'It may be that I will want us all to meet again later, so please be ready if I send word.'

They got to their feet and moved towards the door, some of them muttering together as they went. Haldur lingered, but his father's gaze was directed downwards and he left with the others. As soon as they were alone, Carapethan opened his hands in appeal to the old man.

'*Tell-avar*, advise me!'

The Hound of the Vow smiled. 'First let me acclaim you on two counts: for laying down Sleccenal, and for keeping your temper with Astell. But now, there is something you need to know. Bringing the Cunorad here to Cotaerdon at your call meant leaving Seth y'n Temenellan with none to tend it. Yet though its doors stand wide and it lies empty, open to the air and the sky, it is not unguarded. I have invoked the unseen protection of the *itanardo*, the fire that feeds only upon itself: no locks or bars are needed while it burns within. That fire will live until we return, and while it burns, none from among the Earthborn may cross the threshold. But the As-

Geg'rastigan may pass, if they will; and one has done so.' Cunor y'n Temennis paused, and held Carapethan's eye. He spoke gently. 'Artorynas entered in, to stand before the firebowl. He came to us as one of the *as-urad*, and so he left us: but I have to tell you that he returns numbered among the Starborn. Now, you tell me, *gerast-is*: do you still need my advice?'

Carapethan sat mulling over what the old man had told him. 'I saw it in his eyes when he stood before me with the arrow,' he said at last, 'but it comes to me now that even before that, I realised when I saw how the Cunorad looked at him. They know, don't they? And Astell, too… He made me angry today, but he was right, as he often is. I should listen to whatever reason Artorynas has for wanting Haldur with him.' Carapethan smiled ruefully, even rather sadly.

'I'm sure you're aware that my lorekeeper and I frequently don't see eye to eye; in fact on the very day that Artorynas left Cotaerdon last year, he… well, I was angry then too, and he said things that alarmed me. But the truth is, he will be a difficult man to replace when the time comes. That day is probably still far off, but it is a thing I sometimes think of. If only Heredcar had lived, Haldur could have followed Astell as his brother would have followed me. Of course, in life matters rarely turn out so neatly, and Haldur now follows a different path, albeit not one his heart would have chosen. Ah well, no man can turn back time.' Carapethan turned to the Hound of the Vow.

'You know, I think I see the way forward with Astell. He is a learned man, and I would be foolish not to utilise his insight. I will let him select his own successor and encourage him to do it soon, so that the apprentice may learn from the master for as long as possible.'

Cunor y'n Temennis noticed how much more like his old self Carapethan sounded. The decisive manner, the pragmatic judgement, the shrewd assessment of himself as much as others had all returned.

'You see, my advice was not necessary after all; you have taken your own counsel,' he said. 'I think I may foretell that you will be remembered as well worthy to lead Rihannad Ennar.'

Hearing the smile in his voice, Carapethan smiled back at the old man, cheered by a twinkle in the newly-bright eyes. No need to wonder any more at his air of youth renewed, when the great hope of his lifetime had at last been rewarded.

'If so, credit should be given to your guidance of me, *tell-avar*,' he said.

With that, the two of them embraced like father and son; and then, drawing his dark blue robes close against the cold spring night, the Hound of the Vow left Carapethan to await the return of Artorynas.

At last he came, alone and quietly.

'Carapethan, I owe you an explanation for the request I made. If I ask you to let your son leave your side once more, then both as father and lord you deserve to know the reason.' Artorynas placed the arrow between them where the lamplight played upon it.

'When we reach Caradriggan, if all is to be fulfilled as it should be, then this arrow must find its target. There is only one man whose skill is equal to the task, and that is Haldur. Only if Haldur's hand and eye set the arrow on its way will it fly true to the gold, and then all will be well. I ask you again, Lord Carapethan: let Haldur ride south.'

Carapethan stared at the arrow as if fascinated while Artorynas' words echoed ominously in his head like the mutter of thunder in the mountains, far-off but threatening. *Only one man… all will be well… true to the gold*. He dragged his gaze from the arrow, forced himself to look at Artorynas, and met the golden eyes as steadily as he could.

'Very well.' His voice sounded strange in his own ears and he began again. 'Very well, Haldur may go with you. Vorardynur shall stay here in his place.'

'My lord, no. If Haldur is to go, then Vorardynur must go also. Haldur will need his help: Vorardynur must be with him. Let Asaldron stay here with you.'

'Both of them!' Carapethan had never expected this; he shook his head, not as if forbidding it, but as if dazed by what he was being asked to permit.

'I give you the promise of the As-Geg'rastigan that both Haldur and Vorardynur will return to Rihannad Ennar. I swear it to you.'

Artorynas spoke quietly, but Carapethan heard it again in his voice, that new note of authority he had half-recognised in the moment of Artorynas' dramatic return that afternoon. So short a time ago! And already the world had shifted under their feet: Carapethan knew instinctively that some hidden line had been crossed, another boundary to divide the rest of his life from what had gone before. He drew a deep breath, unable to prevent it sounding like a heartfelt sigh.

'Thank you, I am grateful. I should say also that… You know how reluctant I was to call for the sword and I am glad that your appearance meant I could lay it aside. At least I do not have that on my conscience.' Carapethan sighed again and then spoke in more robust tones than before. 'Very well then, both Vorardynur and Haldur may go, and let Asaldron stay here in Cotaerdon.'

And so it was that within the week, Carapethan stood on the steps of his hall as those who were to set out assembled below him. Word of Artorynas' return had flown to such effect that more had come in who once rode with the Cunorad; so that now, with these reinforcements and the addition of Haldur and Artorynas himself, two hundred riders prepared to depart. Two hundred! What can two hundred hope to do, groaned Carapethan inwardly. Have I taken leave of my senses, to permit this? He glanced around him. Vorardynur, rather pale but resolute; Asaldron, his relief not quite disguised by an air of newly-acquired responsibility; Haldur, wrapped in a kind of solemn elation, that faraway look, so familiar to his father, in his eye: three young men who thought themselves happy, now that their wishes had been granted. The morning air was fresh and keen, the early spring sunlight shone down, gleaming on the golden-brown coats of the small, swift horses of the Hounds of the Starborn. The Cunorad looked to none but Artorynas, and Carapethan saw that it was upon him also that the gaze of Astell and Cunor y'n Temennis rested. I wonder, he thought,

I wonder if they too know what I have been told. In the deep blue of earliest dawn, while the stars of morning were still in the sky, Artorynas had sought out the lord of the Nine Dales where he waited for the day, unable to sleep. Even as Carapethan gave the word, even as the two hundred began to move, even as they rode away and the dust of their going settled like a pall on those left behind with only their hopes and fears for company, still he heard Artorynas' voice in his heart.

'I come to say farewell, Carapethan. I promise you once more, your son will come safe home and Vorardynur with him. But you and I will not meet again. For me there is no return to Rihannad Ennar.'

CHAPTER 58

No more secrets

'It'll be all right, I know it will. He'll come, we've just got to wait.'

Haldur and Vorardynur were sitting on an old log near the river bank. The broad water flowed placidly along, curving in a wide bend; over the passing years, as its course had gradually changed, it had left behind it within the curve a water-meadow whose flat surface was divided into a series of terraces by the ancient river banks. Here, on the higher levels and also within the trees, the force was encamped. From where Haldur sat, he could see people moving to and fro, watering the horses, checking equipment, preparing whatever they would eat that evening; but they went about their tasks quietly. Around them the endless miles of forest whispered, and the golden calm of mid-afternoon lay over all. No-one would ever have guessed that the two hundred were there: secret, silent, purposeful. Waiting. Haldur picked up a small stone and threw it into the river in frustration. He was worried enough as it was, without having to listen to other people's fears; he had come out from the camp to sit by the river, hoping that solitude would help him to set his thoughts in some kind of order, and now here was Vorardynur, fretting because there was no sign of Sigitsinen.

'And another thing,' persisted Vorardynur. 'Ten men, from the forest? Only ten? We're going to be in a mess if we can't count on better support than that.'

Haldur sighed. 'Look, they all came from the refuge we escaped to when Sigitsinen rescued us. I told you before, there's only about thirty people living there altogether: they wouldn't be able to spare more and still keep the place going. The ten who've joined us were all slaves at the mine; we'll be glad to have them with us when the time comes.'

'What about this Cunoreth fellow? From what you said, back in Cotaerdon, I thought he'd be coming to join us too.'

'Vorardynur, I *don't know*. Anything could have happened to him over the winter. You were there when Haldas told us they've not seen him for quite a while in the forest. But regardless of that, he'd not have been bringing comrades with him here. He's based in another hideout, a long way off. If all goes well with us, no doubt his folk will come down from the hills to play their part.' Haldur threw another stone into the river.

'Until it's time to take the mine, we can't risk moving nearer to it than this; but as long as we stay quiet within Maesaldron, the forest will keep us safe from the Caradwardans and I want to talk to Sigitsinen before we go any further, if I possibly can. We weren't expecting what Haldas told us, were we, that Valahald found out we knew about the invasion plans? We need to know what's happening now; and placed as he is, Sigitsinen will have inside information. And so we'll wait.'

'But we can't wait!' Vorardynur gestured at the sky above them, where the sun's warmth was increasing by the day. 'Time's going on: if we skulk in the forest indefinitely we're going to throw away the chance of taking them by surprise, and that's one of the few advantages we've got.'

'I didn't say we'd wait indefinitely. If we can get fresh news about how things stand, a short delay will be worth it. But if we can't, then we'll just have to move into action as planned. We're only about three days' journey from the valley where the mine is.'

'Is Artorynas happy enough to wait, then?' asked Vorardynur.

'Well, I think for him,' said Haldur slowly, 'for him… His main concern is whatever awaits us in Caradriggan. So since, in order to succeed there, the plan is to take the mine first, I assume it follows that if he was concerned about our chances of doing that, he'd say so.'

'Mm.' Vorardynur sat in silence for a few moments, making no comment on this, and then he changed the subject slightly. 'I wonder how Valahald got the truth out of Heranar? It must have been him, mustn't it? He wouldn't have told anyone else he'd tipped you off, surely.'

'Who, Heranar? Not in a hundred years. He probably gave himself away… The last time I saw him, he was in a terrible state, practically writhing with panic at what he'd done. Valahald would be quick to spot anything like that and apply the necessary pressure.'

'You mean you think he tortured him? His own brother?'

Haldur laughed grimly. 'I'm sure he wouldn't hesitate, if he thought it was necessary. The rumour was he'd already killed their father. It was never proved, as far as I know, but you could see no-one had any difficulty believing it. Poor Heranar! He was completely out of his depth – but by now he'll probably be dead. I wonder what's happened to his family.'

To Haldur's great relief, Sigitsinen did indeed join them a few days later, appearing round the upstream bend of the river in a small coracle.

'Saves time,' he said. 'It's light enough to carry on my back on the trail over the pass and then it's faster to travel by water than on my feet. See, I was right that you'd come to help us, wasn't I? How many of you are there? I'm glad you waited until I could get here. There's a lot you need to know.'

'Yes, we've heard enough already to realise that. And we've got something to tell you, too.' Haldur's voice was gleeful. 'There's someone with us I think you'll be surprised to see. Remember how you told me you wished Artorynas could come to us? Well, he's here now!'

'Artorynas?' Sigitsinen straightened up from gathering his things out of the coracle, obviously at a loss. He looked doubtfully round at the men who had come down to the river to meet him.

'No, that's my cousin Vorardynur,' said Haldur, introducing them with a grin, 'and this is Cureleth. You've met Aestrontor before.'

227

'Yes,' said Sigitsinen, shaking hands in greeting but looking now beyond Haldur towards the camp. They saw his pale eyes suddenly widen in shock. 'You've brought *women* with you?'

'Oh yes.' Haldur glanced over his shoulder. 'That's Esylto, but you'll hear her called Cunor y'm Esc, because she's here as one of the Cunorad y'm As-Geg'rastigan. All twelve of them are riding with us, and there are other women too among those who were once numbered in the Hounds of the Starborn and who answered my father's call. But our archers are all bowmen, the best from every valley in the Nine Dales.'

Sigitsinen stood there, his gear slung over his shoulder, and stared at Esylto as if he could hardly believe his eyes. He had never seen any woman so beautiful, but it was an apprehension, almost a kind of dread, rather than desire that woke in him. Suddenly it struck him: if the rest of the Cunorad were of similar kind, what terror might they inspire in those who saw them? But Haldur was taking his arm, pulling him forward, talking about Artorynas. An uneasy shiver ran over Sigitsinen at the name. How could this be the Artorynas whose name was whispered in hope? How could he be here, hidden in the secret depths of the forest? Baffled, he left his belongings in the tent they showed him and hurried to catch up with Haldur, who had continued ahead and was now talking to someone partly hidden from view as people moved to and fro. Then this man stood up, and Sigitsinen saw who it was.

For one wild moment, Sigitsinen wondered if he was the victim of some strange enchantment of the forest, under some spell such as those the children of Caradward were brought up to fear. First Esylto, and now this... this face from the past... Was he awake or was this just a dream? Did he look upon a ghost or a living man? He gaped at the dark hair with the white lock at the temple, the amber eyes, the small scar on the lip... How could it be anyone else, and yet... The face was subtly different: stronger, sadder, sparer... but years had gone by, after all... Say something, Sigitsinen told himself, don't stand here staring as if you've lost your wits...

'Maesrhon?' It came out as no more than a croak. The man exchanged a half-smile with Haldur and the truth dawned on Sigitsinen.

'Maesrhon – it's you, *you're* Artorynas! When you said Artorynas would return, you meant yourself! And now you're coming back! But where have you been?' A new idea struck Sigitsinen. 'The forest… Have you been in Maesaldron all the time after all? I thought… My kin in the south were sure it was you, but the traveller they helped disappeared into the marshes…'

Artorynas smiled. 'No, I've not been in the forest. I've been journeying for more than five years, searching… But the search is over now and it is time for me to return to Caradriggan. Haldur has business there, as you know; and so have I.'

Sigitsinen felt his hair lift slightly as he heard a change in Artorynas' voice; but then its warmth returned as he smiled at Haldur again. 'But it hasn't all been lonely wandering. I spent almost two years in the Nine Dales, to whose friendship and help I owe much.'

'You've been in Rihannad Ennar? But then…' Sigitsinen turned to Haldur. 'That must mean you already knew each other! Why didn't you tell me? I told you about Maesrhon: I mentioned Artorynas, but you never said anything.'

'I know, I'm sorry. It was because of a promise I had made to my father, never to reveal that we knew of Artorynas in the Nine Dales.'

Sigitsinen said nothing, frowning as he looked from Haldur to Artorynas. Haldur's face fell: he felt as though he had somehow let Sigitsinen down.

'It wasn't that I didn't trust you,' he insisted, willing Sigitsinen to understand. 'I wanted to confide in you, but we all, all six of us who travelled south, we all swore an oath before witnesses that we would say nothing. It was so that Vorynaas wouldn't suspect our motives, so that we wouldn't put our homeland at risk.' He ran his hands through his hair. 'Things haven't turned out that way in the end, of course. But

Artorynas is here now, he's here with us, so we've no more secrets from each other.'

'See if you recognise these.'

Artorynas intervened, drawing one of the slim throwing-knives from the side of his boot and offering the hilt to Sigitsinen; and in his other hand showing him a small box made of horn, its lid open to reveal needles, hooks, a sawing-wire. Once more Sigitsinen found himself at a loss for words. He looked up from examining the items.

'But these… these are from my father's workshop! These are work of his skill, and my brother's also. I remember we looked at them together, when we were training in Rigg'ymvala, but you didn't buy anything even though my father thought… So how is it you have these?'

'I sent another man to purchase in my place, with silver my grandfather had given me,' said Artorynas. 'I saw how disappointed your father was, but I hope he was pleased with the sales he eventually made, even though he never knew the goods were for me. They have all served me well.'

Sigitsinen laughed, his greenish-grey eyes brightening with pleasure as he handed the things back. 'No more secrets, eh? Well, well. I hope I get the chance to tell the old man, one day. You're right, he will be pleased.' He laughed again, and clapped a relieved Haldur on the back. 'Well, I suppose we'd better get down to business and make some plans. Oh – but hold on a moment.' He turned back to Artorynas.

'You've been gone five years and more, and you said you'd been searching? What was it you were searching for?'

'For this,' said Artorynas, laying the arrow before Sigitsinen. A sudden stillness seemed to fall upon them, as if for one moment the afternoon stayed its progress towards evening. The sunlight played upon the silver of the arrow's shaft, the red gold of its feathers, the white gold and sky-steel at its point. Sigitsinen felt dazed: how many more suprises was the day going to bring? Then he looked up into

Artorynas' golden eyes, and another shock hit him. He was jolted into an exclamation in the Outland tongue as he made the sign; but Artorynas took his hand and smiled.

'No more secrets,' he said.

Into action

Haldur had half-expected Sigitsinen to be concerned that there were so few of them, but it seemed this was not so. He paused briefly to watch the archers at their practice and looked with interest and approval at the small, tough little golden-coated horses they had brought. But all the time they walked about the camp, even while they lent a hand to pull in the fish-traps from the river in preparation for the evening meal, his eyes were drawn to the Cunorad and most of all to Artorynas. Eventually it was time to eat: there were Haldur, Vorardynur and Artorynas, with Aestrontor, Cureleth and the other company leaders; the twelve Cunorad sitting together; Haldas, slightly apart from the others; and Sigitsinen. Most of the food was fresh, and came from the forest or the river. It was the time of year for nesting waterbirds and fresh new growth, so there were green shoots and eggs in abundance together with fish, cooked in the ground ovens together with a small allowance each of meal baked into flatbread. Sigitsinen rummaged among what he had taken from his coracle and produced a bag of dried fruit.

'A present for you from Hafromoro,' he said with a grin. 'You knew what you were doing when you flattered her cooking.'

'It wasn't flattery, I meant what I said,' replied Haldur. He smiled a little sadly. 'I wonder if she and her husband will ever be able to go back to running an inn, even if it's not the one she spoke of, the *Corn Dolly*. All this' – he waved his hand around their encampment – 'all this will be worth it, it seems to me, if only the Hafromoros of this world can be free and content once more. But nothing will ever be quite the same as it was, no man can turn back time. Now,' and he turned to Sigitsinen, putting the moment of introspection behind him, 'maybe you're thinking we're being a bit reckless with our stores, eating bread with our supper, when as you've seen we don't have much meal with us. Well, we've travelled light deliberately. We're counting on restocking from what we find at the mine. To do that, we've got to take the mine. And to do *that*, we're trusting to the advantage of a surprise attack and the panic we hope it will cause, rather than weight of numbers. With the mine in our hands, the idea was to move down the valley and secure the bridge before assailing Caradriggan, while meanwhile the rising began behind us in Gwent y'm Aryframan. But we've already heard from Haldas here that somehow Valahald found out we knew about the plan to invade the Nine Dales and I imagine this changes things significantly. We need to know whatever you can tell us about what Valahald's up to now, and how things stand back there.'

'Well, you can leave Valahald out of your reckoning, for a start. He's dead.'

'What! *Valahald's* dead? We thought probably Heranar…'

'Yes, it's not what you'd expect, is it?' Sigitsinen laughed briefly and without much mirth. 'You've given me one shock after another today, so it's only fair I should surprise you in turn. I'll tell you what I can about what happened. As you'll guess, things moved pretty rapidly once you'd escaped. Valahald came north from Framstock to take over the investigation, but that wasn't all he took over. Heranar was relieved of his duties, demoted from his status as governor, and by the year's end he was imprisoned in Framstock; but unfortunately for him, when the alarm was raised he'd panicked and sent off his wife and children to her own family: no doubt he thought they'd be safely out of the way there. Valahald of course has always been suspicious by nature and he smelled a rat immediately. As soon as Heranar was under lock and key in Framstock, he had Ilmarynvoro and the children brought back from her father's place. I expect his idea was to question her and Heranar separately, hoping they'd incriminate each other, and it does seem to have worked, although obviously we'll never know exactly how it was…

'After you told me, last autumn, that Heranar had revealed the invasion plan to you, we thought we might have to get him away somehow, but he was incarcerated in Framstock before we'd had the chance. Then about a month ago, we heard he was to be sent to Assynt y'm Atrannaas. Well, whatever he may have done in the past, he didn't deserve that; so we got one of our men, an Outlander who's been attached to my group of irregulars as part of the recent postings up north, included in the escort. It was a long shot, but we thought maybe this Sigisstir might be able to rescue him after the others had forced him towards the dark.

'But things never got that far, because who should turn up but Valahald. Couldn't resist the chance to gloat, by the looks of it. He took over the escort, but when they got to the place where the prisoners are made to go on alone, he started taunting Heranar. He said…'

Sigitsinen stopped speaking suddenly, breaking eye contact with his listeners. He picked up his cup and drank before continuing, and though the others seemed not to notice anything strange, it struck Haldur, when Sigitsinen continued, that he had decided to leave something out of his account.

'Sigisstir, I mean, said Heranar just seemed to crack. Well of course more prisoners than not run wild at the end, throw themselves on the soldiers rather than walk into the dark, so probably Valahald assumed this was what Heranar intended, and expected his guards to kill him. But apparently Heranar never hesitated: he went straight for his brother. Planted his boot right where it hurts most, leapt on him where Valahald was moaning on the ground, got him round the throat with his knee in his back and broke his neck.

'You'll be wondering: what were the guards doing? And the answer is, nothing. Stood there and watched; not one of them raised a finger to help Valahald. Interesting, eh? Next thing, Heranar jumps to his feet and makes to run off, but Sigisstir grabbed him. Better to keep an eye on him rather than have him at large where he'd be as much of a danger to others as to himself, so Sigisstir took them all off into the wilds as fast as he could and eventually they managed to make it up north and linked up with the Salfgard folk, which is where they are now – well except for Sigisstir, obviously, and also for Heranar. Apparently *he's* since vanished without trace, and let's just hope he stays that way. So Cunoreth's people have gained six fully armed and trained recruits – and you'll remember one of them, Haldur: Temenghent, who used to be based at Seth y'n Carad? Valahald had him transferred to his own staff for some reason, but it seems he was glad enough of the chance to change sides – and Sigisstir's back at base. Officially, he's under something of a cloud. We want him to be able to continue working with us, naturally, so he had to concoct some tale about being overpowered and kidnapped before managing to escape. He got Temenghent to rough him up a bit to make it look convincing – when I saw him he'd got an impressive black eye. He's been temporarily demoted from patrols, but our commanding officer Naasigits will make sure it's not for long. He's one of ours too, as I told you before.'

They sat for a few moments, digesting all this. It came home forcibly to Vorardynur what a fine line they were treading between success and disaster. One false move, one captive forced to speak, and all would be lost.

'What happened after Valahald's death was discovered?' he asked.

'Well, this is the best bit, although you might not think so at first hearing,' said Sigitsinen. 'Valahald had put a man called Wicursal in Heranar's place as a temporary measure and it looks as though he'll keep this position. He's ambitious, but not particularly bright: he'll do what he's told. And the man doing the telling is Valestron, who's taken over from Valahald. Top brass, right enough, and the reason is that since they know that by now you in the Nine Dales are forewarned of the invasion, they've decided to bring the attack forward. Valestron's already in Framstock overseeing the plans. He's brought troops with him from

Rigg'ymvala and more are to follow. Wicursal and his men are working flat out to establish a huge forward base: stores, equipment, temporary living quarters, the lot; and the plan is to surge north at speed towards the end of the summer. They reckon that with back-up in place, and with numbers and surprise on their side, they can risk a late advance. "In Cotaerdon by autumn" is what they're telling each other.'

'You'd better explain what you think's good about that.' Aestrontor's voice was grim; Cureleth looked stricken and Haldur was staring at the ground, frowning.

'It makes things easier once you get to Caradriggan,' said Sigitsinen. 'With Heranwark practically emptied, the city will be defended mainly by conscripts. My feeling is they'll crumble as soon as you appear, and remember our own men will be waiting for the moment to intervene. Once Caradriggan's in your hands, then Valestron and his forces will be effectively cut off. They'll have to rush back south, and our people will rise behind them. And don't forget what I told you about the disaffection among the regulars – didn't raise a finger to save Valahald, did they?'

Haldur was apparently still deep in thought, but eventually the lengthening silence caught his attention and he looked up to find his comrades all watching him, evidently waiting for his reaction to what Sigitsinen had told them.

'I remember poor Cathasar saying he thought Temenghent was half-tempted to come down with us to Tellgard, when we went to talk to Arval,' he said, 'and it seems maybe that was right, if he's thrown his lot in with us now. Let's hope the other hints of similar kind we picked up during our time in the south turn out the same way, because it certainly looks as though we're going to need all the help we can get. But in a way, this news about what the Caradwardans are planning now doesn't really change anything, for us. We always knew we only had one chance: we either succeed, or we die. So that brings us back to our first objective, taking the mine. Can we do it, with the small numbers we have here?'

'Well, I've something else to tell you first,' said Sigitsinen. 'In a couple of days' time, a detachment is due to arrive at the mine to transport a consignment of gold back to Caradriggan. My advice would be to edge nearer to the Lissa'pathor, so your scouts can let you know when it's been and gone; and once it's well away, that's the time to make your move.'

'Surely it would be better to attack while they're at the mine loading up?' suggested Cureleth. 'Why let them go back to Caradriggan, when we could at least thin the ranks of its defenders, even if it's not by that many men?'

'Because this way, we keep our advantage of surprise,' answered Vorardynur before Sigitsinen could say anything. 'If we knock out this transport, someone will want to know why it hasn't come back from the mine, and will likely send to find out. Not to mention the fact that if even one man escapes us, he'll raise the alarm – and I'd say these bullion consignments are well guarded, Sigitsinen?'

'Yes, by heavily-armed troops.'

'Vorardynur's right. And let them take their gold away too, it means nothing to us.' Haldur smiled suddenly, his gaze sweeping round to take in Artorynas and Esylto with the Cunorad beside her. 'We have our own, more precious by far.'

Sigitsinen followed his glance and again felt his hair rising slightly. *In my wildest dreams*, he thought, *I would never have imagined that Haldur would come out of the north with companions such as these.*

'Indeed you have,' he said, 'and to answer your earlier question, there is no doubt in my mind that you will carry the day. Haldas here, and those he brings with him who endured the living death of slavery at the mine, are your guarantee of that. But I tell you now, no matter how many may rally to your cause, it is the two hundred who will give the name to any legends that are handed down from today, Na Devocatron whose story will be told in years yet to come.'

And so next day, after Sigitsinen went back to keep up his cover with the auxiliaries, they struck camp and moved stealthily through the forest, nearer and nearer to the mine, halting again when only one more range of tree-clad slopes stood between the valley where they lay and their objective. Here they waited for two anxious days until Aestrontor and those he had taken with him returned to report that they had seen the wagons of bullion move off under guard down the southward road along the Lissa'pathor. Then Haldur called all his leaders together.

'We'll wait here one more day, to give them time to get over the bridge,' he said, 'and then we'll strike. Haldas, you and the other nine who have personal knowledge of the lie of the land will each take nine bowmen with you and move into positions encircling the head of the valley. My father's household men, together with half of those who once rode with the Cunorad, will divide into two groups. Aestrontor, you will take command of one of these and Vorardynur, you the other. You will station yourselves on each side of the road, hidden in the trees just south of where the mine compounds begin; your task will be to intercept any who try to escape. With me will go the rest of our forces, to block the southward road. If anything goes wrong, we'll attack at the full gallop. I don't think that will be necessary, but we've got to be prepared to act if it does. Are there any questions?'

'Who are we to go with?'

Two champions had come with their bowmen at Carapethan's call, from Rihann nan'Esylt and Rihann y'n Riggan. It was Arellan who spoke for both of them, but as Haldur answered, he looked rather at Ennarvorad from the Golden Valley.

'I want you both to come with me,' he said; and Ennarvorad, not knowing what lay behind his leader's smile, smiled tentatively back; but Haldur was remembering, as if from another life, an evening of friendly rivalry with the bow; hearing again, as if from an old story, the unconscious irony of words spoken: *you must have the eyes of the As-Geg'rastigan.* Ennarvorad seemed so young: Haldur hoped desperately that he would live to return to his home again. There was a pause, and since it appeared that there were no more questions, Haldur was about to dismiss the gathering when to his surprise Haldas spoke up: Haldas, usually so silent, so bleak of face, with seldom a word for anyone.

'What will *they* be doing?' he asked, nodding towards the twelve Cunorad. Haldur noticed glances being exchanged here and there and realised that others too had wondered about this, but before he could answer, Artorynas leaned forward.

'Their time is yet to come,' he said. 'They will be needed at Caradriggan.'

As he looked at Artorynas an unreadable expression passed over Haldas' face. For a moment it seemed less set and closed, but then, making no verbal reply, he bowed his head as if in acceptance.

'Right then,' said Haldur, 'if no-one has anything else to ask, let's get ourselves organised. We'll start early tomorrow. The archers will move off first, and the rest of us will move to our stations when we get the word they're in position. And the next day... There'll be no turning back, after that.'

All too soon, evening was upon them. The bowmen ate first, and then, after a final check of their arms and equipment, gathered for a short briefing to make sure all knew which guide to follow and what to aim for when the time came. The ten who had laboured at the mine before their escape ran over the plan, each of them using a roughly sketched layout of the buildings and other features they would be looking down upon. Once more they described the uniforms worn by the overseers and gangmasters, once more they traced the routes the slaves followed at the shift-change, which was the time chosen for the attack as being the moment when the greatest numbers would be above ground. At last the gathering began to break up, as men got to their feet: there was nothing left to say, now. But something had occurred to one of the archers, a man from the broad, generous fields of Rihann y'n Fram.

'Don't you think our cover's a bit thin here at the head of the valley?' he said, putting his finger on the map his guide had been about to fold up. 'What if they make a break for it this way? Shouldn't we spread out to block them off, rather than dividing to put five groups on each side?'

'They'll not run that way, whatever else they do.' Dusk had fallen now, but the shaded glow of a small lantern picked out the scar of the man's mine-mark as well as his teeth when he laughed harshly. 'Though if they did, I'd be inclined to let them get on with it. I'd let the Waste take every last one of them, if I had my way; and it's Na Naastald that waits there, just beyond. And that reminds me: fill your water-bottles here before we set off, so you drink from the Lissa'pathor as little as you can.'

Fears at daybreak

The night passed, its slow hours measured out in watches. Haldur found it difficult to sleep: his rest was disturbed by confusing dreams and interrupted as the guard was changed, quietly though this was done. Each time he woke, the thought of what lay before them over the next two days made his stomach churn. Eventually, opening his eyes once more and seeing that now a faint light was beginning to grow, he sat up, putting on his boots and outer garments. Maybe activity would cure his nerves. He went across and spoke briefly with the guards, confirming that all was well. Day was still some while off and the cold of earliest dawn chilled the air, drifting with the ground-mist that curled among the trees. Beads of condensation dewed the guards' cloaks and hung in their hair. Haldur moved off, chafing his fingers in his sleeves. As he walked through the camp he wondered how many still slept, and how many lay wakeful with their fears as he had done. Gradually the darkness thinned, the impenetrable black of the forest night waning to a deep green gloom. Glancing up automatically, Haldur realised he would have to wait for a while yet before he knew whether the dawn would be fair when it came, for the sky was obscured by a thick canopy of the new season's leaves.

His senses at full stretch, he heard soft movements from the horse lines, the occasional faint jingle of metal harness; smelt the piercing freshness of the new day. He leaned against a tree for a while, lost in thought, and then his attention was caught by a stir over where the archers and their guides were sleeping. It was almost time for them to be on their way.

He headed towards them, thinking to wish them well with words of encouragement, but suddenly heard a small, almost furtive noise away to his right where the ground dipped away in a gully through which a little stream wandered. At the same moment a new smell came to him, sour and unpleasant, jarring on the sweetness of the morning. Quietly he pushed through the trees and a white, woebegone face turned towards him: Haldas, huddled up alone out of sight of his fellows. Surprised, Haldur hunkered down beside him.

'Are you all right? The others are getting ready; you should join them and eat something. You've a long day in front of you, you don't want to tackle it on an empty stomach.'

Haldas looked away. 'It's already emptier than it was. I couldn't sleep, I came down here and now I've puked. Thrown up what I ate last night.'

It flashed into Haldur's mind that though the Cunorad were trained in basic first-aid and healing, they had brought no specialist medic with them. If this was something infectious or contagious, their whole enterprise could be at risk.

'What's the problem? Was there something wrong with it? Have you got any other symptoms?'

A breath of bitter laughter escaped Haldas, but it was more grimace than smile that twisted his features; when he spoke, his voice was heavy with self-loathing. 'Yes, I have: a bad case of yellow belly. I'm too scared to face this. So afraid, I can't even hold my food down. How does it feel, to have a coward like me on your hands?'

'Now you listen to me,' said Haldur, settling himself more comfortably on a tree-root. 'There's no call to name yourself a coward.

Don't you think we're all afraid? I'm afraid myself: I couldn't sleep either, that's why I'm out here.'

Staring at the ground, Haldas shook his head vaguely; it was obvious he was not listening. 'When I ran from the mine all I wanted was to die a free man: I had nothing to go back to. But when I would have killed myself, the folk of the forest who helped you prevented me. They offered me a refuge, fed me and clothed me as they have done Morancras and others, restored my strength. I owed them the debt of life and I was prepared to pay it, if it was required: I had nothing to go back to. My father was put to death and my mother is dead also; I don't know what's happened to my sisters... except for Asanardo. I saw her once at the mine.' His lips retracting in fury, Haldas bared his teeth like a dog. 'She was being used as a whore by Haartell the mine overseer.'

'I am truly sorry,' said Haldur, surprised at how freely the usually silent Haldas had spoken, 'but after all, even those with happiness behind them cannot turn back time. You have most of your years still before you: can you not look forward now? Surely, if you've thrown your lot in with Sigitsinen and the others, you have hope for the future?'

'You forget, I didn't join them of my own accord. And I'll always have the mine-mark on me.'

'No man has the right to enslave another,' said Haldur. 'The mark is on your head, not your heart. You are free now.'

'Ah, it's easily said. It's more difficult to make it mean something... I'm sorry, I shouldn't have said that. There's... there's something I do want to say though, now while there's still time. That day when you set out home, when I guided you over the pass... I'm sorry I didn't stay with you when you asked me, up there on the mountain where you said it was a *numiras*. I was ashamed straight away, though I couldn't bring myself to admit it. But when I went back, I told Morancras that you can see the village from up there, like you suggested, and he was glad.' Haldas fell silent and then added, rather awkwardly, 'You're a good leader.'

'Well, thanks!' Haldur's face broke into a grin, he assumed Haldas had got a grip on himself now. The first birds were beginning to call overhead and time was running on. 'So will we go back now, and join the others?'

'Wait, you don't understand. I've been talking about how it was with me, before. I did believe you'd come back to help us, but I assumed we'd all die anyway. That meant nothing to me then, and in any case I would have forfeit whatever time I had left for the chance of vengeance on Haartell. But now that you've brought *him* with you ...'

'You mean Artorynas?'

Haldas was pale and miserable. 'I still think of him as Maesrhon, but it doesn't really surprise me, to see what he is. Even when he was a boy, there were whispers ... I remember him from years back. I was enslaved as a child, and he was kind to me then, me and another. We would have done anything for him, and I suppose,' he added with a sad half-smile, 'I suppose you could say we paid a high price for it. But anyway, that's not the point. Now he's come back, maybe we really can put things to rights again. And I realise now I want to see it, I do want to see the world restored, I want to live to see it! But now that I want to live, all I can think about is how afraid I am that I'm going to die! Oh, Haldur, look!'

Far beyond the trees, the sun must have lifted clear of the earth. Down on the forest floor, its first rays were broken into numberless red-gold spangles of moving light, while one bright beam, momentarily unobstructed, pierced the green shade to fall beyond the little stream on a misty glade of bluebells. The chorus of hidden birds swelled to greet the new day, and the earth gave back a mingled scent of moss and pine, new growth and the leaf-mould of a thousand autumns. When Haldas spoke again, his words were muffled, his head in his hands.

'It's as if the world is new-made with the new day. I've already fouled this dawn with the stink of vomit and I'm ashamed to think we'll ruin tomorrow's sweetness with murder and death. But worse, I can't bring myself to face the battle. I'm afraid I might let you all down, that I'll run away when the killing starts… I've seen plenty of dead men in my time, but I've never had to fight before. I'm afraid of what I'll see then, I'm afraid of being wounded, I'm afraid of the pain… Even thinking about it made me throw up. I hate myself, I can't bear the shame.'

Haldur pulled the young man's hands away from his face. 'Look at me. There's no need to feel shame for fear. Don't imagine that there's a man in this camp who's not afraid; it's just some of them hide it more easily than others. If you went over to the latrines now, there'd be half a dozen of them green in the face as their stomachs griped and their bowels emptied: what price the stink there! It took nerve to say what you've told me just now; plenty of people would never have been able to do that. And you know what, you're wrong about something else too. Being afraid of pain and death isn't the worst thing, it's not as bad as inflicting them. You're ashamed that that's what we're going to do, and you should be honoured for it, not hate yourself. I wish you could meet my father, that's how he felt too. Listen, Haldas. There's no point pretending. Some of us will die, and I can't promise it won't be you, any more than I can be sure it won't be me, or any other of my comrades. It hurts me to think about it, because every life lost will be one that need never have been taken away. But we'll do everything we can on our part to limit the killing. And I *know* you'll be steady when the time comes. You're as brave as the next man, believe me. You're here of your free will, aren't you? It's not like when you were being forced into the mine.' He heaved Haldas to his feet with a grin.

'Come on, now. Haldur and Haldas, eh? Sounds a bit like one of the old comic stories, but who cares – I think we make a good team.'

Haldas managed a shaky smile in return.

'That's better,' said Haldur. 'Don't worry about tomorrow, just keep thinking about the day after that, when dawn will break over the Lissa'pathor.'

'Dawn? Over the gold mine?' said Haldas sceptically, then suddenly his voice changed. 'What is it?'

'Nothing.' Haldur had shuddered slightly before he could stop himself, but he bit off as unlucky the old saying about someone walking over his grave. 'Nothing, it's still a bit chilly and I'm hungry. Come on, let's get ourselves a bowl of hot frumenty before you have to set off. We can have some of that dried fruit in it that Sigitsinen brought.'

Counting the cost

Before nightfall on the day of the attack, it was all over. In the sullen glow cast by the lamps of the mine compound they gathered to count the cost of victory. Still bewildered by their sudden liberty, several hundred mine slaves huddled together silently. There had been soldiers stationed at the mine, after all: some forty men of whom ten were younger sons forced into their year's service. Two of these conscripts were injured and the rest had rushed to give themselves up; of the regulars, three were wounded and four taken prisoner; fifteen had changed sides as soon as they realised what was happening and the rest were dead. These eight lay to one side, along with the slain overseers and slave-drivers; and separated from them lay those others who had paid with their lives: three bowmen, who would never return to their valleys again; two from among the former Cunorad, both women; Aestrontor, who had been killed in an attempt to save them; and two of their guides, one of whom was Haldas. Some of the slaves had died too, cheated of freedom by the very impulse that had made them fight for it alongside their liberators.

Haldur stepped onto the mounting-block outside the stables so that all could see him. There were tears on his face but he ignored them, concentrating all his efforts into keeping his voice steady and calm.

'Is there anyone here with medical knowledge, who can help the injured?'

After a moment or two of whispering and murmuring, he saw movement and out from among the crowd of slaves came three men, middle-aged and grey-haired but all branded with the mine-mark.

'We are slaves now, kept to tend the overseers and guards,' said one of them, 'but we were free men once, who all received our training in Tellgard, if that means anything to you.'

'It means much,' said Haldur. 'I have stood within the sanctuary at Tellgard while Arval the Earth-wise spoke the rite. I am Haldur son of Carapethan, who is lord of Rihannad Ennar. We come to tell you there will be no more slaves here: you are all free men now. If you and your colleagues will treat the wounded – all the wounded – we will be in your debt. Take anyone you need, if you require help. And there is something else to ask. Are there those among you here who worked in the kitchens?'

This time there was a much longer pause. Eventually half a dozen women and girls crept out from the throng, but their eyes flicked from the women standing with the former Cunorad to the women lying dead on the ground, and Haldur could see they were too frightened to come further forward.

'There's no need to be afraid,' he told them. 'There must be stores here. If you can find enough food, we'll all feel better for it if we can eat. Perhaps you would organise a meal for everyone, while the rest of us work to bury the dead.'

Vorardynur stepped up. 'Right, we'll get on with the burials. I'll sort things here; I expect you'll want to take ours into the forest, it's the best we can do for them…'

'No.' Haldur spoke up clearly again. 'We will bury all the fallen together. Every life lost is a life wasted, a waste that should not have happened.' A buzz of comment greeted this and under cover of it Haldur spoke quietly to Vorardynur. 'When they bring Haartell out, make sure his body is kept covered.'

Years later, if Haldur looked back, the thing he remembered most clearly about that night was the whispering. The darkness seemed full of it, a soft, sibilant muttering that shifted as the breeze sighed above. From where the wounded lay to where the freed slaves gathered, from soldiers to Cunorad, from one watch fire to another it passed to and fro: sometimes louder, sometimes the merest breath of sound, but never completely ceasing. Whether exhausted or elated, fearful or hopeful, glad or grieving, there was none who could simply sleep without the comfort or companionship of speech. Except the dead, thought Haldur. They lie now in a silence that will never break. A quiet footfall approached and Artorynas sat down beside him without speaking. Time went slowly by. Haldur was glad not to be alone, but his heart ached with bitter regret for Aestrontor and Haldas. He wondered whether the young man might have lived, had he not gone seeking revenge on Haartell. The two dead men had been their own witnesses: Haldas must have struck first and Haartell, though dying, had lived long enough to inflict a mortal wound in his turn. Haldur dropped his head onto his knees, too sorrowful to sleep. He would never know, now, whether Haartell had taunted Haldas about his sister, or whether what Haldas had done had been in his mind all along. They had found him, slumped against a wall inside Haartell's handsome residence; and a gory trail, sticky and smeared, led them to Haartell, who had crawled only a short distance before his own life flowed away on a tide of blood. And when they turned him over and saw where the blood came from, saw what Haldas had done to him... and for what? Haldur had enquired among the slaves, but no-one seemed to have so much as heard of Asanardo.

'I remember once, when I was a boy, asking my grandfather about Maesaldron,' said Artorynas softly. 'I wanted to know what it was like, in the forest. And he said it was dark, and full of secret life. An unhappy man, who allowed himself to be overwhelmed by the burden of his past.'

Haldur looked up and his heart warmed. Artorynas knew without being told that what troubled him was the weight of lost lives laid to his account.

'Isn't it strange,' he said, 'to think that he once lived here, in that very house. And stranger still to think that I've met him myself. I'm so sorry about what happened to him. I really don't think Arval expected he could live, after he fell as we were leaving Tellgard. It's such a shame: he was holding on to the hope of seeing you again.'

'You should really try to get some rest,' said Artorynas; and Haldur was too tired to notice that his friend had made no response to his words. Indeed he was almost too tired to sleep, but he lay down and eventually dozed a little.

When night drew on to its chilly end, he raised his head and looked about him, drawing his cloak close for warmth. People were beginning to move about, stirring up the fires; smoke hung in the air before slowly rising. Haldur saw that the freed slaves and others from Caradward were looking upwards, running to wake those who still slept, pointing at the sky in wonder. For himself, he felt only a kind of dull disappointment. Dawn might indeed have returned to the Lissa'pathor, but it was obscured by cloud and to him it seemed sullen and dour. If Haldas had lived to see it, would he too have been disappointed?

'I promised Haldas he would see dawn break over the mine,' he said, almost as if speaking to himself.

'The true dawn will be at Caradriggan.' Artorynas, on one knee lacing up his boots, now got to his feet. 'It will be then that the light returns.'

'But I promised him. And I promised Cathasar that he would see the Nine Dales again; but now both of them are dead. Must all my promises be blighted like this?'

'Did you also promise them life?'

'No, but …' Haldur stood frowning, chewing his lip.

'Listen, Haldur. Men *will* die, when we get to Caradriggan: you cannot prevent this completely, but as few lives as possible will be wasted. I promise you this, as you promised Haldas. You may think I cannot be certain, but the arrow is my surety.'

247

'Arval said something like that to me, something about how if you found the arrow, it would change everything.'

'Well then, we should put our trust in Arval's wisdom.'

Haldur stared doubtfully at Artorynas, but before he could say any more, someone called his name. Vorardynur came tramping over towards them and it was time for Haldur to immerse himself in the business of the day.

CHAPTER 59

Waiting

If Ardeth, or Gillis and Geraswic and others whose deaths lay to Caradward's account, could have returned and strolled through the once-familiar streets of Framstock to the *Salmon Fly*, they would scarcely have known the old place. True, its mellow stone walls still stood; the wide hearth, the uneven staircase, the deep windows overlooking the river were all unchanged; and yet they were not the same. The living heart was gone from the inn, its friendly charm faded like the sunlight. The companionable air it had once worn so easily was harder to maintain now that conversations were guarded, faces watched, ears alert for an incautious word. Yet in spite of all, the *Fly* was still there and folk still frequented it; and on an evening whose darkness mocked its spring-time date, an undercurrent of excitement was noticeable in its low-ceilinged rooms, where a larger than usual number of customers had gathered, muttering together in corners. And although those in the *Fly* could not have known it, similar scenes were being played out in other inns and *gradsteddan* up and down the land: from Rossaestrethan and Rosmorric, Gwent y'm Aryframan in happier days, to Staran y'n Forgarad in the far south. In barracks and messes too, men had their heads together, from Wicursal's headquarters in the north to the training-grounds of Rigg'ymvala; and down in the Outlands, in bright tents the wandering *sigitsaran* gathered, hailing the news in their own tongue, drinking to it in the peppery spirit they kept for auspicious occasions. Even in the heart of

Caradriggan the rumour ran, in the *Sword and Stars* as in the *Golden Leopard*, in the streets and in the barbican garrison; among the guard in Seth y'n Carad itself, the word passed swiftly along: and the name that everyone whispered was Artorynas.

The seeds had been carefully and cleverly sown. While the two hundred moved down the valley from the mine and lay hidden once more in the forest, watching the road for any who might travel up it from Caradriggan and waiting for the moment when it was time to take the bridge and sweep down to the city, their agents were already at work. For almost six years now, the story had circulated of what happened in the feast hall on the night Maesrhon vanished from Caradriggan. Everyone knew what he had said to Vorynaas, that he had taunted him with the name of Artorynas, warning him he would hear it again; everyone knew that Vorynaas had taken the threat seriously, searching everywhere for any hint of the whereabouts of this unknown man. So the tinder lay ready to hand, wanting only a spark to set it ablaze, and now the story was running out of control like a wildfire with the breath of a thousand rumours behind it. The more attempts were made to stamp it out, the stronger it sprang up again: in no time 'Artorynas will be among us soon' had become 'Artorynas is here'. Men remembered more of what Maesrhon had said, that the light would return too, when Artorynas was seen; and those who had remained steadfast roused themselves, looking up again, while the downtrodden met each other's eyes and saw there instead of the old despair the beginnings of a new hope. And those who had risked all to keep the secret resistance alive recognised the awaited signal, readying themselves with quickened breath and beating hearts for the action to come.

Great efforts were made by the authorities to find the source of the stories, but in vain. No-one, it seemed, had heard anything at first or even second hand. Soldiers, merchants, innkeepers, farmers; housewives in the shops, craftsmen at the workbench, traders in the streets, servants at the waterpump: all were hauled off unceremoniously for questioning, but all their frustrated interrogators got from them were variations on a theme of 'They were talking about it at the inn in Rihannark, they said a man heard it from the drovers who came in from the Rossanlow'; or 'My brother lives in Staran y'n Forgarad, he came on a visit and said one of his apprentices said he heard some *sigitsaran* brought the story with them into the city'; or again, 'The youngsters came back from training-leave and one of them said his parents mentioned a rumour the wife's cousin brought home from market'. Though some of those detained were roughly handled, and none were treated too gently, they were eventually released unharmed; but all were burning with a resentment that was shared by their families and friends. The ripples that spread from a stone-cast may not be seen for long before they subside, but they leave behind them a deceptively smooth surface beneath which the stone itself still lies, and so it was now. Matters quietened down, but it was a sullen calm heavy with a sense of injustice that served only to intensify the hope that the whispers might be true.

For some reason he was unable to analyse, Vorynaas felt curiously oppressed by the whole episode. However he was more annoyed than disappointed when the report on Valahald and Heranar reached him. They weren't worth the trust I placed in them, he told himself. Heranar, now: I should have taken his province away from him long ago, he wasn't up to it. The only thing that surprises me really is that he was the one who betrayed our plans. I'd never have given him credit for that much nerve, regardless of why he did it. And Valahald, well, he's no great loss. I would never have been able to trust him, especially after that business with his father. Too devious by half. An unpleasant smile crossed Vorynaas' face briefly. Quite funny when you thought about it, that it appeared the only man who had tried to fight off Heranar's attack on his brother had been an Outlander, and after all that whingeing I had to listen to from Valahald about them! No, if his men stood aside to let him die, then clearly Valahald had failed to instil either loyalty or fear in them with sufficient success. And he had let me down before, thought Vorynaas, his mood darkening further as he remembered how and when. Ah, if only Ghentar had lived, then the sons of Valafoss would never have enjoyed such favour from me! But with the practice of a lifetime, Vorynaas' mind closed itself automatically to the regret and loss that haunted its weaker thoughts, and turned instead to his current preoccupation. The whispers about Artorynas had ignited a fury in him and he felt his rage building now as he stood, remembering as vividly as if it had happened yesterday how Maesrhon had defied him to his face in open hall. That cuckoo in the nest, that changeling! Let it only be true what Valahald suspected, that he is hiding up in the Nine Dales! If I could have one wish, it would be to see his face once more, to watch him as he dies. The world could do what it would after that, it would mean nothing to me...

'Have you taken a vow of silence? A half-*moras* for your thoughts, my old friend.'

'What?' Vorynaas swung round to where Thaltor lounged at his ease, drink in hand and a grin on his face. 'Oh, nothing.'

He sat down himself. 'Curse the peddlers of these damned rumours, though,' he burst out. It had been Thaltor's report of an investigation he had conducted into loose talk among the troops under his command in Seth y'n Carad that had prompted his bout of introspection. 'If ever I do find who started it all, I swear they will pay. By my right hand, they'll wish they were facing whatever lurks in the Waste rather than what I'll make them suffer.'

'Ah, it's only idle talk, there's nothing in it that any of us have been able to find. I wouldn't let it bother you. Not worth letting it distract you from the bigger picture. It's all going well up in Rossaestrethan, by the sound of it.'

Vorynaas looked at his old crony. Thaltor's one great virtue was his loyalty, but against that it had to be said he was lazy, both physically and mentally, and it was a trait that was becoming more pronounced as the years went by. Look at him, thought Vorynaas. He doesn't really care whether we take the Nine Dales or not: no drive, no ambition, he'd happily spend the rest of his days sitting about here in Seth y'n Carad, and he's a good ten years younger than I am!

'It would do, with Valestron to make it happen,' he said experimentally. 'He sorted things out up there in no time.'

'Yes, he certainly doesn't mess about.'

Thaltor's reply came readily, and one of Vorynaas' thick brows lifted. He knew Thaltor disliked Valestron, but had hidden it as far as he could, not knowing whether he or Valahald would ultimately win their struggle for supremacy. But with Valahald dead, and his brother never in the reckoning and now on the run, it seemed Thaltor had hitched his wagon easily enough to the new heir-apparent. Lazy, and no principles at all, reflected Vorynaas without a hint of irony; but we go back a long way, I know what to expect from him. He left unsaid the sardonic comment that had sprung to his lips and leaned back more comfortably in his chair. At least there was no need to keep up appearances with Thaltor; the two of them could relax together.

'Well, I'll tell you one thing,' he said. 'I wouldn't be in Heranar's shoes, when Valestron catches up with him – which he will. Just shows you, doesn't it? You'd have said those two lads of Valafoss had it handed to them, but look what they did with it.'

Hill-country hospitality

Shortly before this conversation took place, a bedraggled figure peered down the hillside from behind a rough stone wall that snaked its way up the fell. Since vanishing from his place of safety among the Salfgard folk, Heranar too had heard the name of Artorynas mentioned here and there as he fled from one hiding-place to another. But neither the name nor the rumours meant anything to him, whose heart had room for one name only. Waking and sleeping, he was haunted by the memory of Valahald's final words, those tormenting, filthy boasts that had maddened him into the murderous assault on his brother. When he heard that sly voice in his mind, a red glow of fury filled him anew, a fire of hate that sustained him through days and nights spent in the open, cold and hungry… but there was just a chance that Valahald had been lying, had taunted him for the pleasure of it… and he had to know, had to find out if he could… So here he was, exhausted and filthy, drenched in the rain that had been falling for hours, but looking down at last on the little settlement where his marriage-father was lord.

Gillavar was anything but pleased to see him: indeed for a moment or two could scarcely credit that the pathetic suppliant at his doors was the same man who had been governor of Rossaestrethan, whom he had last seen wearing the chain of his office but who now was dressed in tattered hand-me-downs that looked as if they might have been stolen from a peasant's washing line.

'What do you want?' asked Gillavar, showing no inclination to move from the threshold where he stood. 'Aren't you supposed to be in hiding? If so don't imagine you can claim sanctuary here.'

'I'm not looking for safety,' croaked Heranar, leaning on the doorpost. 'You can turn me away without food or shelter, I don't care. But I must talk to you: just let me in so we can speak. Please, please!' He clutched at Gillavar's sleeve desperately.

Brushing his hand away, Gillavar stepped back and called over a servant. 'Let him get washed and give him something to eat.' He turned back to Heranar. 'I'll talk to you after you've cleaned yourself up, but remember I mean what I say: you'll not be staying here.'

Within the hour, Heranar was back. Gillavar received him alone except for a frightened-looking man of middle years, balding and rather scrawny, who had clearly given himself a hasty shave in the meantime and left a cut on his cheek in the process.

'This is my lorekeeper,' said Gillavar, 'who's here as witness to what you've got to say, and what I say in reply.'

Heranar barely glanced at the man, although not so long ago he would have smirked openly at the thought of such an unimpressive person holding office as a lorekeeper even in this forsaken valley in the hills. He huddled closer to the fire, rubbing the rough fabric of his garments with his hands.

'My thanks for food, and the change of clothes. I'm in your debt.'

Gillavar waved this aside, frowning. 'Oh no you're not.' He noticed Heranar's fingernails, cracked and broken but no longer gnawed right down as of old. Must have stopped chewing at them once he had something to really worry him, thought Gillavar: nothing like a genuine crisis to concentrate the mind. 'I've done no more for you than I'd do for any traveller in the mountains. You can rest here tonight, if you wish, but you'll be on your way when morning comes. You wanted to talk to me, you said, so you'd better get on with it; although I'll tell you now I've got nothing to say about this Artorynas, whoever he is. I've heard the rumours, like we all have, and I don't care who he is or where he is or if he even exists, and I don't care what he might do or what anyone else might do in response. On the day we first met I made it clear to you, governor though you were then, I told you straight I wasn't going to meddle in affairs: I'd keep my people out of trouble and I'd keep them safe. That was my position then and that's where I still stand now.'

Gillavar had not bothered to conceal his satisfaction at his marriage-son's humbling; Heranar wondered wretchedly whether there was anyone at all who did not dislike him. Except, of course… He sat up straighter.

'I'm not here to talk about Artorynas. I want news of Ilmarynvoro. Have you heard anything? I thought maybe you might know what really happened…' He faltered into silence, stopped by the look on Gillavar's face, but when the older man said nothing, he continued. 'I can't believe what Valahald said, but it torments me. I am glad, glad I killed him! But he was capable of anything, I'm afraid of what he might have done. If I could only find her, or even just news of her… I was so sure she would be here, I don't know where else I can search, now…'

He stopped, brought up short as Gillavar laughed briefly. 'Ilmarynvoro? Oh, she's here all right.'

'Here!' Heranar stared, colour flooding into his face. 'She *is* here? Can I see her? Will you let me talk to her?'

Gillavar laughed again. 'No, you can't see her.' He turned to his lorekeeper. 'But we might let him talk to her, what do you think?'

The man had shifted about awkwardly when Ilmarynvoro was first mentioned, and said nothing in answer now, unwilling to meet his lord's gaze, obviously ill at ease. Gillavar stood up. 'Yes, let's bring him into his wife's presence.'

All his attention fixed painfully on his marriage-father, Heranar had completely failed to notice the other man's discomfort. He jumped to his feet eagerly, but when he saw how Gillavar had to force the lorekeeper to lead the way the first hint of fear brushed at him; and when they went out into the rain-lashed darkness a terrible premonition began to grow in his mind. They walked down a muddy lane, round a corner or two and out to the edge of the settlement and then Gillavar stopped, holding up the torch he had taken from above the hall door. The rain hissed and spat on it, making the flames flatten and smoke.

'There she is, governor of Rossaestrethan,' said Gillavar bitterly. 'Talk to her all you like, she'll not interrupt you.'

Heranar stared down wordlessly at the narrow mound at his feet. There was nothing to mark the grave yet, it was too new. He dropped to his knees on the sodden grass, the rain soaking through his borrowed clothes and his newly-dried hair almost as fast as the pain flooded his heart. A dreadful, animal-like cry broke from him as he heard Gillavar's voice above his head, coming as if from far away.

'Whatever you may have heard from Valahald, this is what my daughter said, the night before she died. They took the children away from her, locked her up alone. Valahald questioned her, over and over again, insisting that she must know something about why and how the men from the Nine Dales made their escape, and that she must tell what she knew. He told her you were under arrest: sometimes he'd say you were already dead so she might as well speak; other times it would be you'd confessed under torture so why not save herself by doing the same thing; or, you'd been condemned to death but he would spare you if she broke her silence. Though she swore she knew nothing, he refused to believe her, tormenting her for days on end: what do you think that was like for her?'

'I know, he did the same with me, but I...' Heranar's agonised groan was cut short by Gillavar.

'Don't waste your breath looking for sympathy from me. I've no interest in anything you might want to say. You can keep quiet, and hear me out. So now Valahald had a better idea. Some of his soldiers brought the children in. When they tried to run to her, he had them dragged out, screaming and crying for their mother. Then he threatened her: speak, otherwise the next time you see your daughters they'll be dead. She threw herself at him, trying to hurt him enough so he couldn't stop her getting out to them. I don't suppose she so much as scratched his face, but in the struggle her clothes tore. You know what's coming next, don't you? He found the amber she was concealing. That stopped them both in their tracks. She was weeping, trying to cover herself, and he stood there watching her, tossing the amber from hand to hand – smiling. "No need now for any more of these pleasant little family chats, is there?" he said. "This is all the proof I need of what I suspected all along. Well, I must get on, I've an important order to sign. Within a couple of days my little brother will be on his way to Assynt y'm Atrannaas." She begged him to send her too, the stupid girl. "Oh, there's no need for anything as drastic as that," he said. "However, this does mean your marriage is over, doesn't it? I'd better have you sent back to your father." She arrived here on foot, bruised and bleeding: she'd been raped by every man of the escort and then turned out on to the road. They'd told her the children were here and if she wanted to see them again, she could walk the rest of the way.'

Gillavar paused for a moment. 'You fool, why couldn't you keep your mouth shut? Why did you have to take the amber? And why, why did you make her hide it?'

Slowly Heranar stood up and wiped the wet hair from his eyes. His hands were mired with dirt from his wife's grave and streaks of clay mingled with his tears. He ignored Gillavar's questions: there were no answers he could possibly give. 'How did she die?' he whispered. 'And where are my daughters?'

'We found her next morning, hanging from a roof beam. The children weren't here, we've never seen them. I've no idea what may have happened to them.' Gillavar pointed with the torch, which flared and spluttered. 'There's a shed over there, it's fairly weather-proof. You can spend the night in there but make sure you don't cross my path in the morning. I never want to see you again. If I could turn back time, my daughter would never have been wife to you.'

Heranar shook his head. 'I can't stay here. I'll go now.'

'Do whatever you want,' said Gillavar. 'You are no longer a marriage-son to me.'

With a jerk of his head to the lorekeeper, he turned away and went back to his hall. Heranar took a last, tear-blinded look at his wife's grave and lurched off into the night. He was holding on to one thought only, that somehow he must find his little girls. But his freedom lasted barely another three days before he was taken and brought this time before Valestron himself, who eyed him with great satisfaction.

'Well, well,' he said. 'How disappointing you and your brother both turned out to be. But still, it seems you at least will have a small claim to fame. As far as I'm aware, no-one else has managed to be consigned twice to Assynt y'm Atrannaas. Unfortunate, but at least unique.'

Heretellar's resolve

Down on the family holding in the Ellanwic, Heretellar leaned on a fence staring at the mules in the paddock without really seeing them. He too had heard the rumours: Meremvor had come home one evening, his face alight with unaccustomed animation, to tell the story of what they were saying in the *Barn and Byre*, down in the village. He turned the name over in his mind, Artorynas, but was no nearer than he had ever been to knowing what Maesrhon might have meant by it. Now if only *he* would return – but what good would that do, unless he brought the arrow of his quest with him? And Heretellar had to admit to himself that he had small hopes of this. It would be like something from one of the legends of olden times, he thought, something great and glorious that just could not happen in real life. He prodded the coarse turf with his foot. The grazing deteriorated year on year; the mules, unthrifty and in poor condition, fetched less and less at market. For all his careful management, it could not be long before the estate failed to pay its way and they would be forced to begin living on capital in order to keep going. It hurt him to see the thin faces of those who worked with him. To him they were as a family and he felt he had failed them. His parents, too, had looked pinched and under-nourished when he had seen them last. But what could he do? It had been his father's decision, not to sell when Vorynaas and his supporters had been buying up land for their great schemes in the Cottan na'Salf. And selling now was scarcely an option. Land prices had dropped and then fallen even faster when the growing-houses had failed to provide the surplus that had been so confidently predicted. Meanwhile the cost of what they did produce had gone up and up, so that only the rich could afford it. Heretellar's face set as he remembered his most recent visit to Caradriggan, when he had been among those shoved aside in the street as the latest consignment of gold bullion rolled into the city. The wealth that should have benefited all had been sadly misused, and now was being diverted into funding this insane, deluded assault upon Rihannad Ennar.

With this, memories of his meeting with Haldur came into Heretellar's mind. Without thinking what he did, he set his face to the north, turning round to sit on the cross-piece of the stile in the paddock fence. For a while his thoughts drifted and then, catching himself wishing he could be with Haldur, back in the homeland he had talked of with such love and longing, he was brought up sharply.

Am I losing my grip on reality, he asked himself; am I really sitting here, envious of a man whose country is about to be invaded? Shame filled him, followed by a kind of angry sorrow for Haldur who was gone to meet his fate, his people doomed. Heretellar reminded himself that in fact there was no way of knowing whether Haldur and his companions had actually arrived safely home: after all, anything might have happened to them. But at least Haldur had taken action, had braved the wilderness for the sake of his father and his folk, had come on the long road south to find out what danger threatened them, against all the odds had managed to escape. And what have I done, thought Heretellar. Ancrascaro and Rhostellat keep faith with Arval in Tellgard; my father too, determined to endure in Caradriggan. Even Meremvor did what he could and now lives with the consequences of what he sees as his mistake. And Maesrhon, Maesrhon is gone and even if he comes back to Arval as he promised, who knows what his return will mean. Heretellar sat, head in hands, and gave in to his black mood. He remembered what he had said to Haldur about the rot at the heart of Caradward. Must we all go down into the dark? Ah, what more do we deserve! Let the end come, and quickly, thought Heretellar in despair.

But after a moment he looked up, and again he felt ashamed. Those dear to him had not given in to despair; but then, they had all stood firm against the darkness. While he… And now Heretellar's sombre reflections caused him to remember another thing. He had heard it said that word had reached Vorynaas of what he had told Haldur about Assynt y'm Atrannaas, that Haldur had denounced the Caradwardan leader's use of it, that this had inflamed Vorynaas' anger all the more against the men from Rihannad Ennar. One black thought led to another, and Heretellar found himself considering the horror of this chasm of darkness. Arval had foretold that it would devour more than the lives of the prisoners cast into it, but what had he meant? What more could it take, what could be worse than consuming the innocent lives of those forced within? And eventually, as he pondered the question, the answer came to Heretellar. He thought of his boyhood studies, of the 'bad time', the 'bad thing' that the shame of succeeding generations had disguised with a childish name; of Haldur's speech in Tell'Ethronad that showed he had the knowledge that even Arval lacked; of the day when at last, along with all those others who gathered to Tellgard to hear it, he had listened to Haldur recite the terrible truth contained in the tales of *Stirfellaerdon donn' Ur* and *Vala na Naasan*. While our ancestors may have been at fault for their deeds and then their failure to remember, thought Heretellar, we ourselves cannot be blamed for not knowing what had been forgotten. But Assynt y'n Atrannaas we used deliberately, knowing what we did. It has indeed taken more than the lives of its prisoners: it has devoured our innocence.

This was a bleak conclusion and it lay heavily on Heretellar's heart, the more so when it came to him that innocence once lost was gone for ever. And then, almost before he was aware of it, he heard another voice in his mind. Arval, speaking with the power and authority only he could summon; speaking, as men said, as if with the voice of the Starborn. Arval, standing before them all in Tell'Ethronad. Arval, warning Vorynaas that if he put Assynt y'm Atrannaas to evil use, it would devour more than the lives of prisoners and *only be appeased by a willing sacrifice*. Heretellar shuddered. A spasm of icy horror crawled over him and he felt his stomach contract with panic, but then he steadied himself. He stood up, gripping the wood of the fence rail, holding on to reality as he contemplated a fate more terrible than he could ever have imagined. I have no wife or children yet, he said to himself. My parents will be grieved beyond consolation, but I must hope that Ancrascaro and her boys will bring them comfort. Meremvor will take my place here. Someone must bear witness that not all Caradwardans have been seduced by Vorynaas' lies. This is for me to do. I will walk into the night under the mountains to sate the appetite of Assynt y'm Atrannaas. I will make the willing sacrifice.

A last message of love

'Back again already! Well, this is an unexpected surprise,' said Forgard
when his son turned up in Caradriggan. 'Your mother will be so
pleased, I'll just go and tell her you're here while you get sorted out.
We've got Arval coming to dinner tonight. He'll be glad to see you...'
He hurried off.

On any other occasion Heretellar would have been delighted at
the prospect of an evening in Arval's company; but not now, not in
view of what he was about to do. He sat at the table, going through
the motions of eating, talking... It seemed somehow pointless to be
helping himself to the dishes before him, when so soon he would
be gone where he would never need food again. The conversation
turned to the rumours that were circulating and he mentioned that
even away south in the Ellanwic the name of Artorynas was on men's
lips. At this he thought Arval turned a sharper gaze than usual upon
him, indeed several times during the meal he got the impression that
Arval was watching him, but no awkward questions were asked. They
had eaten early and to his relief Arval rose to go soon after supper was
over. As Forgard paused to bid his guest farewell before opening the
street door, Arval turned to his host.

'So Heretellar doesn't know that Maesrhon and Artorynas are one
and the same, or that he reached the Nine Dales: am I right?'

Forgard smiled slightly, a strange mixture of pride and sadness in his
face. 'I have kept faith with the trust you placed in me, Lord Arval.'

Arval looked steadily at Forgard. It had struck him more than
once during the evening that a stranger, going on appearance only,
might easily have mistaken himself, Forgard and Heretellar for three
generations of the same family; but it occurred to him now that
they had more than a physical resemblance in common. He gripped
Forgard's shoulders.

'Truth such as yours is beyond price. I know it has hurt you to
keep your knowledge from Heretellar and I see that some shadow lies

on him tonight. Confide in him now, if you wish. He will be steadfast, as you have been.'

Glancing at the stairs, Forgard hesitated. 'Maybe it's only that he's tired, he has already gone up to his room ... I will think it over and perhaps speak to him tomorrow.'

But in the room that had been his own from boyhood, Heretellar sat wakeful, slowly composing his last message to his parents. After begging their forgiveness for leaving them, and trying his best to explain what he was about to do, he asked them to make sure Meremvor was rewarded for his loyalty. 'If ever it should happen that our hopes are fulfilled and the light returns, I would like him to inherit in my place, in the Ellanwic,' he wrote, 'but I leave the actual decision on this to rest with you.' Then he listed various keepsakes which he wanted specific members of his household to have, and finally he asked that if Ancrascaro and Rhostellat should ever have a third son, they would name him Heretellar for remembrance. No, that was unfair, such a request was a self-indulgent weakness. Heretellar crumpled up the page and started again. When he had finished, he sat for a long time staring at what he had written and then, deciding there was nothing more to say, simply added his love. He sealed the message and left it in a drawer, but found himself unable to sleep; and when night was drawing to a close he put the rejected letter in his pocket and slipped quietly downstairs, out and away. His father encountered Isteddar while breakfast was still being prepared and heard that he had exchanged a brief word with Heretellar in the stable.

'He asked me to say goodbye for him; he'd decided to make an early start and didn't want to wake you,' said Isteddar. 'Is anything wrong?'

'No, it's nothing,' said Forgard. 'It's just something I wanted to tell him ... I wish I'd done it last night, now. Strange that he's away so early, he didn't say anything. Oh well, it will keep. I'll tell him next time I see him.'

An unexpected reunion

For those who waited, biding their time while rumour did its work, these were anxious days. Haldur left Arellan in command at the mine, to guard it behind them with men drawn from those liberated, both former slaves and soldiers, reinforced by some of the archers from the Nine Dales. He and Vorardynur led the rest down the valley where, trusting to the fear that Maesaldron inspired to protect them, they lay quiet not far within the forest, watching the road and preparing themselves for the day when concealment must be laid aside at last. Well-provisioned now from what they found at the mine they had no need to forage, but Haldur encouraged his bowmen to daily practice, having discovered what every leader finds, that it is when troops are forced to idleness that fears and doubts creep in and affect morale. He had no such worries about the Cunorad or those who had once been numbered among them. They knew their time was near, and sustained by an inner certainty of their own kept themselves to themselves. Esylto spoke for them in council and sometimes led them in the rite, but at other times Artorynas would speak the words. Haldur had mixed feelings about this: for every occasion when his heart filled with a kind of solemn joy, there were others when he could not shake off a feeling that a distance had somehow grown between them, a gulf filled with sadness that Artorynas seemed not to notice. But there was no time to either remedy this or to dwell too much upon it: they had to keep guard constantly and be ready to intercept any who might appear, travelling up the road towards the Lissa'pathor. Those who did were taken and questioned, most of them opting to join their captors. They were sent to swell Arellan's ranks further up the valley, while the few who refused were held securely there also. So it was that the two hundred would hear accounts from time to time of how the word put about by their agents was spreading through the land; and then their eyes would meet in a shared understanding that the signal for which they waited must come soon.

Some two weeks after they took the mine, the day arrived at last. To Haldur's surprise, it was Cunoreth who appeared down the road through the forest; with him was Temenghent and a rather shy, gangling youth who was introduced as Cunoreth's cousin Urancrasig.

'Yes, the word has gone round all right,' said Cunoreth, who seemed keyed up with a kind of reckless excitement, 'and we knew, Sigitsinen had arranged it so that the signal was the name, Artorynas, we knew when we got the message using the name that the time had come. It's seemed a long wait, but it's over now at last!' He laughed on the old, gleeful note and then as if remembering something quietened down and took Haldur's arm. 'Er, I wonder if I could speak to you privately for a moment.'

'Of course.' Haldur moved a few paces off, drawing Cunoreth with him. 'What is it?'

'It's about Urancrasig. He's only a boy still, he shouldn't be here; but he slipped away from his family and joined us when we were already well on our way. It was too late to send him back, so I've had no choice but to bring him with me, as no doubt he counted on, the young devil. If there's anything you can think of to keep him out of danger, so far as that's possible, I'll be in your debt, because the last thing I want is to have any rift between my uncle and myself. I, well, I'm hoping to be wed when it's all over and we're back home, and I'm going to need Mag'rantor's support. I've no home or wealth of my own to offer, you see.'

Haldur smiled. 'I'll do what I can. I'm glad to know you're counting on our efforts here being successful.'

'Oh, yes. As you can see, I've been letting my hair grow again.' Cunoreth laughed again, brightening once more. He peered over Haldur's shoulder. 'I heard you brought these Hounds of the Starborn with you, I can't wait to…oh!' The smile vanished from his face, to be replaced by an expression Haldur could not identify. 'I don't believe it.'

Haldur turned to see what Cunoreth was looking at. 'What's the matter?'

'That's Maesrhon. It must be ten years, and he's... but I'd know him anywhere. You've got Maesrhon with you.'

'Indeed we have. Maesrhon is Artorynas, that's his true name.'

'Why didn't Sigitsinen tell us?'

'It was just too risky: imagine if it had got back to Vorynaas! The way things stand, he thinks maybe Maesrhon is with us in Rihannad Ennar: it's one of the reasons for his assault.'

Cunoreth stood silent. All his enthusiasm seemed quenched and Haldur wondered what could have got into him.

'You knew him when he was a boy, I think,' he said, 'so you must guess the man he has become. Come and talk to him! Believe me, he has tales to tell, if he will share them. You'll see how the Hounds of the Starborn look to him. With them before us, and him to lead them, surely none will be able to withstand us. They will be our weapon against which there is no defence, if only we can keep them secret until the moment comes.'

'I don't doubt it,' said Cunoreth, but his voice sounded dull. He turned and walked a few steps further away. Haldur followed him, but before he could ask what the trouble was, Cunoreth stopped and set his back against a tree. 'When he was a boy in Salfgard, some said he was one of the *as-urad*.' Haldur heard the unspoken question in the words.

'They were right. I don't know if you're familiar with the legends that speak of Asward donn'Ur and the Golden Strand; but since the days you speak of, Artorynas has journeyed there and walked on Porthesc nan'Esylt. He has returned to us numbered among the Starborn.' Haldur swallowed. 'So our lorekeeper says.'

Cunoreth's shoulders drooped. 'The woman I want for my own has loved him since childhood. When Salfgard is rebuilt, I hoped to take her there with me; but she won't have me now.'

'But...' Haldur could feel his own heart growing heavier as he tried to cheer Cunoreth's. 'If you plan to live in Salfgard, then... I mean, I don't... I don't think Artorynas will be returning there.'

'It won't make any difference, if she knows he still lives. If he walks in this world, no matter where or how far away, she will never turn to me.'

At these words, all the forebodings Haldur had tried to force down seemed to take shape. They settled on his shoulders like great black scavenging birds whose talons dug into his flesh, whose mocking caws rang in his ears. He had been so glad to see Artorynas return, so glad to ride south together; he had closed his mind to fears about the future. But Cunoreth had opened the door to that future now; if he looked through it, what would he see? Momentarily he actually squeezed his eyes shut before forcing himself to smile at Cunoreth.

'We shouldn't try to look too far ahead. We're still in the dark, here, but when we stand in the light once more, who knows how different things may be?'

Although he shook his head, Cunoreth seemed to pull himself together. He laughed, though rather grimly. 'Well, it's true we've business to finish in the south here first.'

A gift regretted

As Haldur had said, it was indeed dark where they lay hid. They were close to the road, within the confines of the Lissa'pathor, and such light as had returned to the valley after their seizure of the mine scarcely penetrated to their encampment among the trees. As evening drew on they sat talking quietly, their plans for the next day now complete. Haldur looked at the faces dimly illumined by the faint glow of the shaded lantern and wondered whether Vorardynur suffered the same qualms as he did, or whether he simply hid them better. Tomorrow evening they would be across the bridge: how many gaps would there be in the circle then? There was Esylto, calm and quiet, as if armoured by her own radiance, impervious to the awestruck glances of Urancrasig; young Ennarvorad from the Golden Valley, methodically checking his arrows; and together as ever were Cunor y'm Eleth, Cunor y'n

Gillan, Cunor y'n Vala and the rest of the Hounds, still waiting for the moment when they should be unleashed. Temenghent was talking to one of the soldiers who had joined them from the mine guard; in the morning, some of those who had changed sides would be riding with them but Vorardynur had dispersed them among the two hundred, just in case: their loyalty had yet to be tested in action. The man who sat with Temenghent now leaned forward, looking across at the two cousins from Rihannad Ennar who were his new leaders.

'It can't be more than a month to midsummer. Will it still be as dark as this, even then?'

Vorardynur and Haldur exchanged glances. Vorardynur was tempted to remind the man that it was thanks to the deeds of his fellow-countrymen that those who had come from the Nine Dales were risking their lives to save their homeland from ruin; while Haldur, though he wanted to reassure him, was haunted by the memory of his promises to Cathasar and Haldas. But before either of them could say a word, Artorynas spoke.

'A new day will have dawned before then. When Arval speaks the rite in Tellgard, the stars of summer will be shining above once more.'

At this, Cunoreth looked up. 'Yes, tomorrow we've got an important job to do, but it's nothing compared with the day of days that's coming soon,' he said.

Haldur had seen him talking with Artorynas earlier and noticed that since then Cunoreth seemed much more his old self: he wondered very much what had passed between them. Cunoreth laughed now, and shook his hair back. It was almost shoulder-length again; he would braid it for the battle, but for the moment it was still loose. 'And I for one wouldn't exchange my place alongside the two hundred with any man on earth.'

'Nor would I,' said Temenghent in a sudden burst of new self-confidence. He still carried the tiny capsule of poison he had bought from Sigittor, and more than once had been afraid that the moment when he would have to swallow it was upon him. But now, sitting here, he felt as if the sun was already shining on him. Though it was true that he might not survive whatever was to come, as indeed any of them could be dead before they ever saw midsummer, still it was also true what Sigitsinen had said, that the name of Na Devocatron would resound down the years in the mouths of men yet unborn. And he had a place with them! He looked across at Esylto and the Cunorad, and at Artorynas, and then at Haldur. The men from Rihannad Ennar had been civil to him, even when they were confined in Seth y'n Carad and it was his job to guard them. He remembered Cathasar urging him to go with them to Tellgard. It was too late now to tell Cathasar his advice had been sound. But Haldur – he cast about in his mind for a way to show Haldur how grateful he was that he had been made welcome, to show that his change of heart was genuine. He turned to the man beside him, with whom he had been talking.

'This is nothing. If you had looked on Assynt y'm Atrannaas as I have, you'd know what true darkness is. And it's a blackness we brought on ourselves: you and I should be glad we've the chance to do something to put things right again.'

The man subsided sheepishly, but Haldur answered Temenghent. 'I have seen it myself: only from a distance, but that was enough. I'm glad that Heranar escaped.'

Cunoreth put down his cup and gulped back the drink in his mouth. 'No, I've the latest news on Heranar, I meant to tell you earlier. Should have stayed up in the hills with us, shouldn't he? But as anyone could have guessed, he fell foul of Valestron and you might know *he* wouldn't have another mistake. Sent him straight back, and made sure he went in, this time.'

'Condemned to Assynt y'm Atrannaas, *again*?' Haldur looked stricken. 'Oh, no.'

'I wouldn't waste sympathy on him – although at least he got rid of Valahald for us. I can't think of a better use for your amber than what Heranar did with it,' said Cunoreth. When he saw they were puzzled by his words, he raised his eyebrows. 'I assumed you'd have heard all this from Sigitsinen,' he said, 'but if not, Temenghent here can supply the details, he was there. Go on, you tell them.'

Temenghent felt uncomfortable with all eyes upon him. 'Well, Valahald turned up and he said he'd got things to tell Heranar, things for him to think about once he went … went into the dark. For instance, he said, "Don't worry about your wife, I'll see to her," and then he said, well, he said, "In fact, I've already seen to her."' Temenghent cleared his throat and shot an embarrassed glance at the women present. 'If you see what I mean. Well, Heranar shouted and struggled, it was all we could do to hold him back. He was screaming that he didn't believe it, that she would never, cursing his brother, generally going mad. Valahald came right up to him and hit him across the face, and before he could start yelling again, he said she'd been so pleased to get rid of Heranar she was glad of the chance to tell it had been him who'd tipped you off' – a quick glance at Haldur this time – 'and then he said, "She was so delighted to receive the attentions of a civilised man for a change that she insisted on giving me a little present, the very same one you sold your loyalty for." Heranar raged at him, said he was lying about Ilmarynvoro and about himself, that she would never let Valahald touch her, that he'd taken no bribe from anyone, but Valahald put his hand in his sleeve pocket and brought out a big piece of raw amber. He held it right under Heranar's nose and gave that smile of his. "I think you'll recognise this," he said, "and I think you'll know where I took it from."

'That's what did it, really. Heranar gave this terrible scream, tore himself free and kicked Valahald in the … er… Well, then Valahald was down and his brother leapt on him, shovelled dust and dirt from the ground into his face, grabbed the amber and forced it into his mouth, right in. Valahald's eyes and nose were streaming and his throat was blocked by the amber – he couldn't breathe. Heranar got up and stood over him, he cursed him again and told him to choke on his lies. Then he watched, and waited for him to die.' Temenghent dropped his eyes and lowered his voice. 'And we watched too,' he muttered.

Haldur sat frozen. He realised now why Sigitsinen had altered the details of Valahald's death when he brought them the news. The Outlander, remembering how Haldur had blamed himself for Cathasar's death, had thought to spare him the full story of what had happened between Valahald and Heranar in order to prevent him taking guilt on himself there too. Part of Haldur's mind registered this delicacy of Sigitsinen's: there was a gentle side to him which those who saw only the hard, pragmatic fighting man would never guess. But mostly he dwelt with a painful intensity on Heranar. Why, why did I give him the amber, thought Haldur; what have I brought on him, what has really happened to his wife? And his children too, those lovely little girls. He looked up.

'I swear on the memory of Ellaaro my mother and Heredcar my brother, Heranar told me of his own free will that the Nine Dales were to be attacked. I left him the amber on the night before we made our bid for freedom, as a gift to be kept in trust for his daughters; but I take the Starborn for my witnesses that I wish I had never done so.'

A long silence followed this and eventually Haldur got up and walked away into the trees. After a few moments of subdued conversation, the others gradually dispersed to their sleeping places. Cunoreth and Urancrasig, lying side by side, exchanged a quick whisper before settling for sleep.

'Myself, I think we're well rid of both brothers.'

'So do I. Haldur takes things too much to heart.'

But next day, as they rode out from the forest and over the bridge, Cunoreth revised his opinion slightly. Out of Maesaldron, down to the bridge and across it, and on into Caradward they stormed; and when they took shelter in their next camp the bridge was theirs as well as the mine: the Lissad na'Stirfell was behind them, and Caradriggan lay ahead. They swept all before them with no losses to the two hundred; and Haldur rode at their head like a man possessed, crying *'Na Devocatron!'* as he led them.

CHAPTER 60

Light to light

'So far, so good.' Vorardynur wiped the sweat off his face with a terse laugh. 'All this tension is putting years on me. I can't make up my mind whether to be glad we've still got a couple of days to wait, or to wish we could get on with things and have it all over one way or the other.'

They had made as much speed as they could after taking the bridge, heading, on Artorynas' advice, for the broken country where he had hidden briefly during his flight from Caradriggan. Here they were barely twenty miles from the city, trusting to a small river each side of them and the generally deserted nature of the land about to give them refuge for the final hours before concealment was put aside for good. After watering the horses and setting a watch they settled down to eat, rest and make what plans they could.

'Yes, I know what you mean.'

Cunoreth's battle-braids were still too short to swing behind him as he moved: instead they stood out all around his face, giving him, when combined with the excitement of the ride which still showed in his eyes, a slightly wild look. He had persuaded Haldur to insist that Urancrasig, in spite of the lad's furious protests, should stay to help guard the bridge behind them; freed from that responsibility, and torn now between hope and despair over Astirano, he was full of a nervous energy that needed some outlet.

'But it's action for me, every time. We've waited long enough. I reckon our next move is for *them* to show themselves, would you think?' He tilted his head in the direction of the Cunorad.

'I'd say so, but it'll likely be for Artorynas to decide that with them.'

'Why? Aren't Haldur and you our leaders? Where is Artorynas, anyway? I can't see him anywhere.'

Cunoreth, tall and lanky, stared around the camp over Vorardynur's head, one foot tapping the ground, his hands moving all the time: hitching at his belt, smoothing his clothes, tweaking at his hair. Vorardynur sighed, and then laughed again.

'Cunoreth.' He looked up into the thin, restless face. 'Will you just calm down? Listen, neither Haldur nor myself would be here at all if it wasn't for Artorynas. But in any case, you must know he has his own reasons for coming back to Caradriggan. Surely it's our good fortune that his path runs with ours. Whatever he says or does is fine by me: if I can't trust one of the As-Geg'rastigan, then I can't trust anybody. I think our hopes rest with him.'

As evening drew near, Haldur paused to look up at the sky as he walked through their camp. The usual thick cloud was deepening and darkening as night approached, but over towards the horizon, slightly north of east, it almost seemed that the cover was less uniform. He looked more carefully, frowning. Certainly there was no actual break in the cloud, no sign of clear sky – but surely he could see texture, shapes in the smothering blanket, a hint of thinning? He eased his shoulders where they chafed under his harness in the heat: it was so sultry, the evening felt close and threatening. Unslinging his quiver, he stooped to lay it with his other equipment and belongings when he heard someone call his name.

'Let's go up the slope a little way,' said Artorynas, 'where we can help to keep the watch while we talk.'

They followed the stream for a while and then turned aside, brushing through the scrub until they emerged from the bushes and sat down where a small thicket grew on top of a bank. Artorynas looked around.

'We came here sometimes when I was training with the auxiliaries,' he said. 'In fact it can't be all that far from here where I got this.' He touched the lock of hair which showed up white in the twilight. 'Then when I left Caradriggan, I used the streams to lay a false trail for my pursuers. And now I have come here again; the wheel has turned almost full circle.'

There was something about these words, something in the tone of Artorynas' voice, which stopped Haldur from replying. It was so quiet and still: the only sounds the rustle of some small creature moving through the undergrowth and brush, the occasional sleepy note of a roosting bird. Suddenly a breath of wind came out of the gathering night; they heard it approaching moments before it sighed across them, strangely chilly, and then it died away, leaving the sticky heaviness still hanging untouched. A loud burst of defiant song made them look up to see a mistle-thrush swaying, black against the dark sky, in the bushes above them; then as quickly as it had appeared it was gone, hastening away to some hidden perch. Artorynas laughed softly.

'We should take it for a sign,' he said. 'Do you call it the storm-cock in Rihannad Ennar, too, and say that it sings to welcome tempest and battle? It knows that doom is near.'

Haldur bit his lip doubtfully. 'Then you think we should go straight on, tomorrow? I had counted on one more day, to steady our minds and steel ourselves.'

'No, keep to your plan. Let the Cunorad prepare themselves; let the others do whatever they must to be ready. I need tomorrow also: there are things I too must do. And so now is the moment when I should give you this.'

To Haldur's amazement, Artorynas drew out the arrow and held it towards him.

'Me? Why? I can't take it – surely it's for you, only you can use it!'

Artorynas shook his head. 'No, only I could find it. But only you can use it so that its flight is true. Take it, this is for you to do.'

Haldur took the arrow. Although he had gazed at it, awestruck, when Artorynas brought it back to Cotaerdon, he had never touched it before. His fingers shook slightly as he turned it over in his hands. Even in the dusk he seemed to see its perfection, as if the details were revealed by the light that somehow it contained. There was a life force in it too: he felt it, a sense of hidden energy that was answered within him. His hair lifted as a kind of shiver ran over his skin. He looked up and saw how the silver and gold of the arrow had wakened the amber in Artorynas' eyes.

'But why me, why must I use it?'

'Because only you have skill enough, and when the time comes, this arrow must reach its target.'

For a moment or two Haldur sat staring at the arrow. He imagined what it might feel like, to set it to the string, to send it on its way, flying like a ray of light from the heart of the sun itself. 'Is this why my father let me come south, after all?' he asked. 'Did you tell him this? Is this the reason he changed his mind?'

'Yes; when I told him you were the one man whose aim was true enough for the task, he agreed to let you go. And then I promised him that afterwards, you would come safely home to him.'

Silence stretched out between them. Once again it seemed to Haldur as if the door to the future was held open before him, but he could not bring himself to look through it. He dragged his mind back to the present. 'What is it, then, that I have to do?'

'At Caradriggan, you will let the arrow fly: light to light, and the dawn will return once more.'

'But ... if only I can ... if the aim must be true, then what will be my target?'

'You will see a light: small, but as piercing and bright as if a star came down to earth. Send the arrow straight into the heart of it, light to light.'

This was not what Haldur had been expecting. It sounded almost too easy: he sensed some significance in the words but the meaning was hidden from him. 'Are you sure this starlight will appear? Will I recognise it?'

'Absolutely sure, because when the time comes for the light to be revealed, I myself will cause it to appear. And yes, you will know it for what it is.'

Again Haldur felt that eerie tingle in his fingers as he ran them over the arrow. It knows too, he said to himself: somehow the arrow knows, it knows its time is near, it is impatient to fly. He sat thinking about what Artorynas had told him of the finding of the arrow, wishing he too could have shared the quest, and suddenly the question that bothered him more than any other sprang so urgently into his mind that he could not stop himself asking it, nor prevent himself from thinking that he should do so before it was too late.

'What is going to happen, afterwards?'

Artorynas replied with a question of his own. 'What do you want to happen?'

Haldur drew a breath and looked up eagerly. His answer was ready: there was no need to think about it. I want the Nine Dales to be saved, I want the light to return for those in darkness here, I want the world to be restored anew so the Hidden People may show themselves once more, I want to spend my life in peace in Rihannad Ennar, I want you to return with me there. Yet the words stayed unspoken. There was no need to tell Artorynas all this, he already knew: why else were they brothers in their hearts, if not because each knew the other's thought like his own? And I know, thought Haldur, I know without being told that Artorynas will never return to Cotaerdon. The Hidden People have taken him to themselves. His shoulders sagged under the burden of this truth.

'Why does it have to be like this?' he muttered.

'When you talked with Arval, did he ever say anything about the fate of his own family?' asked Artorynas.

Haldur shook his head.

'Well, many years ago he told me a little of what happened. His father was as-ur, or so Arval thought, because his father disappeared and never returned. To use Arval's own words, he was driven in spite of himself to seek what he could never find on this earth. Even though he had a home, a wife and a small son; even then, he was unable to bear his restless yearning for the Starborn. And he never returned;

Arval scarcely remembered his parents, because with his father gone, his mother lost the will to live and died, leaving her little son alone.'

Haldur sat considering this, reflecting on how he had met Arval, spent time in his company, and never guessed at the sadness that lay hidden in his past. The sorrow of the tale brought the words of *Maesell y'm As-Urad* to his mind and the anger and resentment he had felt towards his own father were replaced by a new understanding. He saw better now what Carapethan had feared when Artorynas lived among them, and realised why he had ordered Astell to spoil a feast-day's mirth by reciting the old story. If parting was painful now, how much worse would the hurt be if the day was delayed? And how would it be once he succeeded his father as lord: what if men said he was not his own master, that he followed Artorynas' word; what if Haldan don Vorygwent felt belittled or ignored? What would befall Torello? And maybe other women too, if their hearts also turned to the Starborn – look at the fate of Numirantoro. Haldur looked up and found Artorynas watching him.

'Listen, Haldur. Remember how you told me you would have stayed with the Cunorad? That if you could have had your wish, you would have spent your whole life seeking the Starborn? I too, I don't remember a time when my own heart didn't turn to them with longing. Think, then, how it was when I awoke on the Golden Strand with the arrow, and knew I had found the Hidden People, had seen them with my own eyes, that they had been beside me, but were gone. I tell you now what I would tell no-one else, the sorrow of that moment was almost more than I could bear: it was as if every hurt I ever suffered came back to wound me again twice over, as if the weight of loss would crush me into oblivion. In fact I came close to wishing it would, that there could be an end. But… there was the arrow, so much hope had depended on whether I could find it… And my mother, one of the few things she left me was the promise that if I succeeded, it would help me with a choice I must make. I don't understand why it is that I have that choice, either to belong to the

Earthborn or the As-Geg'rastigan: it is a mystery that Arval has not explained to me, at least not yet; maybe he will tell me when we meet again. Perhaps it seems an easy decision, but that wasn't so. I hesitated before I made my choice. You know without my saying it that if I were to stay, I would wish to be nowhere else but the Nine Dales. But as it is, I take our friendship with me into the life of the Starborn: you go with me to the Hidden People, carried in my heart.'

As he listened to this, once again Haldur sensed a kind of shock run through the arrow he still held. Surely it was made from more than metals, precious though these were: the life of the Starborn had woken within it, too. He began to see how it was that only Artorynas could have found it. Then a new thought struck him.

'What is it that you have to do, tomorrow?'

'I must enter Caradriggan once more.'

Haldur exclaimed in dismay. 'But you can't! You won't be able to get in!'

'I think I will. I must, if I am to keep my promise to Arval. I swore to return and stand beside him again.'

'But how will you do it? They'll recognise you; you'll be captured. Why not wait? Once we take the city you can see Arval then.'

'I won't be captured. People see what they expect to see. They're looking for Artorynas, whose face they think is unknown, not Maesrhon whom most believe dead. Trust me, this is how it has to be.'

Haldur stood up. He could hear the pain dragging at his voice. 'You won't come back.'

Artorynas got to his feet also. He lifted his hand and touched Haldur's forehead in the dedication used by the Hounds of the Starborn. 'I want you to know that I too wish we could have stood together on Porthesc nan Esylt. But remember that the Hound of the Vow once said that for you, the search is not yet over.'

At this, back into Haldur's mind came Artorynas' assurance that he would live safely through what lay before him. The words weighed on his heart more like a sentence of death than a promise of life. 'What is there left to seek for?'

'You are still Cunor y'n Tor, and Rihann y'n Temenellan leads down to the sea. Now I must delay no longer. If I set out now, I can make enough speed on foot during the night to get around the south of Caradriggan and enter the city tomorrow on the far side from here.'

For a moment or two Haldur stood, afraid to speak in case he was overcome by tears. 'So we will not meet again?' he said eventually, once he was sure he could keep his voice level.

'We will see each other at Caradriggan,' said Artorynas. 'Aim true when the time comes, brother of my heart!'

And so they parted, with no other farewells. Haldur stood, the arrow still in his hand, as Artorynas slipped silently away and vanished into the oppressive night of Caradward.

Arval and Artorynas

At the approach of the new day, the guard was changed around the city walls and those who looked out westward saw men and animals milling about just within the range of the torchlight. Sometimes it happened that travellers and traders mistimed their journeys and failed to reach Caradriggan before the gates closed at evening, and today there was a temporary camp of just such a group of wayfarers some distance out from the walls. As the huge west gates clanged open, they began to move forwards, dust rising from feet, wheels and hooves. Under the archway there was little room to spare as several heavy wagons trundled through, pedestrians squashed together as each tried to be first into the city; and a man on horseback heading out found himself forced to pull over sharply. In the press there was some pushing and shoving, the guards attempting to restore order with shouted threats. The horse, unsettled by this, began to play up; and under cover of this brief flurry of activity a plainly-dressed man slipped through with the other pedestrians. The rider, occupied in calming his mount, failed to notice the face shadowed by a hood drawn against the dawn chill; and the man on foot, intent on entry as quickly and unobtrusively as possible, never glanced up to see who it was who wrestled for control of his horse. Heretellar and Artorynas, each going open-eyed to his fate, passed unknowingly within hand-clasping distance of one another.

As he walked swiftly towards Tellgard, his senses alert for any hint that his presence had been noted, memories of the night when he had fled away from Caradriggan came back to Artorynas. He remembered how he had felt shielded by the protection of his Starborn inheritance, buoyed up by its power, invincible, invulnerable; how men had hidden themselves within doors, afraid of some nameless force abroad in their streets. It was different today as he passed through the city. Only those whose business required them to rise early were out and about; they hurried along, sleepy-eyed, no-one giving him a second glance, and the new day held no promise: it was stale, flat, without hope, and the faces he saw seemed shut in and closed. But he himself… The great task was almost done, now. The quest was achieved, it was already behind him. All the fears, the toil, the sorrow were finished: soon, very soon now, all would be finally fulfilled. Then the pain he carried with him from his parting with Haldur, the old childhood hurts, the sadness that came from *maesell y'm as-urad*, all would be gone. But that was for tomorrow: for today, if he was not prevented, he would be true to the oath he had taken and return to stand beside Arval once more. Artorynas turned the last corner and saw Tellgard ahead of him. Tomorrow, he thought. Tomorrow, I must be steadfast; only so will I pass through the light into the life of the As-Geg'rastigan, only so will light and hope return for the Earthborn and the circle be truly complete at last. Putting all concealment aside, he lowered his hood as he reached the colonnade and ran up the steps. With a long, lithe stride he crossed the court, the light breeze of early morning lifting the dark hair away from his face. A door opened and

Arval, coming out from a vigil in the shadowed hall, heard a footfall and turned. Artorynas walked forward steadily, the years and miles of wandering forgotten in the joy of seeing the guide and guardian of his youth again. Arval looked at the face before him with its spare, proud lines; austere, yet lit from within by a kind of stern serenity; at the strong nose and jaw, at the tall, lean frame; and in spite of the white lock at the temple and the small scar that marked the lip, despite the amber eyes whose gold was wakened by the lamp on the wall above, for him yet more years rolled back and he saw Arymaldur before him once more: a lord of the Starborn who smiled a little, holding out his hands. Wordlessly, Arval raised his own hand in the threefold sign and then, still speechless, spread his arms in welcome.

If ever Arval, for all his wisdom, could have been tempted if offered his heart's desire, it was that day. Careless of the consequences, he would have wished to turn back time, so that he could have heard all that Artorynas had to tell him over and over again, so that he could have lengthened out the hours indefinitely, savouring anew the delight of their longed-for meeting, delaying what he quickly discovered must happen on the morrow. He hastened to draw Artorynas with him up the stairs, away from any who might see; and closing the door of his study behind them turned to feast his eyes on the wanderer for whose return he had waited so long. There they sat, as they had done so often in years gone by, as if master and pupil once more; but Arval sensed, as he noticed that the lamplight itself seemed diminished by the brightness of the presence within the room, that the old relationship was changed.

'When Haldur told me you had reached the Nine Dales safely and gone on in search of Asward donn'Ur, I never thought I should see you so soon, before even a year had passed from then! But now that I do, I see also that you have made your choice: and therefore I know that you must have found the arrow. Where is it, *Is-torar*? May I see it once more?'

'You will see it tomorrow,' said Artorynas. 'I have left it with Haldur, whose fate is now also bound to it.'

'With Haldur!' exclaimed Arval. 'You have seen him since he left Caradriggan, then? Where? He sat with me, in this very room, before travelling north once more, and shared his fears that Rihannad Ennar was in danger from Vorynaas, that the man was not to be trusted. And his suspicions were well-founded: even now Vorynaas is poised to attack. I have heard that Heranar, of all unlikely people, warned Haldur of what was planned, and that he and his companions escaped. Did he come safely home? But if he has the arrow with him in Cotaerdon, how is it that you say I will see it tomorrow?'

'Vorynaas will never set foot in the Nine Dales,' said Artorynas. 'The evil deeds that lie to his name cannot be undone, but his time is very nearly over. Haldur is not twenty miles from this city: by dawn, he will be outside the walls. From tomorrow, those with the will to do it may begin to mend things once more; and in that, he and they will need your wisdom and guidance above all.'

'My guidance? What of yours?'

Arval's dark eyes locked with the golden gaze before him and never flinched, but the pain of knowledge half-guessed and long denied pierced his heart at Artorynas' reply.

'I shall not be here.'

Artorynas took out the As y'm Ur from where it lay next to his heart, and fastened it about his neck so that the jewel lay in the hollow of his throat.

'I have told Haldur what to aim for. In his hands, the arrow will not miss its mark.'

Arval's hands were clenched into fists within his sleeves as he fought to control his emotions. 'Haldur loves you,' he said. 'Are you sure he will be able to do this?'

'It is because he loves me that he will do it,' said Artorynas. 'But afterwards, though his name will be renowned as long as tomorrow's deeds are remembered, that will mean nothing to him. He will need help and support, which is one of the reasons why I insisted to Carapethan that Vorardynur must ride south with us. He is here to shoulder the burdens of responsibility that Haldur will be unable to bear, at least at first. But it is you that Haldur will need most. Care for him, Arval. Guide him, comfort him, as you have watched over me. I love him also, he is the brother of my heart.'

Suddenly Arval was overcome with weakness. He covered his face with his hands and Artorynas saw how he trembled. When he drew breath to speak, it was almost a groan. 'But how can this be what Arymaldur foretold? He spoke of hope returning.'

'Yes; but Arval, remember his words. "Let that which is left seek for that which is taken. When the two are united, hope shall return." You have said yourself, many times over the years, that there is always hope if men know where to find it; but hope needs fulfilment. I see now that Arymaldur left us with a deed also to do, that possession of the arrow alone will not bring to pass what must be.'

'Why must it be so soon? Are we to have no more than one day together after all these years, little son?'

'Vorynaas has forced our hand. We cannot wait, if we are to save Rihannad Ennar from our darkness. Now, there will be light for men, in a new sunrise; this world renewed; and for me, the straight road revealed that leads to those I have yearned for through all my years, and whose life I have chosen to join. The works of hand and mind of both my father and my mother; the life called into being by her love; past, present and future, all will be as one; and then, truly, hope shall return.

'But we have more than a day, because why need we waste the night? Let us talk on, and I will tell you all you wish to know. You can drink from the strengthening spirit of Tellgard if you feel the need.'

Yes, reflected Arval bitterly, there will be time enough later to rest: for me to sleep, if grief permits; and for you – who knows if the Starborn suffer weariness and if so, how they assuage it? But he raised his head and agreed, hiding his thoughts; and indeed before long was so engrossed in listening to the tale of Artorynas' wanderings that he forgot his sorrow in the vast new landscapes that became visible to his mind's eye, the hidden treasures of knowledge that were unlocked and laid before him, the immense perspectives of fresh learning that were now revealed. The business of Tellgard went on its quiet, orderly way, those who dwelt or worked there recognising that its master seemed closeted with his books and leaving him undisturbed until his private study should be finished; and in the streets beyond, the noise of daily life in the city rose in its usual hubbub as the day wore on. Arval and Artorynas ignored both alike, deep in converse as they were. Even when, shortly before mid-day, shouted orders, screams of fright, clattering hooves, all the sounds of a sudden tumult, drifted up to them from outside the walls of Tellgard, their eager talk never faltered: to Artorynas, such alarms held no meaning any longer, and Arval seemed not even to notice.

A warning and a promise

Outside on the steps of the colonnade, a woman sat in shock, staring at the blood welling along her arm from a whip-cut that had torn her sleeve away. A toddler who had been knocked to the ground and scraped his knees was bawling loudly while two older children scrambled around, picking up the packages that had tumbled out of the woman's basket and come to rest here and there. Two men were struggling, one yelling abuse at the troopers who were rapidly disappearing up the street, the other desperately trying to calm him down.

'Shut up, shut up,' he hissed, 'or they'll come back for you. Do you want to end up in the Open Hall?'

'Ah, what do I care!' snarled the first man. 'They could send me to Assynt y'm Atrannaas, as long as I got my hands on the bastards first! Look at her, what did they have to do that for? What's so urgent that they have to use whips on their own people?' He glared around him. 'When's this Artorynas we've all heard about going to appear, eh? Maybe then they'll all be driven into the Waste to rot, here's hoping!'

The small group of bystanders that had gathered began to melt away at this, several people exchanging frightened glances. But hands moved in the sign and Isteddar, who had been on his way home from the early shift at the *Sword and Stars*, changed his mind. He turned from where he had been standing at the back of the crowd and headed for the inn again. There might be some news worth hearing in due course. The man who had been doing the shouting hunkered down beside his wife.

'Come on love, we're right outside Tellgard here. Let's take you in, they'll patch you up.'

Meanwhile the soldier who had whipped his way clear was dismounting in Seth y'n Carad, calling for Thaltor. He had three other men from the barbican with him: one was Tirathalt, now hauling to his feet a man who, with hands tied behind his back, had been lumped like a sack across his horse's neck in front of the saddle. All of them disappeared into the guardhouse but very soon hurried out again with Thaltor, hastening towards the main building.

Ordered to speak by Thaltor, the fellow with tied hands stammered out his tale, wilting with fright at being thrust before Vorynaas himself. Tirathalt stood listening, scarcely able to believe his ears. He wanted to sneak a look at Sigittor, but dared not take the risk. They had been gathered up at random to form a quick escort and the third man was unknown to him: it was uncertain where his true loyalties might lie and clearly the captain was not to be trusted, given the speed with which he had rushed his informant up to Seth y'n Carad. Vorynaas sat stroking his beard, his dark eyes moving over the men before him, considering in silence what he had been told. Abruptly he got to his feet: the bound man flinched visibly and even the troopers started slightly before recovering themselves to stand at attention once more.

'Thaltor will assume overall command in the city; he will come down to the barbican shortly,' said Vorynaas. 'Meanwhile you, captain, sound the alert, have all the gates closed. Have a despatch rider made ready; I shall want an order taken immediately to Torilmarap on the border.'

'Sir. Er, sir…' The captain faltered as Vorynaas raised his brows. 'Er, what am I to do about *him*?'

'Ah yes, our friend from the countryside.' Vorynaas smiled at the fellow's obvious fear. 'Well, I think you'd better take him back to the barbican and keep him there for me until we find out whether he's told us the truth or not.'

In Tellgard the hours passed unheeded as Arval sat listening to Artorynas; sometimes asking a question but mostly simply listening, caught up in the tale of his quest, drinking in his words like parched earth soaking up rain after a drought. Even though he had heard something from Haldur of the early years of Artorynas' journey north, now he wanted to be told at first-hand. The lonely emptiness of Ilmar Inenad, fading into the western glow of sunset, the silent heights of the Somllichan Asan, pathless and mighty; blue lakes bustling with life in springtime, freezing snows under a winter's moon; rivers in spate, woods in leaf, starry skies, golden dawns, summer heat-haze, autumn gales, winter storms raging over the wanderer's solitary refuge: all were conjured into being before him.

'When I was a boy in Salfgard, Ardeth often used to say how lovely this world is,' said Artorynas. 'In fact, Fosseiro and others would tease him about it sometimes, tell him he said every season in turn was his favourite. But he was right, this world is fair beyond our powers to describe.'

As he spoke, he glanced at the shelves: yes, Numirantoro's books still lay there in pride of place. He took one down and leafed through it until he found the page with the standing stones. There they stood, exactly as he remembered them, watchful upon their bleak upland plain.

'Here is a mystery. This circle of stones is not just a picture from my mother's mind. Far to the north of Rihannad Ennar it lies, the work of long-forgotten hands, but solid and real: I have seen it and walked past it.'

286

Arval's dark eyes widened in wonder. He leaned forward and turned the book towards him. 'You think perhaps it was raised by men in the years before... before the fires of death on earth, before *Vala na Naasan* ruined all?'

While Arval lives, the bad time will never be dismissed as legend again in Caradriggan, thought Artorynas with an inward smile; but before he could reply, there was a soft tap at the study door. Arval sat up straight, suddenly tense. 'Who is it?'

'It's Forgard. May I come in? I have news,' came a voice from the corridor, where Forgard stood in some surprise: usually Arval bade callers enter without question.

There was a moment's pause in which Arval glanced quickly at Artorynas for his agreement. 'Yes, of course,' he replied.

Swiftly the door opened and closed as Forgard slipped into the room. Artorynas was struck by how quietly he shut the door behind him, how careworn, almost furtive he seemed. Then Forgard, turning towards Arval, saw that he was not alone. He faltered, almost as if he had struck some invisible barrier, and groped for the back of a chair to lean on, staring at Artorynas with shock etched onto his face. Arval jumped up to help his old friend into a seat.

'Quick, *Is-torar*, in the cupboard there,' he said, and Artorynas reached down the flagon of strong feast-day wine, pouring a cup which Arval pressed upon Forgard.

'Drink this.'

Forgard took the cup but put it down again untasted. He still had not uttered a word, but continued to stare at Artorynas. Tears gathered in his eyes and spilled to roll down his cheeks, and still he could not speak; then slowly his hand moved in the ancient sign and he found his voice. 'How, how have you come here? When?'

'At dawn today, among the first incomers,' said Artorynas. 'Come, drink, I am sorry to have startled you like this.'

Beginning to recover slightly, Forgard shook his head. 'Startled! I am just amazed, I cannot believe it... but... if it was this morning, maybe you saw Heretellar?'

'Heretellar! Has he left already?' asked Arval rather sharply.

'Yes, Isteddar said he decided to make an early start,' said Forgard, still gazing at Artorynas but now sipping at his wine.

'No, I saw no-one I knew,' replied Artorynas, 'but Heretellar would have left the city by the south gate, surely, and I came in from the west. What is your news, Forgard?'

Now Forgard turned to Arval. 'You must have noticed the upheaval in the city this afternoon? No? Well, in the circumstances that's understandable enough.' He smiled for the first time and then became serious once more.

'Isteddar says word has come that an army is drawing near; he heard it in the *Sword*. Some fellow from the countryside brought the news: I gather Vorynaas has him under guard in case it's not true – it does seem incredible, I have to admit – but he's taking no chances apparently. Thaltor's been put in command here in Caradriggan; they've closed all the gates, and a messenger's been sent to request reinforcements from the garrison on the old border.'

'So it's true, then, that the city is only lightly defended?' said Artorynas. 'That the balance of forces has been shifted north, in preparation for the advance on Rihannad Ennar?'

Forgard stared in surprise. 'Yes, that is so. But how…?'

'How do I know?' Artorynas laughed slightly. 'I heard it from Sigitsinen, an officer in the auxiliaries, a leader of the secret resistance, and a friend of my youth with whom I trained. We are well informed. And we are well prepared, athough there was always the risk that our approach could not be kept concealed from every eye. Does Vorynaas know how many move to assail him, or that I was with them?'

'Well…' Forgard glanced at Arval as if hoping for some kind of guidance. The shock of finding Artorynas in Tellgard, this calmness, the lack of apparent reaction to the news he brought, were putting him off his stride. He pulled himself together.

'Of course, it's true that I can only tell you what Isteddar overheard, and the tale may have become garbled in the telling. But as he heard it, this fellow who came in with the news told Vorynaas that he'd seen a small force only, but he maintained he recognised some Caradwardans among it and swore he'd seen Haldur also. Thaltor scoffed at this and said it was impossible. He reckons he's simply dealing with a band of rebels; but Vorynaas is taking no chances, as I said before: he's sending for more men in case this is just an advance party of some larger force. He can't know about you, the word would have been all over the city in no time if he had. They've got the messenger locked up in the barbican. You'd think they'd be grateful for the warning he brought, but no doubt he's quaking in his boots wondering if he's going to meet the traditional fate in store for the bringer of bad news, especially as he must have got it wrong about Haldur, surely.'

Artorynas stood up. He closed Numirantoro's book and replaced it on the shelf. For a moment he stood with his back to the room, then he turned.

'This fellow deserves better of Vorynaas, because his report is accurate, so far as it goes: east of Caradriggan Haldur lies, and with him there are indeed some who once obeyed Vorynaas. I left them at nightfall yesterday. The mine and the bridge are already in their hands; by dawn tomorrow, they will be outside the city walls: Na Devocatron, whose name will be written in books like these in the days and years to come. There is no need to fear that their numbers are so few. Among the two hundred are the Cunorad y'm As-Geg'rastigan, all oath-bound; and they have brought to Vorynaas what he wishes for above all else, the chance to see me again.'

Artorynas raised Forgard to his feet. 'Greet Heretellar for me, and Ancrascaro and Rhostellat; remember me to Isteddar. I am sorry we cannot talk longer, but time is running short and I have promises yet to fulfil to Arval during what remains. Go home now, Forgard, sleep in peace. Tomorrow the nightmare will be over.'

Master and pupil

When Forgard had gone, having embraced Artorynas with tears once more in his eyes, silence fell in the room. Evening was drawing on, and with it the quiet that came when the sounds of day faded and died.

'Heretellar is someone I should very much have liked to talk to again, if it could have been possible,' said Artorynas.

Arval moved the lamp and as he did so the light passed over his silver hair and thin face, throwing his dark eyes into sudden shadow. 'He arrived unexpectedly at his parents' house only yesterday, having been in the city not long before,' he said. 'I do wonder very much what has caused him to leave again so suddenly.'

'His father seems untroubled about it,' said Artorynas. 'Heretellar is well named, wise beyond his years. I have never forgotten his assessment of poor Geraswic: it was not only accurate, but both shrewd and compassionate also. Maybe now he will come into his own. He will want to help you in your support of Haldur.'

This served to remind Arval painfully of the grief to come. He dropped his eyes to his hands where they lay on the table. '*Is-torar*, you might have chosen the Earthborn,' he said sadly, and then looked up. 'If you stayed with the Ur-Geg'rastigan, little son, how would things fall out?'

'Yes, I might. And it was not a decision taken in haste. But Arval, although I spent time on the choice – indeed you could say that in some ways I have spent all my life in reaching that choice – yet in other ways my mind has always been set. I think my mother knew it; she saw my heart though she looked on me only once. At any rate her words proved true: it was following the arrow's path that brought the light of understanding. If I had chosen otherwise, I think that tomorrow you could look for what you have always warned us against: evil deeds that men may only excuse by claiming that the end justified the means. And who knows whether my life too might then have been one of those required in payment? This way, I cannot promise that there will be no deaths: there have been too many already and they lie heavy on Haldur; but at least we may hope that sorrow may be curtailed and fade the sooner.'

For a while Arval sat, pondering all he had heard. I am the pupil now, he thought, a glow of sad pride warming his heavy heart. Yet in spite of all, his intellect was feasting on the new lore laid before him; the questions crowded unbidden into his mind.

'Do you think that for the Earthborn, the road to the As-Geg'rastigan must lead through death?' he asked.

Again Artorynas stood up. He paced softly about the room, and though his eyes moved over the hundreds of books crammed onto the shelves, his face had an inward look. 'I don't know. Maybe it must, if one would walk the straight path. My mother... if my life had not woken within her, so that you kept her alive until she could bring me to birth, surely she would not have endured the fire that burns in the Starborn. You know, in the Nine Dales they call them the Hidden People... Astell thought they were hidden from us in a world that is perfect; that they can pass from their world to ours if they will, but we cannot go to them because their world is the earth as it should be, not the world as we have made it. When I followed the Starborn, far in the north, it was as if I stepped from this world to theirs; but when I came to myself, I was alone and never saw them again. Yet who else could have set the arrow beside me? Who can explain the mystery? Not I, not Astell – and, it seems, not even Arval, Arval the Earth-wise.'

Arval could not help a smile at this. 'Haldur tried to persuade me to go back to the Nine Dales with him, and after all I have heard, I cannot deny I should like to talk with Astell. But today is for you, little son, and already night is drawing on. Tell me now of your journey to Asward donn'Ur, of your days upon the Golden Strand. Speak to me of the As-Geg'rastigan.'

So Artorynas sat down once more, and spoke on. The hours passed, and Arval listened with rapt attention to all Artorynas had to tell: about the dread of Aestron na Caarst, where some unknown terror dwelt; about the loveliness of Asward donn'Ur; about the boundless sea that washed the sands of Porthesc nan Esylt. He looked at the shells Artorynas had brought back from that untouched shore, and it seemed he too heard the voice of the deep waters, saw the golden path laid dazzling upon the waves where the *astorhos* blossoms floated. He sighed, scarcely able to bear the longing that woke in him too, a yearning that pierced his heart, a hopeless wish to see that unspoiled northern land. And now Artorynas began to tell him of the Starborn themselves, as he had seen them sweep into the sunset, calling to him, fleeting away from him even as he ran in desperate pursuit... But here Artorynas' voice faltered, and he broke off. He looked across at Arval, shaking his head.

'There was something else, something I had never heard, or heard of, before, and I must try to describe it, although I don't know how.'

He sat, lost in memory; then he took a deep breath and tried to find the words.

'It was just before I saw them,' he said at last. 'I realise now that I knew in my heart they were near. I sensed some change in the light, the very air was charged with life. But it was what I heard...' again he faltered into silence. 'I heard a sound – sounds – no, a blend of sound. It was lovely beyond endurance: so sweet, yet at the same time a mighty force; it both crushed me and sustained me. Hearing it was a torment, but... but if it had stopped, I could not have borne it. All I wanted was for it to go on for ever, to overwhelm me. And then, when the heart was torn from me, when even the strength to think was taken away – they were there. A great host of the As-Geg'rastigan passed before me, as if what I had heard had taken a form visible to my eyes. As if...' Once more Artorynas stopped, and then he spread his hands, thwarted. 'It's no good, I don't think there is any way to explain what I'm trying to say.'

'You underestimate your skill with words.' Arval was facing Artorynas, but his black eyes were wide and dark, as if they looked on something far away. 'It must be that you heard *Haellem y'm Asan.*'

'A song of stars?' said Artorynas doubtfully. 'I've not described it well enough. I mean no comparison with the warble of a robin – or notes the storm-cock may fling at the sky,' he added, a memory of the previous evening suddenly coming back to him. But then he paused, thinking. 'Although yes, maybe both are somehow a part of what I heard.'

'You hear with the ears of the As-Geg'rastigan, little son,' said Arval, his gaze now focused intently upon Artorynas. 'The *Song of the Stars* is indeed said to carry echoes of all other songs within it. I have found only one reference to it in all my long years of study, and that was while you have been away, which is why we have not discussed this before. It is said that men once knew how to make songs of their own, and they too were somehow born from *Haellem y'm Asan*; but no doubt this knowledge was forgotten like much else when the fires of death swept the earth. Maybe the lost skills will one day be recovered, to be at once the balm and bane of men's minds. Whether I should envy you or not, for having heard *Haellem y'm Asan*, I do not know; but I think I understand now what prompted the choice you have made.'

'Yes, you are right that I would pay whatever price was asked to hear it once more,' said Artorynas, 'but there is another reason. From as long ago as I can remember, what I wanted more than all else was to *know*. No doubt you have not forgotten how when I was a child I pestered you for more teaching, more lore, more knowledge. It seems to me that if even some of what I have been told by you, or some of what Astell guessed, is true, then surely the Starborn must know, in the same way that I wish to understand.'

Arval leaned forward. '*Is-torar*, if you take a brother's bond with Haldur into the life of the Starborn with you, do not go to them with any thought that you ever pestered me.'

At this Artorynas smiled, and for the last time Arval saw Numirantoro in him as well as Arymaldur. 'Arval, when I was a boy you were not only my beloved teacher, you stood to me for father and mother, brother, sister and friend. You rescued what could be saved from my childhood; it is you who made me what I became. I owe you a debt I can never repay. I take you also to the As-Geg'rastigan with me in my heart, where you will always hold a father's place.'

Tears he could not check overcame Arval when he heard these words, but Artorynas hastened to embrace and comfort him.

'There is still a little time, before day comes,' he said. 'Let us go down together and watch the morning stars fade above the *astorhos* trees in the secret court. Then I will go through the hidden door, out to where my fate awaits me in the dark dawn.'

CHAPTER 61

Under arms

What was that? Was there really something to see, away over there to the east, or was it just tiredness and fright playing tricks with his eyes? The young man stood, one hand gripping the stonework of the wall as if for reassurance, staring out into the dark. His breathing was quick and shallow as his heart began to race. Should he raise the alarm, or wait till he was sure? As he stood there dithering, another long, low growl of thunder sounded above, muttering in dull echoes from one horizon to another. It had been going on for hours now, all through his watch, doing nothing to calm his fear. He almost wished there would be lightning or rain, that the storm would break and have done; it would be better than this sense of constant threat. None of his fellow-sentries were near him at present, where he stood on the wall-walk trying to decide what best to do. His watch had begun at midnight; he'd had hours now with nothing but his thoughts for company. Why, why did this have to happen during his time for military service? As it loomed nearer, the unavoidable fate of younger sons, he had so much dreaded being sent up to Rosmorric or Rossaestrethan and maybe caught up in the fighting, that the posting to the barbican garrison had come as a huge relief. But now... His thoughts strayed to his parents, far away in Staran y'n Forgarad. They thought he was safe; who would ever have guessed that Caradriggan itself would be in danger... Again, he peered into the distance. Surely, there was something odd about the sky. When he was a boy, there had once been a huge fire in his home city; some accident in a workshop had sparked a blaze that consumed several other properties and a warehouse before it was brought under control. He had been on a visit to his grandparents at the time and remembered that even at a distance he had been able to see how the clouds were stained by the reflection of the flames below. But this was different. Away to the north-east there, as the night grew old, horizontal lines of red had slowly appeared: shifting, indistinct, they glimmered and glowed as the clouds changed shape. Like blood seeping through cloth, came the comparison he could not prevent. Now stop it, he told himself, get a grip. Look again: there underneath the red, can you really see anything? Frowning, he screwed up his face in concentration, trying the old trick of focusing his eyes to the side of where he thought he had seen something. And yes, he was sure there was movement; and now, look, lights too! Torches? It must be this army they'd been warned of: it was out there, creeping closer! Had no-one else seen anything? Oh why, why does it have to be me? He clamped his teeth together to stop them chattering and looked out again. There could be no doubt. Leaving the wall-walk, he ran down the stone steps and along to the nearest guard chamber to tell the officer of his watch.

The two hundred had struck camp and begun their advance soon after midnight. All through the previous day they had lain close, preparing themselves in body and mind, and now they moved quietly through the dark at a steady pace. Haldur led the way, and Vorardynur kept guard at the rear; Temenghent and others who had joined them, each accompanied by men from the Nine Dales, formed a screen on the flanks some distance from the main force in case of the alarm being raised in any of the villages they passed near.

'And after all, we don't know for certain that no-one has spotted us already,' said Haldur. The Cunorad y'm As-Geg'rastigan, led by Esylto, rode together in silent purpose a few ranks back, shielded from view for the present by their comrades around them. At last they could see, still far in the distance, regular points of light on Caradriggan's walls. Now they halted, bringing in the outriders once more. The leaders gathered together for a final check that all knew their place and plan; then they lit their torches and moved forward towards the city. It had been agreed that when secrecy was no longer possible, they should make their presence as obvious as they could. Haldur had been insistent on this point.

'We've got to do something to start an alert,' he said. 'We're not in a position to attack the city, but we must make sure they react in defence sufficiently to let Artorynas know we're here. Remember he'll be in Tellgard with Arval: neither of them will be able to watch out for us.'

Yes, that's if he's managed to get into the city – and if he's still alive, thought Vorardynur. He had been dumbfounded, at first, to discover that Artorynas had left them to make his own way into Caradriggan, and others too had murmured in surprise and alarm when Haldur broke the news to them. Hiding his own misgivings as well as he could, Haldur had spoken quickly in reassurance.

'He had to go; he was bound by his promise to Arval. Don't forget it's our good fortune that he has his own reasons for coming back to Caradward, that his fate is twined with ours. He told me this is how it has to be, and I trust him.'

'So do I.' Unexpectedly, it was Cureleth who spoke up, as he had done in Cotaerdon. 'From all we've heard about this Vorynaas, I only wish we could see his face when Artorynas appears in their midst with the arrow!'

This caused a general relaxation of tension and some smiles, though Haldur bit his lip. He was sure it was right not to reveal that he now had the arrow, but he could feel dread pressing on him like a burden he was unable to shake off.

And so here they were, advancing upon Caradriggan with torches held high as the dark clouds showed ominous and red behind them and the thunder, muted and sullen, rumbled on above. Then the moment came that told them they had been seen. All along the city walls, more lights sprang up: torches flared, cressets blazed, lanterns shone out. The sudden glow illuminated towers and battlements, the stonework seeming pale in the glare; they saw movement as men ran to their posts and then distantly the sounds of action could be heard in a confusion of shouted orders. At last the two hundred halted and Vorardynur and Haldur dismounted. The cousins spoke quietly together for a moment.

'The walls are within range of our archers from here, but we're not within theirs,' said Haldur. 'The defenders don't realise how much more powerful our bows are: when our embassy came south last year, I took care that we didn't show all our skill when we were invited to compete. Wait here with the others while I go forward, near enough to hail them.'

'But what if they shoot at *you*?' objected Vorardynur.

'They won't, at least not until they've heard what I've got to say. And anyway, I know I'll be safe. Artorynas has promised my father I will live to return home, so it stands to reason that for me it's not the risk it would be for anyone else.'

Vorardynur had no time to wonder at the curiously flat tone in which Haldur spoke of this piece of good fortune. He found himself watching as his cousin walked slowly forward, a torch in his left hand and his right held out empty before him. In a breathless silence Haldur stopped, planted the pole to which his torch was fixed in the ground, and bent to lay his arms before him: quiver, bow, throwing knives and sword. Then he straightened, scanning the walls above the east gate. His voice rang out.

'I speak to Vorynaas of Caradward. Yield this city to us, and give yourself up, or be called to account for the evil deeds that lie to your name.'

Inside Caradriggan

Within Caradriggan, few who lay down to rest at evening slept peacefully through the night. Hope and fear alike wrought upon men's dreams; and lamps were lit in many houses long before the usual time, when those whose slumber had been interrupted found themselves too wakeful to settle again. Even Vorynaas had woken more than once, disturbed above all by a feeling that he had failed to notice some vital point. He lay thinking things over again. How could it possibly be true that Haldur was among those who approached? Unless – maybe he had never gone back to the Nine Dales at all, but simply hidden up in the wilderness somewhere. If so, then Thaltor was probably correct that his followers were just a disaffected rabble of some sort. But in that case, why come back? Why risk a direct march against the city? Haldur had seen enough, they had made sure he saw enough, to know any such attempt was doomed. It made no sense, especially considering that he knew of the planned invasion. Surely it was far more likely that he was back in Rihannad Ennar by now, doing what he could to shore up their defences. Suddenly Vorynaas, sitting on the edge of his bed, punched his pillow angrily. It was a cursed nuisance to have to deal with this unexpected alarm, just when everything was going so smoothly and he wanted nothing to hold up arrangements or distract men and resources from where they should be deployed. Then another idea struck him and his eyes narrowed. All these Artorynas rumours could have started this, he thought. After all, a man as successful as I have been must have enemies who would like to see him thrown down from his position. Maybe those who are envious of my power and wealth have deluded themselves into thinking this is the moment when they can topple me. Yes... that could be it. Vorynaas smiled, his good humour restored. What an unpleasant surprise these fools are going to get tomorrow, he said to himself. Whoever they are, they must be men of no account whatsoever, or else some hint of what was afoot would certainly have reached me earlier. But their fate at least will live long in memory, when it is seen what vengeance I will have upon them.

Deeply asleep at last, he was dragged into reluctant consciousness once more by light in his bedchamber and the anxious shuffling of his steward.

'Well, what's happening? Get on with it, man, don't just stand there,' he snapped.

'Sir, Lord Thaltor is here and wishes to speak with you at once.'

'All right, send him in.'

Thaltor clanked into the room. He was in uniform and fully armed. 'They've been spotted approaching the east side of the city. We're on full alert and I've got the men of the garrison at the ready, drawn up inside the barbican.'

Vorynaas began dressing at speed, his mind working fast. 'Right, that's good. Have that fellow you've got under guard brought up to the east gate and I'll meet you there on the wall-walk.'

Shortly afterwards the two of them were standing gazing out when a soldier climbed up to them, shoving the unhappy messenger ahead of him. Vorynaas, now fully accoutred in the most expensive, high-quality arms his gold had been able to buy, turned his intimidating gaze on this man who, having spent a sleepless night in the cells, was now convinced his last moment had come. He wished with all his heart he had never had the idea of coming to Caradriggan with a warning: his hopes of a reward had been cruelly overtaken by panic that death, either in a siege or at Vorynaas' orders, would be his lot. Vorynaas now beckoned him over.

'Have a good look out there. Is this the force you told me of yesterday? Is this all of them? Look carefully before you answer.'

The fellow peered out over the wall. In the far distance, just visible against the ominous red streaks in the dark sky, he saw movement and a faint twinkle of lights. Night was barely over, yet already the air hung still and stifling. He gulped, trying to estimate how many men approached.

'Well?' barked Vorynaas.

'My lord, I, I think this must be the men I saw. Their numbers seem about right, but they are still far off... If they were nearer, and I could be sure of those I recognised...'

Impatiently, Vorynaas cut him short. 'Well, obviously. If that's all you can tell me, you've not been much use.' He jerked his head at the soldier. 'Take him along to the guard-room there. I might want him again later.'

For a while they watched in silence as those who approached came nearer. Then Thaltor spoke. 'I reckon there's not more than around two hundred of them, all told – that's the best rough estimate I can manage. And I've got two thousand under orders in the barbican.'

These overwhelmingly favourable odds had already been calculated by Vorynaas, who was half-regretting now that he had sent that message off to Torilmarap. But still, if this was it, if this was all the threat amounted to, then they could deal with it and send word before the day was out that reinforcements were not necessary after all. Closer and closer the small force advanced, steadily riding forward, keeping together.

'Mm. You know, there's something odd about this,' he said. 'Are they out of their minds, these fellows? Whoever they are, what do they think they're doing, setting themselves against a walled city under full defence? Maybe they've got a death wish.'

Thaltor laughed. 'Well in that case, they could be in luck. Let's make their day!'

'Ah, the old ones are the best ones.' Vorynaas laughed too, then an inspiration came to him. 'Listen, we're in no danger: that lot out there can't attack us, obviously – there's far too few of them. And by the same token, they can't sit down to a siege; or at least, if they try it, you can give them a warmer welcome than they'd probably like. We've got time to use this situation. Send some of your men through the streets. Have them sound the signal for attendance at the Open Hall, but when everyone turns out, your fellows can chivvy them along to anywhere they can get a view of what's happening. Even the wall-walks, so long as we're not impeded. I want people to see this.'

'You'll allow them on the walls?' said Thaltor dubiously.

'Why not?' Vorynaas glanced out again. 'They'll be in no danger. These heroes aren't going to come within our range unless they've completely taken leave of their senses.'

When Thaltor still hesitated, Vorynaas stepped closer to him. His quiet tone belied the menace of his words. 'I've told you, I mean to demonstrate what happens to those who take arms against me. I gave you an order: I expect to see you carry it out immediately.'

Thaltor turned on his heel and marched off and Vorynaas went back to his watch. Soon he heard the sounds that told him his instructions were being implemented. Doors slammed, cutting through the formless crowd-noise of voices and footsteps. Before long every window or tower parapet that gave a view beyond the city was crammed with anxious faces; bolder spirits had climbed to peer from the walls; and in the streets, those left below called up to friends with vantage points to tell what they saw. The two hundred were very near, now; they had lit even more torches as if determined to be clearly seen, and Vorynaas sensed rather than heard the name as those within the city recognised that Haldur was indeed their leader. Suddenly his dark eyes widened. By all that lurked in the Waste! That fellow who brought the warning was right, there *were* Caradwardans with them: surely that was Temenghent who had been among his own guards in Seth y'n Carad! Vorynaas clenched his fists, vowing he would make such an example of these renegades and northerners as would never be forgotten. At last they halted and he saw Haldur and another man dismount and speak together briefly. They had stayed beyond the range of his bowmen, as he had surmised they would, but then Haldur began to walk forward.

The captain of those guarding the east gate, inhibited by his commander-in-chief's presence, hesitated and looked to him for guidance.

'Not yet,' said Vorynaas. His lip curled. 'I want to see these mice scuttle about before I pounce. Hold your fire for the moment and let's hear what he's got to say.'

At the city walls

By now Haldur had stopped and laid down his weapons. He looked up as if scanning the defences of the east gate and the walls to either side of it.

'Vorynaas of Caradward! Yield to us, or be called to account.'

Vorynaas waited until the silence had lasted for the space of a few breaths, then with a mocking laugh he showed himself, stepping up into view where the light fell on his rich garments and armour.

'The last time we spoke, Haldur son of Carapethan, you gave me to understand that your place was beside your father; but it seems that your sense of duty is as unimpressive as this band of outlaws you've gathered together. Or maybe you enjoyed our hospitality so much that you prefer to die here rather than in your homeland?'

'Everyone knows I was your prisoner, not your guest, and you a treacherous host who plotted our murder and now think to bring your darkness to the north. Think again, Vorynaas! You failed then, you will fail once more. You will never set foot in the Nine Dales. Open the gates of the city, come out and give yourself up to us. You have brought only ruin and despair to your people, but we come to bring them hope. Your day is over.'

'Are you out of your mind? Listen to me. You are ten times outnumbered by the garrison of this city alone. They will wipe you from the earth, to the last man. Inside the barbican they await only my word to attack, which I would have given already were it not for the small amusement of this exchange with you. And I have more armies, other resources at my call. I will take Rihannad Ennar before the year is out.' Vorynaas laughed again, carried away by his own words. 'My reserves are infinite, I shall do what I will. Give me just one reason why I should yield to you.'

Now it was Haldur's turn to laugh. 'I will give you more than one. Do this, and you may yet be remembered for good as well as evil. But if that means nothing to you, here are other reasons for you to consider. You boast of your power and your wealth, not knowing that your words are empty. Your people scrape and scratch for food so that your soldiers can fill their stomachs. Will they fight for you if you cannot feed them? You seized Gwent y'm Aryframan, but all that followed was the darkness that already lay over Caradward. It would be no different in the Nine Dales; but in any case, I tell you again, you will never take Rihannad Ennar! As for your wealth, hear this Vorynaas! The gold mine is yours no longer. Its slaves are freed, Haartell and his overseers are dead or captive. The mine is in our hands, and so are the road and the bridge that lead to it. What price your riches now?'

At this, a clamour arose among those who listened. All along the wall there was movement and a chime of metal as guards and sentries, captains and soldiers turned to each other with questions, exclamations, curses; but among them were some whose eyes met in silence. They had no need of words because they knew the moment they had waited for, and risked all to bring about, was near. They steadied themselves for whatever was to come, hands ready to their weapons, their senses alert. Amid the sudden disturbance, a man began to move forward through the crowds in the street below the wall, slipping unnoticed through the throng as it milled about in a gabble of amazed comment. Meanwhile Vorynaas, stunned into momentary silence, was recovering from his shock. Shouting to his captains to restore order, he turned back to Haldur with a sneer.

'Who do you think will believe that, you fool? My patience with you is running out. Tell your followers to lay down their arms if they want to live until tomorrow. And move back to join them yourself, or I will have you shot where you stand.'

'Too many deaths already lie to your account,' said Haldur. 'Your time is over, don't try to ease your loss of power by wasting more lives. Look well, soldiers and citizens and you too, Vorynaas! There are faces here you will recognise: by them you will know that what I say is true.'

Then out from the main body of Haldur's followers stepped those who had joined them at the mine. There was another growl of muttering, but more muted, more apprehensive this time. Those within the city whispered to each other, pointing out here a friend, there a relative who had laboured or served under arms in the Lissa'pathor; and there was fear now in their voices. Surely there would be nothing Vorynaas was not prepared to do to win back the mine, and how could so few withstand him? They watched apprehensively, expecting the onset of battle; and those who waited strove to remain calm as the tension stretched almost to breaking point. Haldur too, though he had spoken out boldly, wondered how much longer he could maintain a defiant stance. He sensed that Vorynaas' tolerance was almost at an end and peered up at the walls desperately for some sign of Artorynas. What if his presence in the city had been discovered? No, in that case Vorynaas would doubtless have paraded him as a captive for all to see. But what if he had failed to get in, or having done so could not reach a vantage point to give the signal he had promised? If Vorynaas ordered an attack, then… Haldur closed his mind to the thought and called up once more.

'I am not out of my mind, nor do I lie. Open the gates, tell your captains to yield the city, come out to us in peace. Your gold is gone, and with it your power. Men shall fear you no more! Not only in the Lissa'pathor, but throughout your lands, even as we speak here they are already rising to cast off the yoke of doubt and despair.'

Vorynaas, wild with fury, screamed at the guards beside him to shoot at Haldur. Seizing bow and ammunition from the man nearest to him, he let fly himself. Arrows thudded into the earth all around Haldur, sending up spurts of dust, but none bit except for one which sliced through the leather of the knife-holder at the side of his boot. He leapt back, and instantly his companions sprang to action. As one, those who held torches swung them down, grinding out their flames in the dirt at their feet; while others bent the longbows of Rihannad Ennar and sent arrows whistling up towards the walls. But rather than warheads, these carried damp rags bound in wads about their tips. Before those looking out had any time to react, every torch along the stretch of wall where Vorynaas stood had gone, knocked from the hands of those who held them or left askew in their holders. Acrid smoke drifted on the air as Vorynaas whipped round, momentarily at a loss as to what had happened. The only illumination remaining came from a cresset that burned on the wall of the east-gate tower: it shone on the gold with which his clothes and armour were adorned. He turned back as a voice called from where the two hundred waited, now only dimly visible in the half-light of Caradriggan's dark dawn.

'Your defences are within our range, though we are out of yours. Were we as treacherous as you, we could pick you off like pigeons from a roost.' And now, right across the sky from one dark horizon to the other, thunder rolled again in another long rumble of menace.

'Hear that, Vorynaas!' cried Haldur, and his voice rang out with a new strength. 'Look where the sky shows red in the east! It is a final warning: do not stain with blood the morning on which Artorynas has returned!'

The strangest sound greeted this, a kind of sighing gasp as a thousand throats drew breath sharply as one. Vorynaas glared about him. 'Cowards!' he snarled at the soldiers who were already edging away, making for the refuge of battlement or tower, leaving him isolated where he stood on the wall-walk. Again he addressed himself to Haldur, his voice thick with rage and hate.

'Save your breath for running, then we'll see how far you get before my troops hunt you down like dogs among rats! But since you talk of treachery, let me tell you something: something you can think about in the few moments you've got left to live. Do you think I don't know who's hiding up there in the north? That I don't know you've given sanctuary to Maesrhon, unnatural changeling, outlaw and renegade, traitor to his country? He too once threatened me with this,

this *Artorynas*, and his threats were as empty as yours; but hear me now, and die knowing that I keep my word. I will be revenged upon Rihannad Ennar, I will raze its dwellings to the ground; I will spare your father's life only long enough to tell him I took yours! The day cannot come soon enough when I see Maesrhon again, and I swear I will make your people bitterly regret that ever they set eyes on him.'

In after years, when the story of this day had grown to full flower, it was often said that Artorynas simply appeared out of nowhere, such was the effect of the shock his appearance caused. But though the truth was simpler, it had taken root in the memories of those who were there, so it was not so strange that it should put out branches and leaves of wonder. As night drew to its end, Artorynas had slipped out of Tellgard, his hood drawn close; and when Vorynaas called out the citizens he mingled with the crowd and took his chance of edging right up to the eastern wall. And now, when every eye was on Vorynaas who leaned out, screaming abuse at Haldur, the moment came. From Tellgard, Artorynas had brought an old sparring-stave. Hefting it in his hands, he shrugged off his hood, took three swift steps, leapt on to a mounting-block, planted the stave there and in one fluid movement levered himself to fly up and across on to the wall-walk. It was so quick, so light and lithe, that as men said afterwards, it was as if he materialised from thin air; and the first Vorynaas knew was the sound of a quiet voice behind him.

The arrow

'You will never set foot in the Nine Dales, but you need wait no longer to see me once more.'

Vorynaas spun round, speechless with amazement, while on every side a clamour rose, a ragged roar as the names of Maesrhon and Artorynas were shouted both within and without the walls, ever louder as a formless hope began to wake in men's hearts, a faint inkling of what marvels might now appear. Artorynas raised his hand, and the noise died to a breathless silence. He glanced out to where Haldur and the two hundred stood and then turned his gaze on the man he had once called father. Vorynaas stared back. There were some among the onlookers who had cried the name of Arymaldur, and he knew why. He could see him now in the hated face before him: he was there in the tall, spare frame, the dark hair flowing back from the high forehead, the hollows under the proud cheekbones, that maddening, unearthly air. Vorynaas bared his teeth in revulsion, seeing also Numirantoro in the calm self-possession, the lack of fear, the blend of gentleness and strength. By the Waste! He could swear he saw a hint of that old fool Arythalt there too, something in the set of the lips. But the eyes, those amber eyes he had always so detested, they were fixed on him now, the flames from the cresset waking the sun-gold in their depths... An incoherent cry broke from Vorynaas before at last he found words.

'So *you* are behind all this! You have taken the name of Artorynas to yourself and come creeping back to bring war to your own people!' He drew his sword. 'I will give you the traitor's death you have avoided for too long.'

'You will not. You cannot touch me, and you know it.' Artorynas took a step forward and Vorynaas gave ground, lowering the sword; many in the crowd, and some among the soldiers, moved their hands in the sign.

'You will never call me Maesrhon again. Artorynas is my true name, given me by my mother, and given with a reason. I told you when we faced each other last, you would hear the name again when the sun rose once more upon Caradriggan. I do not bring war, I bring hope. I have walked in Asward donn'Ur, I have looked upon the Starborn, I return with the arrow that Arymaldur made, that you in your madness tried to use against him! What have *you* brought to your people? Despair and darkness, desolation and death. But the long night is about to break.'

He put his hand up to his throat where, Vorynaas noticed for the first time, a small gem hung on a fine chain, and cried aloud. 'Haldur! Aim true, light to light, in dawn returning!'

Suddenly a point of star-like brilliance appeared, burning so intensely that men shielded their eyes from its brightness. The radiance shed by the As y'm Ur was such as to consume all other nearby lights: its heart of fire seemed to hide, rather than reveal, Artorynas. The crowd surged forward towards the foot of the wall, scrambling to reach the steps, holding out hands to Artorynas, repeating his name, trying to touch him. Arval began shouldering his way through those who blocked his path, determined to reach Artorynas' side. Vorynaas was shouting, but his words reached Arval as if from some great distance, as if the storm of grief and love and loss within him was a barrier to the emotions of others. Dimly he heard Vorynaas curse and yell, and order his guards to whip the people back or force them down with their spears; and then, loud and suddenly clear, he heard him shout for Thaltor and his men to attack, heard the signal repeated as it passed along the wall towards the barbican: almost he could have sworn he heard the crash and rattle of chains and bolts as the barring mechanisms were released and the great gates began to swing open. Then above all the voice of Artorynas rang out again, clear, fearless, exultant.

'Now, Haldur, do it now! Let the arrow fly! A new day, my brother!'

For Haldur, it was as if years passed for every moment after Artorynas appeared. In the flurry of activity after he was attacked and the torches were doused he had scrambled back to the two hundred, snatching up his weapons as he went; and then, even as it crossed his mind that time had run out, that Vorynaas would set upon them, even as the thunder still echoed overhead, there was Artorynas above them on the wall. Haldur's bow was already in his hand and now he took Arymaldur's arrow from his quiver. It gleamed, despite the dim light, and from behind him Haldur heard Vorardynur's muffled exclamation and the sudden stir that told him the horses of the Cunorad had reacted to the heightened awareness of their riders. He set the arrow to the string, but held it only loosely. Vorynaas and Artorynas still confronted each other, talking, talking. How long would it be before Artorynas gave the promised sign? Haldur's senses swam. There was a buzzing in his ears and the ground seemed to tilt under him; his heart was racing, making him faint and disorientated. Desperately he planted his feet in the archer's stance, and then he sensed it. That eerie life had woken in the arrow again. The shock ran through his fingers where the gossamer filigree of the red-gold feathers brushed them. He raised the bow, his eyes travelling down the silver and gold of the arrow's shaft until they reached the sky-steel of its point; and above him, there on the wall, a star burned and from it came Artorynas' voice, bidding him aim true.

Haldur drew back the string, but his hands shook. That point of light was so tiny: could he be sure that even his skill would suffice to guide his aim? And it was so bright. Now that he had looked at it his vision was impaired. From nowhere, a memory came to him of a golden afternoon in Rihann y'n Wathan when he and Artorynas had swum and dived in the mountain pools. Artorynas had gazed directly into the sun as he lazed beside the river, but he had the eyes of the As-Geg'rastigan... Haldur squinted painfully up at the walls again and now it seemed to him that a kind of silver nimbus enclosed the dazzling starlight. Out of the radiance Artoryas called again: a lord of the Starborn and his truest friend, the brother of his heart, whom he had sworn to help.

'Now, Haldur, do it now! Let the arrow fly! A new day, my brother!'

Blinking the tears from his eyes, closing his mind to what he had understood too late, the best archer in the Nine Dales took aim once more. Back to his ear he drew, and released. The great bow of the north straightened as the arrow soared on its way, flying true, sky-steel to sky-steel: completing the circle, fulfilling men's hopes, setting a seal upon Arval's work, taking Artorynas into the life of the Starborn, breaking Haldur's heart.

Sunrise

Vorardynur was beside him, leading Haldur's horse by the bridle. 'What have you done? No, there's no time. They're coming, look. Come on, quick, get up, get up!'

Haldur looked round. Already the front ranks of Thaltor's forces were advancing upon them and the rest were pouring out through the barbican gates: ten times their number, as Vorynaas had said. Haldur could not bring himself to care. He put his foot to the stirrup, thinking only to ride to a quick ending. Then as he swung into the saddle, he saw the eastern sky and sheer wonder drove all else from his mind. Those ominous lines and bars of angry red were brightening, spreading; the clouds were moving as if pushed aside by mighty hands. Between them dazzling shafts of light now appeared, golden rays like spears from heaven. Thunder again sounded above, no sullen muttering now but rather a crash and boom that jolted the very earth as if worlds had collided; and as the echoes died away, the clouds parted to reveal the sun at last: the sun, rising in glory. True dawn had returned to Caradriggan for the first time since the day on which Artorynas had been born.

Light seemed to flood through Haldur. 'Follow me!' he shouted, turning his horse, spurring wildly to the gallop. 'Na Devocatron! The Two Hundred are upon you!'

Behind him the Hounds of the Starborn rode, the Cunorad y'm As-Geg'rastigan surging in his wake, crying the name of Artorynas. Temenghent and others for whom the long nightmare was over had the name of their own homeland upon their lips, while those who had come from the north called upon Rihannad Ennar to fire their hearts.

Thaltor's forces faltered. Even the least warlike among them had been confident of an easy superiority, given their numbers, but they had not bargained for what faced them now. They were advancing into the full sun of a midsummer dawn and the blinding glare of its overwhelming power hampered them. And now, coming straight for them as if riding out of the sunrise itself came the Cunorad y'm As-Geg'rastigan, hurtling forward as the ranks of the two hundred finally opened to reveal them. Reckless, heedless of risk and danger, they galloped headlong as if possessed, the Hounds of the Starborn giving tongue with the name of Artorynas: golden and gleaming on golden horses. Though there were but twelve of them, when they burst from the heart of the new sun with Esylto at their head they fell upon the men of Caradward like avengers given form and substance by the golden glory of the sky. Panic broke out among Thaltor's troops. Confusion that he was unable to control turned rapidly into a milling, dusty chaos. Though he had two thousand men at his command, a good five hundred of these were young conscripts doing their service in the city guard. Heedless of his orders to stand and fight, his threats of retribution for any who refused, they turned and fled. And now Thaltor saw that others, many of whom he had regarded as battle-hardened rankers, were also abandoning the conflict, throwing down their weapons; and worse, many too of his officers were leaving their posts, putting all their efforts instead into drawing off those who had surrendered. He recognised an Outlander, whose name escaped him in the heat of the moment, rushing over to organise and steady the youngsters. Sword in hand, Thaltor attempted to rally those around him before the two hundred reached them. But it was some years since he had fought in earnest; he was slow and already out of breath and his resolve was draining away. Was he really prepared to die, when Vorynaas was safe within Caradriggan? Could he trust the loyalty of the few who still stood with him? He saw in their eyes that they knew he was wavering, that they would save themselves before these golden maniacs crashed upon them rather than resist to the last.

The two hundred streamed forward. Vorardynur glanced at Haldur as they rode. He seemed fired with a kind of battle-fury such as old stories told of, yet there were tears on his cheeks. Suddenly Vorardynur was afraid that he might give himself to death, or deal it out to others, while his mind was unbalanced by grief: he had never seen such torment on his cousin's face before but could guess well enough at its cause. He yelled, and Cunoreth, who riding neck and neck with Haldur had begun to pull ahead, checked until he was alongside.

'Stay with Haldur,' shouted Vorardynur. 'Look out for him, he's not himself. Don't let him do anything he'll regret afterwards.'

Cunoreth lifted a hand to show he had heard and understood and then spurred onwards again, braids flying, lying low to urge his horse forward, riding like one of the Cunorad themselves. Vorardynur pulled right a little and turned in the saddle to remind the others too of what they had agreed.

'Don't attack those who give themselves up! Show as much mercy as you can. *Rihannad Ennar!*'

'Rihannad Ennar!' rose many voices after him, mingled with shouts of *Artorynas* and other names dearest to those who cried them, as the two forces crashed together.

The new day was not one hour old before it belonged to the two hundred. The blazing summer sun, still low in the sky, shone slanting through clouds of dust that hung swirling in the air and settled alike on the wounded and whole, horse and foot, victor and vanquished: on the living and on the dead. Vorardynur looked about him and saw young Ennarvorad lying lifeless, along with six other bowmen of the Nine Dales and three who had answered Carapethan's call, remembering their days among the Cunorad. Some of those who had ridden with them from the Lissa'pathor had also lived only long enough to see the darkness lift, but Vorardynur noticed the man who had doubted, when they lay waiting in the forest. He was hurt, but seemed not to notice as his eyes turned to the sky lifting blue and clear above the choking dust. Cunoreth was bleeding from a wound in his leg and his horse, maimed beyond healing, struggled on the ground. As Vorardynur watched, Cunoreth gave it a swift and merciful end and then ripped a strip of cloth from his sleeve to tie round his thigh.

Others were moving among the survivors, reassuring those who had surrendered, comforting those in pain. Losses on the Caradwardan side were greater, but the swift capitulation of so many and the quick intervention of those who had been numbered among the partisans had prevented matters turning out worse than might have been. Thaltor, together with a dozen or so who had refused to yield, was a prisoner. He sat glowering with his hands tied, his gold-adorned clothes and arms all dulled and soiled. Vorardynur turned away from him, staring around in growing fear.

'Where's Haldur?'

Temenghent pointed towards the barbican gates, which stood wide. 'He went into the city, following the twelve.'

'What? They've gone in there?'

Itantoro spoke up. 'You and I have both ridden with the Hounds in our time, Vorardynur,' she said. 'Remember they are oath-bound to seek the Starborn. When the day was ours, Esylto would lead to where their pledge took them.'

Vorardynur bit his lip. It had never occurred to him that Haldur would not be there to take charge, but he saw that for now at least the responsibility fell upon him. Calling over his captains to help, he began on the task of bringing some order to the situation on the field. There were many matters needing attention there before he could think of entering the city himself.

Within Caradriggan, all was tumult and disorder as people ran to and fro leaderless. There had been some wild shooting from the walls, but eventually those such as Tirathalt who had been waiting, waiting for the signal to act managed to assert themselves and either marshal the remaining defenders to their side or secure them under guard. It was at the city gates where the stoutest resistance was encountered: there the captains were mostly Vorynaas' men and some tried to fight it out. But before anyone could begin to think of whether the great barbican gate should be closed again, the Cunorad were upon them. They had carved a path right through Thaltor's forces, who fled from them in terror; and then turned, following Esylto, and rode straight for the city. Never pausing in their headlong course they thundered through the gates, through the barbican, through the inner gate and into the streets of Caradriggan. Soldiers and civilians alike leapt to avoid them, women snatching up children into their arms. Some screamed and cried out, calling upon the Starborn. How many more wonders would the day bring? First the two hundred outside their walls, then Artorynas within them; the sun, so long yearned for and now risen in splendour – and now these golden riders! They shut their minds to the arrow: that was a matter too charged with awe and dread for thought to dwell upon yet. Instead they stood gaping, staring amazed at these uncanny, half-naked golden riders, these wild horsemen and women with rapt faces whose eyes seemed fixed on a sight unseen, whose voices rang with the name of Artorynas. But the Cunorad y'm As-Geg'rastigan looked neither to right nor left; as swift and sure as the arrow itself, the twelve swept on, never stopping until they reined to a halt in the heart of Tellgard.

By the time Haldur arrived they were standing silently together, quiet now as if at peace. Were they waiting for Arval? He was nowhere to be seen but Haldur knew, somehow, that he was within, that he would have brought Artorynas back here. Vaguely he recognised faces he remembered. Rhostellat and Ancrascaro, and many more from the Tellgard community, were busily at work tending the wounded and hurt; Haldur saw that Forgard too was there, with Isteddar and Merenald and others whose names eluded him. And now he noticed that the dead were being brought to Tellgard also, laid to one side under the shelter of the colonnade. He slid from his horse and walked over towards them, moving like a man in a nightmare. Lifting the covering that had been laid over the bodies, he looked down at the first face. It looked back at him, blank eyes open in a young, fresh face without a mark upon it: the death-wound had been dealt to the chest. It was Escanic. Feeling a hand on his shoulder, Haldur turned to see Isteddar and remembered that the two of them were distantly related.

'He stayed on in the army after all, then?' said Haldur eventually.

Isteddar nodded. 'He'd no choice, really. Family pressure.'

'I know, he told me about it. I'm so sorry.' Haldur bent to cover Escanic again, but Isteddar stopped him and knelt.

'Just a minute.' He closed the young man's eyes, covered his face once more and straightened. 'We all knew there'd be casualties. Some were bound to be unlucky. At least he saw the sun rise.'

'How do you know? Did you see how he died?'

'Yes.' Isteddar looked at Haldur. 'I was there when Maesrhon – Artorynas – appeared. I think Escanic must have been stationed on the wall somewhere between the barbican and the east gate. You can imagine what it was like when the sky began to clear, after… Well anyway, Vorynaas had given the order for Thaltor's men to attack, your people were charging forward…' – Isteddar glanced over to the corner where the Cunorad now stood – 'and suddenly it was obvious that there were those within the city too who were throwing off the shackles, rising up against Vorynaas. They were shouting to their comrades not to fight, to change sides, to protect the citizens. I could see that Vorynaas grasped the situation in an instant: whatever his faults, he's a quick thinker. He sprang off towards the steps; he can move fast for a man of his age. And then…' Isteddar broke off, tilting his head at the motionless, shrouded form beside them.

'Then out of nowhere, Escanic appeared, running along the wallwalk. He stood at the top of the steps, blocking Vorynaas' way, yelling something – I don't know what. Vorynaas never hesitated: just ran him straight through, leapt down the steps and disappeared into the crowd.' For the first time, Isteddar's voice shook. 'Escanic hadn't even drawn his sword.'

'Where is Vorynaas now? Have you got him under guard somewhere?'

Haldur and Isteddar turned to see that Vorardynur had now arrived. He spoke again to Isteddar. 'Where is he? Is he dead?'

'No, he's not dead.' Isteddar recognised the air of authority about Vorardynur and realised he must be a leader of the northerners. 'They say he made it across the city to the east gate, killed another of his own men there when they weren't quick enough to open the gate for him, grabbed a horse and galloped off up the border road. He's got away.'

CHAPTER 62

Partners in evil

As soon as Vorynaas reached the first posting-station, he sent a younger rider ahead of him with orders to spare neither horse nor man in getting word to Torilmarap on the border to speed up his gathering and despatch of reinforcements. Yet after only the briefest pause for rest, he commandeered another horse and set off again himself, his dark will driving him on in defiance of age and exhaustion. But swiftly though he rode, and speedily though his despatches went through, when he arrived at the fortifications that stretched between the Red Mountains and Maesaldron he found that bad news other than his own had preceded him. He sat in the headquarters building with wine on the table beside him, evaluating what he had been told. Though bathed and fed, he was aching and sore from almost three days in the saddle and his mind felt as bruised as his backside as the thoughts ran round and round in his head. Torilmarap sat in anxious silence, afraid to speak while Vorynaas pondered matters; it had taken all the nerve he possessed to break the news that Heranwark was theirs no longer, Rigg'ymvala in the hands of the partisans and its commander Rhonard a prisoner. He quailed inwardly now as Vorynaas raised his head and looked directly at him; but the dark eyes were focused inwards as Vorynaas, mentally sorting events and information, began to concentrate his energy on a strategy to deal with the crisis he found himself so unexpectedly confronting.

So Rhonard was captive: at least that implied he'd put up a fight like Thaltor. But clearly there were turncoats everywhere, traitors who had waited for their moment.

'Any news of Lemered?' Vorynaas asked.

'Nothing as yet,' replied Torilmarap, failing to suppress the wish that he could change places with his colleague of the garrison in Staran y'n Forgarad.

Well, thought Vorynaas, the bold Lemered didn't show up too well when I called him to the council in Caradward. He was the first to speak against the idea of invading the Nine Dales. Whatever is happening in the south, it's only too likely that we can't rely on any help coming to us from that direction; not to mention that if Lemered's dead, or a prisoner, or has changed sides, then quite possibly the mines in the Somllichan Ghent are in danger too, if they haven't already fallen into enemy hands. But the gold mine is the crucial loss, and Caradriggan itself… He sat up straighter, planting his hands firmly on the arms of his chair.

'Right. This is what we're going to do. My priority is to re-take Caradriggan and the Lissa'pathor. Once we do that, everything else will be simply a mopping-up exercise: support for this rebellion will melt away and then I'll show just what happens to those who raise their hands against me. So how many men can you mobilise to march tomorrow?'

'Tomorrow!' Torilmarap cleared his throat nervously as Vorynaas raised his eyebrows. 'Well, I was going to explain, my lord. It's just that, when your second message arrived, and in view of the news from Heranwark, I thought if things were so serious then maybe you'd need more men than just those stationed here, so I sent to Framstock asking Valestron to help us. If you can wait a little longer, my understanding is that he should be here himself by the day after tomorrow.'

When Valestron arrived, he left an officer to settle his men into temporary quarters and headed straight for Vorynaas.

'I suppose you do realise that I've got problems of my own? I've had to leave Atranaar in my place in Framstock and trust to Wicursal to hold things together up in the north. There's trouble breaking out everywhere; we've even been ambushed a couple of times on the march down here. We'll not be in Rihannad Ennar now before this year's end, that's for sure.'

Vorynaas waved this aside. 'When there are difficult decisions to be made, it's the man who chooses the right option who comes out on top. We can put the invasion plans on hold if we have to: after all, the original idea was to advance next year, not this. Looked at in a positive light, things could even work to our advantage. These fools who've deluded themselves into opposing me have picked the wrong moment to make their move. If they'd waited until we were already on our way north, well… But as it is, this way, we'll be able to march in the reassurance that all opposition has been dealt with. And let me tell you, Valestron, that by 'dealt with' I mean completely crushed: I won't be showing any mercy. So what we do is this: we sweep straight back down on Caradriggan and we take it before there's any chance of reinforcements moving in to hold it against us; and then we repossess the gold mine. After that, by the Waste! I'll have my revenge, and I'll turn my attention to the Nine Dales once more.'

For a few moments Valestron digested this in silence. For himself, there was no real choice. His rivals, real and potential, had eliminated each other and Thaltor, who in any case was now in enemy hands, had never posed a credible threat to his ambitions. His position as natural successor to Vorynaas was now unassailable – but this would be small consolation if the older man did not regain power completely and quickly; and from the rumours he'd heard, this might not be as straightforward as Vorynaas seemed to think.

'You're not too worried about events that side of the border, then?' he asked, with a jerk of his head to indicate the road up to Framstock and beyond.

The hand that stroked at Vorynaas' beard hid the grim smile he permitted himself at this. In spite of the trouble Valestron had described, he'd responded promptly none the less to Torilmarap's plea for aid. I know where he stands all right, thought Vorynaas. If he wants what he's schemed for all these years, he's got no choice but to support me and he knows it. And he knows I know it, too.

'No more than you are, seeing you've apparently decided your talents will be better deployed down here,' he said. When no reply to this was forthcoming, Vorynaas got to his feet and began pacing the room, ignoring his aching legs and the stiffness in his back.

'Listen, Valestron. None of these peasants and runaway slaves and *vigurtan* of one kind or another are going to even think of coming south; all they'll want is to kill as many of their masters as they can before they're killed themselves. And if Atranaar can't deal with a disorganised rabble of that sort, he's not the man I take him for.' Vorynaas raised a dark brow to add a final sting. 'He's another who knows just where he stands.'

Valestron decided to ignore this and help himself to wine, as no offer of hospitality had so far been forthcoming. 'Is it true about Maesrhon?'

At this Vorynaas sat down again, replenishing his own cup and leaning forward to emphasise his words. He remembered only too well how Valestron had indulged in sly hints and insinuations in years gone by, but that was no matter now. All three of those he hated most were dead at last, while he was still alive, who had sworn to be revenged. He narrowed his eyes. Let Valestron pay full attention now!

'Oh yes, it's true. He came creeping back with the men from the Nine Dales and took an arrow from Haldur through the throat for it. Now listen to me. You'll not have forgotten what I did to Arymaldur, and remember this too. I vowed to give Maesrhon a traitor's death and that's just what he got when he defied me once too often. Listen again, Valestron: I swore I would destroy Arymaldur and Maesrhon, or else let the blindworms of Na Naastald take me. Now *you* speak to your men: make sure you tell them I keep my word, and how I keep it. And here's another thing you can think over as we go about our business. Haldur will never succeed his father in Rihannad

Ennar. When I take the Nine Dales, a new lord will be needed in Cotaerdon.'

Valestron was indeed pondering these words as they began their advance down the road to Caradriggan. Presumably Vorynaas meant him to assume that he would rule the new lands in the north when they took them, that this would be the reward for his loyalty now; but Valestron was not so sure he relished this idea. Cotaerdon was so far away, too far for his liking. What if out of sight were to mean out of mind: suppose another was to take his rightful place as heir in Caradward? Many times over the years he had regretted that Vorynaas had produced no daughter. If such there had been, then regardless of beauty or temperament she would have been wife to me as soon as was legally possible, thought Valestron. But as it is, better to delay no longer. As soon as we restore control in Caradriggan, I will make the best match I can and get myself a son. There is still time: he would be adult before I am the age Vorynaas is now. He reflected on what Vorynaas had said about Maesrhon. As instructed, he had roused his men with the story of Vorynaas' daring oath and its outcome, and Vorynaas himself had addressed the troops in similar vaunting style; but to Valestron their response had seemed somewhat muted. And indeed, though the men were too afraid of their commanders to speak, among them rumour had run quicker than any despatch-carrier could have brought news, spreading like wildfire, becoming more fantastic with each telling: but even the most fanciful tale was nearer the truth than the version Vorynaas had told. Valestron glanced at him as they rode. Rested and invigorated, his attire and equipment burnished up and restored to its former splendour, their leader was the very picture of ruthless, determined confidence. Then Valestron's eye was drawn by a distant darkness. They were passing the turn that led to Assynt y'm Atrannaas: in spite of the summer morning's sunshine that played on their harness and armour, still it loomed, black and baleful, a horror waiting under the mountains beyond. He turned hastily back to the road before him. Surely they must prevail! Any other outcome was not to be contemplated.

Into darkness under the sun

Once Heretellar was clear of the city on his fateful journey, he took to byways and little-used country roads. He wanted no human contact that might weaken his resolve and in particular was anxious not to be recognised. It would not do to meet anyone who knew him, who might take word to Forgard that his son had been seen heading for the Red Mountains when he was supposed to be on his way home to the Ellanwic. But though he forced himself to push on, he rode slowly, telling himself he was sparing his horse while knowing in his heart that every mile of the way was a greater effort of will than the last. On the second morning, he woke to stare with incredulous eyes as dawn broke in a summer sky of unclouded blue. The day wore on and he hesitated, unsure of what to do. Without any doubt, momentous events must be afoot and the temptation to turn back to Caradriggan tormented him. But he knew well that if he returned now, he would not have the strength of mind to set out again even if, despite the new day, darkness had not lifted from the pit of horror to which his road led. And he was certain that it would not have done, for Arval had said nothing to justify such a hope. Far from it: his assertion had been that only a willing sacrifice would end the evil. Heretellar reproached himself for wasting a day, for allowing fear to tempt him from his chosen course. He was scarcely showing himself to be willing, by dragging his feet like this. So he set himself to go on, until on the fourth day the mountains were tall before him, red in the rising sun, and he turned right to ride through the foothills towards the doom that awaited.

It struck him as he went that the world seemed as if it stirred from a long, uneasy sleep. Every crag of the Somllichan Ghent showed clear-cut in the bright mornings; if it rained, when the sun shone out again he could swear the withered grasses were already sweeter and greener. There was blossom breaking in the hedges and birds were busy everywhere, flying through the warm air or foraging on the ground. Or maybe it was just that Heretellar, knowing it was likely he looked on these things for the last time, noticed them with a particular intensity. But there was one thing about which there could be no doubt. It was becoming more difficult to stay solitary. There were people everywhere, working with a renewed energy in the neglected fields, repairing and repainting houses, hurrying along the roads. Even on the lanes he had been using they passed him, men with a cheery greeting, women and children with smiles. Heretellar rubbed with his sleeve at one of the metal trappings his horse carried and squinted at himself in the burnished surface. Although its curve distorted his reflection, he could see that almost a week's growth of beard, contrasting darkly with his silvery hair, was a passable disguise. And anyway, who was likely to know him here? It was a part of Caradward he had never frequented and had scarcely visited since he passed through the border area to bring Ancrascaro home from Salfgard. Curiosity got the better of Heretellar and at evening he turned in through the gate of a small, low-built *gradstedd*.

Here, sitting quietly in a shadowy corner, wiping out the last of a bowl of broth with some flatbread, he listened as the talk went round. There was plenty of it, and though Heretellar guessed not all he heard was true or wholly to be trusted as accurate, it was astonishing enough. So Caradriggan had fallen to men from the Nine Dales, and Maesrhon had returned! There was some argument as to whether or not Maesrhon and Artorynas were one and the same, but as soon as he heard it suggested, Heretellar knew instinctively that this was so. He could think of no explanation as to how he came to be in the city. Despite vociferous support for the theory that he had simply materialised on the wall ('I don't care what you say, I was always taught the Starborn could walk unseen,' one fellow was stoutly maintaining), Heretellar was not convinced; but how could it be true that, as others insisted, he had come south with Haldur? Yet all the stories agreed that he had called upon Haldur; that it was at his bidding that Haldur had fired Arymaldur's arrow.

'Of course I'm sure it was the same one,' said a squarely-built middle-aged man, flushed in the face. 'I was apprenticed to Poenmorcar when he had the contract for work on Seth y'n Carad: I saw it then and take it from me, once seen never forgotten.'

'And now the poor lad's dead,' sighed a woman, but her words were drowned in a confusion of voices.

'Arval took him into Tellgard, remember how he saved him before?'

'It was always rumoured Arymaldur was the boy's father, maybe he…'

'Right through the throat…'

'Yes, but they say that's where the light came from, he had a jewel…'

'And then the sun rose again.'

Heretellar could bear no more. The whole mystery seemed suddenly clear to his eyes and he spoke up before he could stop himself.

'Arval used to say Arymaldur told him there is always hope, if men know where to find it. Vorynaas thought Maesrhon had fled from him, but he was wrong. He went as Maesrhon, seeking the arrow: and because he was indeed Arymaldur's son, he found it. And he came back to us as Artorynas, bringing us hope in light returning.'

Silence fell as every eye turned to Heretellar. He gritted his teeth, regretting immediately that he had drawn attention to himself, wishing he had not spoken. Then an ancient elder sitting by the fire leaned forward, arthritic fingers rubbing at his bony knees, filmy old eyes brimming with glee.

'You seem well-informed, young stranger.' He looked round at the familiar faces of his friends and neighbours. 'I've a notion where you get your facts from, and I mean no disrespect – it's long enough since we've had cause for mirth like tonight!' He cackled in delighted mischief. 'If your beard matched your hair, you'd be the very spit of Arval. I reckon you're his love-child!'

Howls of laughter did indeed break out at this, but before Heretellar could do much more than sit there feeling foolish, completely at a loss for a reply, the door burst open and two soldiers came into the room.

'Friends, friends!' they shouted, holding up empty hands as folk scrambled away from them in panic. 'We've made a break for it from the border garrison. Valestron arrived there yesterday, he's brought men down from Framstock. You want to keep out of the way tomorrow, they'll be marching past on the road to Caradriggan. Yes, it's right: the city's fallen, Heranwark too and maybe other places as well. Folk are rising up all over the old Gwent y'm Aryframan. Thaltor and Rhonard are prisoners, but Vorynaas got away; he's leading the counter-attack. He's going straight for the kill now he knows the gold mine's been captured.'

Heretellar saw that the moment had come to make a move. Everyone was talking at once, so that only disconnected fragments of speech reached him. Not much of it made sense, but he realised that some kind of co-ordinated resistance was at work, which so far at any rate had mostly met with success. And yet he felt a shadow on his heart: remembering the tale his father had many times told of the day on which Arymaldur had vanished from Caradriggan, he knew that Maesrhon too was gone for ever. Under cover of the noise and confusion, he slipped out to the stable. For a moment he stood, his horse's head against his shoulder in silent companionship. Then he took down his bag and turned away. If he left on foot he would be quieter and he could leave without anyone noticing he had gone. He hoped the animal would find a gentle new master, but any fate would be better for it than the darkness to which he journeyed. Softly he strode off into the gathering dusk, and as he went he looked up. Once more the summer stars twinkled above, a diamond-dust of beauty against the blue twilight. Heretellar took a deep breath, feeling suddenly lighter, almost free of care. He had not forgotten Arval's warning against civil strife, but could he dare to think that the longed-for return of light and hope would trample its evils underfoot before they took root and spread too far?

326

But all his doubts returned next day. He heard the sound of their approach in the afternoon, and saw them as the soldier had said he would. Lying hid in a rocky dell surrounded by bushes he watched them go by, Vorynaas and Valestron leading a great company of troops with Torilmarap bringing up the rear, and it occurred to him when he saw their faces that the expression 'going for the kill' was only too apt. He thought of Haldur, who had escaped with his life once already and got away to his own land. Was he to die after all, so far from home? And then he thought of his own parents and wondered what might befall them if Vorynaas was victorious. Heretellar clenched his fists. The noise of hooves and marching feet was fading, drifting away with the dust they had raised. He broke from cover and set off on the final stage of his journey, all those he loved behind him now and only the dark horror of Assynt y'm Atrannaas ahead.

Drawing breath

On the morning of sunrise in Caradriggan, after the alarms and wonders at daybreak and the raw emotions that tore men's hearts this way and that, a kind of exhausted calm finally settled over the city. The crowds dispersed as people returned to their homes, but the day was too momentous for them to stay behind doors for long. Gradually they ventured out once more, at first only whispering neighbour to neighbour, doubtful of the newcomers' intentions, unsure if rejoicing was permitted, subdued and watchful. In Tellgard the Cunorad, who for all their wild mountain rides had never before stood in a *numiras* such as this, settled their horses themselves as they always did and then withdrew into the hall. Men saw by their faces that they were not yet free from whatever rite they followed, and respected their silence. Forgard guessed that they waited upon Arval. The old man had not been seen since he returned from the city wall, belying his age by bearing the body of Artorynas in his arms. It seemed likely to Forgard that they had passed through the secret door whose existence in Tellgard he had long suspected. He glanced at Haldur as he passed, Haldur who sat staring blankly, still grimed with the filth of battle, ignoring those about him, speaking to no-one. Maybe Arval would be able to rouse him from his grief, but time was passing: someone would have to take charge if Haldur could not. So Vorardynur gathered the leaders to him, both his own comrades and those who had thrown off their old allegiance to resist their erstwhile masters; and together they went up and down the streets, round the walls, through the courtyards and markets, into the guardrooms and messes, with reassurance that the men of Rihannad Ennar had no thought of conquest: that there would be slaves no more, that in due course Caradward and Gwent y'm Aryframan must work out their own justice between themselves but meanwhile all must stand together in face of the threat posed by Vorynaas in his attempt at vengeance.

Vorynaas had been both right and wrong in his assessment of the disorder that Valestron had left his deputies to quell when he hurried south to answer his leader's call for help. Correct, in that many of those who rose up against oppression had revenge in their hearts rather than the righting of wrongs; but far from the mark in assuming that they would be easily dealt with. As a result, all over Rossaestrethan and Rosmorric violence flared and could not be stamped out: it smouldered to spark again, like the embers left smoking after men have beaten out the flames of a forest fire; and though the new sun shone down upon Gwent y'm Aryframan once more, its light fell upon many who lay needlessly dead, turning blind eyes to the clear blue sky. But although as the days went by not a few old scores were settled in vindictive relish, gradually the leading figures among the partisans began to restore order and calm. Within a week Wicursal, finding himself surrounded in Heranar's old headquarters and his men lacking heart for a fight, surrendered when called upon to do so by Naasigits. Only in Framstock was there still resistance, where Atranaar and a small company of irregulars held out grimly.

'We've got to deal with this,' said Naasigits to Sigitsinen when he heard what a weary messenger arrived to report one evening. 'Atranaar's a strange character: he'll not give up like Wicursal and he'll know he can't rely on the old 'only following orders' excuse. And if the men still with him fight to the end as well, think what a legacy of bitterness that will leave, not to mention Framstock in ruins. But it's not so long since you trained under him that Atranaar won't remember you. If you can somehow get word to him, you might be able to negotiate. Take Sigisstir as your second and whoever else you want.'

Framstock in flames

They hurried south, a small force of tough volunteers; but though they moved fast, matters outpaced them. Even from a distance they could see the smoke rising and knew that Framstock must be in flames. Atranaar ran through the streets, sword in hand, attempting to rally his men, to organise some kind of containment of the blaze, to clear the people out of danger, by force if necessary. But he knew in his heart that it was beyond him. He was outnumbered and the panic was breaking out even among his own men. He paused for a moment, panting for breath, wiping the sweat and soot from his face. Curse the fools who started the fire, he thought bitterly. Did they think to smoke us out? The wind is picking up; soon anything that will burn in this town will be reduced to ashes. With a roar, the flames leapt across a narrow alley and began to devour the next building. Atranaar turned to the few who still stood with him, noting that even in the brief moment while his attention had been elsewhere, several men had slipped away.

'This is beyond our control now,' he said. 'Save yourselves as best you can.'

Atranaar tried to think clearly. He was in the district where Valahald had made his headquarters, in the central part of the town.

Best to get away south, if he could, down towards the old border; but the wind was blowing from that direction, pushing the fire before it. He ran down a side-street, hoping to work his way around. Suddenly he heard high, terrified screaming, and looked up. At a first-floor window he saw two children, small girls with long, dark-red hair. Their eyes were fixed on him, their little fists beating on the glass. He hesitated. There was no-one but himself in the street and his own life was in danger. Two children, he thought, what do I care about two children? Where are their parents? A blast of hot air, thick with smoke and sparks, scorched his face and at that moment the screaming began again on an even more frenzied note. Right through the pit of Atranaar's stomach a most peculiar sensation ran, a kind of icy shiver. He wrenched at the door, but it was locked. Throwing down his sword he kicked the door in and stumbled up the stairs. The house was already full of smoke, thick and choking. He burst into the room on the left, where the children were still at the window. Some part of Atranaar's mind registered that bars had been fitted across it: what had been going on in here? He grabbed at the girls.

'Come on, quick, come with me.'

They pulled away from him, the smaller of the two seeming immobilised by fear; but the elder was refusing to move, shouting something about a baby.

'There's no time,' gasped Atranaar, beginning to cough.

He dragged them bodily from the room, only to see that the stair by which he had entered was now on fire. Desperately he lurched through another door and found himself at a window without bars but hidden behind locked shutters. Fear gave him the strength to tear at them bare-handed, pulling one away with ripped and bleeding fingers. The second one broke more easily and he saw that the window gave onto a small enclosed garden where, right underneath, there was a raised bed where shrubs grew, reducing the drop and offering some kind of softer landing. He smashed the window and turned to the children.

'Through here, we'll have to jump. It's the only chance.'

'But my baby sister!' wailed the older girl.

Atranaar assumed she must mean the smaller child. 'She'll be all right,' he panted, and picking her up he dropped her out through the window. But when he turned to seize her sister, she ran from him across the room, sobbing and crying. His lungs seared by heat and smoke, sweat blurring his eyes, Atranaar found her screaming unbearable. Cursing and choking, he staggered after her but was met by a wall of flames. He backed away and fell against a staircase leading to another storey. Now prevented by the fire from getting back to the open window, he clawed his way up the second stair. For a moment he thought he heard her, still crying about a baby, but then there was only the greedy roar of the fire, the crash of timbers falling, and smoke, blinding, suffocating smoke; it was impossible to see, to breathe, to think… and he was unable to remember where the door was, or find his way out…

By the time Sigitsinen arrived in Framstock, its centre was a smoking ruin and its people almost too dazed to savour the fact that they were oppressed no more. But though there was no longer any need to think in terms of negotiation, Sigitsinen could see that swift action was necessary. He called together all survivors of the secret resistance and any who yet lived who had attended Val'Arad in the old days of freedom.

'It's all over, now,' he said, 'the worst of it, anyway. We owe it to those we've lost to make sure there are no more deaths. Put your trust in those who have risked their own lives to bring about a new day; work with them to rebuild and heal. If you need more help, send a message to my captain Naasigits. The names of Rosmorric and Rossaestrethan shall be heard no longer: let us all taste the sweet sound of Gwent y'm Aryframan upon our lips!'

A ragged cheer greeted this, but Sigitsinen knew it was only too likely that there were still hard times ahead for those who hung on his words unless more aid came to them from Caradriggan, and this could only happen if the threat posed by Vorynaas was snuffed out once and for all. Though it was true enough that the north, had Vorynaas only known it, was already lost to him before ever he began his march upon the city, that the further he advanced, the deeper he went into territory already held by his foes, yet Sigitsinen did not underestimate his ability to turn desperation to victory if brought to bay. He was determined that Vorynaas should have no chance of retreat, no hope of a second escape; and before the next morning had dawned, he and his comrades were already hastening down the southward road, spurred on by a shared resolve that those who had freed Caradriggan should not have striven in vain.

The unspoken secret

The long day finally drew towards its end in Caradriggan, and the city that had woken to a sunrise of new hope now lay under the golden glow of evening. Gradually the sky filled with stars innumerable: old folk wept openly for the joy of beholding once more what they had thought they must die without ever seeing again; parents waked children from their beds and carried them outside to gaze on the splendour that arched above. In Tellgard Vorardynur and the others gathered to deliberate their next move, but silence fell when the door opened and Arval joined them. He glanced swiftly round at the faces turned towards him.

'Where is Haldur?'

'Outside, in the colonnade,' said Forgard. 'He has sat there throughout the day beside the dead, staring before him, silent. We cannot rouse him.'

Vorardynur stood up. 'He is overwhelmed by grief for what he has done, and the sorrow is too deep for us to reach him. But if you would go to him, Lord Arval: all this past year, I have heard him speak of you with love and respect. He would hear your voice; you could lift the burden that weighs upon him.'

The creases round Arval's dark eyes deepened as he smiled a little. 'You are Vorardynur, I think?'

'Yes; I'm sorry, I should have…'

'No need, no need. You have done well today; I'm glad you're here. I have every confidence in you. You can all manage without me for the matters you must discuss this evening and you are right, Haldur needs me now. We'll talk again tomorrow.'

Arval went out again and soon was standing beside Haldur in the darkness. 'Look at me,' he said.

Slowly Haldur raised his head and looked at Arval. Blank, empty-eyed despair was stamped on his face; but when Arval bade him stand up and follow, he obeyed. Arval headed into the pump-house of his own quarters and turned towards the young man, who had still not uttered a word.

'There is warm water here and clean house robes. Get washed and then come up to my study.'

In due course Haldur entered the familiar room with its many shelves of books, its papers and writing instruments and all the other paraphernalia of scholarship. Arval pushed a tiny measure of liquor across the table towards him and wordlessly Haldur drank when told to, recognising as he did so the secret distillation of Tellgard.

'Look at me,' said Arval again; and then holding Haldur's eyes he said, 'Speak, give the pain words.'

When they came, the words were plain and bare, a stark expression of torment. 'I cannot bear what I have done.'

'But why? No other man could have done what you did. You obeyed the word of the Starborn, and through you hope has returned to us. Your name will be honoured for generations to come.'

Haldur shook his head. The lamplight winked on drops of water that clung to his damp hair, but his eyes were still deadened and dull.

'Generations to come! Since dawn this morning, it seems to me as though age upon age of this world has already passed, and the day is still not ended. Tomorrow is a desert that stretches before me like the Waste.' He dropped his face into his hands and the words were muffled. 'And somehow I must endure the rest of my life.'

This hit so near to the pain that Arval also felt that tears stung his eyes, but he blinked them back. 'Haldur, you and Artorynas were brothers in your hearts: you both told me so. I will freely admit that I doubted whether you could do what he wished; but he assured me, in this very room he told me, that it was your love for him that would enable you to act. Did you not wish many times that you could help him in his quest? And once he had made his choice, who did he turn to but you?'

At this Haldur wept. 'He said to Sigitsinen in the forest, before we took the mine, *no more secrets*. But there were, oh, there were, and I think I half knew it. Why, why didn't he tell me?'

'Would your aim have been true, if you had known too far ahead what it was you had to do?' asked Arval. 'As it is, he has taken us both in his heart into the life of the As-Geg'rastigan, the sun shines once more, and your homeland has been saved – although maybe one should not tempt fate by saying that, when the threat of Vorynaas must be faced at least once more. Sleep now, Haldur, and do not waste your strength in useless grief. Tomorrow you must be ready to help Vorardynur.'

For a few moments Haldur sat in silence, occasionally brushing the tears away with the back of his hand, gradually mastering his emotions. Then he looked at Arval, suddenly alert once more.

'That's it, isn't it! That's why Vorardynur and I are both here! I know Artorynas persuaded my father to let me come because I had to use the arrow, but he must have asked for Vorardynur as well so that he could stand in for me afterwards.' He laughed bitterly. 'And now I must help him, you say. Yes, let him lead us. I will ride with the Cunorad y'm As-Geg'rastigan as Cunor y'n Tor. I have been told twice now that my search is not over, though what could there be still to seek? *Let the Hidden People show themselves* was our watchword, but I see now why it is said men should be careful what they wish for.'

'Yes, indeed,' said Arval, smiling a little sadly as he remembered Numirantoro. 'But you and I will harbour no regrets. There are mysteries here, Haldur, and we will study them together. Artorynas promised that the Nine Dales would be safe. We will first make sure his words are fulfilled, and then this time I will go with you when you return home; this time, when the north calls to me, I will answer.'

Where once this would have delighted Haldur, now it seemed but small comfort. Nonetheless it was something to hold on to, to steady him when despair would otherwise have robbed him of the will to endure. Over the next few days, he took his share of responsibility in the work of bringing order to the city and preparing for the clash with Vorynaas. But he had little to say, and Arval noticed that although he must have seen that the arrow rested once more beside the lamp, secure in the casket from which long ago Haartell had wrested it, he never once mentioned Artorynas, nor asked what had befallen when Arval brought him back to Tellgard from the wall. Eventually the expected word came that Vorynaas was fast approaching, already a day's march the Caradward side of the border. On the morrow they would have to set out to stop him.

They rode at dawn, as many as possible taking the road while still leaving the city well-defended. From what he had been told, Vorardynur estimated that this time the opposing forces were more evenly matched in numbers, although according to his informant the advancing column was being harried every mile of the way, men being picked off from the outer ranks by ambushes and night attacks. He wondered about this: would it affect morale, or were the troops as determined as their leaders to exact revenge? As the second day's afternoon wore on, three men approached, holding up empty hands in sign of peace, bringing the news that Vorynaas was only about two hours away.

'He's staking all on this throw, because he's brought Valestron with him,' they said. 'He must know it's winner takes all, now. But if you defeat him, he's finished, because Gwent y'm Aryframan's risen up behind him and if you can overcome him here, then it's all over. We want to be able to tell our grandchildren we did our bit: we've come to join you, to stand with these riders you've brought, the ones everyone says fight without weapons and can't be killed.'

They looked around eagerly, craning to see this legendary company, and Vorardynur smiled at the new reputation the Cunorad had acquired.

As the city waited, its fate still in the balance, Arval and Forgard took a brief rest together, sitting side by side in the courtyard of Tellgard and enjoying the early evening sun. Forgard tipped his head back, his eyes closed, feeling the warmth on his face.

'You know, I'm surprised not to see Heretellar back again,' he said. 'He can't have been further than a day's ride from the city when the dawn came. We waited for it long enough, I'd have thought he would have turned for home straight away.'

'Oh, I don't know,' said Arval, as lightly as he could. 'Didn't you tell me he'd already made a couple of journeys in quick succession? He probably wanted to share the moment with your people down in the Ellanwic.'

'Yes, I expect that was it.' Forgard smiled, but he looked exhausted – as well he might, having worked tirelessly for days on end with Arval, helping his fellow-citizens. 'He's a good boy. It's been hard for him, keeping things going, but maybe there'll be easier times ahead. He's held the estate together where another young fellow might well have given up; he deserves to see it revive.'

Arval heard the love in Forgard's voice and glanced swiftly at his old friend, but his eyes were still shut against the bright light. He himself, unable to shake off the slight feeling of unease about Heretellar that had bothered him ever since the evening they had all eaten supper together, found nothing to say in reply.

Willing sacrifice

There came a point when Heretellar could force himself no further towards Assynt y'm Atrannaas. Some way back he had seen the last military outpost where troops had once been stationed. Its buildings were abandoned and its guards fled, leaving bits and pieces of equipment scattered to lie where they fell. Surely it could not be far now to the place where prisoners were forced to go on alone, the place where many had flung themselves on instant death rather than face the waiting horror alive. For a while now the track he followed had been leading steadily downwards into an impenetrable darkness. Behind him there was still light in the sky, but the sun, declining behind the mountains, had disappeared behind ominous clouds that added their gloom to the menacing shadow of the Somllichan Ghent that towered before him. He stood, fighting the fear that rose in his throat. At last his breathing slowed and steadied once more, and he walked on again. Now the dark was all about him, more dense and black than anything the worst nightmare could conjure: a brooding, suffocating, breathless, hopeless pit of despair. Heretellar faltered again. His knees felt like water and he sank down to sit on a rock. He must be very near now. If he went on but a little way further, the darkness would close over him; he would pass through this black door of night and never return. He clenched his teeth, ashamed of the small sounds of fear he was unable to stop himself making. Then, drifting out of the darkness, he smelt it: the unmistakeable sickly-sweet, vile, rotten stench of death. Strangely, although his body reacted with automatic revulsion, it seemed to steady his mind. What else had he expected? Death comes to us all eventually, he thought. We live with this knowledge from our earliest childhood, yet we do not spend every day in constant fear, so why be afraid simply because we know the moment has come? And whatever form death takes, we can only die once. It occurred to him that if he had been brought to this spot and ordered to go on, he would have found the strength to do it without compulsion. He stood up. If I would have denied Vorynaas the satisfaction of seeing me show fear, he thought, then surely I can master myself for the sake of those I love, and those whose lives have ended in this terrible place. Once only he looked back; then with open eyes and firm tread he walked into the dark, and the black night of Assynt y'm Atrannaas under the mountains closed behind him.

The Two Hundred

With battle now imminent, it was time for the leaders of the Two Hundred and those others who had since swelled their numbers to make their final plans. Esylto, grave and fair, spoke first.

'This is the day of destiny on which Artorynas asked that those who had once been arrayed in the gold of the Cunorad should wear it again. Let all who are willing withdraw to prepare themselves.'

Quietly but without any hesitation men and women detached themselves from the ranks of their comrades and led their small bright-coated horses aside. Though some of those who had come forward in Cotaerdon had fallen, still there were more than sixty who would ride once more with the twelve Cunorad, who were themselves yet all unscathed; and Haldur made to follow them. When he saw this, Vorardynur excused himself from the council and hurried after his cousin. Conversation between them had been brief and stilted in the days since dawn brought freedom to Caradriggan, but urgency left no more time for awkwardness.

'Why are you doing this?' said Vorardynur. 'You are our chief captain: you should be leading us now the moment has come!'

'I will lead you,' said Haldur. 'How else will the Hounds run? There will surely be nothing of the Starborn for them to seek among Vorynaas' host. But Arval has entrusted the arrow to me: I have it with me once more. I will go first, and the Cunorad y'm As-Geg'rastigan will follow me.'

Vorardynur began to interrupt, but Haldur held up his hand. 'Remember, it has been promised that I will return safe to the Nine Dales. Since my life is protected, who better to be our standard-bearer?'

They stood looking at each other in silence. Vorardynur had heard the bitterness in Haldur's voice, but had no time to answer it. He reached up to touch Haldur's forehead. 'Very well. You shall lead us, Cunor y'n Tor.'

'My rallying-cry will be *Warriors of the Sun*,' said Haldur. 'For after all, that is what we are; although the tale of that name, which is a favourite with the Caradwardans, tells a very different story. When they hear the shout, we will strike panic into their ears as well as their eyes.' For a moment, a shadowy smile appeared briefly on Haldur's haunted face, and he returned the traditional salutation of the Cunorad. 'The Starborn keep you, Cunor y'm Ardo.'

It was evening when battle was finally joined, a golden, serene evening of early summer. Vorardynur watched the enemy approach, his thoughts racing in a strange, detached, disjointed manner. Not knowing that his survival too had been predicted, he wondered whether his death was only moments away. And he wanted to live, wanted it with an almost painful intensity. How ironic that Haldur, whose survival was assured, seemed not to care either way! If matters had turned out differently, it might have been Haldur in his place, and he among the Cunorad... Vorardynur glanced quickly over his shoulder at the oath-bound company, sitting silent and calm on their horses, waiting, waiting: yes, there was an eeriness about them, no wonder they inspired fear... and Haldur had used the name that had been his when he was one of the twelve, the Hound of Fire... Vorardynur turned forward again. Cunor y'm Ardo... it had been a name well given. Since his days in Rihann y'n Temenellan, he had learnt to master his quick temper, but now he felt a fire within him. He *would* live! Or if not, he would sell his life as dearly as he could. He gathered the reins more securely in his left hand. Was Vorynaas going to order his troops to halt for a parley? If so, they would call on him to surrender, but if not ... And then suddenly, he realised the waiting was over. Dust rose into the evening air as the front ranks of the enemy broke into a gallop. Vorynaas, bent on a quick kill, had decided upon a sudden onset without warning. Instantly, his foes responded, putting into action their pre-arranged plan. Every archer of Rihannad Ennar drew, aimed and released. Arrows flew from the mighty bows of the north, bringing down men and horses before the enemy's advance had gathered its full speed. And then, even as a second flight of missiles whistled on its deadly way, the shout went up. Vorardynur and the other captains, already spurring to the charge themselves, drew aside to part the front line and through it burst Haldur, eyes wide and wild, anointed with the golden salve of the Cunorad, riding recklessly forward with Arymaldur's arrow raised aloft in his hand, the Hounds of the Starborn streaming heedless of danger in his wake. *Warriors of the Sun, Arythaltan y'n Tor* they cried, and the words were taken up on all sides, swelling from every throat among Na Devocatron.

Having seen the Cunorad before, Vorynaas had forewarned his troops and thought by this to discount any element of surprise. But his glimpse of them at Caradriggan had been brief, nor had he himself stood against them. Not only was he unprepared for their increased numbers but also he had not reckoned on the influence the changed hour of the battle might have. This time, the sun was behind his men; and as it sank towards setting its level rays fell directly upon those who assailed them. Even as the first arrows fell among his troops and the screams of the dying rang in their ears, those still unhurt now saw with terrifying clarity the gleaming tide that poured forwards, its very strangeness unnerving and unmanning. No warning they had been given had prepared them for this thunderous cavalcade of tossing manes and streaming hair, these riders who were not simply without armour but actually stripped to the bare golden skin, these faces held in some trance, these eyes filled with light, these voices lifted in wild exultation. Surely too there were many more of them than they had been led to expect? And now they saw that some of these battle-crazed madmen were in fact women! Warriors of the sun? Who were these unearthly foes, how could they be fought? As a second flight of arrows found its mark, Vorynaas and Valestron exchanged glances in which an understanding passed. This was the panic that had undone Thaltor's men; if it was not countered immediately it would be too late.

'Stand, stand!' shouted Valestron. 'Ignore them! Go for the others, and give no quarter. Archers, fire back! They're within range now. Follow me, forward!'

But the Cunorad, riding as only they could their agile, specially-bred golden horses, were galloping this way and that, turning and changing direction with bewildering speed, cutting swathes through Valestron's men, dividing one company from the next, preventing concerted action. Vorynaas brandished his sword.

'Kill the women!' he screamed. 'Bring them down, don't let them put a spell on us!'

Esylto heard this and turned headlong towards him. The man at his side, swearing desperately, was trying to pull out of her path. With a snarl of rage, Vorynaas tore the spear from his hand and hurled it. He saw Esylto's face, at once terrible and beautiful, saw the slight smile as she tilted her golden head aside. The spear passed harmlessly over her and buried itself deep in the breast of the woman riding behind. Itantoro fell without a cry, her arms flung wide, her eyes still open to the evening sky, and disappeared under the crushing welter of hooves and trampling feet. Vorynaas laughed wildly and urged his own horse onwards. But even as he shouted to Valestron, a throwing-knife came flying, slender, wicked and razor-sharp, and Valestron was gone: gone for ever before they could share the triumph of the kill. The smile froze on Vorynaas' face. Refusing to acknowledge the cold fingers of despair that now for the first time began to tighten about his heart, he wheeled around and plunged back into the fray with a ruthless resolve. But even as he killed and killed again, he heard a new shout raised above the clamour. His foes were crying *Warriors of the Sun* no longer. Instead they called to his men, urging them to surrender and lay down their arms.

'Come over to us,' he heard, 'don't throw your lives away! We will show you mercy if you yield!'

Desperately though Vorynaas attempted to rally his forces, he felt control slipping from him. Some on the outer fringes of the fight were heeding the call to give themselves up, the instinct for self-preservation now stronger than their fear of him. Suddenly, over to his right, he saw a whole company turn. He caught a fleeting glimpse of Torilmarap at their head and then they were away, galloping back up the road towards the border. One or two fell as they rode, but the rest held on with some semblance of order. Vorynaas found that he had made his decision without conscious thought. Surrender he would not, and while there was any chance to re-group he was not going to fight to the death. He would go after those who had withdrawn, whose discipline seemingly still held – and when he caught up with Torilmarap he would pay for abandoning his commander. But that could wait; for now, he must look out for himself. He cut his way through the chaos, moving gradually towards the rear, and then slid from his horse, running low through the swirling dust. Not far from the road a tree, half blown over in some gale, thrust roots into the air and below them, where others still remained in the ground, was a sort of burrow. Into this earthy refuge Vorynaas was forced to creep, too spent to flee further as yet. He crouched, his chest heaving, grimly ignoring the weaknesses of age that pained his body at every point. Uneven footsteps approached, and the sound of ragged breathing. Vorynaas gripped his sword in readiness. Then not two yards away, a man fell to the ground. For a moment or two he gasped and moaned, then with a final shudder lay still. An idea came to Vorynaas. He dragged the dead man nearer by his booted foot, ignoring the body's convulsive twitching. Quickly he removed the fellow's jerkin and cap, plain and quilted to double thickness with some metal plating. There was no need now to abandon his body-armour. Over it he put on the anonymous leather, all slimed and bloodied as it was. Then he pushed his own helmet into the soil under the tree roots, put the disguising cap on his head and settled himself to wait.

From his hiding-place, Vorynaas knew by what he heard that the battle was over. Now they would be gathering up the dead and wounded, sorting the weapons, securing any captives, deciding on the next move. The search would be on for himself, too. His eye fell on the dead man from whom he had taken his disguise. What if they came to collect him, and he was discovered? He heaved at the corpse, bringing it in to share his den, shoving it to the back, forcing the lifeless limbs to bend into a more compact bulk. Then his ear was caught by a new sound. Coming rapidly nearer, he heard the hooves of horses ridden to the limits of their endurance. Could it be that reinforcements were arriving? He listened, all his senses at full stretch, and gradually it dawned on him that this was Torilmarap and the men who had fled the battle coming back again. But clearly they had not come to renew the fight: there was no mistaking the panic and fear in the voices he heard. He heard the jingle of harness as the newcomers dismounted, a louder metallic noise which he took to be weapons thrown to the ground, a confused blur of many voices all talking at once that gradually faded and then, approaching down the road from the same direction as the riders had come, the sound of heavy wagon wheels. Nearer and nearer the dull rumbling came, an oddly ominous noise, and then stopped. For several moments there was complete silence; then voices again, in which this time, Vorynaas heard a new note of horror and disbelief mixed with fear.

What could possibly be happening? Curiosity gnawed at him until eventually, barely breathing, he peered stealthily out from his hiding-place. The battle had raged for two hours or more, and now there was only a lingering summer twilight in which he saw men crowded round two bulky wagons. There was a babble of animated voices, and much milling around. Vorynaas saw that his moment had come. Better to go now, while his enemies were preoccupied and there was still that last trace of twilight to prevent the darkness of true night giving him away by making him stumble or fall. He crept out and began to steal away, slowly, cautiously, leaving the lights and voices behind him, pausing often to take stock and listen. On one of these halts, as he crouched warily, his nostrils suddenly flared in disgust. The stink of his own sweat and dirt, of blood from the dead man's jerkin, were already foul in his nose; but now something much worse reached him out of the darkness. He felt his hair lift under the filthy leather cap. There was something close by, something so vile he had no name for it. Then before he could get to his feet he was pinned to the ground and a voice hissed in his ear, its words borne on a fetid stench.

'Don't move until I tell you, don't cry out. One sound, and you're a dead man.'

CHAPTER 63

Horror at sunset

It was after sundown now, although a golden glow still stretched across the western sky; but dust hung in the air, dimming the warm summer twilight, and the onset of dewfall intensified the sharp, metallic smell of blood. The aftermath of battle lay strewn across the road and on each side of it: the storm-wrack of conflict, left behind as the surge of violence abated. Some of those who lay on the ground called for help; but there were others too badly hurt to move or cry out and many more whose stillness and silence was final. Vorardynur took off his helmet, shaking out his sweaty hair and wiping his face with the backs of his hands. Although he knew all resistance was broken now and victory was at last theirs, he felt cold and blank as the heightened perceptions of battle faded. Maybe joy would follow in time, he thought wearily; for now, there were urgent tasks to do before they could settle to rest. He called to him those captains who were unhurt.

'Help the wounded first. Find me somebody who knows this area, who'll be able to tell me how close the nearest village is. If we can get hold of some wagons, we can get the worst cases off to the city tonight. Collect the dead, keep our people separate. And check both the living and the dead for identification; we need to account for Valestron and Vorynaas.'

'Valestron's dead, I can tell you that.' Two men, passing close by carrying a fallen comrade, had heard him. One of them jerked his head. 'He'll be somewhere on the road. I saw him come off his horse right in the thick of things; he took a hit from a throwing-knife.'

'Right. Well, we still need to…' Vorardynur broke off, listening. Hoofbeats, hammering down the road, coming rapidly nearer! He raised his voice in a shout to carry over the groans of the wounded, to reach his scattered forces. 'Mount up, rally to me! We're under attack again. *Na Devocatron!*'

Ramming his helmet back on, he threw himself into the saddle and wheeled his horse; all around, men were doing the same, picking a way through the casualties as fast as they could, spurring to meet the new threat. But as soon as the approaching riders saw that the road was held against them, far from charging forward, they reined to a plunging, sliding halt. Vorardynur and the others waited, frowning: was this some new trick? Then the leader of the newcomers dismounted, yelling at his men to do likewise. They began to hasten forward on foot, stumbling as they ran, throwing down their weapons, holding out their hands. Suddenly a man behind Vorardynur cried out in amazement.

'By my right hand! It's Torilmarap! From the border garrison,' he explained when Vorardynur turned to him. 'He turned tail and fled while the fighting was still going on. Why's he come back?'

Why indeed, thought Vorardynur, as Torilmarap came near enough for speech. 'Are you giving yourselves up?' he shouted. 'If so, keep your hands high.'

It seemed the troop could not surrender fast enough. As one man, they rushed to submit, almost dragging their captors with them in their eagerness to get off the road. Torilmarap himself clutched at those restraining him.

'You've got to understand, I was only following orders. They've escaped somehow, they're coming! But listen to me, I had to follow orders! I was forced to do it, we all were; we wouldn't have done it if we'd not been afraid for our own lives and our families… I tell you, I'd no choice! You've got to believe me, listen to what I'm telling you before they get here…'

Not much of this meant a lot to Vorardynur, but he decided it was something he could deal with later. 'Take him away with the others,' he said, turning to resume his interrupted work.

Yet not long afterwards, a warning shout alerted him that something else was indeed approaching down the road. Dark against the north-western sky two large, heavy farm carts drew slowly nearer. Nearer and nearer they rumbled, clumsy and ponderous, their wheels squeaking and grumbling, finally lurching to a halt some yards away. The man who had been walking in front, leading the two pairs of oxen, threw the reins over the animals' backs. They stood patiently within the shafts as he came forward, but Vorardynur and the others barely noticed him in their horror at those who rode in the carts. Pallid, emaciated, some with hair pulled out from their heads, others with unhealed cuts and rips in the flesh of their meagre limbs, they looked like the slain of some primeval battle, torn from their graves and returned to haunt the dying hours of day. They had apparently been separated from each other, for while in the one cart they slumped motionless and silent with sunken, lifeless stares, those in the other fidgeted constantly, gibbering and muttering, wild eyes flickering from side to side as if they feared some threat. It seemed somehow indecent to stare and the onlookers wrenched their gaze away to the man on foot. Suddenly Haldur, scarcely able to believe what he saw, realised who stood before him.

'Heretellar! What are you doing here? And who, who in the name of the Starborn are these? Where have they come from?'

'I've been into Assynt y'm Atrannaas. It's gone, now: closed up again after we got out. There was a rock-fall when the ground quaked. But these were the only prisoners still left alive, inside.'

There was something strange about Heretellar's voice: it was toneless and strained, as if he spoke from a great distance; but when they surged forward, exclaiming in shock and amazement, he became more animated.

'Stay back! Don't alarm them.' He looked at Haldur. 'I heard you'd returned. The tales run everywhere of events in Caradriggan, but what has happened here? I saw Valestron and Vorynaas march past. Did you meet them here on the road before they reached the city?'

'Yes, it's all over now. Valestron's dead, but we're not sure yet about Vorynaas. We were looking for him, checking the dead and wounded. We can't risk him getting away again like he did from Caradriggan.'

'I'll not hinder you, then,' said Heretellar, 'and in any case, I need to hurry on. Can you spare me someone to help with the oxen? If there were two of us, we could drive them and make better speed. The only hope for these poor souls is Arval. And if we could take on water and some food – just bread would do, they can't deal with anything else yet – but make sure you feed those in this cart first, or they'll attack the others and take theirs. They'll fight each other for it in any case.'

Vorardynur glanced up at what those in the second wagon were clutching as weapons and hurriedly looked away again. 'Why are they…'

Heretellar shook his head. 'Don't ask me about it.'

Just then, a soldier came running up. 'Look what we've found!' he panted, waving a gold-adorned helmet all soiled with earth. 'This is his helmet! It was pushed into the ground under some tree-roots: who but Vorynaas himself would have hidden it? Anyone else would have claimed it as a trophy – he must be still alive! He's escaped again.'

Vorardynur exclaimed in angry frustration, hastening to see the place for himself. The others busied themselves in helping Heretellar as he had asked and in the flurry of activity no-one noticed one of the last survivors of Assynt y'm Atrannaas climb down from a wagon and slip away.

A true son

'One sound, you're a dead man.'

Vorynaas lay still in the darkness as his assailant pawed at him, removing his armour and taking his sword. He heard the quick, uneven breathing as he was roughly searched and his dagger taken also; then his hands were tied behind him and he felt the points of both weapons pressed against him.

'Get up, move. Do what I tell you. And remember, the longer you keep quiet, the longer you live.'

With no option but to comply, Vorynaas obeyed, bewildered. He had assumed some looter had found him and was expecting to be murdered out of hand; but now he was being compelled to stagger through the night, forced to go on if fatigue made him slow or brought him stumbling to his knees. These were the only occasions on which his captor spoke, a menacing whisper that left no room for doubt that he meant what he said about killing if necessary. Vorynaas had the impression the man knew who he had caught, so why was he apparently heading away from the place of battle, away from any chance of fame or reward?

'Where are you taking me?' groaned Vorynaas, after he had tripped and fallen yet again.

'You'll find out soon enough,' came the foul breath in his ear, with a hint of gloating in it that made the hairs rise on Vorynaas' neck. There was something about the voice that seemed vaguely familiar; but with a slurred quality to it that prevented recognition. Maybe the fellow had lost some teeth or perhaps was himself wounded. When daylight returned, Vorynaas looked with horror on his companion. He was filthy, with matted hair; covered in bruises and sores, and dressed in rags. But far worse was his manner, which seemed half-deranged to match the crazed look of his face; and worse still was the weapon he brandished. In addition to the sword and dagger he had taken, he was armed with what was clearly a thigh-bone with shreds of stinking flesh still attached to it; and Vorynaas, averting his eyes as the vile thing was waved in his face, could not rid himself of the suspicion that it was a human bone. He lay, now bound at the ankles also, as the fellow slunk off and left him. Had he been abandoned to starve to death? How long should he wait before he risked shouting for help? But after a few hours the man came back, pushed some food at him, untied his feet and forced him to go on.

And so they continued as the days and nights passed: hiding, skulking, making their furtive way; drinking even from puddles if need drove them, only eating when stealing had been possible. Vorynaas was beyond exhaustion, was begging for death in his mind, although he had not yet reached the point where he would plead aloud for mercy. But his captor seemed tireless; indeed he appeared barely to sleep at all. If Vorynaas woke, tormented by pain and hunger, he would be sitting there with open eyes: watching, always watching him. Eventually they reached the river, beyond which loomed the forest.

'Quiet!' hissed the madman, when Vorynaas began to babble in panic. He foraged up and down the bank, and reappeared dragging a large chunk of dead wood, torn down in some storm of winters past. 'If you want to live, hold on to it. Let go, and you'll drown. It's as simple as that.'

Into the Lissad na'Stirfell they went. Vorynaas felt his flesh creep at the cold touch of the river and was unable to prevent his face contorting into a rictus of fear. An age seemed to pass and then he felt something nudge at him. Opening his eyes, he was amazed to see that the current which had borne them downstream had also brought them across to where an eddy gurgled against a tangle of debris caught on some underwater obstruction. They struggled onto dry land, where Vorynaas retched helplessly from a mixture of relief and fear, the river now behind him but the darkness of Maesaldron at hand. It seemed there was to be no escape however; as they stood there dripping with water, his companion was already threatening him both with his own sword and the unspeakable cudgel, forcing him into the trees. Vorynaas cracked.

'Not the forest!' he gasped. 'Not Maesaldron! Don't you know the kind of thing that lurks in here?'

'It's what lives beyond Maesaldron you need to be worrying about. Now get in there.'

Days later, the trees began to thin out, but Vorynaas was so spent that he barely noticed. He knew now that continuous fear saps the strength more surely than hunger, thirst or hard labour: though the forest was not dark and black as he had anticipated, its green depths were an alien world and the terrors bred into him by his upbringing would not let him rest. He lay, propped against a tree trunk, eyes closed, chest heaving.

'Well now,' said a voice beside him, 'we'll be reaching our journey's end today, so now's the time for a little talk.'

He opened his eyes to see his captor sitting looking at him. If Vorynaas was in a bad way, this man looked like an apparition from a nightmare. His eyes were red and inflamed from lack of sleep; the skin on his face had broken out in angry blotches and his hands trembled constantly.

Vorynaas stared at him. 'Who are you? What kind of a madman can go without sleep like you have, to bring me here?'

The other's ravaged face broke into a slow smile for the first time, revealing widely-spaced teeth with a larger gap where several had indeed been knocked out. He saw Vorynaas' eyes widen as recognition dawned at last.

'Yes, you know me now, don't you?'

'Heranar! But why, how…?'

'Heretellar has freed those entombed in Assynt y'm Atrannaas. Let's wish him joy for the courage he showed, though after what he's seen in there, I doubt he'll have it… Anyway, that's nothing to me, now. But before that I'd met an Outlander.' He pulled a pouch from some pocket in his filthy garments and dangled it in front of Vorynaas with a shaking hand. 'I got this from him. It kept me awake in the dark, and it's those who can stay awake longest in there who stay alive longest.' He laughed crazily. 'And then I got out, and heard what was happening… and I had enough left to keep me going while I looked for you, and brought you away…'

Vorynaas cut across him. 'Are you insane? It'll kill you if you swallow it down in quantity like that, you can't expect…'

'Shut it! You listen to me.' Vorynaas recoiled as he was prodded in the chest with the noisome bone, and Heranar smiled again, though his whole body was now gripped by uncontrollable tremors. 'That's better. I know what it does. But it'll keep me on my feet long enough, that's all I'm interested in. So much for how. And you want to know why. *Why?* Because of my family, because of what's happened to my parents, to my brother, to me; to my wife, and my children.' His voice cracked in grief.

'My children! I don't even know if they're alive or dead, or where they are. A whole family, destroyed by the poisonous greed and envy you encouraged! And we weren't the only ones, were we? Hundreds, thousands of lives wasted, and all can be traced back to you. But it's almost finished, now. Your son is dead, your other cronies in evil are either prisoners or dead also. But you've still got me, your son-before-the-law; and I'm going to do for you what a true son should. Now get up, and start walking again.'

It was slow going, both of them now barely able to drag themselves from one footstep to the next. They lurched along, Vorynaas no longer caring about how much noise they made. Within a couple of hours they emerged from the last of the trees into a suddenly much brighter light. Vorynaas looked up and quailed at what lay before him.

'Know where we are?' said Heranar. 'We've skirted round the mine workings and come out of the forest. And here it is, what we were always taught lay beyond Maesaldron: the Waste. Valahald told me, you were so arrogant in your pride that you dared to swear by the blindworms of Na Naastald: *let them devour me, if I do not take Arymaldur's life.* You fool, no man takes the life of the Starborn. You couldn't kill him, or his son either.' A sudden spasm made his teeth chatter and he broke off, wiping the sweat from his upper lip as the unhinged laugh broke from him again.

'But I know you won't want to be remembered as a man who didn't keep his word, so I've brought you here to fulfil your vow. What are you waiting for? Off you go now, make sure you get right out into the open. And don't think you can double back into the trees, because I'll be right here, watching you.' He pulled out the pouch and snatched another mouthful of the drug it contained. 'Yes, I'll be watching. Watching, for however long it takes.'

The future

Arval crossed the exercise court in Tellgard, and seeing Heretellar at one of the windows of the study room next to the library let himself in to join him. He answered the young man's unspoken question.

'I don't know that they will ever fully recover. An ordeal like that… It affects the mind perhaps more than the body. But their physical hurts are healing. Maybe if we can continue to soothe and calm the most disturbed, and keep trying to reawaken the life in the others… who knows. It may take a very long time.'

Well, let us hope that their memories at least do not recover, thought Heretellar. He felt he himself would be haunted forever by what he had seen when he walked into the night under the mountains. Hearing faint sounds – water dripping on rock, furtive scraping noises, hoarse breathing – he had stood rooted to the spot, his feet numb from splashing through icy puddles, his whole body frozen with fear. And then to his amazement the darkness of Assynt y'm Atrannaas had lifted, revealing the spectral survivors, squatting among the remains of their companions in horror: scattered bones, bloated corpses floating in black pools, more recent carcasses torn and rent apart. It was all too easy to understand how those who were not dead had managed to keep themselves alive, but he would never tell what he had seen, no matter how many times he was asked. He knew well enough that there were those who had guessed, but he had said nothing: not to the villagers who had helped by lending the ox-carts, not to Haldur and the others, and especially not to his parents. Thank the Starborn that word of his deed had only reached them together with news of its success and his safety; that he had been able to retrieve and destroy the letter he had written them before they found it. Suddenly conscious that, lost in thought, he had made no reply to Arval, he turned to the old man.

'I wish Heranar was getting the benefit of your care.' He shook his head. 'I can't understand how no-one noticed he had slipped away. I blame myself: I should have kept a better eye on things while we were halted at the battlefield.'

'Heretellar, it's not your fault. Don't take all on yourself like this. Can you even be quite sure it *was* Heranar?'

'Oh yes, it was him all right. He was the only one who was even partially lucid – after all, he must have been among the last prisoners to be sent there; he can't have been inside more than a couple of weeks or so. As soon as the darkness lifted, he seemed to grasp what was going on: there was no need to urge him to follow me like I had to encourage the others. In fact if it hadn't been for him I doubt whether the rest of them would have moved in time. We'd gone no distance when the ground began to shake and then half the mountain-side came down behind us. When the air cleared, the chasm had gone, completely filled up with rock and earth. The landslip hid all traces of what had been there before.'

Maybe it would have been better if the mountain had fallen sooner, thought Heretellar; better if the quick release of death had come to the unfortunates within, rather than the slow recovery of rescue.

Arval moved across the room to look out from the tall central window. He had a shrewd idea of what Heretellar was thinking, but before he could speak he saw Haldur, Vorardynur and several others coming up the steps from the street. He tapped on the glass to attract their attention and show them where to find him. The door opened and in they came: not only the two from the Nine Dales, but Temenghent and Tirathalt also along with Cunoreth; a young Outlander known as Sigittor from the barbican, who had been another of those in the resistance; and with them came Ancrascaro and Rhostellat. As they exchanged greetings and found seats, Arval looked around at them all. It would not be long now before Vorardynur and Haldur and their companions would be gone, back to Rihannad Ennar, and himself with them. He suppressed a smile at the way Cunoreth was twisting about in his chair as if he sat on an ants' nest. Having heard a little about Cunoreth's hopes and plans, he knew how keen he was to set off home.

Temenghent, although wounded, was on the way to recovery now and had a new confidence in his gaze; Rhostellat's quiet, studious air befitted the man who would preside over Tellgard once Arval had gone. Beside him sat his wife Ancrascaro, who had blossomed with maturity into a dark, rather stately beauty. And there was her cousin Heretellar, who despite his unassuming manner and self-doubts was these days hailed as a hero every time he showed his face, saluted as the man who had been brave enough to go alone and willingly into Assynt y'm Atrannaas. I am looking at the future, thought Arval as he met the eyes that turned to him.

'We've just been talking about poor Heranar,' he said, 'and wondering where he is now.'

Heretellar, remembering what he had been told since they had all been back in the city together, looked over at Temenghent. 'Do you think he might be trying to get back where you took him before, to the refuge in the mountains where he was safe?'

'Maybe, although I doubt he would know how to find it again.'

'I'd say it's more likely he would try to make for his old headquarters, or wherever there might be news of what's really happened to his wife and the little girls. Beautiful children, they were. But I don't see how he would have had the strength to get there.' Haldur shook his head sadly, seeing again in his mind's eye the ghoulish figures who had loomed out of the sunset, but Cunoreth looked aside out of the window, tweaking at one of his braids. He could see it would not do to say in front of Arval and the others that he cared nothing for what might have happened to Heranar.

'Kept himself alive in Assynt y'm Atrannaas, though, didn't he?' said Tirathalt, exchanging a glance with Temenghent and then both of them looking at Sigittor. It had already occurred to the young Outlander that Heranar might have found the means to endurance beyond the norm, but he said nothing and his face remained expressionless.

'Well, he's not my main concern.' Vorardynur stood up and began pacing the room. 'It's Vorynaas that's bothering me. The man must have nine lives like a cat. I can still scarcely believe he's escaped us again; I was sure his body must be on the battlefield somewhere. I didn't want this delay. We should be on our way by now, back to Rihannad Ennar. I stand by our pledge that we will let Caradward and Gwent y'm Aryframan work out their own future between themselves, and that includes whatever they want to do with Vorynaas. But he, more than any other, was responsible for what was done here, and he must be brought to some form of justice or be proved dead; and until that happens, I am not leaving this city.'

'Sigitsinen will find him.'

Cunoreth, who had perked up at Vorardynur's first words and then sunk back into gloom again now brightened once more as Haldur sought to reassure his cousin.

'It was our good fortune that he was the leader of those who arrived from Framstock the day after the battle. Believe me, you could put no man more skilled on to the trail. I know what he can do. He'll bring Vorynaas to us, if he's still alive; or if he's dead, we'll either have his body or proof of his death. You can trust Sigitsinen for that.'

Vorardynur sat down again. 'Well, I hope you're right. And I hope it doesn't take too much longer.'

Payment exacted

Two days before midsummer, Sigitsinen returned to Caradriggan; but he was alone. They gathered to Tellgard again to hear his report, and he laid a sword on the table in front of him. There was gold wire gleaming in the decoration of the hilt and guard, sky-steel glinting at the killing edges of its blade.

'Dead,' said Sigitsinen without preamble. 'We're still holding Thaltor with the other prisoners, I take it? Well then, he can confirm this as Vorynaas' sword.'

Vorardynur frowned as he stared at the weapon. 'Was there nothing else you could bring away with you?'

'No, not in the circumstances.' Sigitsinen looked round at them all with his strange, pale eyes and launched into his tale.

'Vorynaas was taken captive, not long after he fled the battle, and I suspected almost straight away who his captor might be. You'll remember that we found Vorynaas' helmet, which he'd probably hidden himself. But much further on, I found the rest of his armour – I sent it back to the city by courier, you have it, yes? – which had simply been left lying. He must have kept that on when he made a break for it; my guess is he concealed it under a dead soldier's jerkin, so why abandon it now? The obvious answer is that he was forced to discard it; which then begs the question: why was it of no interest to his captor? Clearly, this person wasn't after booty, or indeed any kind of acclaim for bringing Vorynaas in – far from it in fact, because the trail led away from Caradriggan. As I followed, I sometimes came across people from whom food had been stolen, and when I heard their descriptions of the thief, I was more convinced than ever that my suspicions were correct. After all, there was someone else unaccounted for, someone who had more reason than most to settle a score with Vorynaas.'

Heretellar made a sudden movement, comprehension in his face. 'Not Heranar!' he exclaimed.

'That's right. And I'm not guessing now, because eventually I came up with them. I was too late, but maybe it would have made no difference...' Isteddar broke off, and the others waited. He stared sightlessly at the table for a few moments and then looked up again.

'Anyway. I tracked them as far as the river. I can swim, but the Lissad na'Stirfell was a risk I didn't feel inclined to take so I improvised a rough raft and crossed on that. My first thought was they'd died there; but no, there were signs on the far bank that two people had climbed out of the water and gone into the forest. I know, who would have believed it? I followed, but I'd been delayed at the river, so it took me some time to catch up. Eventually, I heard voices, and then silence. I crept forward, but the trees were thinning all the time. While there was still some cover, I stopped and parted the foliage to see what was happening and I realised immediately that we'd gone right through the forest, because there in front of us was the Waste.'

Sigitsinen paused and cleared his throat. 'I was taught as a boy what lies beyond Maesaldron. But the Waste, now that I've actually seen Na Naastald… It's beyond me to describe it to you. It's empty, blasted, barren, and yet I've never felt such a sense of menace, of evil…' He shook his head.

'I can't find the right words. Vorynaas had gone a little way out into it and I saw him stagger slightly. Heranar was standing at the edge of the forest, watching. When Vorynaas looked back, he brandished his weapons and Vorynaas turned again and walked a bit further. It was obvious he'd been told to keep going or come back and be killed. Then… then this noise started up.' Sigitsinen swallowed.

'Within moments, it was so loud, I felt I might go mad – or even worse, lose control and run into the Waste myself, in panic. I was actually crawling on the ground, moaning in fear, I'll admit it: that should tell you how bad it was. Then it stopped and I forced myself to look up. To my amazement, Heranar was still standing – well, I say standing; it looked like his knees had given way, but he'd grabbed hold of a branch as if to support himself. He'd never taken his eyes off Vorynaas.

'So I looked out myself. I'd assumed that Na Naastald was lifeless, but I'd been wrong. I saw this… thing, this… creature, dropping out of the air on to Vorynaas. He'd fallen to the ground but it swept him up into a tight, crushing hold, lifting him easily. And then… It had no eyes or ears, or even jaws that I could see, only slits almost like gills where its neck might have been and a line of small round markings along the length of it. If it had stayed still you'd scarcely have seen it against the background of the Waste: its hide was a dirty creamy-white colour. The head and body were all one, it was like… like some vile maggot you'd find in a rotten fruit, but huge, and winged. And at the head end it had a sort of long snout that writhed and burrowed its way inside Vorynaas' jacket. He screamed and twisted, but his struggle was brief. There was a noise like, I don't know, water going through a sluice. For a moment the markings on the creature's body showed red, then the thing took to the air again, now completely silent. As it went, it let go of Vorynaas, and what was left of him fell back to the ground like a child's puppet, all head and hands in empty clothes. He'd been sucked dry, pulped from the inside.'

A horrified silence filled the room.

'A blindworm!' whispered Temenghent. 'So they do exist, after all.'

'Is that really what it was?' asked Ancrascaro. Her dark eyes were wide, fixed on Arval; but he and Haldur were staring at each other and it was her husband who answered.

'Surely it must have been,' said Rhostellat, 'or at least, this must be the creature that gave rise to the legend and the name.'

Arval and Haldur, remembering what Artorynas had told of his journey beyond the Nine Dales, were sharing the same thought: that this creature, evolved from who knew what blighted begetting, must also haunt Aestron na Caarst far to the north. Artorynas had heard it and found the evidence of its feeding, but never seen it. Thank the Starborn it had not seen him!

Sigittor now spoke up. 'I heard that Vorynaas bragged before the battle about how he'd sworn to destroy Arymaldur and Artorynas, or let blindworms take him. He boasted that he wasn't afraid to bind himself by such an oath.'

Heretellar leaned forward. 'What happened to Heranar?'

'Well, when the creature, the blindworm or whatever we're to call it, had gone,' said Sigitsinen, 'he just stood there, still staring. So I called to him, and then I moved out of hiding and into view. When he heard his name, he whipped round to face me. I could see straight away what he'd been doing to keep himself on his feet: his eyes were dilated and bloodshot, his lips were cracked, he was shaking from head to toe. I held my hands up, I said, *See, it's Sigitsinen, you know me, nothing to be afraid of*. He peered at me, and repeated my name. Then he pointed to where Vorynaas lay and broke out into hysterical laughter. "Did you see that?" he said. "Did you see? Wasn't I a good son, helping him to keep his vow?" He sounded completely deranged, so I tried to calm him down. *Yes*, I said, *I saw, but it's all over now. Come with me, let's go*. I took a step towards him, but he snatched up Vorynaas' sword from where he'd let it fall. "Don't come any nearer," he said. He looked at me, and suddenly he seemed calm and quiet. "You're right, it's over," he said. "It's finished now." Then without any hesitation at all he put the hilt of the sword against the nearest tree with the point under his ribs, and walked up the length of it. He fell right at my feet with his eyes still fixed on mine. I buried him there as decently as I could, but after what I'd seen I wasn't about to risk messing with what was left of Vorynaas. I took his sword and brought that back instead.'

Another silence fell in which Haldur sat staring at the sword at it lay before them, the sword that had drunk Heranar's blood. It was clean now, burnished bright, a masterpiece of the swordsmith's craft, but how many other lives had it taken since it was made? His thought strayed to Sleccenal, the ancient sword of the north that his father had been so reluctant to take up. Carapethan had been spared the decision in the end, but what about when his own time came? He shifted his feet under the table and felt the slight pressure of the throwing-knife in its holder at the side of his boot. Haldur remembered the wild joy he had felt in killing Valestron, exulting in his own life and strength at the very moment of deliberately dealing another man his death-blow. The Accursed Battle, he thought; *Vala na Naasan*. Let me never again feel that terrible craving to spill blood. He looked up from his dark memories as Arval began to speak.

'Well, to echo poor Heranar's words, it would seem that all is indeed over. Now we need to turn our attention to the times that lie ahead, to make sure that they are better than those we have put behind us. We should gather the people together; and I think,' he said, looking at the captains from Rihannad Ennar, 'I think one of you two must speak to them first.'

'Let it be Haldur,' said Vorardynur. 'I am known here only as a fighting man and words of peace from me might sound hollow; but many will recall that Haldur came south in friendship last year. When the events of these days are recorded for men to read, in the years to come it will be his name that is remembered by all.'

Haldur shook his head. 'There are other names far more worthy of honour than mine.' He looked at those who sat around the table and his eyes met Heretellar's briefly before resting upon Arval. How glad he was that this time, the old man would be travelling with them when they returned to the Nine Dales. He smiled slightly. 'But I will speak, if you wish me to.'

Passing on the burden

So it was that late in the afternoon of the following day he found himself facing a huge crowd of people who had thronged into the parade-ground in Caradriggan. The assembly was being held there because, in spite of its unsavoury associations, it was the biggest open space within the city. Today though, the dais was left unoccupied; instead, a temporary wooden platform was built at the opposite end of the arena and it was here that Haldur stood to speak. He paused for a moment, waiting for quiet. The background noise of hundreds of conversations gradually died away; then a momentary lull was overtaken by a groundswell of anticipation that built and then itself faded to a breathless silence. Haldur looked down on all the faces turned to him, and in the last moment before he began to speak a sudden bright jangle of notes reached him, a brief, wistful cadence like a scatter of jewels thrown carelessly down. Somewhere close by a robin was whistling, heedless of the tides of human history ebbing and flowing below him. In an instant, Haldur was transported in mind back to Cotaerdon where, though it was a bird that sang throughout the year, the robin was often known as the winter-warbler; a pair nested every spring in the flowering climber that scrambled over the porch in Astell's garden. A longing for his own country swept over him so powerfully that he felt the ache of his homesickness lodge in his throat. He had been anxious about what he should say; but now that the moment had arrived, he raised his hand and simple words came readily to him.

'I speak to you now at the request of Arval the Earth-wise. If there are any here who do not know me, I am Haldur son of Carapethan, who is lord of the Nine Dales far away in the north. I came south with my comrades here beside me, those who are known as the Two Hundred, although it grieves me to say that fewer than that number will ride home again with me.'

He saw movement in the crowd as heads craned, those further back trying to get a glimpse of Na Devocatron and in particular to see the fabled Hounds of the Starborn.

'We had two purposes,' continued Haldur. 'First, to save Rihannad Ennar from the evil designs of Vorynaas who intended to enslave our land as he had done Gwent y'm Aryframan; and also to support those among you who had asked for aid in throwing off the yoke under which you laboured.

'I think it is fair to say we have achieved these aims, but who knows whether we should have done so, if we had not ourselves been helped beyond hope. We are all indebted alike, for freedom, life and light, to him whom you once knew as Maesrhon son of Vorynaas but whose true name was Artorynas: the son of Arymaldur of the Starborn and Numirantoro of Caradriggan. In Tellgard now there lies once more the arrow that Arymaldur made, a wonder of both art and craft, work of the very hand and mind of the As-Geg'rastigan. Guided by the wisdom of Arval, Artorynas sought that arrow through years of toil and danger. Arymaldur foretold that its finding would mean the return of hope for men: we now have that hope. Numirantoro promised her son that if he followed its path, light would shine again upon the earth, upon men's hearts and upon a choice that lay before him.'

Here Haldur paused, dropping his gaze briefly from the thousands of eyes fixed upon him, mustering his strength for what had to be said before he ended. His audience waited in absolute silence. He looked up and continued.

'We now have that light. And Artorynas made his choice. He is gone from us, released by the arrow to take a path directly into the life of the Starborn.

'And we too will soon be gone, those of the Two Hundred who still live. Let me reassure you that we of Rihannad Ennar have no wish for influence or domination in a land not our own. But there is much that must be done to heal and repair the damage we have all done each other and the sooner it is started, the better. Who will you have to speak for Caradward in the days to come? We will stay to help begin the work and to celebrate midsummer tomorrow with you in fellowship, if we may; but afterwards we will return to the Nine Dales and leave you to order affairs as you wish here in the south.'

Maybe Haldur's listeners were caught out by the brevity of his speech, or taken aback by its sudden end; or perhaps after years of oppression by Vorynaas they were unsure how to respond when free to express their feelings. At any rate his words met with a confused, rather muted reception as if no-one was quite sure whether acclaim was appropriate, or confident that it was permitted. He stepped forward once more and they fell silent.

'I ask you again: who will you have? There are demanding days ahead, before Tell'Ethronad can once more take up the burden of governance. Until then, who do you trust to represent you?'

For a second time Haldur saw movement ripple across the crowd as people put their heads together, whispering and muttering. Then suddenly a voice rang out, cutting through the confused murmurs.

'Heretellar! Let Heretellar speak for us!'

At this, the noise level surged upwards as many more took up the name. Haldur could distinguish some of what those who stood nearest were shouting: men and women calling for Heretellar, Heretellar who was untainted by association with Vorynaas, who had braved Assynt y'm Atrannaas for the sake of the innocent. He looked to his left, to where Heretellar was standing beside Sigitsinen and Temenghent, and gestured to him. Hands reached out from the crowd, hoisting Heretellar up to join Haldur, and now a huge wave of enthusiasm broke over them. When it finally ebbed away, Heretellar stepped forward.

Renewal and return

'If I am to speak for you, I must first speak to you,' he said. 'It will be for Tell'Ethronad to decide the fate of those who have refused to yield. Until that time, let them be held securely, safe from sustaining or doing further harm. Valestron was killed in the battle and we have now received proof that both Heranar and Vorynaas are also dead. All those who held positions of power until recently are therefore accounted for, and we are free again.' They cheered wildly at this, but Heretellar had not finished.

'We are free from oppression, but not free from guilt,' he said. 'What happened was done in our names. Is there any one of us who can truly say, *I could not have tried harder to prevent it*? We must all take a share of responsibility. Let us always remember not only the horrors of *Stirfellaerdon donn'Ur*, which we foolishly allowed ourselves to forget, but also our recent misdeeds. But what good will remembrance be without reconciliation? I have two things to ask. We of Caradward dishonoured the ties of friendship and kinship that bound us, time out of mind, to our neighbours of Gwent y'm Aryframan. I ask my fellow Caradwardans here today: if you will join me in asking for pardon, then raise your hands now.'

Heretellar's own hand was the first, and after the briefest hesitation others followed until it seemed the crowd was a meadow where a myriad flowers had all sprung and opened in an instant.

'And now I speak to any Gwentarans present,' said Heretellar. 'I know you stand among us, betrayed, illtreated and bereft. If there are any who can find it in their hearts to forgive, then let them take the hands stretched out in entreaty; and if there is anyone here who shared my foster-years with Ardeth of Salfgard, then I ask them to come forward now and join me in making a new beginning.'

He waited. Then here and there hands reached out and touched; slowly, cautiously and then more readily there were handshakes, tentative smiles, an easing of tension. His attention was caught by movement near the front and he looked down to see a man whose arm bore the corn-sign struggling through the press. Heretellar leant forward to take his proffered hand. As he did so, he heard his name called and turned to see two men and a woman who had climbed on to the platform from the other side. These men also had the corn-sign on their arms, and the woman's left ear had been pierced though the amber drop swung there no longer.

'We were with Ardeth of Salfgard in your time,' said a man of about Heretellar's age, of robust build and a broad, open face in which past hurt and present hope both showed.

Heretellar stared at him, scarcely daring to believe. 'Framhald?'

'Yes. I wasn't sure if you'd remember me. And here's Cottiro, too.'

Heretellar looked at her and his heart ached to see how the fresh, country prettiness of the girl he recalled had been overwritten by lines of sorrow and loss. 'Oh yes, I remember well. Happier days, but together we can make them return.'

Smiling now, they embraced in friendship. Meanwhile more Gwentarans had come forward, and Heretellar beckoned Rhostellat and Ancrascaro to join him together with some of their colleagues from Tellgard; and there too were Isteddar, Sigittor and Tirathalt, and Meremvor, who had travelled up to the city just as fast as he could when news of what was happening in Caradriggan reached him; and suddenly Cunoreth vaulted on to the platform beside them with a whoop of his old exuberance. He was from Salfgard, he wanted to be part of things in the better times to come! The people cheered and cheered again. Heretellar, looking down, saw Arval and waved his arm, wanting him to step up also, but with a smile the old man shook his head; then as Heretellar's gaze was held by his parents, who stood watching him, tears on their cheeks even though their faces were lit up with love and pride, Arval caught Haldur's eye. An unspoken message passed between them. Under cover of the continued jubilation, they withdrew from this happy scene, followed quietly by those who were left of the two hundred.

And very soon, even before the midsummer days had begun to shorten, they set out for the north once more, true to their word that they would not meddle further in the affairs of other lands. Cries of farewell, promises of friendship, hopes to meet again hung in the air as Vorardynur and Heretellar, Urancrasig and Isteddar, Arellan and Temenghent clasped hands and parted. Cunoreth was cantering up and down the line, braids flying, his horse catching the excitement of its rider who was impatient to be away, to start his new life, free now of the vows he had made. Arval's dark, deep-set eyes were bright with anticipation. In spite of the sorrow he carried, he had laid down his burden. All the long years of waiting, watching, warning, were over now. There had been moments of weakness and he had been hurt, but he had done the best he could: without regret he left Tellgard to its new guardians and turned his mind to the pleasure of new knowledge, new exchanges of learning in the time remaining to him. He smiled inwardly at himself: I feel like a six-month-old puppy, he thought, ears turning to every sound, nose lifted to savour all the scents of the fresh morning. Then his eye fell on the Cunorad, riding together slightly apart as usual. It seemed almost beyond belief, but the Hounds of the Starborn had all come unharmed through the desperate venture that brought them south; all would return to Seth y'n Temenellan where the *itanardo* burned, awaiting them. There was Esylto, Esylto the golden, Cunor y'm Esc: as fair as the Starborn, fearless and serene, oath-bound. Arval looked again, more closely, his heart seeing a change that was invisible to the eye. So there was another task awaiting him, after all. Haldur was finishing his farewells, embracing Heretellar and Forgard, speaking with Sigitsinen, smiling at Ancrascaro. Arval, watching as he settled himself on his horse and rode forward to take his place beside Vorardynur, saw how the early sun sparked a flash of gold from the torc at his neck and wondered what the eye that looked inwards saw in his heart. The road lengthened behind them, mile upon mile, day after day; and Arval, often riding beside Haldur either in companionable silence or whiling away the hours in talk, noticed that he never once looked back.

Afterwards

CHAPTER 64

The lazy afternoon slipped by, its serenity almost palpable. I could put out my hand and touch its softness as I would fondle the fur of a sleepy cat, thought Arval. He and Astell were sitting side by side on the open green space at the centre of Cotaerdon. Six years had passed since Arval came north when the two hundred returned home, and by now the two of them knew each other well enough to spend time together comfortably without much talking. Arval heard children's voices from the water's edge where some youngsters played and splashed in the shallow river, ducks quacking as they dabbled, doves crooning unseen amid the leaves of nearby trees. He felt warmth move slowly over the skin of his face and hands as the sun progressed across the sky, saw its light reflected in a thousand flashing, sparkling ripples on the surface of the water. His gaze roamed with pleasure over the low-arched footbridges, over the honey-coloured stone of the buildings beyond, over the roofs with their mixture of thatch, russet tiles, grey slates. There was no need to wonder at the strength of the tie that bound Carapethan to his own land; and Arval could see too why it had been a wrench for Artorynas to leave the Nine Dales, even after his choice was made. He also had loved Rihannad Ennar from the first, delighting in its every valley as he rode its highways and byways, feasting his eyes on its snowy mountains and clear rivers, its orchards and pastures. Over on the parapet of the nearest bridge he saw Lethesco sitting, her head bent over the small bundle in her arms. Beside her stood Vorardynur, holding their little daughter by the hand. The imminent birth of his second child had made it sensible for him to stay in Cotaerdon to deputise for his leader while Carapethan rode around the valleys this summer and now he turned from contemplation of his new son and waved a greeting to Astell and Arval. After a moment he loped across with an invitation to join his household for supper in the high hall that evening. Having accepted with pleasure, the two older men watched him return to his family.

'The mantle of leadership sits easily upon his shoulders,' said Astell.

'Yes,' agreed Arval, 'and I think they would be strong enough to bear the burden of lordship also. It surprises me a little that Carapethan, shrewd reader of men though he is, seems not to see this.'

'The most keen-sighted man cannot see what he has closed his eyes to. Carapethan has always been afraid that Haldur would be taken by the Hidden People: that is why he was so relieved when the first thing Esylto did after your return from the south was to make her vow lifelong. And now that old Cunor nan Haarval is dead, and she has taken his place in Seth y'n Temenellan as Hound of the Vow, he has persuaded himself that the future will turn out as he wants it to be. But I told him to his face seven years ago that Haldur's heart would always belong to the Starborn.' Astell gave a short snap of laughter. 'Carapethan should remember that no man can turn back time. And Haldur needs to learn that not all sorrow and loss need be barren, if one accepts them.'

This man is a sterner taskmaster than ever I was with my own pupils, thought Arval; but he spoke quietly. 'Well then, what better guide could he have than yourself?'

Astell's beaky features seemed to sharpen as he shifted in his seat to look directly at his companion. 'I had begun to assume you would see out your days with us here in Cotaerdon, but am I mistaken?'

Arval smiled. 'Not entirely. I mean to indulge my pleasure in the Nine Dales for a little while yet.'

At this Astell raised his eyebrows but did not respond further; and as it seemed Arval had no more to say, they fell silent again. Shadows lengthened as the drowsy afternoon wore on, the sun burning to a deeper gold as it neared the horizon. Arval lifted his face to the light. Yes, he sensed it: even today, somewhere within summer's golden heart there was the faintest hint of autumn frosts, a tiny chill that floated upon the air more as a scent than anything else. It would be cold after sundown, this evening. The long years of witness in Caradriggan had not been without their cost, but this sojourn in Rihannad Ennar, where he was able to savour the changing seasons as they turned, was almost reward enough. He realised how much he had missed the sense of the earth as somehow a living thing, breathing and moving only slowly maybe, but full of a secret life and hidden wisdom of its own, gathered and garnered, age upon age. Once more Arval felt that barely perceptible breath of autumn. When the year turned, Haldur would be coming back to Cotaerdon. There were still things to say to each other, but soon Haldur would not need him any longer; and then, just as he had lingered in Caradriggan, enduring until all was fulfilled before he followed his heart, so now also he would soon be free to go on again. This time, thought Arval, it will be Haldur's turn to help me.

Away in Rihann nan Esylt, Carapethan's business was almost concluded for the year. Although they had been fortunate to lose so few of those who rode south, risking all to snuff out the danger that threatened the Nine Dales, even so there were households in every valley where sorrow rather than joy had been felt, where there were empty seats at table, clothes lying unworn in the chest, familiar footsteps no longer heard at the door. Carapethan never forgot this, and each year he made sure he spent time under every roof where the safety of the land had been bought at the price of a life: it was well said that he was the father of his people. His was an example Haldur took care to follow. There was a new champion now in the Golden Valley, an amiable man whose skill made him worthy of his status, and Haldur had enjoyed his companionship; but today he had done as he did each year, and ridden up the dale to visit young Ennarvorad's parents, to show them their son was remembered with gratitude and honour. Now, heading back to re-join Carapethan's entourage, he let his horse set its own speed. A memory came into his mind of the day when Haldan don Vorygwent had tested his suitability to follow Carapethan into the lordship of the Nine Dales, and again he saw Ennarvorad with the other champions, the coloured ribbon of office tied at his knee. Young Ennarvorad, said Haldur to himself, that's how I still think of him: but if he had come safely home again, he would not be so young now. The years would have passed by for him, as they have for the rest of us.

He sat up straighter, intending to shake off these sombre reflections by speeding up, and at that moment the sun, shining out from behind a passing cloud, fell directly upon a group of buildings high on the hillside to Haldur's left. The brightness of their freshly-whitewashed walls caught his eye and then suddenly he felt it, that sense of a *numiras* close by, the silent call to which the Cunorad were oath-bound to respond. Turning his horse, he found a place to ford the stream that splashed down beside the road and then set the animal to the climb. The track wound this way and that, following the easiest gradient, and eventually emerged at a small level area of ground where the buildings, crouched under their roped-down heather thatch, backed into the hillside behind for shelter. An old fellow, bent and slightly lame from a lifetime of hard work on the land but brisk enough nonetheless, came round the end of a barn.

'Thought I heard a horse. Good day and good health to you, master. Come for the *numiras*, I expect? It's round the back here, I can show you where to go.'

'Dad! Dad, just a moment.' Before Haldur had the chance to say anything, a younger man had come running, staring at Haldur while he pulled at the old fellow's sleeve, muttering into his ear. 'Dad, it's the lord's son, it's Haldur who's here.'

'All right, all right, no need to get in a state about it.' With filmy old eyes he peered at Haldur, who had now dismounted. 'Yes, I can't make out the face too clearly but I can see you've the torc at your neck. Well, if you're lord Carapethan's son, you're welcome twice over. Hitch the horse here, I'll take you round to the *numiras*.'

With a grin at the younger man, who seemed slightly embarrassed by this display of old-style Nine Dales directness, Haldur handed him the reins and followed where his guide led. 'How did you know I'd come to see a *numiras*?' he asked.

'What else would bring you up the hillside to a place like this? The *numiras* has been here time out of mind, but once word went round that we'd had one of the Hidden People with us, we get two or three come up most weeks. Everyone knows about it in this part of the country.'

Haldur looked down at the little spring, cold and clear, that trickled out from a rocky bank surrounded by ferns. It fell into a small pool around which forget-me-nots grew, their intense blue matched by the delicate harebells that nodded on the slope above. A low wall enclosed the *numiras*, clearly formed from the offerings of many former visitors: it seemed the traditional thing here was to place a stone for remembrance. The old farmer answered Haldur's question before he had even had the chance to frame it.

'See that stone, that one there? That's the very stone Artorynas put there, the day he went up the dale and away. Aye, he slept under our roof, and helped me in the top field, and then he put that there. Only think of that. And then mother cooked him an egg to put him on his way. I'll never forget it, never. Nor what he said to me. See, I'd told him: the Hidden People took my son when he rode with the Cunorad, none will come after me here like I followed my fathers. And he was that kind to me, he said he'd have stayed if he could.'

The old fellow's voice had become gradually quieter, almost as if he was speaking to himself; then, seeming to notice Haldur's silence, he looked up.

'You shouldn't be sad, young sir. You and Artorynas, between you, you saved the Nine Dales. Look what's happened here. Him you saw in the barn there, he's my marriage-son's brother. He came calling up here, the next spring after Artorynas was with us: wanted to join me and help work the land, see? And then at the midsummer, didn't my daughter appear after we'd not seen her for four summers; and my grandson, well, do you see, the lad had changed his mind? Wanted to learn farming after all. I'm a happy man now, with my family by me: we've even had to put up another house-place. Aye, it's right what I say. You and Artorynas together, you went south with the arrow and put things to rights. You saved Rihannad Ennar.'

Haldur drew a long breath. 'Don't you know what I did with the arrow?'

'Of course I do! Everyone knows. We've all heard the story that's gone up and down the dales. Come over here a moment.'

Haldur, his arm taken in a surprisingly strong grip, found himself led over to a turf seat below the bank in the sunshine.

'Now I'll tell you something, young man. It's right what they say, old folk remember things from years back better than what happened yesterday – you'll find out in time, like we all do, lord's son or no.' The old fellow chuckled and then sighed a little. 'Aye, well. So, things I was taught when I was a boy, from my bit of schooling down there in the village, must have stayed with me, or maybe they come back to me now. How men drove the Starborn away, but if ever they returned, all would be well with the world once more. Ah, why go seeking the Hidden People, like my poor boy, when we're taught they can walk unseen? But now, now there's no call to look for them any more. I know they're among us again. Haven't I seen one of them myself?'

The old fellow had been sitting forward, elbows on knees, but now he straightened up. 'For all that though, there's been some who've paid the price of it, my own lad and others, and you too, I can see. But listen to me now, master. I'll tell you something, and it's right what I say. If Artorynas hadn't brought the arrow back, if you'd not used it how he told you, whatever the cost, the Golden Valley might have been dark today and me lying dead in the ruins of my home, picked bare by the crows. As it is, well, it's like he said to me: "You and your land will lie in love together." Aye, whenever it comes, my last sleep won't bother me now. You and Artorynas, you saved the Nine Dales and more besides.'

Clapping Haldur on the shoulder he got to his feet, testing the weight gingerly on his lame leg. He passed a calloused hand over the stubble on his cheeks; Haldur heard the scratchy sound as he turned to him with a sudden grin. 'I'll be getting wrong from mother for not cleaning myself up, but how was I to know the lord's son would come calling? Never mind: come on in and let her see who's honoured our hearth.'

When Haldur saw his father rein to a halt as Cotaerdon first came into sight on their homeward journey, saw him sit his horse, gazing down on the valley, saw the love in his face as his eyes swept the familiar scene, his heart went out to him. He wanted to tell him about the trust and wisdom he had seen in Rihann nan Esylt, to share with Carapethan what Artorynas had said to the old farmer. But this was not the time: they were pressing on now, keen to put the last miles behind them; and in any case, he found these things so difficult to speak of, especially to his father. He never mentioned Artorynas, or the deeds of the two hundred in Caradward, unless someone else spoke of them first. It was very different with Astell, whose acute mind matched his predatory face, forcing Haldur to confront what he would have avoided, to probe the shadows, to analyse the mysteries, always urging acceptance through understanding. Haldur sighed as they trotted along. He should try harder with Astell, but still found him somewhat forbidding. It was as if he had turned his own sorrows into an enduring strength; whereas I, thought Haldur, I have let mine weaken me: how then am I worthy to follow my father? Passers-by and those working in the fields alongside the road ran to cheer and he acknowledged their acclaim, marvelling as he always did at their expressions of love and loyalty. Carapethan glanced across at him. He was not quite so blind as Astell thought, having long ago noticed what Haldur never spoke of; but still he hoped that time would lift the shadow that lay on his son. He set a quicker pace, eager for his hall again, wondering what tidings awaited him.

In recent years, since a safe road south had lain open once more, very occasionally a traveller would journey up with news, or one from Rihannad Ennar would venture down and bring back tales of his own; and it turned out that this had happened while they were away from Cotaerdon.

'If only we'd set off a week later, or he'd got here sooner!' said Haldur the next day.

'Yes, he was sorry to miss you.' Arval had been telling Haldur that in his absence, Urancrasig had turned up with news. Cunoreth was a father again, to a baby daughter whose name was given in remembrance for Fosseiro. She, as she had always maintained she would, had lived long enough to see Salfgard flourishing once more and now lay at rest beside Ardeth, on the hillside overlooking the farm. Cunoreth's little son Ardeth was three years old, sturdy and thriving; and his step-daughter Cottardo, said Urancrasig, seemed well enough, but had still never uttered a word.

Haldur sat thinking over what Arval had just told him. When they all journeyed back north from Caradriggan, he went with a few others at Cunoreth's request, making a detour out of the direct way to see the new Salfgard already beginning to rise from the old. He remembered vividly his shock on seeing the small child for whom Astirano and Fosseiro were taking the place of mother and grandmother: a little girl with huge brown eyes, golden freckles over her nose and long dark red hair. She turned a blank, silent gaze on him; and when he discovered that she had been found wandering in the smouldering ruins of Framstock and had not spoken so much as one word since, even after being rescued and then taken to Fosseiro's care, he kept his suspicions of her identity to himself. Surely, there could be no doubt that she was one of Heranar's daughters: but what could be gained by using Tiranesco, the name he remembered, when her new family called her Cottardo? Haldur saw how Cunoreth treated her with gentle kindness, probably remembering his own inauspicious childhood: he might not feel the same if he knew who she really was.

He came out of his reverie and shook his head. 'I'm as certain as I can be that Cottardo is really Tiranesco, Heranar's middle child. I wonder what happened to the other two.'

'I don't suppose we'll ever know,' said Arval. 'Poor Heranar, he suffered more than most. I'm glad if even one of his children has been comforted by Fosseiro's love.'

'Heranar and his wife had gone in for the most grandiose names for their daughters,' said Haldur, smiling, 'although admittedly they were fair enough to carry them off successfully. Cunoreth and Astirano have settled for much more workaday choices. Do you think the child will ever speak again?'

'It's difficult to say, without knowing exactly what kind of shock she experienced,' said Arval. 'If she's happy and healthy, presumably at least she has no memory of whatever happened to her. Maybe, given time and the security of her new family, she will eventually recover.'

'You know, Arval, I think Astirano might not have turned to Cunoreth for all his pleading if her heart had not been softened by the little girl's plight. She felt a mother's love first, and so was able to respond to his. He should be grateful to Heranar, if he but knew it.'

Arval glanced at Haldur. 'And you think Torello may not be so fortunate, am I right?'

Haldur looked up quickly, his face colouring a little. 'You don't miss much, do you Arval? My father told me once to speak to her about Artorynas, but it was already too late. It's hard on her parents; though Tellapur is married now, they'll have grandchildren through him. They'll have to accept that some things can't just go back to how they were.'

'Maybe you're absorbing more of Astell's precepts than you think,' said Arval with a smile. 'I notice, though, that your concern is rather for her family than Torello herself.'

'Well, yes, because I am beginning to believe that there are – experiences, occurrences, whatever we decide to call them – that are worse if you fight against them. To accept, you have first to understand; but of course, it's very difficult to understand without accepting first. And some people struggle more than others.' Haldur dropped his head. 'I wouldn't say, myself, that I'd come anywhere near the achievement Astell expects of me. Then there's my father.'

'Mine also, long ago.' At this, Haldur met Arval's eyes and the old man saw that he had heard the story. 'Your farmer friend up in the Golden Valley saw clearly when he said the cost is higher to some than others, when there is a price to be paid. But your father has Vorardynur and his family: there is no need for Carapethan to worry about his beloved Nine Dales.'

The colour came up again in Haldur's face when he heard this. He looked at Arval as if not sure what to say. The straight, heavy hair fell down again onto his forehead as he ran his fingers through it, showing the silvery summer sheen that would soon fade as autumn advanced. When it seemed he would stay silent, Arval spoke again.

'You asked me, on that day of days in Caradriggan, what there could be left for you to seek: but it was a question wrung in pain from your sorrow and loss. You did not expect an answer, because you thought you knew there was none; and in truth I had no answer to give. But you have been told twice that your search is not over, and I think we may certainly trust those who made the promise. So today, let me ask you whether you feel now that there is anything you still look for; and if so, whether you know what it is.'

Haldur stood up and moved away, his immediate concern to school his voice so as to hide the bitter retort that sprang to his lips. Arval did not deserve that, when he had been so gentle, had always shown such understanding. Then as if from nowhere, a new stillness seemed to fill his heart and his answer came without conscious thought.

'Yes,' he said slowly, sounding slightly surprised, 'yes, for the first time it comes to me now that maybe there is something I still seek, although I don't know what it is. But I should rather ask you, Arval: is there anything *you* seek? You have lived among us here in the north for over six years now, always giving of yourself in advice and guidance to those who asked or needed it. We are all in your debt for counsel and wisdom, myself most of all. Is there any way in which I may help you, to repay just a little of your kindness?'

'I would appreciate your company on a journey I have in mind.'

'You're not thinking of going back to Caradriggan?'

'No, no.' Arval laughed, hearing the note of incredulity in Haldur's voice. 'They don't need me any more in Caradriggan. But now that I've come north to Rihannad Ennar, I have discovered what Artorynas found before me: that though the lodestone may point to the north of this world, yet there is a north beyond, for which the heart yearns. The road leading there is hidden from me, but before my time comes, I would do what I can to find it.'

By now Haldur had sat down again. He leaned forward, staring at Arval. Surely he did not intend to attempt the crossing of Aestron na Caarst? He must have heard what Artorynas had to tell of it, a wasteland where blindworms lurked; and who could forget Sigitsinen's description of what he had seen one of these creatures do to Vorynaas! Haldur suppressed a shudder. Would he find the courage to go north with Arval, if this was what he was about to ask? Then it struck him that in any case his father would never allow it. He bit his lip, frowning.

'I would be honoured to travel with you, but ... You mean to follow Artorynas?' he asked eventually.

'Not exactly, although we should be retracing some of his footsteps,' said Arval. 'I propose to follow the valley of the Lissad y'n Cunorad to its end and look upon the sea.'

Arval, watching Haldur closely, saw his face light up with a strange blend of exaltation, eagerness, anticipation: for a moment he looked like his younger self again before his features clouded once more. He glanced at Arval briefly and then looked away as he spoke. 'Astell says Rihann y'n Temenellan will not lead to the Golden Strand.'

'I know, he has also told me this; although it can happen that even the wisest man may be wrong. What did Artorynas tell you?'

'He believed that he wouldn't have found Porthesc nan Esylt if he hadn't crossed Aestron na Caarst first. But he did tell me to remember that Rihann y'n Temenellan leads to the sea. It was one of the very last things he said to me.'

'Well then! And there's something else to think of. We'd be passing the grove of *astorhos* trees that grows where the valley opens out towards the sea. Didn't you say Cunoreth had promised Fosseiro that if he could, he would set one to flower above the place where she and Ardeth lie on the hillside? When you come back to Cotaerdon, you can bring seeds with you. Then if the opportunity ever comes for you to travel to Salfgard again, you can give them to him.'

'Yes, I could do that.'

Haldur sat for a moment, his thoughts drifting; but then suddenly his attention was caught. What did Arval mean when he spoke of his time coming? And there was something else… 'When I come back to Cotaerdon? What about you? Where are you going? Will you not be with me?'

'No, my days are almost finished now.'

Haldur ran his fingers through his hair again, and Arval heard him swallow. 'Oh no. Please, no.'

'Listen, Haldur. Everyone's time comes in the end, even mine. I am fortunate that I have been able to choose the moment.'

After a long silence, Haldur looked directly at Arval. 'When?'

'I suggest next spring. We can travel light, and quickly: by midsummer we should be on the shore. Coming back, you can use both horses, turn about to keep them fresh; that way you'll make good speed. You'll be in Cotaerdon again long before the weather breaks for winter.'

Haldur forced himself to smile. 'I see you have it all well thought out.'

'Yes.' Arval smiled in turn. 'But then, I've had many years to think about it. Now my long wait is almost over. Will you come with me, to look on the sea?'

'I will. Yes, we'll go together, next spring.'

Each in their season the named days came and went, the time-honoured festivals that marked the year's progress: harvest, midwinter, seedtime, until it was time for the Spring Feast once more. Arval and Haldur slipped away without much ado during May-tide, setting off in the early morning with the dew still glittering, the fresh scents of the new day sweet upon the air and a high blue sky overhead. At the last turn in the road, Haldur turned to wave, shading his eyes from the low sun. Carapethan, standing on the steps of the hall, raised his own hand in return. This leave-taking had none of the tension that attended the departure of the two hundred. Although he knew he would be missed, Haldur could see that Carapethan was comfortable about his son's temporary absence. Beside the lord of the Nine Dales was Aldiro his wife, with Vorardynur, Lethesco and their children; and the air of togetherness that enveloped the little group struck Haldur forcibly: even a stranger would have known them for one family. I am the odd one out now, he thought, with a sudden insight into the loneliness that must have marked Artorynas' life. Arval glanced about him as they rode. This would be his last sight of Cotaerdon's shallow sparkling streams, its graceful bridges and mellow stonework, yet there was no sadness in his heart. He was sure he had made the right choice: like Artorynas before him, he was about to complete the circle. He thought back over the previous evening, which he had spent with Astell. They had sat outside in his sheltered garden until twilight was far advanced, talking quietly as the flowers around his porch showed pale against the darkening sky and bats swooped overhead; and when the moment came to part, their farewells had been simple.

'Let the Hidden People walk with you.'

Arval smiled to himself, hearing Astell's voice in his mind. The words, so plain yet full of dignity, well matched the people among whom they were traditional. Like the folk of Rihannad Ennar, like the Nine Dales themselves, they were direct and straightforward, but below their surface there was a depth of wisdom and kindness, a

383

wellspring of trust and hope. The Hidden People. Did the Hidden People have a hidden road? Their own way, one that only the Starborn, who could walk unseen, could use; one that led to the north of the heart, the north beyond, that only they might look upon: the path that Artorynas had seen them take? Arval looked back over his long, long life. I waited for Numirantoro, he thought, yearned as she did for the Starborn, promised to guide and guard Artorynas; spoke out against Vorynaas, warned against bloodshed; never wavered in my pursuit of learning. But did I achieve all I could? I was unable to prevent deaths, I was ignorant of the dark misdeeds of the past; Numirantoro, Arymaldur and Artorynas are all gone. Yet it was through them, and with my help, that hope has been renewed for this world: is there hope for me, that I may have my one remaining wish, to look upon the As-Geg'rastigan, to hear *Haellem y'm Asan*?

It was almost midsummer when Haldur and Arval stood beneath the *astorhos* trees. They moved gracefully in the light breeze, flowers occasionally drifting loose to float down onto the river and be borne off upon its waters to the sea; as day drew on towards evening, the scent of the blossom seemed to intensify in the warm dusk. Haldur gathered up some seeds and examined them as they lay cupped in his hand. They were like tiny acorns, held in a case patterned with regular markings, but the nuts themselves were smooth with a deep red, almost translucent hue. He held one up against the setting sun.

'I can almost see through it: they remind me of amber.' Then as he closed his hand upon the seed, he turned to Arval. 'To think of the life it contains! This tiny thing, with a mighty tree sleeping within it, awaiting its time. And I can hold it in my hand, something that can awake into growth to thrive and flourish, living on long after I am gone and forgotten.' Then he put the seeds in his pocket and laughed rather shyly. 'I do realise this is scarcely an original observation.'

'That doesn't make it any less true though, does it?' said Arval. He hesitated for a moment, and then came to a decision. 'Haldur, there's something I want to say to you. Artorynas told me, the night before he left us, that I had always held a father's place in his heart; and from the day he was born, I can say I loved him as my son. I can't tell you how hard it was to hide my sorrow when he left to spend five years away in Salfgard, and then to lose him again to face all the dangers of the search for Arymaldur's arrow. And when he returned, to let him go, free to follow his choice, to have only one day together: that was the worst hurt of all. But it had to be so, and Astell is right to say that not all sorrow and loss must be barren. I have had time to reflect, during my years of peace and serenity in the Nine Dales. Artorynas said I saved his childhood by giving him what I could of a parent's love; but you brought the love of true friendship to his youth. So it is, that he has taken us both into the life of the Starborn, carried in his heart as father and brother. I think we should have joy in this; but also, before we two part in turn, I would like you to know how grateful I am for the happiness Artorynas knew through you.'

As he realised what Arval was going to speak of, Haldur felt the summer's evening glow grow chill about him. He stood frozen, braced for pain, wanting Arval to stop, wondering why he chose now of all moments to open all the wounds again. Then Arval fell silent, and Haldur looked up. The sunset was warm once more, the distant sea whispered, the scented air was soft against his cheek. And, as had happened during their conversation in Cotaerdon, to his surprise he felt the old bitterness comforted; for an instant it seemed his mind stood on the brink of knowing what it was he still sought. Then the moment passed, but seeing Arval's deep, dark eyes fixed upon him in understanding, suddenly he found it easy to reply.

'No more thankful than I, for the wisdom you have shown me.'

He glanced up at the bulky headland that rose steeply above them, dark against the deepening blue of the sky, blocking out any sight of what might lie beyond it to the north. Even for himself it would be an effort to climb up: for Arval it would surely be impossible. 'I am sorry I could not help you reach the Golden Strand.'

At this Arval smiled. 'Ah yes, I do indeed wish I could look upon Porthesc nan Esylt. But even if I cannot, I would like to go down to the sea. Will you come with me, tomorrow?'

So at last they stood on the shore, gazing on the boundless sea. For the most part they did without speech; for what words, thought Haldur, could do justice to the fairness of what we see? And so he respected his companion's silence, walking along the sands, letting the moving water wash over his feet, looking back inland to where the *astorhos* trees stood, and far away seaward to the distant horizon. Arval sat, lost in contemplation, all his senses at full stretch. He felt the warmth of the sun as it climbed into the morning sky, smelt the life contained within the sighing sea, heard the little birds call to each other as they ran along the sand or wheeled and turned with flashing wings, tasted the salty breeze upon his lips. It seemed to him as if he was a vessel, gradually filling with the beauty of what lay before him, until his earthborn heart brimmed over with its loveliness. Yet even this was not Porthesc nan Esylt. In his mind Arval compared what he saw with what Artorynas had described to him. Maybe the Golden Strand was for the Starborn alone; in which case, how glad should he be, that he had spoken with one who walked there!

Hours passed until the golden day drew on towards evening. In the blue twilight Haldur and Arval sat together, sharing food and drink; and then as dusk deepened to reveal the summer stars above they prepared for rest.

'Sleep well, Haldur,' said Arval.

The young man leaned up on his elbow. 'We sleep in a *numiras*, I think,' he said, 'so maybe we shall dream of the Starborn. Let the Hidden People keep you, Arval.'

'And you. Until the dawn, then.'

They lay down, and soon Haldur slept, but Arval was wakeful. He sat beside Haldur as the heavens wheeled above, and the silence of night was broken only by the voice of the sea, quiet but never still. At last Arval walked down to the water's edge once more and his thoughts ran back and forth like the endless waves. Were the As-Geg'rastigan of the earth but not in it, or in it but not of it? If the Hidden People could indeed walk unseen, how could the Earthborn reach them? Arval smiled to himself in the darkness. I am never content, he thought. No matter how much I learn, always I seek to know more. But an end must come. Starlight sparked on something in his hand as he unstoppered a tiny bottle, and into the sea he poured the last few drops remaining of the secret spirit distilled in Tellgard that had sustained his life for so long. A weight seemed to lift from his shoulders. All was fulfilled now; there were no more burdens to carry. He was content to abide whatever came. Glancing back towards Haldur, he found that he could no longer see the place where his companion lay sleeping. Arval stood alone in the silent, empty darkness. Then, as long ago he had felt it, he sensed an other-worldly life upon the air, as if it awoke and danced. He looked up: the stars burned huge and bright. Arval's heart began to race with painful eagerness: he strained to listen, but there was nothing, nothing... Then faintly there came a thread of sound, so lovely it tormented his ears, growing inexorably in power, becoming unbearable, irresistible in its glory... he could have wept for joy, but there was no longer any need of tears.

The early sun shone onto Haldur's face, making him turn over away from its brightness. Not opening his eyes, he stretched out, half-aware that waking was inevitable but trying nonetheless to hold on to the dream that still possessed him. It was fading though, as dreams did; and he squeezed his eyes tight shut, trying harder to remember, willing himself to keep the memory of what he had seen and heard: the vast, dark night, silent and empty, flowering into a melding of light and sound as a great host of the As-Geg'rastigan had been revealed to him in their majesty and might. He could see them still in his mind, but was unable to call back what he had heard; it had drifted away, beyond recall. Haldur sat up with a start, suddenly fully awake. *Haellem y'm Asan*! Had Arval heard it too? And then he saw that Arval was gone. He got to his feet, looking wildly around. Everything was as they had left it the previous evening: the gear for their journey neatly stacked in a small heap, the horses quietly grazing; but he was alone. There was not so much as a footprint in the smooth sand. Then his dream returned to him with bittersweet force, and he understood. While he slept, peaceful and unheeding, the Starborn had swept Arval away, bearing him with them to look at last upon that unreachable north he had so wished to see, the north beyond.

Haldur found that there were tears on his own cheeks and he brushed them away, realising in surprise as he did so that it was not sorrow that he felt. Loss, yes; awe, certainly: he found himself trembling slightly at what had happened. As he stood, trying to come to terms with the suddenness of Arval's leaving, his eye fell on the promontory that bounded the northern side of the estuary. Leaving the dunes where he had slept, he ran as fast as he could to the foot of the slope and began clambering up, wild hope lending him strength for the climb. What if, when he reached the top, Porthesc nan Esylt lay below him? Fear and excitement battled within him as he wondered what he would do if he saw footsteps there, on the Golden Strand. At last he found himself in a kind of rocky gully that led to the summit, and ran leaping from boulder to boulder across the rough ground until he reached the far downward slope. Then he stood, out of breath, staring in disappointment. Was it sea fret, rolling in with the tide, or a mist from another world that hid from him whatever lay below? It drifted and swirled, and its chilly message was plain to understand: Porthesc nan Esylt was not for him. Slowly Haldur turned away and retraced his steps, feeling the sun warming him once more as he climbed down again. He saw to the horses, ate some food and then packed everything up for the journey back to Rihannad Ennar.

By the time he reached Cotaerdon, there was frost at nightfall and morning as often as not and Carapethan was already home from his progress around the dales. Haldur was welcomed back to his place at the lord's side and drawn into the embrace of his family. Everyone was eager to hear his story, to know why he had returned alone, but his report was brief.

'We followed the Lissad y'n Cunorad to its end,' he said. 'We walked on the shore, and looked on the sea. It seemed to me we had found the fairest of *numirasan*. And on the night of midsummer we rested there; but when I awoke next morning, Arval was gone. It is my belief that he was taken by the Hidden People; he told me even before we set off that his time had come.'

Those who heard this tale exclaimed in wonder and made the sign; and some pressed Haldur for detail, especially if they had come to love Arval. To them he described the place where Rihann y'n Temenellan met the sea; but only to Astell did he speak more fully of those last few days with Arval, telling of what he had seen in his dream, of how he was thwarted when he would have gazed over Porthesc nan Esylt: and while winter gripped the Nine Dales, keeping folk close in Cotaerdon, the two of them spent many hours together in study and thought.

One spring day three years after he and Arval had set off down-dale, Haldur and Carapethan walked together around the streets of Cotaerdon as usual. But when his father returned to the hall to eat, Haldur strolled over a low bridge onto the green at the centre of the town and sat for a while, letting his mind drift as the sounds of morning floated across to him. As he looked around at the familiar scene, his eye fell on a seat not far from a stand of may-trees on which the pink blossom was yet to break from the bud. To think that fourteen years had passed since he and Carapethan had sat there: fourteen years since the day his father had told him he must face up to his fate as heir, fourteen years since he had put on the torc. Fourteen years! He jumped to his feet and headed back over the bridge, taking the steps of the hall porch two at a time and catching Carapethan before he finished his meal.

'Father, I want to ask you something. You know I'm in debt to Cunoreth for helping to save my life and he in turn has made a promise I'm now in a position to help him keep. It's still very early in the year; I'd like to go down to Salfgard and take him the *astorhos* seeds I brought back from Rihann y'n Temenellan.'

'If you go, it will mean another year when you don't ride round the dales with me.'

'I know, but… it's a debt I feel I should pay. And if I'm going to do it, there's no point in putting it off from year to year; and if I'm travelling this summer, then I should be preparing to start almost straight away.'

'True.' Carapethan pushed his plate away. 'Who will you take with you?'

'Oh, there's no need for more than three or four of us. But I wondered whether Vorardynur would like to come, to see how they're getting on down there, you know.'

Carapethan looked up quickly. His blue eyes were as penetrating as ever, the thick brows still fair; but his hair was almost all grey now, and there was white in his beard. After contemplating his son in silence for a moment, he glanced over at his wife. Aldiro was rocking a sleeping baby on her knee: Vorardynur's second son, now some six months old.

'Well, why don't you ask him and see what he has to say?'

Vorardynur hesitated only briefly when Haldur approached him. 'It's not that I don't want to; in fact in some ways I'd love to come with you. But… well, I can't see myself ever leaving Rihannad Ennar again unless it was absolutely necessary. And now that the children are older, and Aldiro can help Lethesco with the baby, I'm free to go with Carapethan round the dales every summer. I don't want to miss that… But you'll give my greetings to those who remember me, won't you? And tell them how welcome they'd be if they ever travelled up to us here…'

'Yes, of course.' Haldur nodded in agreement, but he had stopped listening. He knew now why his father had told him to approach his cousin directly: it had been a shrewd move, letting him see that Vorardynur was at one with Carapethan in the love of his own land. They were growing more alike with every passing year.

In the end, Asaldron went with Haldur: quite keen to ride south again now that the darkness and danger he had once faced were no more; and glad of this unexpected break from routine. He was in high spirits as the miles went by, comparing their easier route with the hazards he remembered from their crossing of the wilderness, taking in good part some teasing from his companions on the subject of his unmarried state.

'It's all very well for you fellows to laugh,' he said. 'I think the secret of success must be to get yourself a wife as soon as ever you can. If you don't, the years slip by and then somehow you find that all the women are already married and suddenly all the girls are too young.'

'Maybe you should look out for a nice widow?' suggested Cureleth, causing yet more mirth.

Eventually they arrived in Salfgard, to find it unrecognisable from the barely-begun farmstead Haldur had seen taking shape in the ruins of the old: it bustled with activity and purpose, crops and animals thriving. Numerous youngsters in their foster-years came running to see them arrive, and Cunoreth was his usual bundle of nervous energy, wanting to rush them round to see everything almost before they had their horses unsaddled. A guest-hall had been built, rather in the style of the Nine Dales; and they slept here but ate in the main house-place with Cunoreth and Astirano. Mag'rantor was away, although Cunoreth expected him back soon.

'He went down to Framstock but I'd say he'll be already on his way home,' he said. 'You'll stay till he gets here? He'll want to see you, and I think it would be only right if he was with us when we plant the *astorhos* seeds.'

In the end they stayed some three weeks in Salfgard. Mag'rantor arrived after a few days and Haldur found himself spending a lot of time with him, walking together around the fields, sitting on the riverbank or just leaning on a fence somewhere watching the world go by. One evening they sat together, taking the air on an old wooden seat beside the path.

'Little Cottardo has still never spoken, then?' asked Haldur. 'She's not so little now though, of course.'

It had been the one shadow on his visit, the silent child whose huge eyes followed him everywhere he went, making him wonder uneasily if it was possible that she remembered him.

'No, not a word,' said Mag'rantor. 'I sometimes worry over what will become of her as she grows up, but at least she'll always have the security of a place here, and she's good with the small children. They seem to share a kind of understanding that doesn't need speech.' He shook his head. 'I don't know: it seems to me that when there's a price to be paid, sometimes it's the wrong people bear the cost.'

'Yes, that's true,' said Haldur. 'In fact, something very similar was said to me a few years back by an old fellow up in the Golden Valley, at home.'

Mag'rantor smiled. 'Makes you wonder why it's always the old wives who get the credit for wisdom, eh? We old boys know a thing or two as well. Do you know something, Haldur. I was sitting on this very seat with Ardeth when Ethanur brought word of the invasion. It killed him, no doubt about that, but I've never forgotten what he said to me before he died. It was evening time, much like this, and the same time of year. We used to take a walk around the farm; I realise now he wasn't a well man, but he liked to look at the fields, see the crops coming on. He'd said this was his favourite time of year, which made me joke that he said that about every season. He just laughed and I thought he wasn't going to answer, but after a while he did try to explain, to put into words what he felt about the fairness of this world. But he couldn't do it, not how he wanted to, anyway. Then just like this, he put his hands behind his head, his feet out into the path, and he said to me, "I've been a lucky man." Well, I didn't know what to say, and to tell you the truth, I was amazed because he was no stranger to sorrow and loss. Then he said, everyone he'd loved had loved him in return, which was something no-one could ever take from him. A wise man, Haldur: a great man, in his own way. You'd have got on well with him.'

Haldur turned to look at Mag'rantor, this man who had risked all in a desperate attempt to reach the place where he trusted Ardeth to give him sanctuary, who had made a life for himself here at Salfgard. His face was deeply lined with age and weather, his hair had receded to leave a pate burned brown by the sun, he had lost a tooth or two over the years; but there was an air of contentment about him.

'Yes, I think I would. I can see why Cunoreth has named his own children Ardeth and Fosseiro.'

'You're right, and the old fellow would have been so pleased. I'm glad that Fosseiro lived long enough to see them. But that reminds me, there was something I wanted to ask you…' Mag'rantor broke off as running footsteps came nearer, mixed with giggling, and round a bend in the path panted little Ardeth, torn between panic and glee at having eluded his mother at bedtime. He danced about, just out of reach of his great-uncle's grasp.

'I guessed this was where you'd be! Let me stay up, I want to walk round the fields with you!'

'You little rascal! You'll do no such thing. We're going back now anyway, and you're coming with us.'

'Oh…' The little lad stood crestfallen, digging at the path with his toe.

'I'll tell you what, Ardeth,' said Haldur. 'How old are you now?'

'Seven. Well, I'm nearly seven.'

'Hm, nearly seven? And you're tall for your age: you're going to take after your father. Maybe it's time you began to use a bigger bow, so how would it be if tomorrow, you and I went together to choose one for you, and then we'll have a little session with the targets? I'm not a bad shot myself – I could show you a tip or two.'

Smiling to himself at this understating of Haldur's abilities as the boy jumped up and down, breathless with thanks and anticipation, Mag'rantor took hold of the child and swung him to his shoulders. 'Let's be having you. Time for bed if you're going to be able to aim straight tomorrow.' He looked down at Haldur, who was still sitting on the seat. 'Coming?'

'No, you go on. I think I'll sit on here for a while yet. But what was it you were going to ask me?'

'Oh, yes. Well, the thing is this. My son Urancrasig's to be wed this summer, and he wondered… He and his girl would be willing to bring the date forward, if you could wait, say, another ten days to let them re-arrange things, so you could be with us for the ceremony? It would mean a lot to him, I know. Of course, we realise you can't stay too long, because of getting home again.'

'I'd be delighted,' said Haldur warmly. 'Tell him we'll all be there.'

Mag'rantor and the child went off towards the farmstead, the sound of little Ardeth's chatter and Mag'rantor's deeper voice in reply gradually fading. Haldur was left alone as the last of the daylight slowly waned. There were feathery clouds across the sunset, just enough to make a dramatic glory of the north-western sky. An escaping ray of light, on the very edge of disappearing, flooded across the land almost at ground level, causing even the wayside flowers and grasses to throw long, thin shadows. Haldur's eye fell idly on the path before him. No rain had fallen since his arrival in Salfgard and the earth was dry and crumbly; where the child had scuffled the ground, the surface of the track had begun to break up. In the brief moment of illumination, the small divots and hollows, accentuated by their own shadows, appeared to Haldur's fancy like the peaks and valleys of a mighty mountain range, seen from a huge height or distance. Then, even as he smiled at his own thought, his gaze sharpened. He dropped to his knees to examine what he had seen and there, embedded in the ground but now half-revealed, was a carved wooden object. Careful work with his knife soon freed it and he returned to the seat, staring at what he had found. There in his hand, dulled by the years it had spent lying forgotten in the soil, was a small wooden robin. Haldur knew, without any doubt, that this must be the carving that the boy Maesrhon had made and given as a keepsake to Ardeth. How often had Artorynas told him about it! And now this evening he had heard from Mag'rantor that this was the place where Ardeth had died. He could imagine the scene: the old man, letting the little robin drop as he fell, darkness hiding it in the panic of the moment, trampling feet pressing it into the earth. Haldur turned it over in his fingers, holding it so the last of the daylight fell upon it. One of the tail feathers was broken and there was a scratch in the wood of the breast; its patina was gone. But he could clean it and oil it, and the smooth shine would return, the wood-grain would glow again. He closed his fist over it, holding it tightly for a moment. It had been given to Ardeth, but Ardeth was gone where such things had no meaning. Were they to open his grave to give it back to him? Surely not. No, thought Haldur. All these years it has lain here, waiting; and now it has come to me, for me to keep.

He sat on as twilight deepened to dusk and stars awoke in the sky above him. The summer night was quiet and still; Haldur could smell the fair-weather scent of warm earth, hear the distant babble of the river as it ran through the pebbly shallows and over the falls. A peace he had not known for years began to steal into his heart. All those who are and were dear to me have returned my love, he thought. Ardeth was right, that is good fortune beyond price. His mind drifted to Arval, to conversations they had shared, especially on that last journey together. Haldur felt ashamed, now, that he had made such a claim upon his kindness and compassion when Arval's grief at losing Artorynas must have been as great as his own – and Arval had been parted from him twice already before the end. Yet not once had Arval blamed him, that it was by his hand that Artorynas was taken from this world: rather, he had actually been grateful, that through him the man he thought of as a son had found true friendship. In fact, no-one had held the deed against him, but had acclaimed him for having the skill and strength of will to perform such a feat. I have found such praise unbearable, Haldur reflected now, because I have eaten out my own heart over what I did. Be careful what you wish for! Arval's old precept came into his thought, and now, albeit rather sadly, Haldur found he could smile a little at himself, sitting there alone in the summer darkness. How many times did I tell myself, and tell Artorynas also, that I wished there was something I could do to help him; and indeed there was, though it's as well I never guessed until that final moment what it would be. But he told me it was for me to do, that only I could do it; so it is true that it was through me that he was able to achieve his choice, and through both of us that all is well once more, in Caradward and Gwent y'm Aryframan as much as in the Nine Dales. A breath of air brushed past Haldur, carrying with it a faint perfume of flowers, but suddenly, just as he felt he was on the brink of finally unlocking the mystery, there was an excited bark and a patter of flying paws. One of the skinny little farm dogs came rushing up to greet him, and the moment was gone. A few yards behind the animal walked Cunoreth, carrying a small lantern. He held it up and its soft glow illuminated Haldur where he still sat beside the path.

'Come on, Haldur,' said Cunoreth, with surprising gentleness. 'Don't sit out here in the dark alone. Let's go back and have a drink together before bed.'

'Right, good idea.'

Haldur stood up and they headed back together, the dog running in circles around their feet, bounding off after fresh scents and sounds and then rushing back to them again. They talked quietly as they went, small matters of the farm, Urancrasig's forthcoming marriage, little Ardeth's progress with his bow. But Haldur's mind was full of the intuition that had suddenly come to him: that soon, soon now what he still looked for would be revealed to him.

Over the next few days he tried hard to find some solitude and quiet in which to pursue his thoughts, but without success. There was Mag'rantor, always keen to have him as an audience for his reminiscences; young Ardeth, mad for ever more sessions of instruction with his new bow; his own companions, looking to spend time together; Urancrasig, anxious that Haldur should know how pleased he was that the men from Rihannad Ennar would stay for his wedding; guests beginning to arrive, some of them to stay as they had come from distance; and then there was the big day itself. This was a boisterous affair, once the formal ceremony was over, with plenty of food and drink, games and storytelling; and as the hours wore on much flirting and match-making. Haldur, giving up as hopeless any chance of introspection in the midst of all the hilarity, entered with enthusiasm into the spirit of things, never for one moment imagining that a life-changing insight would indeed come to him before the day was out. As well as Asaldron and Cureleth, he had brought two other companions with him from Cotaerdon: both members of his father's household, young men barely out of their second ten years. They were having a high old time, making eyes at the local girls, whereas Cureleth, being a married man these days, was devoting most of his attention to the catering. He wove his way over to where Haldur was sitting, flagon in hand.

'Have you seen what Asaldron's up to?' he asked with a grin.

'No – what do you mean? Where is he?' Haldur looked around him, but saw no sign of Asaldron in the throng.

'He's round the other side of the guest-hall.' Cureleth took a swig at his drink and was caught out by a sudden belch. 'Sorry, excuse me. Didn't I say he should look out for a nice widow? Seems he's found one. She's a guest of the bride, someone's auntie I think, but still quite young. Come and have a look!'

Intrigued, Haldur got up and followed Cureleth's somewhat unsteady progress until, rounding the corner of the guest-hall, he found a crowd of laughing onlookers who were clapping and calling out ribald encouragement. He vaulted over the rail onto the raised walkway that ran round the building to see over their heads and was confronted by Asaldron and a woman enacting *Aryfram ac Herediro* for their audience. It came back to Haldur that he remembered being told how Ardeth and Fosseiro had been well-known for their version of this old tale. Maybe their tradition accounted for the way Asaldron's partner was playing up to his ardent farmer as the bashful maiden. Except that, Haldur noticed, a grin spreading over his face, there wasn't much reluctance in her performance that he could see: she and Asaldron were gazing into each other's eyes, and when he swept her into his arms at the end of the story, the embrace lasted a good deal longer than was strictly necessary. Everyone was stamping and whistling as they eventually walked away, still clasping hands.

'See?' said Cureleth, gesturing gleefully and slopping his drink in the process. 'See? I told you!'

'Well, well!' Haldur laughed, raising his eyebrows. 'Looks hopeful, doesn't it?'

As evening drew on, lamps and lanterns were lit. They swung from eaves and over doors and porches, imparting a glow of mellow gold to the scene. Eventually Urancrasig and his bride were escorted noisily to their new home by flower-throwing well-wishers, and then, tired children having reluctantly gone to bed and not a few young couples having disappeared into the summer darkness, the remaining guests settled to conversation and quieter entertainment for the last few hours of the celebration. Haldur felt a hand pull at his arm and stepped out of doors again in response to Asaldron's request for a private word.

'You, er, might not have noticed, but I've been spending quite a lot of time with Rathineno,' he said; adding, awkwardly and rather unnecessarily, 'That's her name.'

'Yes; she seems very nice.'

'Oh, she is, she's … But the thing is, she's from what they call the Gillan nan'Eleth, it's some distance from here. There isn't time for me to travel there and back before we go home, and I can't ask her to come with me, not so soon anyway. So I thought … Astirano and Cunoreth say we can both stay here, over the winter, and then if, if she's willing, I'll bring her to Cotaerdon next spring. But it would mean you'd have to travel without me now.'

'Don't worry about that, you get things fixed up with Rathineno.' Haldur gripped Asaldron's shoulders. 'At last, another cousin heading for marriage!'

'Well, I hope so.' Asaldron grinned. 'Come on, let's go back inside now and I'll introduce you to her.'

Some time later, one of the traditional word-games of Gwent y'm Aryframan having run its course, a contented hush fell upon the company. Then Mag'rantor spoke up. 'Who'll recite a tale for us? Let's have one more story, and then call it a day. Anyone?'

After a moment, Asaldron put down his cup and leaned forward from his place beside Rathineno. 'Haldur, you give us something.'

'Me? Oh no, I've no skill for this kind of thing.'

'That's where you're wrong. You've always had the feeling for it, I remember you even as a child in our lessons. But more than that, I was there in Caradriggan when you spoke in Tellgard. I've not forgotten that day.'

No, neither have I, thought Haldur. The two of them stared at each other, the bright blue eyes and the misty grey locked together. Haldur's mind suddenly flooded with a confusion of memories: Asaldron, speaking out proudly when Vorynaas would have humiliated them in Tell'Ethronad; himself, holding that throng of listeners in silent thrall in Tellgard; Maesmorur, testing his knowledge on the day he put on the torc; Astell, forced by Carapethan to recite *Maesell y'm As-Urad*. But on that same occasion, the lorekeeper of the Nine Dales had also given them a different tale. All these images came and went in an instant, followed by a sudden, piercingly clear vision of his way forward. The shock he felt showed in his face: he could tell from the way they all looked at him as he slowly got to his feet.

'Very well, if you wish it. This is a tale not often told even in Rihannad Ennar, so it may be new to you.'

And with that, he gave them *Numir y'm Aestronnasan donn Porthesc nan Esylt* as Astell had told it for Artorynas on that last evening in Cotaerdon: *Stars of the North Beyond, shining above the Golden Strand.* They hung on his words; and Haldur, once he was caught up in the tale, forgot his nerves and lost himself in its beauty. When he finished, his listeners were too moved to applaud: they murmured thanks and appreciation, seeming slightly overawed; and Haldur was surprised to find that he too was shaken by the experience. Then, while that air from another world still breathed its influence upon the room, Astirano spoke.

'This has been a special day, we should give it a fitting end. Please renew the pledge for us once more, Haldur, before we go to our rest.'

Haldur began upon *Temennis y'm As-Geg'rastigan ach Ur*, his glance falling upon the child who had fallen asleep, curled up on the floor. Little Ardeth and Fosseiro had long ago been tucked up in bed, but Cottardo, being older, had been allowed to sit up. Now, as if sensing his gaze, she opened those huge dark eyes and looked directly at him. This was Tiranesco, Haldur knew it without doubt. He wondered how things really stood between Astirano and Cunoreth and, drawing near to the end of the pledge, spoke the words as if for them alone. Did she truly love him, or had she settled for second best? Were she and Cunoreth happy, or had he to learn to live with her sorrow? Was there a shadow in her face, could he see a sadness that time might soothe but never wholly take away? Could anyone who had ever loved one of the Hidden People then love one of the Earthborn with their whole heart? All around the room, hands moved in the sign as Haldur finished speaking; but he found no answers to his questions. Maybe there were none to find.

The time came for all to sleep, though Haldur lay on his bed in the guest-hall with open eyes, heart beating fast as he contemplated the decision he had made. Soon the short summer darkness began to lighten. The first breath of dawn drifted through the window, the first liquid notes of blackbird and thrush. As silently as ever he could, Haldur rose, creeping boots in hand from the hall, treading quietly out from the farmstead without rousing the dogs, seeking solitude in which to order his thoughts and settle his resolve. It was so early that the world was without colour: earth veiled in mist, sky still flat and white. He climbed the hillside, leaving dark prints in the grey dew, and halted just within the trees of a small spinney. From here he could look down over Salfgard, could see a curve of the river, the hills beyond, the rooftops below, the place on the slope where Ardeth and Fosseiro now lay side by side, waiting for the *astorhos* flowers to open above them where they watched over their home-place. While he was walking, Haldur had been able to keep at bay the memory he knew was waiting its moment, but now he stood and let it possess him. Another wedding, another dawn; a different place, a different time. Himself, wanting time alone on the morning after Sallic's marriage, hoping to find the gateway between two worlds left open in a *numiras*. There would never be another morning like that one. Deliberately, he let the pain of that knowledge fill his heart, made no attempt to ward off the hurt. He waited, and eventually the ache dulled and receded as a new strength replaced it. How many were there who could say, as he could, that they had sought, and found? Only a very few. And now at last he saw what he must do.

Arriving back in Cotaerdon a few days after Carapethan's return from his progress around the dales, Haldur explained Asaldron's absence and his hope that, when he came home next spring, he would be bringing a bride with him. This news was well received, as was Vorardynur's observation that Asaldron and Rathineno would not be able to make the journey alone: travelling companions would be necessary, which in turn meant that they could look forward to seeing friends from Salfgard in Cotaerdon fairly soon. Haldur, although he was spending rather more time with Astell than his father would have liked, was quick to catch up on all that had been happening in his absence and wanted to know when Haldan don Vorygwent would be meeting. There was usually one full gathering of the council before winter closed the passes between the dales and Haldur learnt that this would take place in a couple of weeks' time. To Carapethan it seemed his son was happier, since his return from Salfgard. He watched him laughing with his fellow-instructors and pupils as they headed off to the butts to practise with their bows and felt confident that at last the long shadow of events in the south was lifting from his son.

Haldur however had reasons of his own for wanting to know when the council would meet. He would have given almost anything to tell his father privately, first, what he had to say, but was determined not to yield to the temptation. He knew Carapethan would be aghast and would without doubt try to persuade him to change his mind; and worse, he knew that it was only too likely that, if he saw his father's distress, he would agree. Yet had not Carapethan himself told him, long ago, that to bear a leader's responsibility meant putting duty to one's people before family feeling? Therefore he must address himself first to Carapethan, lord of Rihannad Ennar, as he sat among his counsellors. Afterwards there would be time for them to understand one another as father and son. The day of the meeting came, a blustery autumn day with rain slanting down in passing squalls and leaves flying on a whistling wind, rising and falling like the rooks who rode the air high above. Carapethan and his counsellors moved from their summertime meeting place under the wide eaves of the hall and gathered within instead, although the doors were fastened back so that any who wished could pass the porch and join the debate. The business of the day was gradually dealt with until finally all was done and Carapethan asked if anyone had other matters to raise. One or two items were brought forward and then Haldur got to his feet. He looked round, holding the gaze of all those present in turn.

'There is something I must tell you. My mind is made up and I will not change it: I cannot be the leader of this land in my turn. I am not the man you should look to as your next lord.'

They sat there, speechless. Haldur had expected a storm to break over his head and now felt that such a response would have been preferable: he thought wrath and raised voices would have been easier to deal with than this painful silence that seemed to stretch on and on. He looked round again at the blank, staring faces and shame swept over him when he met his father's eyes and saw the dismay and disappointment there. But he set his teeth, determined to see this through. He took off the torc and laid it down before them.

'I relinquish my position as heir to Carapethan, and I give you back this sign of that standing.'

Haldur remembered how heavy the torc had felt upon his neck when he first wore it. Now there was a strange lightness where its warm weight had rested for more than fourteen years. Still no-one spoke, but then eventually Morescar found his voice. He made no attempt to hide his anger.

'You pledged yourself to this land and its people! Do you find it so easy to turn your back on a promise?'

'No: it has been a harder struggle than any of you could know.' As if he drew strength from Morescar's anger, Haldur felt his confidence increasing. 'And yet it has not been the most difficult thing I have done. I have already served the Nine Dales well, I think. But the cost was high, and I have borne a larger share of it than most. Rihannad Ennar deserves a lord who will love her with an unclouded heart.'

Morescar subsided, his face turned away to hide the pain that showed there. Haldur knew his words had woken the older man's sorrow at the fate of his daughter Torello.

'Lord Carapethan!' They all heard the challenge within Astell's resonant voice; he was now on his feet. 'It is some years ago now since you first urged me to name my own successor. The moment has now come when I can at last do so. My choice falls upon Haldur.'

Carapethan's brows drew down over the fierce blue eyes. He stared at Astell, standing there with the easy grace of his calling, his features more predatory than ever, and down the years the words echoed again between them: *I name in payment the heart of your son Haldur.* The others looked on anxiously at this confrontation between lord and lorekeeper. When Carapethan made no reply, Astell turned to Haldur.

'You are willing, I think?'

'I am. Let me assure Morescar, and all of you, that I still feel a duty to Rihannad Ennar. This way, I hope I may fulfil it.'

'It means we should have to begin again on choosing who will wear the golden torc,' said Devorhon, ever practical.

Haldur caught a glimpse of Sallic, sitting there beside his stolid father but unlike him still gaping in amazement at developments, and felt a sudden wild desire to laugh: a feeling instantly extinguished when he heard the quiet voice of Maesmorur. He realised that his own father had not yet said a word, and now Carapethan's old friend was trying to help, smoothing the path for his leader.

'Does anyone wish to put a name forward for consideration?' Maesmorur now asked.

Haldur, who had tentatively sat down when Devorhon spoke, now jumped up eagerly. 'Yes, I do. Why not Vorardynur? I urge you all, let him take my place as Carapethan's heir. He too has already served you well. He took my place ably when first I was away, he has kept the lord's seat here in Cotaerdon more than once; he is still young and strong, he has ridden both with the Cunorad and in battle. When the two hundred were in the south, no-one was better placed than I to see how he acquitted himself with distinction in a difficult role. He helped and supported me then as I would gladly support him here. Choose my cousin Vorardynur, let him put on the torc!'

Now all eyes turned to Vorardynur. Carapethan, beginning to recover, saw immediately that his own shock was mirrored in Vorardynur's face. He realised that none of this had been pre-arranged, that Vorardynur had been taken by surprise as much as he had himself. From the habit of a lifetime his mind, at some level underneath its surface turmoil, had been gauging the mood of the meeting and now he sensed that the council was settling down again, mollified: Haldan don Vorygwent would accept this new arrangement, if Vorardynur agreed and he sanctioned it. He forced himself to speak.

'I can swear before you all that the dearest wish of my life has been that Rihannad Ennar should be troubled by no word or deed, that no sadness or regret should disturb the order of her days or the peace of her nights. I will admit to sorrow at past events that have shaken our tranquillity, and to distress that I must now contemplate a future very different from what I have become accustomed to expect.'

He paused and then directed a penetrating blue stare at Astell. 'But I must accept that no man, however much he might wish to, can turn back time; and I have also to acknowledge that in spite of everything the Nine Dales, though storm-tossed, have not been shaken from their course. My personal wishes have always taken second place to what is best for the Nine Dales and that will never change so long as I live. If all is well with Rihannad Ennar, then when the time comes, I shall lie happy in the embrace of her earth.'

Haldur's heart jumped at his father's words, so similar to what he had heard of the exchange between the old farmer and Artorynas, away in the Golden Valley. He looked up, and for a long moment his and Carapethan's eyes met. Then his father turned to Vorardynur. 'Are you willing to undergo testing by Haldan don Vorygwent?'

Before Vorardynur could answer, a murmur of voices broke in and then Poenellald spoke for all. 'There is no need, we are happy to abide by Haldur's acclaim and assessment.'

'Very well.' Carapethan addressed himself once more to Vorardynur. 'You are our choice. Will you wear the torc?'

Vorardynur got to his feet, the colour high in his cheeks, his blue eyes bright with solemn pride. 'I will.'

Carapethan set it on his neck and the two of them stood side by side. How alike they are, thought Haldur.

So Haldur went to Astell and though he felt respect and affection rather than love, they became closer as time passed. But apt pupil though he proved, he knew he would never quite have Astell's bardic skills or his knack of timing and delivery. Towards mid-day one chilly spring morning, the two of them dismissed the youngsters from the little schoolhouse in Cotaerdon and walked back towards Astell's house. As they reached the gate, Haldur held its topmost bar when Astell would have pushed it open.

'Tell me: why did you choose me?'

The lorekeeper turned. 'Why did you accept?'

When neither spoke, Astell brushed Haldur's hand aside and unlatched the gate. 'It is too cold to stand out here.'

The living-room of Astell's cottage retained a residual warmth from the heating system he used for his plants, but he lit a small brazier before busying himself with assembling a simple meal for the two of them. Afterwards he served them both from a pan of mulled ale and then returned to their unfinished exchange.

'You questioned me first, so it's only fair that I should answer first. It was more a claim than a choice: one made long ago, in fact, so that it was the timing, rather than the choosing, that was significant. You will not have forgotten how your father bade me recite *Maesell y'm As-Urad* amidst the mirth of a feast day, telling me I might name my fee. What you may not know is what passed between Carapethan and myself the following morning. I warned him then that the price would be the heart of his son. He was alarmed, and angry… It was necessary to remind him that all actions, even his own, have their consequences. He sought by means of *Maesell y'm As-Urad* to dislodge Artorynas from the Nine Dales; but he failed to realise that this deed, and the memory of the tale, would influence Artorynas in his choosing the life of the As-Geg'rastigan over that of the Earthborn. And having made that choice, he in turn needed you to help him achieve it. I told Carapethan that as a result your heart, already turned to the Starborn, in the end would be given to them for ever. He was filled with fear, believing you would be taken by the Hidden People, but this was not my meaning. But though the payment was named that day, it had to wait until you renounced the torc yourself before it could be claimed.'

Haldur sat silent, struck with astonishment and regret to hear of this fear and sorrow his father had carried but never spoken of to him. No wonder Carapethan had been adamant that he would not permit Haldur to leave Cotaerdon again, when the two hundred were sent south on their desperate errand! Yet he had changed his mind in the end: clearly he must have believed the promise made him by Artorynas and had trusted his son's safety to the word of the Starborn. After a long pause, during which Astell waited, examining with gentle fingers the leaves and petals of one of his delicate indoor flowering plants, the lorekeeper repeated his own question.

'You have my answer: what of yours?'

'Well... When you named me before Haldan don Vorygwent... I hadn't expected it and I would have to admit I was surprised when you spoke. And if I had foreseen it, I don't know what my feelings would have been. So you will see from this that I had no plan already made to come to you in this formal arrangement.'

Astell arched a rather sardonic eyebrow, but said nothing, so Haldur continued.

'If Heredcar had lived, it was my secret wish to stay among the Cunorad, to make the vow lifelong as Esylto has done. In those days, I thought nothing would content me so well as to be Cunor y'n Temennis in my turn. Then my brother was killed and I knew this could not be.'

He put up his hand and touched the empty place on his neck. 'I think I was never truly happy with my position as heir to the lordship; but the inward-facing eye on the torc I wore could bear witness to how hard I tried to live up to what was expected of me. I do not believe I am being boastful in saying that if all had gone as my father hoped, I would have made a worthy leader when my time came: I would have done well by the Nine Dales and they by me. But as you know, fate intervened.

'There is a fault-line running through my life now. Those who have tried hardest to understand have assumed that it falls on the day of dawn in Caradriggan, and why would they not? At first, I myself felt the same. It is fair to say, after all, that a man who handles something made by one of the Hidden People, who uses it as I did, who fires the arrow that takes the Earthborn life of his truest friend and sworn brother even though he was bidden to do so, who sees the sun rise in splendour, the darkness lift, the days both great and terrible that followed – that man will be changed for ever. And truly, I am not the same; but I see now that the turning-point came long before, in the moment when I found Artorynas lying close to death in a *numiras*, the moment when the gate between our two worlds stood briefly open.

'My heart goes out to any whose path has crossed with that of the Hidden People: Arval and others of his family now long gone, Torello, Forgard and his son Heretellar whom I met in Caradriggan. Even for Numirantoro herself the cost was high, willingly though she paid that price. Maybe, if I had not been destined for the high hall here in Cotaerdon, things would have been different... Who can say? It seemed to both Artorynas and myself that friendship is the best and least perilous bond that can be forged between the Earthborn and the Starborn – or one who is of the As-Urad. But we both foresaw the divisions that might follow, if others were envious of our closeness or believed I favoured his advice in council. My father is not wrong, to take heed of the warnings contained in *Maesell y'm As-Urad*.

'I see you are surprised to hear me say this. I would add more. You also were right, to say that the true love of my father's life is the Nine Dales; and further, that not all sorrow and loss need be barren. As I tried to explain on the day I renounced my heritage, I cannot love Rihannad Ennar as my father does, as its lord should. This is not only because I have taken a hurt that can never be completely assuaged, but rather because my heart now yearns to love all this earth: to embrace it so wholly, so fully, that perhaps one day I may take the path to that other world, go through the gate that once stood so briefly open. You're a wise man, Astell. I know what you said to Artorynas when he asked you about the Starborn: your words deserve to be remembered no less than the most beloved of our traditional tales. Now that fellowship is restored between Caradward and Gwent y'm Aryframan, now there is no longer any threat to Rihannad Ennar, now that Heretellar and Cunoreth will ensure that knowledge of what they called "the bad time" is not forgotten again, perhaps we may hope, a little, that this world will so renew herself as to become as she should be, as she could be, perfect as the world of the Hidden People is perfect.'

Suddenly Haldur laughed. 'But all this doesn't answer your question! Well, despite all, I do love Rihannad Ennar. I don't wish to leave the Nine Dales, and I would serve my homeland as best I can. And so, when you named me as your successor, suddenly it came to me that I was willing, that this was how I might fulfil my duty and still follow the promptings of my heart.'

He glanced across at his companion, but it seemed Astell had no reply to make. The lorekeeper had lowered his eyes and appeared to be studying his hands; but though his face hid the emotion he felt, his heart was wrung with pain. He too, like Carapethan, could see Ellaaro again when he looked at Haldur. But Carapethan at least had the comfort of remembered happiness. He had nothing: year after year of emptiness, of hurt that could still leap into life to wound him again at the slightest prompting. And how bitter it was that he had never spoken, that Ellaaro had maybe never known he loved her. That was almost the hardest thing of all to bear.

The silence lengthened, making Haldur uncomfortable. Had his words given unintended offence? 'What's the matter?' he asked. 'I hope I haven't upset you by what I said?'

Astell stood up and turned away. This is her son, he said in his heart, hers and his; and even the words had the power to hurt him. Ah, if things had been different! Would the son she and I never had have been like this? Haldur saw his hands clench, but after a moment Astell sat down again, his voice steady, his face composed, his manner as detached as ever.

'Not at all; I am pleased that you have confided in me so fully,' he said. 'You have spoken skilfully and choose your words with care. We will deal well together. I suggest that we should devote ourselves above all to the recording of the great events of our time. It should not be only the deeds of the past that are honoured with eloquence and memorable phrases.'

Day followed day, season after season. Vorardynur's new role fitted him as if he had been born for it, while Rihannad Ennar adjusted to the unexpected changes, settling down peaceably under the different order. And Haldur also found a kind of contentment. He was sure he had done the right thing in stepping aside for Vorardynur and in taking on the role of lorekeeper instead; he felt he had achieved sufficient understanding to be able to accept his sorrow and turn it into a force for good, as Astell urged him. Yet as time went by he began to realise that he was after all still seeking, albeit even now without knowing what it was he looked for. He would rise early and watch the dawn, and, especially in summertime, linger under the twilight long after the sun had set, feeling somehow that it was at these times, half way between day and night, that he might find the door between two worlds open once more and, looking through it, might finally see to the heart of the mystery. When chance permitted, or his duties took him to remoter valleys of the Nine Dales, he would journey up into the hills until he found some high place with a wide prospect. Then he would sit, chin on fist; or stand, heedless of the passing hours, gazing around him as distance shaded the green into brown and finally into grey, blending with the blue of the sky; and while the clouds drifted over his head, and their shadows followed across the ground below, so scenes, faces, words, came and went in his mind.

He knew he would never again set foot in Caradward: for him, those memories would always be too raw. But having seen it, fallow under its darkness, he could imagine how rich and plentiful its wide acres must be now, could easily envisage the beauty and elegance of Caradriggan restored. When it came to Gwent y'm Aryframan, there was no need for speculation. Several times he had returned there, and had seen for himself how Framstock had risen from the ashes, how the abandoned fields and pastures were desolate no more. His mind moved on to the refuge in the forest where he and his companions had been sheltered and helped, and a pang touched his heart at the thought of the little plot where Cathasar lay buried. The trees would long ago have reclaimed both settlement and graves. He remembered the autumn leaves, falling in a cascade of gold out of a sunlit morning sky to the blue frost still lying in rime on the ground below, and the loveliness of what he saw in his mind brought back other memories equally fair: the Somllichan Asan, towering white with snow, far-seen on a clear evening from Salfgard; summer sunrise, sending a river of light flooding up Rihann nan Esylt; the *astorhos* trees, flowering within sight of the shore where he and Arval had walked. It was commonly said that *astorhos* grew only where the feet of the Starborn had walked, but the last time he had visited Salfgard he had seen how blossom already spread wide above Ardeth and Fosseiro on the hillside and Cunoreth had shown him how, encouraged by this, he had set other seeds and now young *astorhos* saplings were growing vigorously in many of the places Ardeth had particularly loved.

Haldur frowned, thinking over what he knew of Ardeth, recalling anecdotes he had heard from those who remembered him. 'You'd have got on well with him,' that was what Mag'rantor had said. Maybe, thought Haldur; but after all, I never met him, so who knows. The familiar feeling of being somehow apart passed over him. Then a new thought began to grow in his mind. All these circles in which he was not included, they all overlapped; and where they did so, that was where he stood. He might be outside each separately, yet where they interlocked, he was within them. A picture formed in his imagination, an immensely long chain joining Rihannad Ennar to Gwent y'm Aryframan to Caradward to the Outlands beyond; Arval to Astell, Astell to Ellaaro; Ellaaro to Carapethan, Carapethan to himself, to Vorardynur and Lethesco, to Aldiro, to Heredcar... Heredcar, immortalised in memory as always young, forever strong, golden, smiling. The memory of his long-lost brother broke his thought temporarily as he remembered his parents' sorrow, and this in turn made him think of Astell's lifelong unrequited love for his mother Ellaaro. I wonder, thought Haldur, who would I have married, if things had turned out differently? Maybe without realising it I actually know the woman who would have been my wife, perhaps I have taught her children, or joined in games with them. He had enjoyed many an hour of instruction and play with the children of his friends, of Sallic and Tellapur, of Vorardynur: yes, those were yet more circles in which he had some part. This turned his mind back to the image of the chain. Its links could be re-arranged almost infinitely, but wherever they fell, he could see a way to fit himself within them.

He looked down at the little carving he held in his fingers. The robin was almost as good as new. The wood had responded well to his careful restoration: it was smooth and silky again, the grain glowing as he turned it over. Artorynas had been right to resist all suggestions that he should colour its breast. Even the broken tail feather, tramped into the soil of Salfgard under the farm track, did not really spoil it. Haldur had trimmed away the splinters and now it was only as though the bird added a suggestion of ruffled plumage to its cheekiness. Artorynas, Ardeth, myself, he thought; and then, with a leap of the heart, Rihannad Ennar, Asward donn'Ur, Porthesc nan Esylt. There was a link connecting the ground where he sat with the world of the As-Geg'rastigan! Haldur found himself on his feet. What had he been told of Ardeth? That he was teased because as the year turned, he professed the greatest love for each season as it came; that this world was so beautiful to him that he could never find the words to express how he felt. And now the *astorhos* bloomed above him. Did this mean the Starborn had trodden the hillsides of Salfgard? Did they walk there now, and in the other places also where Cunoreth had planted the trees? Then he remembered the day he had stood at the *numiras* in the Golden Valley and the old farmer's assertion that there was no need to seek the Hidden People: his simple certainty that they were among men once more.

I see it at last, thought Haldur, I understand, I know the answer! This whole world is a *numiras*! Filled with a wild elation, he threw the robin up into the sunlit sky, almost convinced it flew. As it dropped back into his hands he caught the smell of its woody scent, a whiff of the oil he had used on it, and instantly he was back in the shadowy courtyard of Tellgard, saying farewell to Arval after they had sat talking through the night. He remembered the sound of a robin greeting the new day, hidden as the dawn had still been hidden in Caradriggan;

remembered the sweetness of new-sawn wood drifting on the air from the workshops, and remembered what he had thought then: that the life within this earth and the life of men upon it should be at peace one with another. This was the insight that Astell sought to express when he said that as the Starborn were the Earthborn as they should be, so their world was this world as it should be. In some way, maybe beyond words to explain, but truly for all that, in some way the two *were* one.

Haldur stood alone on the hillside, wrapped in the understanding that had come to him. He had a small share in each world; he must, he would, be true to both. Far below, where the valley lay open to the sun with the shelter of the mountains behind, the apricot orchards of Rihann y'n Riggan were thick with blossom, though the lie of the land prevented him seeing Cotaerdon. The afternoon was wearing on; he should make his way back, go down from the hills, go home to take up the double responsibility his fate had given him. But... He remembered lying alone on the shore in a midsummer dawn, left with only a dream to cling to. Would a day never come when he might wake to the dream made real? If only the gate might stand half-open once more; if only through it might come that air from another world, not so much cold as fresh, clear as crystal, dancing with a secret energy, charged with life.

Suddenly Haldur turned towards the north. Let just a touch, a whisper reach him, the merest breath from the north beyond! For a long moment he stood there, eyes closed, the little carved robin in his hand. But he heard no sound, saw only the darkness behind his eyelids, felt only the vastness of the mountains all around him. Silence, darkness, emptiness.